Steven Lang is the author of two novels, *An Accidental Terrorist*, which won Premiers' Literary Awards in both Queensland and New South Wales, and *88 Lines about 44 Women*, which was shortlisted for both the Christina Stead and the Queensland Premier's Literary Awards for Fiction. Steven co-directs *Outspoken*, an extended writers' festival taking the form of occasional conversations with major Australian and international writers. He lives in Maleny, in South East Queensland. www.stevenlang.com.au

Bookclub notes for *Hinterland* are available at www.uqp.com.au

Hinterland

STEVEN LANG

UQP

First published 2017 by University of Queensland Press
PO Box 6042, St Lucia, Queensland 4067 Australia

uqp.com.au
uqp@uqp.uq.edu.au

Cover design by Christa Moffit
Cover photograph by Yuliya Shora/Shutterstock.com
Author photograph by Chris Francis
Typeset in Adobe Garamond 12/16 pt by Post Pre-press Group, Brisbane
Printed in Australia by McPherson's Printing Group, Melbourne

The author wishes to express his gratitude to the Australia Council for
their generous support during the writing of *Hinterland*.

The University of Queensland Press is assisted by the Australian Government
through the Australia Council, its arts funding and advisory body.

National Library of Australia cataloguing-in-publication
data is available at http://catalogue.nla.gov.au

ISBN 978 0 7022 5965 4 (pbk)
ISBN 978 0 7022 5916 6 (pdf)
ISBN 978 0 7022 5917 3 (ePub)
ISBN 978 0 7022 5918 0 (Kindle)

For Chris

one

Miles

At first light he hears the sound of a heifer in trouble. Never mind the empties in the kitchen or the one lying next to the lounge, he's up and out in the cold and the dirt of the yards getting the beast in the crush so he can put his hand inside her and find the calf, working his whole arm deep in her womb where is jammed this extraordinary impossible bundle of legs that'll kill her if he can't get it to turn, she roaring all the while, he talking to her in a long, slow stream of profanity, an affectionate soliloquy of half-remembered obscenities, he is, after all, a doctor not a vet, but the truth is he loves his cows more these days, his cows and his dogs (they, lying in the dirt, heads across their forepaws, watching doubtfully from the corners of their eyes) more than any other thing; a man who hasn't been with a woman since Sonia died two years ago and is unlikely to be with anyone else any time soon, with his arm all the way inside a cow in the early morning, groping for new life.

By the time it's settled, the calf out, fawn fur curled, sticky with fluid, feeding well, butting its pink nose up against its mother's udder like nothing ever happened – the sort of thing that can bring tears to a man's eyes – it's already late and he needs to wash and brew coffee, a bit of toast to settle the stomach, putting the bottles in the recycling out the back with hands he can't help but notice shake, wondering if he can keep himself from it until evening, worried not by the wine but the spirits, his apparent inability now to stop once he's started, lying on the couch into the small hours keeping himself just exactly where he needs to be with ever less carefully measured doses of brandy until it's all gone and the television has descended into even more profound meaninglessness than when he started and he hies himself off to bed, the dogs ignoring him, the dogs out for the night by then, disdaining to follow him further down.

Showered, dressed in shorts and shirt (crisply ironed by Melanie, who comes in once a week to clean) white socks held up by garters, the vertical lines in the knitted-weave straight, his brogues with enough polish on them to last another day, his remaining hair brushed tight back against his skull, he takes the Hilux up the dirt to the main road and onto the Range feeling like something close to half a man. A new house being built on what used to be Carlisle's, which twenty-five years ago was a functioning dairy – you couldn't say *thriving* because none of them had, the dairies had only ever survived – bought now by in-comers from the city, the developers or hippies or tree-changers or retirees, buying them up for hobby farms or to build fancy houses, planting trees on land the old Scots worked so hard to clear, planting so many trees that now you can barely even see the shape of the place anymore. Not that he's complaining. It's just the irony of it, the unimaginable effort of cutting forest the size of which we'll never see again in our lives, big trees, trees that took them days to fell with axes and cross-cut saws, hauling away the timber they wanted with bullock teams, sliding it down the hills to the coast, burning the rest and rooting out the stumps with mattocks, day after bleeding day until there wasn't a tree in sight,

2

until it was all rolling paddocks with fat cattle grazing, milked twice a day, by hand, only to have their effort spurned a hundred years on, to have it all replanted by these people who've arrived with their wholemeal roasted marinated Mediterranean focaccias and espresso coffees and pristine four-wheel drives, their ideas of an *environment* which doesn't include people, which doesn't even include birth and death or only in the abstract, well, that's until it comes to them via the thousand different ways that ill-health visits the human form. Which wasn't what he was thinking about at all. It was the calf in the early morning that's brought this up; the fact of its life (and the life of its mother) given by him, and yet his clear intention to have it killed sometime later, to eat, without remorse or regret; the need to provide grass for its feed between these two events, grass grown on his own land, which had once belonged to another Scot who sold it for a pittance to *his* father; three hundred acres, not enough in this kind of geography – where the Range breaks away into ridges and gullies – to support anybody really, land that was most likely better served being covered in trees in the first place. It is both the requirement and the difficulty of straddling these different notions which is troubling his mind, the impossibility of their coexistence.

Only three cars next to the surgery when he pulls up which is good, as long as there's no disasters over at the hospital. Nick, the new locum, should have been able to deal with what's come in, but when he opens the door he can see on Joy's face that all's not entirely well, there might be only three cars but half a dozen people look up from their *Women's Weekly* and *National Geographics* to note his arrival. He nods to them, smiling good morning, as if to say he's been off on other important doctor-business elsewhere. He picks up two files from his tray and takes them into his room, putting down his bag and looking around the confines, the high bed with the clean sheet laid over it, the little yellow two-step stool for getting up, the cluttered desk with all its pharmaceutical nonsense in jars and packets, the damn computer already switched on and ready, humming at him miserably from beneath the desk. The familiarity of the place exerting its own influence, calming his mind, as if all the years spent in here, the great stream of affliction which has passed before him, asking for his attention, has a force of its own which calls him out of self-destructive pathways of thought. But not his hands. When he goes to type in the password, single-fingered, the others curled back so as not to bump the wrong keys, they are still shaking. He can feel the sweat rise on his skin from the effort.

Joy standing in the doorway. Coffee in hand.

'Trouble with a beast,' he says.

She lets it pass. Joy being of indeterminate age. Two grown-up sons, one in the military, the other a fitter and turner in Sydney, married with children of his own. Photographs of them on her phone and desk, as screen saver. Prone to showing them. She is a woman of unparalleled efficiency from whom it would be difficult to hide anything should you even want to try, chosen years ago by Sonia, when Sonia was alive and choosing such things for reasons not all of which were to do with effectiveness as a practice manager. She is something of a tyrant with the patients, vetting them according to an arcane system of her own devising, but he does not complain; he could not operate without her.

She gives a run-down of the morning's events, the two call-outs to the hospital which Nick has taken care of, the backlog of patients in the waiting room, his home visits which she has, she says, scheduled for the afternoon.

'This is for you,' she says, putting the coffee on his blotter. 'Are you ready? Or shall I give you a minute?'

'A moment,' he says, opening the first file. 'If you wouldn't mind.' When she's gone he gets up and closes the door, gets out a half of brandy from the bottom drawer and pours a shot into the coffee. Enough to steady the hand.

The first patient, Harry Barkham, takes the offered chair with a mumbled comment about the lateness of the hour. He's sixty-five, a former smoker, moved to Winderran ten years ago from one of the big cities after having reached dizzy heights in oil then getting a scare with his heart. Built a mansion overlooking the mountains with the proceeds in which he perches, now, watching over his stocks and shares or whatever it is that ex-oil men do when they're not driving their Mercedes four-wheel drives. He's not accustomed to waiting for anyone, and yet is humbled, *as are we all*, by our doctor, he who has the keys to our happiness. Or some few of them.

'A difficult birth earlier today,' Miles says, without offering further clarification. 'What can I do for you?'

'I have this persistent cough,' he says, and the consultation has begun, the listening to symptoms, the discussion of history, habits, diet. Harry being fit for his age, only carrying a few kilos around his waist. He bicycles with a group of men. Miles sees them from time to time outside one of the cafés in the early morning, bikes leaning against the wall, men his own age unembarrassed by multi-coloured lycra, laughing loud, letting the world know of the ease they've bought with each other through shared exertion.

He lifts the man's shirt to reveal a pale-skinned back with its unique constellation of moles, places the stethoscope on the various points and asks him to take a breath, listening, wondering, obtusely, if Deirdre, Harry's wife, still runs her hands over this skin. You'd think, as a doctor, that you'd know these things, but it's often not clear what people do.

'You've seen the camp?' Harry says. He wants to chat, he wants his money's worth, or, having been made to wait he's going to make sure that others will be similarly inconvenienced. Miles doesn't mind, it's part of the service.

He shakes his head.

'Out along the Elmhurst Road? A bunch of hippies have set up against the dam. Aboriginal flags. Hand-painted banners. Tents, buses, water trailers, the whole disaster. Settling in for the duration. Not that it will do them any good, State's committed. They're not going to let rag-tags like that interfere.'

'You're in favour then?' Miles says. A superfluous question. The man was in mineral extraction, familiar, no doubt, with the accoutrements of dissent.

'It'll be the making of the place, I tell you. Think of the opportunities for tourism.'

Harry has the deep voice of a man who's lived in the tropics, enriched today by catarrh and the need to stop and cough; there's a definite infection but it doesn't appear to have gone to the chest, the sort of thing a course of antibiotics was designed to address. Harry comes in two or three times a year with various ailments, bits needing to be checked – prostate, knees, hips, a great scar on his chest and belly where they went in to do the bypass but no problem since then. Harry assumes that he, Miles, is also in favour of the dam, which he's not, he doesn't have a position. He doesn't have time for positions but if he did it would be against it, if only because Joy's brother, Marcus, has a farm right in the way of it which he and his wife, Lindl, have spent the last three decades or so planting up, revegetating the banks of the creek.

Harry's problem, Harry's *disease*, peculiar to towns like Winderran, has its roots in boredom. He retired too soon. Came up here, spent the first couple of years building his pile, organising the landscaping (he has forty-three varieties of camellia in his 'grounds', which he opens to the public once a year) but once that was done had little else to occupy him. Now he plays bridge three times a

6

week, sits on the committee of the Winderran Heritage Society where he holds forth with what he hopes is the same authority he held in boardrooms across the nation when making decisions that involved hundreds of millions of dollars, but which, ten years later, in a small country town, render him a pedant, a specialist on the musicals of Gilbert & Sullivan, his voice drowning out the others in the room, a spokesperson for a conservative point of view that, whatever his opinion on the damn dam, Miles has never subscribed to. A sometime friend of Guy Lamprey, whose wife, as it happens, Miles will be visiting later that afternoon.

Harry out the door with a script and instructions to alleviate the symptoms with old-fashioned remedies like steam inhalation, he invites in the next patient, and the next. Each with their own problems, many of which are within his scope to deal with, but others that are harder, needing referrals to specialists. These patients, as often as not, arriving with the dreaded screeds of paper bearing internet addresses as headers or footers. At one point he might have been able to dismiss them as hypochondriacs, holding to the pretence that he was the one with the expertise, but those days are past. Knowledge expands in every direction and there is no hope of keeping up. His own authority increasingly in question. It behoves him to take notice of what they bring to him, to sift through the nonsense, the snake-oil, cure-all, self-promoting healer sites to find those that offer new perspectives. Every day, too, the government and the pharmaceuticals deliver great swathes of paper with their lists of wonder drugs and regulations, their research data, their KPIs and side effects, their evidence-based outcomes. He is no longer anything like the doctor he once was, the doctor his *father* was – a good thing that – but is now a kind of cipher, an overloaded spigot whose function is to act as the local outlet for incalculable streams of information, supposedly tailored to each person who enters his room except that the weight of the unknown backing up behind him becomes ever larger, more pressing – talk about dams – and it's no use to reassure himself that nobody can know everything because on the other side are the armies of lawyers (of whom Sonia was one, so it's no use pretending he doesn't understand) keen to capitalise on his mistakes and apportion blame for his failure to pick early-stage cancer from a back ache, to notice an irregularity in ionised calcium as a sign of this or that.

At lunch he drops down to the hotel for a bar meal and a beer, to rest, briefly, in the noise of sport and horse racing, in their deep simplicity. The problem being that the bits of the job he loves most, the interaction with people, have got lost. There are ever more screens between him and his patients, a raft of technology on which he is barely floating, whose bindings threaten to come loose beneath him with every new wave. The young bloke, Nick, has a handle on it. Never out of range of his laptop or smartphone.

In the afternoon he takes the Hilux out past Elmhurst, skirting the edge of this wide valley that the government, given the chance, will flood; noting the camp that so annoyed Harry, where people of all ages, not just hippies, have indeed set up in opposition. Colourful banners tied along the fence line, two people under a beach umbrella at a table by the gate.

He might be tempted to concur with Harry and his friends and support the notion of development for development's sake, he has, after all, seen the living standards in the town improve with the arrival of new wealth and the associated demand for better services, better food, more sensitive design. He's been invited often enough to join them for boozy meals in attractive surroundings, but more recently, since Sonia, he's stopped accepting. Opulence and fine wine aside he finds himself taken with a terrible loneliness around them. A loneliness even deeper than his own. These people always have something to say, but their banter skitters over the surface of things, it is the perfect embodiment of small talk, a constant and often nasty reiteration of the nothingness they've learned to master so as to get on in their world, to serve their own interests, but which has, over a lifetime, emptied them of humanity.

Margaret Ewart has the upper end of the valley, the near edge of her property dipping down into the area affected by the dam, but most folding away to the north and west. Last remaining daughter of Bill and Ida Tainsch, her husband, Jack, her brothers, sisters, cousins, all long dead. She lives by herself in the kind of rural squalor that was commonplace fifty years ago but is now, for the most part, long gone: a kitchen with worn linoleum on the floor, the webbing showing through beneath the plastic and steel chairs around the formica table; the old Rayburn on one wall going in any weather; the meat safe home to her limited selection of dishes; a geriatric fridge in the corner given to miserable sighs before the compressor cuts in and out; the walls dark from age and lack of paint, the only adornment a free stockfeed calendar with a picture of rape in flower, the yellow turned blue with age; light thrown by a bare bulb hanging on a doubtful lead. A radio burbles the local ABC in the corner. Vicious dogs chained up on a veranda, guarding her privacy. She comes to the door despite her hip, resting on a borrowed hospital crutch, wearing a skirt and blouse, a cardigan in need of darning at the sleeve ends. Her face a geological study, lizard-like weatherworn skin on neck and shoulders. She serves him a cup of International Roast and a slice of the cake she's baked for her son who's been up from Brisbane on the weekend to see she's okay, no doubt eyeing off his investment, the millions that must be tied up in the place, never mind the unpainted weatherboard house on its sagging bearers or the tumbledown sheds filled with the bits of machinery Jack gathered over the decades. Martin will be wanting to get Margaret out of there and into a home to realise the profit while he can. The problem being she's not for moving; despite her age, eighty something and in general disrepair, she still has all her smarts, still wants to drive a little white Toyota flatbed in and out of town, picking up her bags of dog and chook food, her staples of white bread and tea and canned ham, going to meetings of the hospital auxiliary carrying plates of cornflake biscuits. Living for who knows what reason. Although that could be said about most of us.

He sits across the table from her and hears the latest on Martin and his wife, the daughters off in other parts of the world, the grandchildren and great-grandchildren. There's a machine working somewhere off in the distance, something large, he can hear its clanking, the occasional demonic beeping of its reverse warning siren.

'That's Mal,' she says. 'Putting in a crossing on the creek. We've got concrete trucks and the lot down there, hardening the lane.'

Mal Izzert, the neighbour, has one of the few remaining dairies on the Range.

'He's still improving then ... even with the dam?'

'You never know with Mal. Could be he's just upping the price they'll have to pay to get rid of him.'

Margaret never short of an opinion. Of the dam she says, 'It's progress, isn't it? That's the truth of it. You can't fight it.'

'So you're not with the hippies on this one Margaret?' he says, for the laugh of it, because they go back, he's known her for as long as he's been in practice, his father would have been present at Martin's birth, almost certainly pulled him out from between her legs fifty years ago. The mystery of it. Martin runs a lighting business down in the city. Doesn't, you'd have to note, stretch to a ceiling fitting for the kitchen, or for that matter to private health cover for his mother.

'You wouldn't know how some of them survive, would you?

Haven't the brains they were born with. I saw one girl the other day on the steps of the IGA,' the supermarket, which she pronounces the same as the mountain, *the Eiger*. 'Feeding her daughter – a wee thing, no more than three year old – raw spaghetti. I'm telling you, I saw it with my own eyes. If that's the future I don't want a part of it.'

He's here about her hip, she's had a fall and now needs a replacement, can't manage the ute anymore. He examines her in the bedroom. Most of the old Queenslanders in these parts are built of solid timber, the walls constructed out of single-skin, vertically fixed, VJ board milled on the Range, the sparse framing on display. At some point Margaret's home has been lined – in a misguided gesture towards what must then have been modernity – with unpainted masonite, walls and ceiling, so it's brown on brown and sagging, the air trapped in the rooms for decades, an internal bathroom with a toilet and a claw-foot bath stained with rust from the furious hot-water heater perched above it. There are other doors he's never seen behind. There will be a parlour, and another bedroom or two, where Martin and his sisters were raised. Not a bookshelf in sight.

Her bed is a double and newer than everything else, its 1970s plush headboard, built-in radio and veneered side tables standing in sharp contrast with the walls and the wardrobe, the latter a looming presence in the corner of the room. The bed's been made. He wonders how that happened, if she did it, on her crutch, one-handed, so as not to be embarrassed by the doctor. She lies down with much difficulty but no complaint and he gently pushes aside the voluminous old woman's underwear to reveal the bruising from her fall, now fading to a jaundiced yellow, the skin, where it's never seen the sun, soft and supple. The muscle starting to fall away.

In the absence of help from Martin or the girls it's a case of waiting her turn.

'I saw your new man in the hospital,' she says.

He waits. She means Nick.

'Handsome, eh? Cold hands.'

'That'll do now,' he says.

'Is this one going to stay around?'

'I don't know. He's a wife and kids in Canberra. Separated.' He helps her to stand again.

'And what about you? By yourself down there?'

'I've got the dogs,' he says.

'We've all got the dogs,' she replies.

He takes the Stapleton Road back into town for the simple pleasure of circling the catchment. It's longer and becomes single bitumen for a time, dipping steeply and rising again, passing through a nice stand of white-trunked eucalypts. It's been a while since he's been this way. Out on the ridge some mining magnate has built a vast pile. During construction they cut half the hill away, but now the building's finished it's tucked into the land, less formidable than it might have been, if you don't count the painted timber rail fences stitching the paddocks around it, or the helicopter pad near the house, the imposing electric gates on the road, just to let everyone know.

Out into paddocks again there's a long view to the west across the river valley, the hills beyond rendered flat by the heat of the afternoon. Sometimes, late in the day, they can step into the distance in different shades of blue, beckoning. Today they're indistinct; no more than scenery. More houses have been built along this way, less grandiose these: one-acre blocks subdivided before the law tightened up, now home to website designers, artists, *feng shui* practitioners, young families. On a whim he goes up to the lookout above the old quarry, from where, when it's clear, you can see forever. Today the flatness fallen over everything. It's an excuse to have sip of something. To stop in the cabin of the truck and feel his pulse racing for reasons that are by no means clear, to tip a portion of the half of brandy into him while looking out towards the indeterminate sea and feel the alcohol enliven not just him but the whole extraordinary vista. Taking a piss through the fence onto the cobbler's peg and *desmodium* the Council have left to grow on the other side. Back, what, *twenty-five years* it would have to be – that anyone might live this long – he came up here one night with Lindl, sneaking away, and kissed her in the glow from Brisbane in the south. Who knows where Marcus was. No doubt about his connection to the world then. Now it's all at a remove. Sonia between him and everything else. Or perhaps that's the alcohol. He fires up the truck and slips a CD into the machine. *Crowded House* thundering out of the dusty speakers, his musical taste, like so much else, locked in another era. Singing along with it as he winds down the steep track to the road.

Perhaps the pulse was to do with visiting Helen Lamprey, recovering from surgery to remove a tumour from her bowel, the diagnosis for which, it is hard to forget, came from the previous locum to Nick because he, Miles, was late on another morning and she'd taken the appointment she could get and Abbas had sent her off for all sorts of tests which Miles had thought were a load of nonsense, and told him so, cross with him for even seeing Helen. Then, of course, the tests were positive and it was all on.

They live in a house that could not be more different from the Ewarts, on the north-east, the better side of town, views to the sea, architect designed. Built long before anyone else lived out that way. When the locals thought they were mad. The living room's long and wide, with lots of glass on the coast side, books and paintings on the others, shelves and shelves of books despite Lamprey having his own studio.

There are low rectangular Italian couches with, at their centre, Helen, a small woman, made smaller by the surgery and the chemotherapy, which is not going well, by herself today it seems, even in these dire circumstances, Lamprey off on one of his projects down in Canberra. The fine bones in her fine face revealed.

He's surprised her husband isn't with her.

'Oh, I'm okay,' she says, 'really I am. I have lots of help.'

She wants him to sit with her, to have a drink.

'I can't drink,' she says, 'but I've got some lovely white in the fridge. It would give me pleasure to watch you.'

She's always been the perfect hostess, brisk, efficient, but now her movements are slow and studied, as if even raising her arm is too much and, after accepting her offer (has she smelled the brandy on him? Is she alert to this weakness?) he must open the bottle and pour for himself, bring her a wine glass with cold water in it ('so I don't feel left out'), wrap the blanket around her shoulders although it's not cold in the house. When he was younger he'd lusted after her. That's not the right word. He'd lusted after several women, and known some, too, even in a small town like Winderran, but Helen had exerted a more significant force. Not simply because she remained aloof. *If there'd been any woman for whom he might have settled*, but she was already taken and anyway she'd been one of his patients. He'd been obliged to admire her from afar. Later, after Alan was killed, he'd had to watch her disintegrate.

'Guy's too busy at the moment,' she says. 'Dabbling in politics now. It seems he's being tapped.'

'By who?'

'Oh, Bain, I suppose. And the Leader of the Opposition.'

'Lonergan?' He can't keep the surprise out of his voice.

'Nothing too grand for our Guy.'

'For what?'

'The Senate, I believe.'

'But, the *Liberals*?'

'Don't sound so shocked.'

'How's he going to write if he's a Senator?'

'He hasn't written anything for a long time. Other than opinion pieces. Can't, won't.' She pauses. 'My fault, I think.'

He waits to see if an explanation for this last will come. The sun has started its tilt towards the west, somewhere behind the house, and the slanting light enhances the view towards the sea, throwing the shadow of the Range across the lowlands, darkening the remnants that linger in its creases.

'Your politics are showing,' she says. 'I'm not keen on Bain and Lonergan but they're not quite the *dark side*.' She laughs briefly. 'Although, now you mention it, my husband quite possibly went over to that years ago, before I met him. It would explain the gift of those early books, wouldn't it?' Holding the glass against her chest with both hands, her fingers entwined around its fragile curve. 'We met in London, me, a girl from down there.' Nodding towards the coast. 'I'd escaped. I mean really. I had a position with Pan Macmillan. How remarkable is that? As an editor. Do you remember Picador? I was with them. Great writers. Have I told you this before?'

'Only the bald facts.'

'That's where I met Guy. A skinny young man, very passionate about things. When he asked I went home with him. He had such ambition. He wanted to recreate the world, reimagine it. I mean, that's what all writers want isn't it? It's what they set out to do. But with Guy it was something more. It wasn't enough just to lift himself, he had to take the entire country with him. Like a kind of Atlas figure, raising the whole continent. Now look at the company he keeps.'

Helen still has remarkable presence, despite the illness, or perhaps because of it. Lamprey must be a fool not to be sitting where he is. But then it's easy to think that when it isn't you. Besides, he's an imposter, the one who didn't pick up on the early symptoms. He feels a sudden overwhelming desire to confess, which he supposes means he wants forgiveness. Not hers to give.

He lifts his glass and empties it, leaving the condensation gathered in a small pool on the table, its meniscus picking up the late silver light.

'Have some more,' she says. 'Please. I think you can manage, can't you? How do you survive without Sonia?'

'It's you doing the talking today, Helen,' he says.

'It is, isn't it? But do fill your glass again.'

He goes to the fridge. Places the glass on a benchtop made of some polished black stone. Everything about Helen has always been exquisite. Expensive. The song he was singing in the truck now lodged in his brain as soundtrack. *Whenever I fall ...*

'It was me who brought him back here. Otherwise I think he'd be living somewhere else. *Provence*, maybe.' Laying on the sarcasm. 'He had an affair. I wasn't going to hang around for that sort of thing, so I flew back here. He followed and by then, of course, it turned out I was pregnant. With Alan. So we stayed.'

That would have been in the late seventies, their arrival not the sort of event that went unnoticed in Winderran. The hippies had a wholefood shop in the main street (*The Store*) with barrels of brown rice and oats, chickpeas and flour, local provenance vegetables, a poor stunted crop *that*, at least in the early days. Helen worked there. The beautiful wife of the famous writer who'd come to live in a fancy house out on the hill. As much a reason as any other to shop there. It had been some months before he realised she was also responsible for the books on the back shelf. Amongst the copies of *Our Bodies, Ourselves* and *Spiritual Midwifery* were literary novels, and not just Lamprey's.

It is difficult to recall the strength of emotion which certain women provoked in him during those years. A disabling intensity. It's not that his sexuality has disappeared, it's still there, latent, but the force of it has dropped away, like a shroud or a veil, so that the world is revealed in an utterly different light. He is not sure if he is the better for it. Certainly it is easier. Women are just people now, like other, more attractively shaped men, with different, and sometimes curious, takes on life. They do not command him by their simple existence. He can see that even if Helen had not been the Beautiful Ice Queen, if she had succumbed (had she ever even noticed his desire? She was always smiling, always friendly, but to *everyone*, you couldn't take it personally) nothing would have come of it except sex – some passionate exchanges in the front seats of cars, people's bedrooms – because the person he'd been fascinated by had not been this woman (with, presumably, some leaning towards the politics of the Right, otherwise how could she have survived all these years with Lamprey and his steady march towards the reactionary) but some other ideal.

After Alan she had come to him several times. He had prescribed various different drugs to help her sleep. She had stopped working at *The Store*. She hadn't been seen much about town. From all accounts the focus of her life became Sarah, her daughter, now living in Western Australia, something in IT.

'It can't have been all bad for him, to be here, can it?' she says. 'I mean there were some good books written in this house. And now, to be considering *politics*. The thing is he likes to be liked, you know. All writers do. And he's had a bad run with his acolytes.'

'I'm sorry?'

'His young men. He likes to mentor young talent. The trouble is they have a tendency to bite the hand that feeds them, a way of proving they've outgrown him. They write bad reviews. It hurts him more than he admits. Recently it's got worse. I have the sense he has become unmoored.'

'From what?'

'Oh. From his work, I guess. From me. No. More than that. From everything. He always had such a sense of things. That's what made him good.' She pauses, seems to consider saying something more but then rejects the notion. 'It's so kind of you to sit with me like this,' she says. 'I'm sure you must have places you're supposed to be.'

'I'm getting less good at being in the places I'm supposed to,' he says.

'Life can be so unfair, can't it?'

'Why do you say that?' he asks, thinking she's still talking about Guy, that maybe she'll articulate the withheld thought; not realising she's turned her attention to him.

'I'm just rambling,' she says. 'But for many years I played the good wife. Guy was so big, there wasn't really any room for anyone else and to be honest I was happy with that, the local girl made good. That's something we have in common isn't it, Miles? Not so many of us locals around. I had my children, he had his books. But the years went by and things changed and I decided to become a bit bigger. Or at least a bit more *me*. And what happens? I get ill. It must be like that for you, too, I guess, with Sonia? You find something valuable and then it gets taken away before you even begin to appreciate it. You don't mind me saying that? These days I discover I'm becoming terribly blunt.' She puts on an English working-class accent. *'I say things as I shouldn't*. I always liked you, Miles. It's an intimate sort of relationship this one, isn't it? You know all my secrets. My pregnancies, illnesses, diseases, losses, unhappiness. I was very pleased when you got with Sonia. She was such a strong woman, a real person, not these bits of fluff you used to go around with. It's strange being from a place and watching it change so much, so many strangers deciding to call it home.'

Everyone left. That's what his generation had done. They turned eighteen and got up and went off to university or to work somewhere else. It was only the timid who remained. Of which he was one, he supposed. After university and his internship Winderran hadn't seemed like such a bad place. His father already suffering with his heart. He *was* timid, always had been. Never mind the women of which there were less than the small town likes to think. Most of the time they chose him. He'd been needed in the practice. This is something he can say, that he is already older than his father was when he died, which, according to the cliché, means every year is a bonus, except he doesn't think that; really, it's just more *life*, indistinguishable.

He met Sonia at a conference in Sydney, she was a lawyer for a firm that specialised in compensation cases, a career woman, the same age as him, no children. They slipped away. The Manly ferry on a bright day, the Harbour all around. They made each other laugh. She was moving to Brisbane. They ended up living half in her flat, half on his farm. She loved having cows and dogs. He had never known a woman change so much in such a short time. When they met she was, not *slim*, but well apportioned. Over the next decade she became positively Wagnerian, as if her position in the company and her relationship with him allowed her to grow in physical stature as well as in personality. A force unto herself. He didn't mind. The sex had remained tremendous. A woman of appetites. Then she got cancer. Being a doctor no help at all. Within months it had all fallen away. Reduced. Fifteen years from go to woe.

The shadow of the hinterland has spread all the way to the sea. Only a container ship halfway out to the horizon – heading south for the Port of Brisbane – still in sunlight, glinting. They are in their own pool of twilight in the wide room, the glass table now liquid black. It seems tears are running down his cheeks. He can feel them wet around his mouth, on his chin. His glass empty again.

'Guy and I barely live together,' Helen says. 'He's away a lot, and when he's here he sleeps in his own room. I think he finds me a bit abhorrent. The sick wife. Like my cancer to me. He'd like to simply excise me but can't find the way to do it neatly, without embarrassment.'

She doesn't seem to have noticed his tears, for which he is glad. *Twice* in one day.

'I think it would be convenient for him if I was just to slip away, but I don't think I'm going to. Not yet anyway. Do you?'

He doesn't answer. There is no good reason for destroying hope.

She talks across the silence. 'If you'd asked me a couple of months ago I would have said it was a close thing. But now, I'm not so sure. Do you want some more wine? There's sure to be some left, it'll only go to waste.'

He does want more. His mind has been measuring the contents of the bottle in the fridge door. But he knows he needs to go, and that he cannot afford to be caught, again, driving like this. Even the local doctor cannot push these rules too far. He needs to go back to his own lair. To his dogs.

'The thing is,' Helen says, speaking from her dark bundle of rugs, he can barely see her anymore. 'I'm on my own now. I'm not complaining. It's my choice as much as anyone's. I wouldn't want it any other way. But I worry about Guy. I no longer know who he is. I don't think he knows either. He seems to be confused about people and wealth. Perhaps he always was and I just didn't notice.'

Behind the wheel of the truck, its headlights following the narrow curves of the road with less certainty than he'd like, he takes note of his condition. He is on the edge of competence, having difficulty making the turns at the right speed, the lumbering beast beneath him lurching unnervingly on the much-repaired road. Pulling himself together so he can at least make it home in one piece. Concentrating on the task at hand. Not so hard really, except that the sleepless nights seem to be catching up with him on this winding road along the top of the escarpment, waves of exhaustion interfering with his will.

A car appears from the opposite direction, its headlights sudden and painfully bright, causing him to brake sharply, and then it's gone, leaving a wash of colour in his eyes. The road straightens and he changes up a gear, gives it a little juice, letting the machine take him home.

two

Nick

The phone pealed out in the darkness, dragging him up from sleep. It wasn't his night on call and in the moments of waking – fumbling for the glowing screen where it was lying on the carpet next to the mattress – his mind put together a scenario in which Miles was shirking his duty again, that he had somehow managed to get the hospital phone re-routed to Nick's number. The resentment surging.

It wasn't the case; it was Guy Lamprey.

'Sorry if I've woken you,' he said. That affable television voice. 'I've a slight emergency and the more I thought about it the more I thought you might be the man to help.'

Nick managing, by way of reply, a sort of grumbling noise. *A slight* emergency. No precedent, surely, for such an adjective? His newly stirred brain going full tilt now, still developing the Miles script: Lamprey's wife was one of Miles's patients, Miles had been irresponsible in some way – not beyond the realms, he was drinking heavily, even, Nick believed, at work (the reason the previous locum had departed) – and now Lamprey had found out. What he couldn't quite get his head around was why he should need to talk about it at this time of night.

'The thing is, I need discretion,' Lamprey said. 'I don't know you well, it's true, but on the basis of our meeting the other night I get the sense I can trust you. Can I speak frankly?'

'Of course.'

Nick rolled over to switch on the bedside lamp, revealing, even within its limited range, the unfurnished hopelessness of the room. The clothes he'd worn the day before thrown over a couple of cardboard boxes. The open sliding door of the built-in displaying his meagre selection of suits hanging limply, like so many shades. Soon he would have to make an effort.

'It's a sensitive matter,' Lamprey said. 'A boy's been hurt at one of those ReachOut places up in the hills. We need a doctor to attend.'

'If there's a medical emergency, why hasn't an ambulance been called?'

'It's not just anyone's boy, you see.' Lamprey calm, collegiate, inviting Nick into his world. It was the *you see* that did it, the affected English upper-class tic which acted as a hook because of course Nick didn't see, and was thus obliged to ask for an explanation.

'So who is it?' The boy, the father, either, both. Still trying to come to grips with the situation.

'I'm not sure I'm at liberty to tell you at this point. The son of someone important. Is that enough?'

'And what's happened to him?'

'He's been in a fight with some other boys. I don't believe it's life-threatening but you can't be too careful, can you? That's why I thought of you. I know it's late but I didn't think you'd mind doing a special favour. I wouldn't ask if it wasn't necessary.'

This strange assumption people make about doctors, that they don't require the same amount of sleep as everyone else.

'I had a couple of drinks before I went to bed,' Nick said. 'Why haven't you contacted Doctor Prentice? He's on call.'

'Can you drive?' Lamprey said. As if his question hadn't been asked.

'I'm sorry?'

'I'm in Brisbane,' Lamprey said. 'You'd need to go out there yourself.'

That would be in the New Farm apartment, a converted loft in an old bond store, close to the city. Lamprey having a way of letting people know about both the company he kept and his possessions. 'Are you capable of driving?' he asked again.

'I suppose so. Where is it?'

There was, apparently, an old training camp up in the hills to the west of town. An area he'd not yet visited, out along dirt roads. Midnight already, had he really only been asleep for a couple of hours? It felt like longer, one of those sleeps where you plunge to the depths.

What was he supposed to do with this boy when he found him?

'See that he's okay, if he's not then bring him back with you, do what you have to. But whatever it is, be, how can I say, circumspect. We don't want the media involved.'

The more Lamprey spoke the more Nick suspected there must be some sort of abuse involved. Was it a church camp? At least he was now awake.

'I need to know more,' he said. 'I'm sorry. I can't be expected to go along with this without knowing what I'm getting myself into.'

'Fair enough. But if I tell you do I have your agreement that you'll go? That you'll be discreet?'

'I'm not undertaking to break the law, you understand that? If there's anything reportable I *will* report it.'

'Well, I hope you'll discuss it with me, and his father, first.'

'Who is?'

24

Lamprey saying a name to conjure with – Peter Mayska. Even someone as disconnected as Nick knew of him. The Queensland billionaire. The actual value of his fortune dependent on both the trade weighted index and the price per tonne of various minerals at present still required by China.

'His son, the boy's name, is Cooper.'

'How old?'

'Sixteen.'

'And what's he to you?'

'I'm a friend of a friend.'

He followed the unfamiliar road down into the valley, spots on the windscreen promising rain, grateful of the choice he'd made of a new four-wheel drive, never mind the expense. Cocooned against the night in its hermetically sealed module, the instruments glowing, nothing visible outside the parabola of the headlights. Nick not being the sort of man who put much store in cars, only persuaded to lease this one by his brother's arguments about tax advantage, agonising over the decision for days as if the question of owning a car was not financial or practical but personal and ethical, a Judeo-Christian conundrum as to whether or not he deserved to own such a fine piece of machinery; a question further complicated by what Abie might think. The same dilemma which contributed to his empty house: it was not only that he'd have to actually go out and shop for the stuff, but that in doing so, in spending money on furniture he would be committing to this place, finally confirming their marriage was over.

After almost an hour he arrived at the bridge Lamprey had described. He took the turn just beyond it, setting the milometer to zero where the road became gravel, dusty despite the promise of rain, starting off wide but getting narrower as it climbed, barely more than the width of the car. Forest on either side, occasional tall eucalypts with white trunks catching in the headlights, big trees. Darker, thicker woods behind, rainforest, high branches reaching out to join their counterparts above the road. He'd not seen another car since he left Winderran and now, on the dirt, not wanting to meet a vehicle coming the other way, he was relieved about that, but at the same time, equally, unnerved. Twenty-three kilometres along this road, Lamprey had said, but although he'd been driving interminably he'd only gone fourteen and the road was getting rougher, rising steeply then descending sharply, in tight, loose-gravelled turns. More up than down. What if it was the wrong road? If he'd made a mistake? Not just with the directions. The longer the journey took the more uncertain he became about the whole undertaking. He had no need to get tied up in some quasi-legal escapade on behalf of privilege. A failure of judgement on his part brought on by Lamprey's charm – one of those men with such an enlarged sense of their own worth that it leads them to expect others will do their wishes, which, by some curious self-replicating mechanism, they then do; people like himself, for example, taking a corner too fast and grinding to a halt, side-on to the road, gravel flying up. The implication being that to do Lamprey a favour was to do yourself one, too. Like those bumper stickers, *What's Good for Halliburton is Good for You.*

The occasion on which they'd met was Sophie Allenby's house concert. To which Nick had been invited by the town's worthies out of a combination, no doubt, of curiosity and the false assumption of a knowledge of the arts in the new locum. The kind of event he would normally have gone out of his way to avoid except that Miles (conspicuously absent himself) had insisted he attend. *You need to get to know these people,* he'd said. *This isn't like Canberra, you can't just ignore your patients, you have to live with them.*

Sophie's house (Mr Allenby apparently long dead) was perched on the edge of the escarpment and boasted a wide room whose curving windows delivered a view across the plains towards Brisbane and Moreton Island, dusk falling over the landscape, those impossible, almost oriental mountains standing up out of the summer haze. Certainly they were all there: Atkinson, the plump little man with the round gold-rimmed glasses who ran the art gallery above the gift shop; the overly perfumed over-bearing woman who owned the same (and, apparently, half the buildings in the main street) – he above her – although it didn't pay to dwell on such things; the cruel-mouthed editor of the local newspaper and his rather glamorous wife; the former big pharma executive turned hobby-farmer; the pianist, Ms Allenby's daughter, a doe-like, sweetly edible blonde twenty-something whose playing, along with a fellow student from the conservatorium, was the attraction for the night. The trouble with being a doctor in a small community being the hidden knowledge, small and large, so quickly developed about people – Atkinson, for example, suffered from dreadful piles, while the host, Ms Allenby, a formidable woman in most aspects of her life, was plagued by a series of disorders, not all of which he could be certain were real; the big pharma man – surprisingly urbane and entertaining – had early-stage Parkinson's. He and his wife had moved to Winderran to enjoy rural tranquillity, raising Charolais beef, and now had different choices before them. There was a need to observe in any gathering professional distance, avoiding not just talk of an individual's ailment, but also the temptation to define them by it.

Seventy or more chairs were set out in a semi-circle facing a small podium in front of the windows. Nick stood awkwardly to the side juggling biscuits and cheese on a napkin along with a glass of wine, praying his beeper would vibrate and free him from the requirements of sociability.

In the break he went out to the deck. With the coming of night the western sky had turned an extraordinary silver, fading to a burnt orange along the line of the hills. Far to the south the lights of the city. Lamprey and another man out there, smoking, talking, their voices swollen with the confidence that their insights would be entertaining, even *educational*, to others. On seeing Nick, Lamprey broke away to introduce himself, holding out his hand and saying his name, as if Nick didn't know it already, hard not to feel flattered that the author and television star had taken the time to find out who *he* was. Introducing the other man as none other than Aldous Bain, local Federal Member and *Shadow Minister for Energy and Employment* in the Lonergan cabinet.

Bain tilted his head towards him and, by way of a handshake, offered the touch of something soft and slightly repellent, managing to maintain in person, despite his exquisite suit, the same impression he gave on screen of being either an undertaker or one of his clients re-activated for the occasion – pale-skinned, sharp-nosed, longish grey hair held back by product, excusing himself with the brusque ease of those who know they must share themselves around.

Lamprey, a tall thin man with a long neck and weak chin that gave him the peculiar appearance, at least in that light, of an inquisitive ostrich, held up the remains of his cigarette between his fingers.

'Exiled,' he said, 'For my sins. The trouble is I like it. Though I shouldn't say that to you, should I? Tell me, are you enjoying the concert? They're good aren't they? For ones so young. You wonder where they get the sensibility to know how to play this sort of thing. You tend to assume that music with such deep emotional resonance must be played by people who're familiar with those feelings. You are a lover of classical music?'

The music had been unexpectedly beautiful, a couple of sonatas by Haydn and Mozart – although, not being familiar with live performance, Nick had been surprised at the raucousness of the horsehair on gut in that refined space, each pass of the bow rending the air. For much of the first piece he'd wondered if the violin was really meant to sound like that, or if it was ever so slightly out of tune, a concern which dissolved when a pair of fruit doves, big birds, landed in the branches of a tree beyond the window and began ripping cautiously at a wire bag of seed, pausing in their work to look in at the assembled guests from cool circles of eye centred within perfect white heads, their silence and staccato movements suggesting that they, too, were affected by the noise from the instruments; and, being a kind of apotheosis of beauty themselves, giving evidence that the music must be the same.

'I like it, but I don't know it,' he said, concerned to discover that, against his wishes, he was about to reveal something of himself, if only as an attempt to contribute to the conversation; as if Lamprey somehow demanded it. 'My father loved opera,' he said. 'Had to be allowed to listen on Sunday afternoons without being interrupted. I think it worked against the genre for me.' The little house in Stanmore drowning in the noise from the tall speakers that sat like sentinels in the corners of the living room. The rows of LPs and the restrictions on touching; the refusal to allow him or his brother to play their music on the system in case they damaged the speakers, as if what they chose to listen to wasn't just a threat to social cohesion, it was physically destructive.

'Now that's a shame,' Lamprey said, stubbing the cigarette out on the sole of his shoe and burying the butt in a pot plant with the fastidiousness of the modern smoker. 'You mustn't let childhood hurt deprive you of such joy. Come and visit. I have the very best sound equipment. I'll play you *Traviata*. An aria or two.'

He wondered at this. Why Lamprey was offering it. Why it is that people offer largesse they don't really mean you to take up, like foreigners met on a train saying, *You must come and see us when you visit Finland*, knowing you never will or that, if you do, it's barely likely you'll land on their doorstep for three days of kayaking in the lakes. It is, he supposed, cheap and easy to say, even easier to add, *We're not just saying that, we mean it.* It was something Lamprey could do because he was famous and Nick wasn't, because it's what grand people do: they make gestures secure in the knowledge that the less grand will never call them on it.

He didn't know why he was so critical of the man. Perhaps it was part of that Australian requirement to take down one's betters, or those who believed themselves so, a way to prick Lamprey's charm, but then it might, also, have been a reaction to the patronising comment about childhood trauma, the dispensation of psychological advice without invitation. Doctors get used to diagnosing patients at first glance. It's a dangerous habit, because you can be wrong, and changing your mind isn't as simple as many believe. But the job is, after all, to appraise people, to attempt to see to the core of their health issue before they can overlay it with personality; never mind that it wasn't what he was supposed to be doing out there on the deck with those curious megaliths sinking into the darkness below them. At the moment when Lamprey had taken his hand in his gruff own and – in contrast to Bain's wet fish – squeezed it hard, that well-met expression on his face, what Nick saw was a man harbouring a nest of vipers. If he'd been asked he'd have said cancer, early stages in the gut, because of a somewhat sallow cast to the face. It was the projection of rationality that confused Nick, that made him critical of his own criticism and dig for sympathy, making it a medical problem Lamprey nursed and not something deeper.

A light on the right-hand side of the road, flickering through the trees. His headlights picking up a couple of white painted tyres planted in the ground to mark the entrance. He took the turn, automatically indicating, but for whose benefit it wasn't clear, passing under a metal archway with words filigreed across the top that probably said nothing like *Work will make you strong*, much more likely *Spring Creek Camp*, but surely the implication was there. A dollar fifty-three on the car's digital clock.

Coming into a wide clearing. Several bunkhouses standing darkly on a gentle slope, the forest beyond. An admin building at right angles to the others. A light on its veranda. He parked. No-one came out to meet him. He switched off the motor, got out. Night all around, silent but for the ticking of the car. The air cold. He had come up several hundred metres. He mounted the wooden steps with his bag. A few brave insects circling the light. One large moth, the same colour as the timber, stuck fast on the weatherboards. The screen door's coiled spring complaining.

Calling out, 'Hello.'

A door down the veranda opened, spilling yellow light. A man emerged, came towards him, grey t-shirt tight across the chest, thick biceps, military-style pants. Army-issue boots, the soft beige leather ones with the thick soles. Number three cut across the scalp. Stopped a metre away from Nick. Didn't say a word. Attempting to intimidate and, quite frankly, succeeding. Extraordinary behaviour.

'Doctor Lasker,' Nick said.

'That's right,' the man said. As if his arrival was unexpected, or forgotten. As if calls hadn't been made. 'Come this way.'

It was a standard issue building. The sort of thing put together by a church group, or a school, for kids' camps. Almost everyone's childhood affected at one time or another, for good or ill, by this architecture and what occurs within it. Weatherboard and fibro. Timber floors. Unrendered besser-block toilets off to the side.

He followed the man through a corridor to a back door and out across dusty grass to a squat annexe. Another light burning outside two rooms. The infirmary. Opening the door and flicking the switch, lighting up a shadeless bulb hanging from the ceiling.

The room lined with pine boards. A cement floor. Two steel-frame beds, one with its mattress rolled up, striped ticking bare to the world. On the other a figure, curled with his back to the room.

'Doctor's here,' the man said. 'Sit up now.'

Nick going around him to perch on the edge of the bed.

'He's right where he is,' Nick said.

The boy somehow larger than he'd imagined, almost a man, a strong pale calf extending out from under the blanket, good muscle tone, the foot still in its vast elaborately stitched running shoe.

'You're Cooper, is that right?' he said. The young man was shivering. He asked him if he was cold. Asked if he could roll over.

Cooper turned towards him, making what was possibly an exaggerated gasp of pain as he did so. The soldier-type produced a small noise; a critical click of the tongue. Nick glanced back at him. At other times, in other places, the intimidation might have been sustained, if only by the man's size, the fit force of him, his surly silence and the unidentifiable tattoo along his forearm, but in this little room, in the middle of the night, Nick was too stupid and too angry for that. The man averted his eyes. A small victory. He went back to the boy. Swelling along one side of his face and around the mouth where there was a break in the lip, the skin split above the eye. Red-blond hair that needed a cut, the first growth of a beard on his cheeks, freckles. A line of blood had run down the side of his face, onto his neck and gathered in the cloth of his t-shirt. He was holding his right wrist with his left hand. There was a contusion on his forearm which suggested a possible break beneath the surface, perhaps only a crack. The sort of injury made by someone raising their arm to avoid a blow. The sort of injury received when a raised arm is hit with something blunt. Further examination revealing bruising to the ribs; signs of having been kicked in the stomach and back, on the legs. The marks received by someone who had contracted themselves into a foetal position.

He took the boy's vitals. Stable. He wanted to check for evidence of rape. He turned to the man behind him.

'You can leave now,' he said.

The man stayed where he was. Arms crossed over his chest.

'I'd like you to go out of the room,' he said. 'And close the door behind you.'

'You have no authority here,' the man said.

Nick looked at the boy. Lying on his back, watching. Frightened. Nick turned back to the man. He wasn't good at conflict. Could be struck dumb by fear at its possibility. Avoided it at all costs.

'When I'm finished here I'm going to take this boy back to Winderran,' he said. 'To the hospital. It looks to me as though there's a green fracture in his right ulna. Right now I'm going to check for evidence of sexual abuse. When I'm done I'm going to want to know what happened here. I'm going to want to know your name, the name of your organisation, the time this happened, who was involved and all the rest of it, and you're going to tell me. You are going to co-operate with me in every way you can because you are in a shitload of trouble. You are so out of your depth in shit that you don't even know you're in it. D'you understand?'

'You don't scare me,' the man said.

Nick stood up. The two of them contained in the little wooden box. Unpainted pine boards on the ceiling as well as the walls. They were about the same height. The man had perhaps ten kilos on him. All of it muscle. As soon as he stood Nick realised his mistake, that this was the sort of man who would use violence without asking questions. But Nick was a doctor and he'd come to understand during his years in ER that there was power in that, too. Not much, but perhaps enough.

'Tell you what,' he said. 'You go back over to wherever you were when I arrived and call up whoever it is that does scare you.' The words coming thick on his tongue, clumsy, betraying him. 'Ask them what you ought to do right now. Okay? Ask them if you should help me or not.'

They stayed like that for a few seconds. Like children daring to stare. Then the man turned and left the room.

Nick turned back to the boy.

'I want to examine you,' he said, the adrenaline high in his system.

The boy just looked at him.

'I want you to take down your trousers and I want you to roll over on your belly.'

The boy thought about it for a minute, then indicated he would do his best but that he couldn't let go of his arm. The mysterious power of the doctor clearly holding for a few moments more. The boy's pale freckled lower back and buttocks had their share of bruising. He checked the boy's anus. No apparent damage. He was familiar with the effects of rape, was grateful for their absence.

'Are you in pain?' he asked.

The boy nodded.

'Your arm?'

'Everywhere,' he said.

'I'll give you a shot of something now. I don't want you taking anything by mouth in case we have to operate. Do you suffer from asthma?'

'No.' The boy awkwardly pulling up his trousers using only one arm.

He left him to it, dug around in his bag for a shot of morphine. Struggled to get the needle to line up with the top of the bottle. Noting how shaken he was by the confrontation. Doing his best to cover such obvious examples of his condition from the boy. Giving it to him in the shoulder, trying to press the plunger in slowly.

'I'm going to get my car,' he said. 'I'll bring it over here. Will you be able to walk?'

Cooper mumbled something. Visibly relaxing as the drug hit his system.

Nick went to the car, going around the back of the other building. He sat in the driver's seat, the door closed, his hands on the wheel. Inside the cabin he felt safe. He wanted to stay there. He wanted to lock the doors and drive away. To never have visited this place. The uniform silence within the car, its false sense of security threatening to undo him. He started the motor and drove over to the infirmary and parked again, opened the passenger door, tilted back the seat. He looked around the camp. The bunkhouses sitting in their forest clearing. Nobody else appeared to be awake. Were there other boys in those buildings? Were they asleep? Had they been training so hard all day, running through the forest, doing rope courses, that now they could sleep through anything? Sleep through a doctor coming to collect the boy they'd beaten up?

Inside the infirmary Cooper was sitting up.

Between them they managed to get him to the car. Nick went back for the blanket and wrapped it around the boy. Closed the doors and walked over to the office. He didn't want to. He'd lost all stomach for a fight.

The man was already at the door. 'He wants to talk to you,' he said.

He showed Nick into his office, with perhaps the smallest amount of deference. A bare, functional sort of room. Rosters on a whiteboard, a desktop computer, a national park poster with a faded picture of a waterfall. An old-style telephone off the hook. He picked it up, said his name.

'Ah, Doctor,' the voice said, 'it appears I'm in your debt.'

'Quite possibly,' Nick said. 'But right now that's not the issue. I have your son in my car.'

'You are perhaps a little confused. My name is Aldous Bain, you've quite possibly heard of me.'

'Evidently.' There seemed to be no point, or advantage, in saying they'd met. 'Why am I talking to you?'

'Mr Mayska is a good friend of mine. Cooper is his son. In this situation I am charged with looking after him.'

'Well,' Nick said, 'Mr Mayska's son appears to have been beaten up by persons unknown.' Unsure where such language came from. Police procedurals? *Persons unknown*? He'd never said such a thing in his life. The other man standing in the doorway, back in his former position with arms crossed. Listening hard, though. Visibly stiffening when he said Mayska's name. In the better light of the office he could see that the tattoo gave the appearance of having been altered at some point, its present incarnation bearing a Celtic Christian theme. 'I'm going to take him to the hospital which is where he should have been hours ago. I'm going to run some tests to see how badly he's been injured.'

'Thank you. I appreciate it. I understand our mutual friend has spoken to you about how sensitive this all is …'

'I'm a doctor, Mr Bain. I have responsibilities …'

'I know you do, and, indeed, so do I, but as I said, I'm deeply grateful to you for looking after this boy. Mr Mayska will be flying up to the Sunshine Coast at first light. He should be in Winderran by mid-morning, perhaps earlier. I would be further grateful though if you could just leave things at the camp. I believe Cooper's injuries come from a, how can I say, unfortunate hazing from his camp mates …'

'Mr Bain, Cooper has, quite possibly, got several broken bones. He has widespread bruising. I'm not sure if there are internal injuries.' This was overstating the case, but he wanted it to sound as bad as possible, immediately regretting the impulse. Bain wasn't the thug by the door and any exaggeration might be held against him later. 'I would hardly describe what has happened as hazing. He's been beaten up, plain and simple.'

'I see. Yes. But the people responsible will be held accountable. I can assure you of that. You do not need to involve yourself in that side of things. Please, I'm asking you, look after the boy and leave the rest to me. I am far from a forgiving man when it comes to these sorts of things. On the other hand I do not forget those who help.'

This was quite the most bizarre phone call Nick had ever been part of. He put the handset back in its cradle. Several quips coming to mind that he might offer the man at the door. On balance he preferred to keep them to himself. He went past him, down the steps to the car.

Cooper slept, curled beneath his blanket. Nick was glad that he didn't have to talk; glad, too, that the boy wasn't watching because he wasn't driving well, going too fast, unable to help himself now that he was out of the place, as if it was only then that he'd come to understand how close the brute had been to injuring him. Muscular Christianity. Suffering from shock, he supposed, cornering hard.

He'd seen Aldous Bain talking about his pet project on *Q&A*. Although why the Opposition should have thought having him in front of the camera was an advert for anything was beyond comprehension, especially in a debate with the slightly sexy government minister – the feisty, articulate one with the Eastern European name.

Bain had been promoting his party's policy for a kind of National Service, based around repairing the landscape. 'In our urban-based culture young people have no connection to this great continent or, indeed, to our society. What we propose will give them a sense of the land they live in while at the same time addressing the real environmental problems we face. Problems with things like erosion, with damaged rivers. At the same time we take direct action against carbon in our atmosphere by sequestration.'

'I thought your side didn't believe in climate change,' the feisty one had said, interrupting.

'What we don't believe in is a big new tax,' Bain answered. 'Listen, political differences aside,' saying this as if he were the rational one, patiently tolerating the interruptions of an hysterical woman, 'over the last few decades in Australia we've created a society which expects the State to offer a safety net. That's fair enough, but it's also a society which doesn't seem to think it has the right to ask for anything back. What we believe is that in any social contract there should be expectations on *both* sides. We are not frightened of having a debate about these things. About what that might mean. Of whether or not we are prepared to ask something of our young, not for their whole lives, just for eighteen months, asking them to give back to the country which, in turn, has given them life. And I know what the Honourable Member is going to say, that this is thinly veiled nationalism and that nationalism is dangerous. But that's only if you make it against something, against some other country or people, this is a nationalism *towards* a sense of ourselves as worthy of value; it is a nationalism that calls on the children of all those races who have come to live here, the British, the Irish, the Italians and the Greeks, the Vietnamese and Sri Lankans, the Afghans and Sudanese, the Lebanese and Chinese, to put aside our differences and work together for the greater good. Other countries do it, why shouldn't we?'

Aldous smarming his way into the camera, pouring himself into Nick's living room.

Cooper's eyes were open. He was staring up at the roof of the car in his thick black t-shirt with its inscrutable tech joke on the front:

```
C://dos
C://dos.run
run.dos.run
```

Not speaking. The kind of soft unformed boy who provokes an irrational urge in adult males to toughen him up. Nick had, before now, felt the same thing about his own son. There had been an awful moment of cognitive dissonance watching *Q&A* when he'd found himself agreeing with Bain. At least about giving back. Grateful to the feisty one for her put-down about it all being a smokescreen to avoid making the people who were actually producing the pollution pay. A sop to the Right wing of the party.

There had been times when Nick had looked at Josh and thought him too soft for the world, that his formlessness was an affront to life; asking for trouble. It was, in some unexplained way, his responsibility as a father to harden him up. For his own protection. To teach him the fortitude that comes out of difficulty, to mitigate that unstinting and often demeaning love – demeaning because it demanded nothing in return – that his mother offered. Unconditional. The love we all crave. Except that love *is* conditional. It requires all sorts of things: he couldn't think what they were right then; respect, he supposed, but also empathy, understanding, loyalty, duty. *Really?* In truth he had no idea, his own record of love hardly inspiring on any front. Only that what had happened in the camp was the logical conclusion to this sort of thinking. *Work will make you strong.*

There being one other matter: Cooper was gay. Nick would have bet the house on it. And if he had picked up on that, the other kids would have, too. They wouldn't have been able to avoid going for him, never mind the billionaire bit (unlikely though it was the other boys were privy to that). And fuckalugs back there wouldn't have stood in their way.

'Are you okay?' he asked.

'Yeah, I'm fine.' The drug slurring his words.

39

No point in trying to talk. And yet the urge for Nick to disassociate himself from what had happened back at the camp was overwhelming. To convince the boy that he had had no part in it, had been co-opted into the situation, his only role to get him out of there.

At the little town in the valley Nick called ahead. A nurse he didn't know answered. He told her who he was and that he'd be bringing in a young man.

'Is there anything else going on?'

'All quiet here.'

The car's speakers exaggerating a foreign quality in the woman's voice, vaguely reminiscent of Greloed, evoking one of those small but disabling spikes of yearning for her which had, gratefully, been diminishing these last weeks.

As they left the small town, the road straightening for a moment so that he could put his foot down in relative safety at last, he had to repress the familiar quickening in his blood raised by this brief exchange. The expectation. Repressing it because it was as unfounded as it was inappropriate. Because, apart from any other consideration, she, the person on the other end of that phone conversation, about whom he knew nothing whatsoever, was a nurse, and he wasn't going there again, had well and truly exhausted *that* particular cliché.

The road starting its climb onto the Range. Slowing, driving more carefully now. Calming himself. The problem was that it didn't seem to matter how many affairs he'd had he never seemed to learn: in every room he entered, every hospital, lecture theatre, office, aeroplane; every elevator, shop, bar, and, it seemed, now, every telephone conversation, he had one eye out, noting, watching, searching for the possibility of connection with the same insatiable curiosity, the same apparently infinite capacity for engagement. He saw it in himself, noted it, *regretted* it, but remained under its sway. Slightly more suspicious than usual of it right then because it had been three months since he'd slept with anyone – something of a euphemism this last, because Greloed and he had hardly ever shared a bed – and he was finding this lack difficult, never mind that it was deliberate, a conscious if hopeless attempt to face up to his history.

It started to rain about ten minutes out of town. He glanced at Cooper. As weird a name as Greloed in its own way. His head resting on the seat, turned towards him. Eyes open.

'Thank you for getting me out of there,' he said.

'You're welcome. They treated you kind of rough, eh?'

'Pretty much. I'm not the type.'

'What type is that?'

'Oh, I don't know. Who thinks sport's good for the soul. Who expresses unquestioning loyalty to an idea.'

'Uh-huh. So what type are you?'

Cooper managing a small smile in the reflected glow of the dash. 'Oh, you know. Subversive. Disruptive. The kind who likes books and gaming and the internet.'

'I have a son who's like that. A bit younger than you.'

'It's not such a bad thing is it?'

'What?'

'To like those things?' Cooper said. 'What I don't get is why people think everyone has to be the same as them. I don't want these freaks to be like me. I'm happy for them to go off for their runs in the woods and sing their happy songs. To *believe* in stuff. I just don't want to do it.'

'So it wasn't your choice to go to camp?'

'As if.'

Coming up onto the plateau, the road more level and familiar but with a terrible surface. Another car appearing around a corner, its headlights shocking after all this time.

'It was my dad's idea.'

Nick not sure what to say to that.

'You know who my dad is, I guess.'

'I've heard of him. He asked someone who asked someone else who asked me to go and get you. So my knowledge of him's not what you'd call direct.'

'That's the way to keep it.'

'Do you live with him?'

'Hardly. I live with my mother. Number two wife. Number three's in charge these days. Lyris. Not as nice as the name sounds. Then there's Michael, my brother. He'd be as old as you.'

'I'm forty.'

'Well not quite that ancient.'

Nick taken aback by Cooper's openness. He didn't know what he'd done to deserve it. He wondered why he didn't have conversations like this with Josh. Maybe it was because he didn't shoot him full of morphine.

The lights of town now in sight.

'I believe I'm a disappointment to him,' Cooper said.

'That's a shame.'

'It's all right. I don't think it's just me. I think the world disappoints him. Anything that's not subject to him disappoints him.'

'Maybe you don't have to take that on board.'

'Oh I don't. Not for a minute. Well. Maybe that's not true. I agreed to go to the camp, didn't I? I guess there has to be some deep emotional need waiting to be expressed, doesn't there? That's what my therapist would say.'

'You have a therapist?'

'Doesn't everyone?'

'No. I'd go as far as to say most sixteen-year-olds don't.'

'Well there you go then. You see, I'm special.'

Nick glanced at him. He was smiling. They were in the town by then. A young man with a sense of humour. He pulled up under the porch outside Emergency, the car dripping, the rain teeming down beyond the pillars.

Nobody coming out to meet them. He went inside, found a wheelchair and pushed it out to the car. Levered Cooper into it and wheeled him back through the automatic doors and into one of the observation rooms. A woman called from two rooms away, through the open doors, the same voice as on the phone, softer in real life; said she'd be there in a minute. Nick got Cooper onto the table. Shoes squeaking on the linoleum. Suddenly very tired. The boy even more vulnerable under the harsh light than he'd been in the camp's infirmary. Dried blood cracked on his skin.

Looking around for the blood pressure unit. 'Are you warm enough?'

'I think so.'

He caught a glimpse of the nurse moving about in the adjacent room, pushing a cart. Slim, tall, dark hair.

'I had another call after yours,' she said, still out of sight. 'There's a child in One if you want to take a look. When you're ready.' He could hear her opening cupboards, taking things down from shelves, clattering something on a tray. 'I know you're not on call, but I thought while you're here, why bother pulling in Miles? I mean, Doctor Prentice.'

Coming into the room pushing a cart. Nurse's uniform, white flat rubber-soled shoes.

'Hi,' she said, addressing Cooper, not him. Just a nod in his direction. 'Let's have a look at you. What's happening here?'

Cooper visibly brightening at the sight of her. The power of the female of the species. Or perhaps just this one. Putting a hand on the boy's wrist and looking at her watch.

'I'm Eugenie Lensman,' she said, looking up at him. 'You must be Doctor Lasker.'

three

Eugenie

She cut the onions at the island bench, the big screen on the opposite wall lighting up the room with the unnatural green of some football stadium's grass, filling the space with the noise of the crowd and the patter of the commentators. David splayed before it in an armchair, a beer by his right hand.

Over the years she'd trained herself to block out the sound, to see it as part of life, and even then not the most offensive. These days, though, with David away for three weeks at a time, she'd grown accustomed to the quiet. Now it didn't seem to matter where she was in the house, what she was doing – cooking, cleaning, reading – the machine's insistence penetrated her defences. It was, perhaps, not even so much the noise that got to her as the self-righteousness which accompanied it: the way he occupied the room, watching *his* sport on *his* television – which, she was more than happy to admit, he was justified in doing, even without having undergone the privations of fly-in/fly-out, earning shit-loads of money, wheelbarrow loads of the stuff, with which the screen, the new Colorado, the tinny, the mortgage, had been bought. Never mind that he was still working at home even now, the mobile always by his side, taking calls from the accountant, supplier, the team on site – it was that it also somehow negated everything *she* did; as if getting the girls to school and their post-curricular activities in town or down the coast, keeping house, still managing two shifts a week at the hospital, things which didn't operate on a three-weeks-on, one-week-off rotation, weren't as important as his work. As if what he did gave him licence to generate the moods which, let's face it, had always been his speciality: the steady production of clouds of negative ions filling their house from floor to ceiling – he was at it right then – viscous but invisible, something you had to push yourself through, but silently, otherwise the anger might be provoked, anger or disdain, one of the two, neither much better than the other.

She finished with the onions, wiping her eyes on the sleeve of her cardigan, a slim woman in her late-thirties wearing a summer dress because it was warm and she'd been to town that afternoon while David had taken a nap after the late-night flight, but also because she'd thought he might like it, her thick hair pushed back, not needing anything these days to stay where she put it, the dampness from her tears glistening on her wide Scandinavian cheek-bones, not beautiful, she'd never claimed that of herself, but striking, statu-esque. Steering the pungent chopped flesh from the board into the hot oil, pouring another kettle of boiling water into the pot for pasta; turning back to rummage for garlic beneath the counter; pausing to look at David, her husband, resolute in his chair before the game; he, feeling her gaze, glancing over at her.

'What?' he said.

'Nothing.'

Turning back to the television.

She'd not been raised, at least for the first few years, with one of the devices in the house. The community where she'd grown up hadn't run to electricity, far less televisions. Perhaps that contributed to her intolerance. The ability to shut them out hadn't been bred into her.

Sooner or later she was going to have to tell him what she'd been up to, what she planned to do. Perhaps he already knew. His mother would have no doubt been delighted to fill him in on her latest outrage. But he'd be waiting for it to come from her. This was the reason for the mood. He was working up his arguments.

It would not be fair to say that this list of activities: children, work, house, described all she'd been doing while he was away. Her involvement with the campaign against the dam had continued to grow, become more than simply something she'd supported out of solidarity with Lindl. After the girls it had become almost the central thing in her life, sometimes resented for the time it required, always engaging.

David had never been keen, claiming he didn't give a shit either way, he just thought the *NoDam* crew were wasting their time. 'What makes you think the government'll listen to you?' he said. 'You lot know nothing about what goes on. These bastards made up their minds about this shit long before you ever heard about it. They've started building the pipeline, for fuck's sake, you think they're going to stop because it upsets you? Because your friends are worried about some trees?' Turning to Sandrine and Emily for support. 'Your mother's whacked in the head,' he said.

And while much of this might or might not have been true his scepticism was, she thought, nothing to do with the politics, it was cover for his dislike of her having a life of her own, interests that didn't include him or have a direct economic input on the household. He wanted to be in control. Not always in a bad way. Would have preferred it if she'd let him support the family instead of going back to nursing when the girls were old enough for school. In this case, though, his dislike of Marcus would have been reason enough. Lindl was *her* friend. She'd invited them both over for dinner, several times. David considered them a bad influence, like she was a child, *easily led*. Marcus, Lindl's husband, was a university professor, older but not much wiser. He'd made the fatal error, early on, of correcting David – as if he was doing him a favour, which he probably believed he was – *It's pronounced kasm not chasm*. Some such thing. Maybe it had been his grammar. *Done* instead of *did*. Marcus not even noticing he'd given offence. David never forgot. He wasn't the type to forget, didn't, anyway, like entertaining. Hadn't grown up to it. He told her once he couldn't think of a single time when people had come to dinner at his parents' house, except for a funeral, and that had been family.

When they'd got together, who their parents were had been the least of their concerns (her mother dead of an overdose, her father back in France ever since the fire). She'd not appreciated that he was a *Lensman*, the son of dairy farmers whose parents and grandparents had worked the land around Winderran. What that meant. She'd visited for the first time *after* she'd agreed to marry him. Even then she hadn't understood. It was only when they came to live on the block of land given them by his parents, subdivided off the farm, that she began to grasp it didn't matter where she'd met David, what drugs they'd done together, what adventures they'd had, what politics they'd agreed on during those heady days, these were his *family*, this was their town; blood would out. His parents were good people, generous to a fault, hard-working, but they were also bigoted, narrow-minded, ignorant. People who by definition regarded her with as much suspicion as she did them even without knowing about her childhood in a hippie community. Their innate prejudices were, it seemed, irrevocably lodged in David's psyche, a subconscious slur against her character that was the subtext behind the description of the *NoDam* campaigners as 'you lot'. Never mind that she had even less time for her hippie heritage than him.

~

48

The community's name, *Bene Gesserit*, had been taken from a sci-fi novel. It meant, in the made-up language of the book, *truth-teller*. The people who lived there, who had named it thus, a bunch of mainly women, preferred to simply call it *The Farm*, though it could never have been such a thing, in anyone's imagination. It sat within a vast eucalypt forest, astride a sandy-bottomed river, the hand-built houses nestled amongst the trees. No possibility of growing anything except more trees. The only access the rough fire trail over the hill from Yowrie, which itself was just a place, not a town.

Her mother's little house, their home, had been built out of sleeper off-cuts, the discarded flitches of former forestry operations; layers of newspaper on the inside to cover the cracks, pages and pages of it stuck on with glue made from flour. The insects ate it. During the night they could hear them gnawing at the walls. The final layer painted over, but roughly, so that snippets of articles and advertisements leached through. Yvette, her sister, when she wanted, could tell the missing parts of these stories. The two of them huddled under a pile of blankets against the cold, Eugenie begging her to tell, pointing with the torch at the words, following them with her finger, *Local Boy Wins*, and sometimes Yvette would oblige with the story of the boy who won a ticket to the moon and what happened there, or maybe, another time, how he won at archery and was sent to boarding school in Sydney where he met a girl hiding in a tree who had special powers and taught him how to defeat the bully – Yvette having no knowledge of proper schools, only that derived from books because *Bene Gesserit* was so far out along bush roads, across fords, along fire trails, that they did home schooling with the other children in different people's houses on a rotation which did not include their own because it was too small and primitive even by the standards of that community.

The stories were always changing, this was part of their magic. It was the same boy, but each time a different adventure.

~

49

She'd made peace with David's parents, learned what could or could not be said in their home, learned to bite her tongue when Harold made pronouncements about women or the government, Aborigines or asylum seekers; found a way to make it all right in her mind that the girls went to his mother when she was off nursing; arranged things so that at family events her own father, Jean-Baptiste, also now a resident of Winderran, wasn't present.

Now, however, the dam had raised its head. They were, predictably, in favour, if only because it was further evidence that the bad old days were gone. The objections to what they regarded as progress confused them. The newcomers, it seemed, had forgotten, or never known, how miserable life had been, milking cows by hand, barefoot in the mud. To cap it off, there she was, just the week before, a *Lensman*, going down to Brisbane with old Mal Izzert to milk cows in George Street, letting the milk run onto the cobblestones in front of Parliament House while the cameras rolled. Standing there with her hippie greenie friends talking nonsense on national television.

Opening a couple of cans of tomatoes and pouring them onto the onions and garlic, slicing them with the spatula.

Really there was nothing for it.

'Can I talk to you? Or is the game at a critical point?' she asked.

'What was that?'

She said it again. He turned off the sound, left the picture on. Which would have to do. Looked over at her.

'Thought you might like to hear what I've been doing.' Watching the sauce as it started to bubble around the edge of the pan. Not looking at him. Giving the pasta a stir. As if she was at ease. 'You'd have heard about the stunt we did down in Brissie?'

'I did.'

'What d'you think?'

'You know that Mal Izzert's as crazy as a cut snake, don't you? The lot of them are.'

'He's making a go of the dairy. Selling cheese into China now. Had a delegation from Sichuan out to visit the farm last week.'

'Doesn't mean he's not fucking mad.'

'He's going to lose some of his best land. Doesn't he have a right to object?'

'They'll more than compensate him. And he gets lake frontage to boot.'

'But has to stop dairying.'

'Yeah, well, that's not such a bad thing, love.'

Claiming a kind of genetic knowledge of the land and the industry she could apparently never attain. She wasn't going to rise. She wasn't going to argue. Keep it calm. Stir the sauce.

'Not sure why you're siding with him, but,' he said.

'I don't believe it's the right policy. On any level. In terms of the site, the economics, the environment. Dams don't work.'

'I don't need a fucking lecture.'

'You asked.'

'What d'you want to tell me?'

'They liked how it went down in Brisbane, you know, me in front of the camera. All the news services picked it up. Good copy. Did you see it? I don't suppose you did. D'you get to watch the news up there?'

'Sometimes. We missed it that night. I guess I should be thankful eh? My fucking mates weren't saying, *Hey, Davo, is that your missus up there running milk in the drain?*'

Taking a sip of his beer. They were allowed four a night in the canteen. The place he worked was like a gaol, he said, except that they paid you. They told you what you could do every minute of the fucking day. When you could eat, have a shit. All of them out there in the morning in rows, doing *stretches*, like they were North Koreans. They called it *Alcatraz*. She'd told him he didn't have to do it but he liked the money, liked the success, liked the fact that his

51

business turned over more every shift than Marcus made in a year. It was part of the bigger plan.

The dinner was almost ready. She'd left her run a bit late. She cut a bit of fresh basil to throw in the sauce. The wide-bladed stainless steel knife large in her hand.

'They've asked me to do all the media from now on,' she said.

'Who's they?'

'You know, the group. Marcus, Mal, Geoff, Alt, Ruth, Sam.'

'And you've said yes?'

'Yes.'

Looking up at him for the first time. Standing up for herself. Proud of it.

He didn't say anything. Looked at the screen. An advertisement showing now. All power to the mute button.

'We're having a debate in town on the weekend,' she said. 'Organised by the uni. In the community centre. I'm representing the *NoDam* crowd. You'll still be here, eh? You could come along. Bring the girls.'

'You don't mind what you fucking do, do you?' he said, straight up, no pause.

Taking a breath. Letting it out.

'What does that mean?' she said.

'You know what it fucking means.'

'It'd be good for the girls to see their mum standing up for something.'

'Something useful. Not this greenie shit.'

Faltering, but determined not to show it. Standing her ground. Unsure where the new-found strength had come from. Scared. He wasn't physically violent; had never hit her, or the girls. Occasionally he'd thrown something. It was just he got so angry. The male potential for violence always there, she guessed. But more often simply cold and mean. A capacity to search out a person's weak spots, to cut directly to the rawest point, without, she thought, even necessarily knowing what he was doing, how much it hurt. Some injury in him that went on the attack in its own defence. That's what she used to think. In the days when she used to want to excuse it, could still forgive it. Going for the girls as a way of getting to her if the frontal attack didn't work.

'I won't have it,' he said.

Putting her hands on the edge of the benchtop. Holding on.

'It's not for you to have or not,' she said.

He turned his back on her again. She could see the tension in his shoulders, those great muscles running up into his neck, pulling his head down like a bull. Years of this sort of thing. Having to fight him for whatever piece of ground she'd gained: about the girls; work; his parents; her father; the house; money, lots of times about money. Going back to work as much to have some of her own as anything else, to buy things for herself or the girls. To not be beholden. Giving way lots of times when she shouldn't have, giving way because she wanted peace, or at least not a fight.

This was perhaps the thing. His going away to work meant she'd been alone enough now to know she could survive without him. Intimacy long gone anyway. If intimacy meant sex. But sometimes just physical generosity, too. The desire to be held. To sleep in someone's arms. You couldn't say they'd swapped it for wealth, it was lost long before the mine work started. Sometime after Emily was born. Or maybe even before that, when her body had started to change with the pregnancy, and this time, with another small child to take care of, there hadn't been the energy for that shared curiosity about her transformation which was both intimate *and* sexual. Her swelling belly, her swollen breasts, she'd thought, disgusted him. Afterwards, they never found their way back.

She didn't know what he did for sex – presuming he did anything. She didn't ask, didn't want to think about brothels in the Pilbara or elsewhere. Or another lover. If she allowed herself to think about it a kind of crushing guilt would overtake her. As if the failure of this aspect of the marriage had to be, by definition, her fault. Growing independent but still tied to him in so many ways. Unwilling to think of alternatives. For all sorts of reasons, many of which had nothing to do with him or the girls but were bound up in her sense of who she was; a substantial investment in the picture of herself as the happily married mother of two girls.

He couldn't contain it any longer. Stood up and came over to the bench with his beer in its stupid fucking stubby holder, like a boy with his teddy bear, working up to a tantrum. Waving it around.

'You don't give a fuck do you?' he said. 'You think you can get together with your crowd of blow-ins and stir up trouble and it doesn't come back, eh? You can plaster your face all over the fucking television, saying all kinds of shit that I don't know where it comes from. You forget I have to live in this town, too.'

'I live in this town. That's why I'm doing this. That's why we're all doing this. Because it's about where we live. It's about caring for the land.'

'Don't give me that shit. You don't give a fuck about the land.'

To which she could answer exactly what? *I do. You don't. I do.* The whole thing reduced to a screaming match.

'What you're really saying is this is about you, isn't it?' she said, just as angry as he was. Hanging onto the bench for dear life. The dinner all but forgotten. The house eerily silent without the television. The girls no doubt listening hard from their rooms.

'Fucking right it's about me. It's about me and my fucking family.' Waving his beer around.

'Which happens to include me,' she said.

'Yeah, well that was a mistake, wasn't it?'

Terrible the way things got said in an argument that weren't meant. Or were meant but not like they sounded. Weren't supposed to come out like that.

'So that's it, is it?' she said. 'Our marriage is a mistake?'

'Was a fucking mistake.'

Watching him standing there with his face distorted by a rage that was entirely out of proportion to what she'd done or was going to do, a rage in him which was always there below the surface, in varying levels of intensity, waiting to spring up, as if it was the only tool he had left to maintain control over his world or at least that part of it which was circumscribed by the home, and to which she'd always been susceptible, had wanted to ease for him, because she loved him or felt sympathy for him, or because it scared the crap out of her for reasons she had no desire to analyse but were probably something to do with her own father and all the shit that had gone down there, none of which had a fucking iota of relevance to the present situation of her wanting to be nothing more than who she was. Tears running down her cheeks despite her fury. Angry, too, that she couldn't hide her emotions. That even if her investment in him had diminished she still put value in their marriage and here he was, articulating things she barely dared allow herself to think as a tactic to win some tiny battle, as if it was just another thing on the table. He'd said this sort of thing before. The threat. Pretending it didn't mean anything to him. And just because it was pretence didn't mean it didn't hurt. The cheapness of him.

'Don't start fucking crying,' he said.

'I'm not *fucking* crying.'

She turned her back on him. Threw the colander into the sink. Lifted the heavy pasta pot off the stove, poured its contents in. Refused to look around to see what he was doing. Threads of spaghetti slithering over the edge and into the drain.

She wouldn't back down. Wouldn't stop doing what she believed in because it inconvenienced him. There were plenty of dairy farmers in the area who thought the dam was a rubbish idea, not just Mal Izzert. The Campbells and the Wyndhams had come down to Brisbane as well, a whole convoy of farmers' trucks blocking George Street, putting the wind up the politicians and the police (who hadn't a clue what to do with *Friesians*. Who to arrest? The cows? The farmers?). Cameras everywhere, the opportunity for media disaster abounding. The *fun* of it. That's what David didn't get, and should have, because he didn't like authority any better than she did, it was just that he'd lost that bit of himself. Lost it in his grand pursuit of money.

The campaign was, in part, the source of her strength. That she could do this thing. That even if she couldn't find the right words to explain it to him there was an excitement in being able to stand up in front of the cameras and be an advocate for something. In other people wanting her to do that. She was a good nurse. Nursing was something she had done, she *did* still, because it paid well and because, when she'd been eighteen and finished school, she'd had to do something and it was what was offered, was one of only two professions for an educated woman that existed in her nan's imagination. But it had never been her passion.

These last months she'd discovered something new in herself: an ability to sit in a room full of people and understand what was going on. She could tell who was there for what reason and act on that knowledge. A talent for activism. It wasn't an alternative profession, but neither could she imagine not doing it because her husband didn't like it.

This was how far she'd come.

Someone, not her mother, had built that house on *The Farm*, put up those timber walls, the dirt floor, the fireplace made from curved sheets of corrugated iron which also served as the cooking stove, the double bed built into the wall where her mum and Jean-Baptiste slept when he was around, which wasn't often. Only one room to the whole thing, a portion cut off by a curtain for her and Yvette to sleep, a veranda with a bark roof where there was a hammock in which she had lain beside her father while he read, curled within his smell, which was tobacco and marijuana, coffee and sweat.

The book he'd been reading was called *The Brother*. She remembered because Jean-Baptiste had told her it was a book about him. Because she thought it remarkable that someone had written and printed and bound a book about her father and when she said that he'd laughed and corrected her and said, 'No, it's not about me personally, it's what happens when you put a young boy in the hands of the Jesuits.'

'What,' she asked, 'is a Jesuit?'

'Ah, now there is a question,' Jean-Baptiste said, drawing heavily on his cigarette, letting the smoke curl back out over his lips. 'Something we hope you never meet. Men in black robes who tell you how wrong you are. Anything you want to do is wrong.' Waving the hand now that held the cigarette, his other arm around her. 'Say you want to go down the creek, that is wrong. Say you want to stay here and read a book, or play music, or simply to think; *that is wrong*. Or it is the wrong book or the wrong music, or you are not sitting up straight enough, or you are thinking the wrong thoughts.'

'What,' she might have asked, 'are wrong thoughts?' except she already knew that because her mind was always full of wrong thoughts, about her mother (even then), or Amanda, the friend who had come to live on the property only recently, a girl her own age, whose mother was an *Orange Person*. They had been to India. Amanda had seen what life was like there. Men, she said, went to the toilet in the street. Yvette had called her a liar. She knew things, too, she said. She wasn't *stupid*.

At eight years old it is impossible to understand context. *Bene Gesserit* had been started by a group of women inspired to go bush through a complex weave of feminism and ill-informed mysticism.

57

Over time the teachings of Osho had taken hold, including an unusual level of sexual freedom, even for those years. Some better suited to the arrangement than others. Jean-Baptiste, for all his liking of women, no good at it at all. He moved out, found someone else's hippie house to rent closer to town, another lover, a local band to play with. The weekend of the catastrophe Eugenie hadn't gone to stay with him. She'd had a sleep-over arranged with Amanda. It was Yvette who was alone in his little cabin when something – a spark from the fire, a kerosene lamp, a candle – set it alight.

In the aftermath – the police, the coroner's report, the inquest, the what-turned-out-to-be-illegal burial on *Bene Gesserit* attended by her distraught and confused grandparents, complete with all-night chanting and dancing by robed members of the community – it was found that Jean-Baptiste had overstayed his visa by ten years. He was deported. In the light of her mother's incapacity to deal with her grief – her need to go to India to process what it meant to have lost a daughter – Eugenie was given into the care of her grandparents.

Turning back with the drained pasta. He was still there, in the middle of the room. A solid man. Like his father. In a singlet that showed off his shoulders, his biceps. Board shorts. Sturdy legs. He'd always had a kind of boyish face, cheeky, but you could see, now that his hair was starting to recede, that there'd come a time, maybe in not so long, when he'd put the tools down for the last time and put on a pair of glasses and take up management completely, and that when he did he'd look like anybody else, like an accountant or a businessman. She almost felt sorry for him.

He looked away. Picked up the remote and flicked on the sound, filling the room with the roar of the crowd. Someone must have scored. His back to her, affecting to watch the screen in much the same way as she had the dinner. A man who lived and worked amongst men most of whom had only a rudimentary interest or understanding of the environment or politics (never mind women). Ripe for manipulation by television and the popular press. There was that phrase she'd heard somewhere: *it is hard for a man to understand something when his salary depends on him not doing so*; but she wasn't sure where the observation left her, sharing the benefits.

'Do you want to call the girls?' she said, pulling plates out from the cupboard. 'Dinner's ready.'

He switched off the sound again, the anger brimming but the protocols of living together still holding sway. For a little while. Going down the corridor to stick his head in their rooms.

Leaving the words he'd said hanging.

She put the plates out on the bench, then stopped, resting her hands on the edge again, her weight on them. Having to, to stop from falling. From the force of holding herself against him. Surprised he hadn't let loose. Wondering if it was still to come. If he would try to use the girls to make his point. Or if, perhaps, something had changed in her that had prevented him. That maybe he sensed she didn't care enough anymore. The awful power of indifference. The idea lurking in the back of her mind that she might have other choices. Not just because of what she was doing with the dam. At three o'clock in the morning a couple of weeks before she'd been in the hospital when the new doctor had brought in a patient. Nothing had been said, nothing done, but she'd felt it in her bones. *In her waters* as her nan used to say. And it didn't matter that nothing would or could happen as a result of it. That all such feelings are, by definition, fantasies. That wasn't the point. Someone had seen her. Someone had taken the time to look. It made all the difference.

four

Guy

What he'd not been prepared for, sitting up there on stage in the carefully choreographed intimacy of armchairs and standard lamps, was the audience's hatred. It caught him off-guard, undermining his sense of self (never as unequivocal as many believed) bringing into question long-held certainties. When he addressed the public – on panels, giving keynotes, during those episodes of *First Edition* filmed in front of a live audience – he was used to admiration, or at least, if that was too strong a word, *deference*. It had taken some time, admittedly, but he'd finally grown accustomed to the vitriol that spooled out in the comments below his online articles; he'd come to understand these rants were nothing to do with him, *per se*, they were an expression of some fundamental disaffection amongst the wider population, an anonymous vein of anger searching for an outlet which just happened to have settled on him, or, at best, what he'd written.

Helen, in one of those blanket dismissals of whole sections of society which had become more common in this last year, the year of her illness, would have it that it was a manifestation of the politics of envy, an attempt to shift responsibility for the shape of people's own lives onto someone else. Which was as may be, but in the Winderran Community Centre it was different. The people in the audience were flesh and blood, several with names he knew, and their anger was personal and immediate. It struck him like a physical attack; if it was envy, he wanted to ask, of what? Which part of his life, exactly, was it that someone else might want?

It was Aldous Bain who'd got him into this. He and Peter Mayska had flattered him, no point in pretending otherwise, and he'd been susceptible to that, even from a man like *Bain*, with his studied use of the vernacular, his *we don't have a dog in the fight*, the idiom as fake as his moleskin slacks and light blue open-necked cotton shirt; the Shadow Minister's knowledge of the bush entirely secondhand, derived from the lesser partners in the Coalition; the man wouldn't know a cattle dog, let alone a fighting one, if it bit him on the ankle. The two of them plying him with excess and privilege so that his judgement was compromised and he'd said he'd do it, having convinced himself, against all evidence to the contrary, that it would be a rational debate. But then he'd refused to look, hadn't he? Social media being beneath his consideration.

Blind-sided from every quarter. Even a glance at the *NoDam*'s Facebook page would have given him notice that his opposite number was to be Eugenie Lensman, a woman he'd barely seen for ten years but who had, nonetheless, come to occupy a significant place in his imagination. When she strode up to him backstage, with that regal bearing of hers, face framed by its mane of tight curled hair, hand outstretched, he was instead caught unawares, lulled into a false sense of security by what he took as a genuine welcome and, how can he put this, the resonance of his own creation.

The first time they'd met her father had been visiting from France. The man, in a wonderful show of Gallic arrogance, had called Guy up, cold, to see if he and his daughter, a resident of the town, might come to visit, to talk about Guy's books – a musician to a writer; a request so unusual that he'd accepted. It was a mistake; the father, for all his reading, had proved to be tedious, wanting to discuss his experience of the creation of art and his fanciful interpretations of Guy's characters. The consolation had been the presence of Eugenie, standing by his bookshelves leafing through various volumes, remaining all but silent throughout, but thus presenting herself as the model for a character he'd been struggling with at the time. The novel – a sprawling early-settlement narrative – had required a female protagonist, strong but wistful, much troubled by external forces, capable of great love but rarely receiving it in return. Eugenie had seemed the perfect embodiment. The problem with such a projection being that, on meeting her again, years later, some part of his brain conflated the real with the imaginary.

The intervening years had given her more confidence. As she shook his hand, telling him he wouldn't remember her, she said that, like her father, she was an admirer of his books, further surprising him by naming several of them, *Magazine Husbands, Indolent Thing,* even *The Brother,* all of them, of course, early works, but no mind. *Husbands* was, she said, her favourite.

'That was the first book I wrote in Winderran,' he'd replied, launching into a description of his process, in thrall to his fantasy of this woman, 'I'd been overseas for a few years and my wife and I had just settled in. It was as if I was seeing the country through an outsider's eyes.'

In actual fact her show of interest had been little more than a tactic to put him at ease, all the better to destroy him in the debate.

'I see you often these days, on TV,' she said, smiling, 'talking about books.'

~

It was certain comments he'd made during an episode of *First Edition* which had got him into this situation. They'd slipped out, unplanned, in response to something his co-presenter, Sheila, had said. The woman had been baiting him for most of the program, which was, on this occasion, being recorded live at a writers' festival. The disagreements between them were the meat of the show, they both understood that – after all, if they liked the same books there would have been nothing to say – and they played to these differences; but any acting involved in the performance was more to do with the pretence they liked each other than in the sparring. Sheila was insufferable. She turned up each month in ever more obscure garments – Nepalese smocks woven from yak's hair, Myanmar silks, a Dirndl blouse – supposedly with the aim of making some sort of avant-garde fashion statement. Clothes which would have looked awkward on a twenty-year-old. Horribly pleased with herself, sitting across from him with her rhinestone glasses hung on a string around her neck and her ridiculous hair; smiling. Never ceasing to smile. They might be discussing the most awful excesses of child soldiers in some African state, or the legacy of Primo Levi, and there she would be with that television presenter's grin on her, all teeth and glossy lipstick.

During the earlier part of the show he'd offended her. They'd been discussing Margaret Atwood's new novel, which he'd hated. She, of course, had loved it, and claimed his criticism was based on prejudice against women's writing. It was an old argument, one she liked to haul out as a way of winding him up. In this case, though, it wasn't so. The writing was simply *bad*.

'Someone,' he said, 'should have had the decency to tell her. An editor, a publisher, *anyone.*' The extraordinary thing, he continued, was that no-one had, with all the implications for literature this implied.

Towards the end of the show, reviewing a slim volume from a famous American which they, unusually, had both agreed was slim not just in size, she took the opportunity to stick in the knife.

'There's a sense,' she said, 'the man's running out of ideas, isn't there?' Looking directly at him, 'Perhaps it's time for him to publish a collection of his occasional pieces, maybe even his letters.' Pausing to let that idea settle, those teeth gleaming in their awful rictus. 'But then that doesn't always work out so well, does it, Guy?'

She had been referring, of course, to his own recent collection, *Correspondencies*, the publication of a volume of letters he and his wonderful friend, Edward, had exchanged over thirty-five years.

He wasn't often lost for words on the show. If, on occasion, either of them stumbled, it could be edited out before the program was put to air. Before a live audience there was no escape. There was a moment of silence. Two or three seconds too long for television. Realising she'd gone too far, perhaps hoping to rescue the situation, she started prattling on about Winderran.

'You're in the news up there at the moment aren't you?' she said. 'They want to build some stupid dam right in your backyard, isn't that the case?'

And there he was, caught by a vast swelling need to humiliate her and all her pusillanimous little hangers-on.

'*Stupid?*' he said. 'Far from it. Most of Queensland, including the south-east, is in the grip of a terrible drought, has been for the last few years. You might have heard about it. The city's dams are at less than twenty per cent. Where I live, at Winderran, it rains a lot, more than almost anywhere else on the eastern seaboard if you don't include the far north, and there's this bit of disused farmland, over-cleared and over-grazed for the last hundred years, a barren plain, which is the perfect site for a dam. The water trapped there would, as it happens, be up on a hill, and therefore could run down to wherever it's needed under its own velocity. In fact you could even generate electricity at the same time. I believe they plan to do so. It's a sort of no-brainer which ticks every box in the green pantheon, not excluding creating jobs during construction and boosting tourism when it's done. It's a kind of God-given answer to a difficult problem, but, of course, every fool and his dog is out there campaigning against it.'

This, or something like it, something more tailored, less abrasive, less patronising, he hoped, was what he gave as his opening remarks at the debate; realising, even as he spoke, he'd misjudged his audience.

The woman, when it was her turn, began nervously, sitting forward in her armchair, straight-backed, a bit Nordic in her frock that just covered her crossed knees, something deeply sexual in her propriety, she had, he thought, aged beautifully in the last decade, coming into herself in the way of women in their late thirties, that exquisite late flowering. She read from notes, the paper quivering, laying out her position on the dam in language that was clear, if pedestrian – but then so, too, were her ideas. There should have been no argument, except that she was applauded for almost everything she said, and so became more enthusiastic, her rhetoric rising to meet the occasion.

The dam, she said, was an environmental disaster in the making, inappropriate for the site for reasons of geology, climate and safety. It was the wrong dam in the wrong place.

More applause.

She wandered into political theory: the decision to build a dam was an attempt by central government bureaucracies to prolong their hold over ratepayers; it would do nothing to alleviate the problem it was designed to solve. 'If a dam is the answer,' she said, to actual cheers, her back ever more straight, quivering with excitement, 'you have to wonder what the question was.'

The moderator, a fellow from the university on the coast, someone he vaguely knew, a professor of that sham excuse for a subject, *Cultural Studies*, himself shambling and overweight, offered him time to address her points before questions were taken from the floor.

'How are people on the coast supposed to be provided with water?' he asked, politely, generously, attempting to bring some rationality back into the debate. 'Or are you proposing that we shouldn't allow anyone else to come here to live? That we lock the doors and keep everyone out? A little enclave of middle-class privilege?'

The set-up on stage designed to appear convivial, as if they were engaged in a fireside chat, the chairs at a slight angle to each other, glasses of water on the coffee table. Familiar territory, except that, being Winderran, the chairs were old lumpy things hauled out of someone's lounge room. You might sink into them without hope of retrieval. And the standard lamps were just for show, the stage was illuminated by a bank of lights which prevented him from seeing beyond the first couple of rows. No sympathy there, just angry people, arms crossed like so many Spartans at the pass.

'Thanks for the question, Guy,' she said, become, it seemed, a budding politician, patronising *him*. 'And you are correct; there *are* some who think we can't allow as many people to live here as want to, who argue there is such a thing as *carrying capacity*. I'm not buying into that debate. What *I* think is if you legislate for water tanks on every new build you won't need to destroy an important part of the hinterland by constructing an expensive and anachronistic piece of infrastructure fifty kilometres from where the water's needed, and then pump it to that location.'

'You can't be serious,' he said, laughing. 'This is gimcrackery.'

'I've rarely been more serious in my life,' she said, her colour rising. 'With due respect, Guy, you're not going to convince us by making smug comments. We're trying to address the way development occurs in our own backyard. Why is that such a radical proposal?'

'Because you're talking nonsense.'

Someone booed. Several others hissed.

'What do you mean?' she asked.

'Well the dam's going to be up here in the hills, you don't have to pump things anywhere ...' he wasn't sure if this was exactly true, but there was a logic to it. *Water tanks for Christ's sake*. 'And then consider the cost ... and the means to monitor and maintain the system, the spread of mosquito-borne diseases ...'

But she'd come armed with statistics, no matter how spurious. 'According to independent studies the cost of a water tank adds less than two per cent to the price of a new build ... these funds would be recycled many times over in the local economy, generating *real* jobs ... if you legislated for this you'd get the same volume of water as in your dam *where it's needed*, for less than a quarter of the price. It's the same principle as solar panels on people's roofs. Are you opposed to them, too?'

'I think,' he said, unable to believe that he had allowed himself to be drawn down this path by a woman speaking in slogans, 'you are proposing simplistic solutions to complex problems.'

'I'm not being simplistic, Guy, I'm being deliberately complex. I'm proposing individual supply solutions instead of major infrastructure. I'm proposing we embrace *that* future. This is a new age of infrastructure delivery. Dams are old technology. They don't work, they don't last, they're dangerous and we don't want one here.'

The hall erupting. The academic choosing this moment to jolly up to the microphone to ask for lights to be brought up and questions taken from the floor. Probably old scores being settled there, too. He'd no doubt offended the man at some point or other. In a place the size of Queensland it was impossible not to have.

If there was anyone in the room in favour of the dam, they held their tongues. Speaker after speaker – they were supposed to be asking questions but the moderator didn't have the capacity or the inclination to discern a question from a diatribe – attacked the dam (and him) for reasons ranging from the specious to the outright mad. It shouldn't have worried him, but it did. It infuriated him. Nobody listening. This hall full of people committed to their little dreams of opposition, their fantasy of always losing out, as if they weren't living in the most prosperous culture in the world.

The point was, he gave opinions all the time. He appeared on *First Edition* once a month with Sheila; wrote for the national broadsheet; was a regular speaker on radio; sat on several Arts boards and contributed book reviews to a raft of magazines besides. For all this he held few illusions about his place in the popular imagination. He'd never made the mistake of assuming a lot of people were paying attention. And yet this little snippet – this little rant at the end of the book show – took off, attracting praise and invective from the most surprising quarters. *How refreshing it is to hear an* artist *standing up for infrastructure*, wrote one pundit in the *Oz, you have your Wintons and your Flanagans wittering on about the environment as if they had a God-given right to lecture us, being given all sorts of platforms to express their utopian fantasies, but here we have one of our better writers calling to account the woolly thinking of the Left, talking up practical solutions to intractable problems.*

Most likely, even then, it would have died a natural death, only that it came to the attention of Peter Mayska. An invitation was passed through Bain to come to his house. 'He's keen to meet you,' Bain said, refusing to give more detail, promising only that he wouldn't be disappointed; the meal would be without par.

A sleek charcoal BMW came to pick him up, driven by a well-built character in a tight black suit and chauffeur's hat who said little but whisked him through town behind tinted windows on the tail end of a Sunday, the sky doing that wonderful thing it does in autumn and spring in these parts, silhouetting the trees, sharply delineating each and every branch, rendering the valleys soft and mysterious; the view, it must be said, enhanced, the uneven surface of the road neutralised, by fine German technology.

Mayska had bought one of the declining dairy farms out past Elmhurst and turned it into a horse stud, complete with imposing wrought-iron gates and painted post-and-rail fences measuring out the roll of hills. Lamprey had never visited, nor expected he would. Australia likes to think itself a classless society, requiring even its oligarchs to dress like their inferiors, to talk in the same way, to appear to want the same things. It doesn't mean they have to mingle.

The house a case in point. It was understated on approach, a long low roof with a raised portico at its centre, very Japanesey, lots of recycled timber. Fine, high-strung fillies tossing their heads and kicking their heels as the car crept past on raked gravel. Broad Moreton Bay figs stretching out their shadows. An impression of humility which was dispelled, however, on entry, when it became clear that the building was vast, cut into the hillside facing away from the road. The owner of Mayska Coal & Gas coming to open the door himself, escorting Guy inside and down wide marble steps to a boundless foyer dotted with sculptures, a grand piano up against five-metre floor-to-ceiling glass, telling him how glad he was that he could come, that he'd been wanting to thank him for sorting out the incident with his son a few weeks previously.

'I did little,' Guy said. 'I simply asked a doctor I know for help.'

'Yes but you knew the right doctor in the right place. Your assistance was invaluable.'

'And your son, he's okay?'

'He's fine. A bit of rough and tumble, no more than that. The usual adolescent stuff. To be honest, the boy needs to step up.' Waving the question aside, encouraging Guy to take in the view, which was as spectacular as it was unexpected. A wide patio giving way to a formal garden that in itself sloped gently to a large farm dam complete with pier and boathouse, ducks on the surface granting perspective; polo fields beyond and from thence the distant hills; glimpses, in the teal dusk light, of ocean off to the east. Wealth on an unprecedented scale, opulence beyond imagination, the little security cameras blinking high up in the corners.

'We'll eat in a moment but I thought you might like to see some of the house first. You are an appreciator of art, am I right? I have a few pieces you might enjoy.'

Mayska in white shirt and slacks, cashmere sweater draped over his shoulders, tall, loose-limbed, fit, grey hair worn slightly long at the back, receding from a forehead shining with that polished skin the wealthy always seem to attain, as if they do actually eat their gold, which, who knows, might be the case, although it's more likely to be a result of something that happens in those curious day-spas; nubile young women buffing their faces with rare rainforest plants or Icelandic stones so that they appear before you radiant with health, *sans* spot or blemish.

Directing him from the foyer through a large square arch into another wing of the building which had, it seemed, been constructed for the sole purpose of housing his private collection.

'Aldous is in here somewhere,' Mayska said, calling out. They followed the disembodied voice, finding Bain at the rear of the gallery, where the face of the excavated rock, lit from below, acted as an artwork in itself.

There were a couple of Rothko's, a Pollock, the requisite Picasso (not one Lamprey found easy on the eye), three Namatjiras and a sampling of bark paintings, but also, amongst the impressionists, a Cézanne; a small painting in an elaborate gold frame hung on a wide expanse of polished concrete, delicately lit, glowing in the perfectly humidified air; its richness, the painter's left-leaning landscape with its pigeon-roofed houses brought into its power against the industrial blandness of the wall, which was probably what it was supposed to do, but Cézanne could surely never have imagined his canvas appearing thus. A painting like that was enough in itself for a day, hard to concentrate on anything beyond it, even on the marvellous Giacometti on a plinth in a room by itself. To have such a thing in one's possession ... this, Lamprey thought, must be the whole purpose of a private collection, to impress, not just with wealth but also taste, a demonstration of sophistication beyond the reach of others.

A meal *was* provided. They chose dishes from a menu. Wines that only the gods should drink to accompany them. The three of them at an antique table against the glass, in their own private restaurant, begging the question of staff and superfluous food, the whole enormous production of which Peter Mayska was the creation, or creator, Lamprey couldn't make up his mind which, wanting to dislike the man but finding him entertaining, a raconteur whose only crime was to like the sound of his own voice (something he'd been accused of himself) and a tendency to draw attention to his journey out of poverty a little too often, even if it was, each time, as part of a story.

On closer inspection, under the disguise of a stylised beard, Mayska's face was deeply lined around the eyes and mouth, showing the marks of his earlier life prospecting in the north and west, lending him a slightly bohemian cast. He sat back in his chair watching them finish their main course, regaling them with an anecdote about his parents' escape from the Bolsheviks. Lamprey was impressed despite himself. It had been a remarkable rise. That, in a single lifetime, a man might climb so high. Come to such estate. Just the mathematics of accumulating all that wealth; the doubling of capital it must have required. Lamprey had recently read a woman writer describe such men as *leading with their dicks*. He'd been surprised by the crudeness of the analogy both in the sense of the approval the woman granted and the practicality of the description, but watching Peter he saw what she meant, age having neither emasculated him nor rid him of his desire for power, possessions, women, dynasty, respect. He wasn't satisfied, was still reaching. On his third wife. Lamprey, taking a mouthful of wine (what was it, *Grange? Hill of Grace?* The stuff had been decanted so he'd never know and was too polite to ask) watched and listened and contributed where possible, but he did so as a writer first, taking notes, savouring each detail for later use, wondering, also, at the naivety of inviting a man like himself to such a place. Did they think he wouldn't use it? That he wasn't alert to their pretensions? Perhaps Mayska believed that when they became as large as this, your own Cézanne in your own gallery, they took on enough *gravitas* to wash critique aside.

The trouble being that for all his close noticing of Mayska he wasn't paying attention to their agenda. Not just the wine having its way with him. It turned out it wasn't his help with Cooper at the camp which had provoked Mayska's interest but his little outburst to Sheila.

'A man like you,' Mayska said, after they'd moved onto the brandy, 'we could use in the Senate.'

'What do you mean, a man like me?'

Lulled by the largesse, but not comatose, not yet. We could *use*? What on earth did they take him for? And why the *we*? Why was Bain allowing Mayska to do the talking on his behalf, or on behalf of his Party?

'Someone who speaks his mind. You have the gift of seeing through to the sense of a thing and then talking about it in terms others can understand. I know that you are a writer – I've not read your books … I am sorry … I don't get time to read fiction – but I've seen you on television and I know something of your background. I think there are other ways you can use your gifts. I think what we need most of all in our country at the moment are people who can communicate frankly and clearly. Without bullshit.'

Biting his tongue; determined not to rise to the suggestion that fiction was somehow the lesser art. So much for speaking your mind. *Our Country*, which was another way of saying *Our Party*. That would be the Liberal-Nationals.

I know your background.

Guy supposed that was part of it. He had a long association with Aldous. They'd bumped into each other at the airport on several occasions and, over drinks in the lounge, he'd found the Federal Member possessed of a droll wit rarely evident in his public appearances. Aldous had been a lawyer before he entered politics and retained his love of literature and the arts. They had more in common than he might ever have imagined. Over the years Aldous had provided him with both material for columns and connection to other sources. It was an arrangement of mutual benefit that Bain would have been unlikely to countenance if there was evidence of some horror lurking in the past. Someone had, without doubt, been rifling through his history. Venice springing to mind; or his more immediate association with a particular establishment in Canberra; not to mention *Alan*. A certain chill at the idea of one of their minions tooling around in his life. But then he'd never been frightened of who he was, the whole purpose and meaning of his books had been to discuss something as grand as the human condition, our awful common failing mortality, and he was unashamed that his own life had been freely employed in its service. If anyone was to claim he judged people harshly, and they did, he held up his own self-analysis as example.

Inviting him to stand for the Senate. Number two on the ticket. A foregone conclusion that they would retain at least two of the slots. How might they not? The other lot were hopeless, clamouring to be sent to the wilderness for at least a couple of terms. Scenarios involuntarily swelling in his mind, their richness enhanced, perhaps, by the extraordinary nature of the company and the remarkable building, its tall windows giving way now to flood-lit fountains in the formal garden, a sixteenth-century tapestry glowing on the wall behind them. He wasn't drunk, even though his glass had been filled many times, this was a different kind of intoxication he was suffering from; besotted by possibility. Trying to ground himself with historical imperatives, *sic transit gloria mundi*.

The invitation tapping, of course, into what he hoped were well-disguised dreams of glory; what was it Peter Carey had said, *who knows the fantasies that lie dormant in a writer's mind*? Something like that. Carey was deflecting a question about the Nobel at the time, but what about the even more terrible fantasy realised by Václav Havel? The one which every writer – world creators all – must nurture deep in their breasts, that eventually the people will come to find them and raise them up to rule over them; even only for a time.

The honour of it.

Except, of course, in this case, Peter Mayska would clearly like to be doing a bit of the ruling.

'Let me make one thing clear,' Mayska said, 'I'm not, and I think I speak for Aldous here too, interested in turning you to my purpose. That is not what this dinner is about.'

An odd idiom even for the correctly spoken Peter.

'Aldous has spoken highly of you, that's all. There is, how can I put it, a dearth of good minds in parliament. We think you could make a difference.'

A waiter was hovering with the decanter and Mayska allowed the man to spill a splash into the deep bowl of his glass, indicating he should attend to the others. At home here in this, one of his many houses, tilting back in his chair, the white shirt stretched across his taut belly. He must work out, didn't mind letting others notice. Perhaps he rode some of the horses. No doubt there was a gym somewhere in the complex, and a lap pool, a media centre, helicopter pad, *everything*.

It occurred to Guy to wonder if the invitation was a test. Nothing being simple with these people. Trying to keep on his guard. But it wasn't so: continuing to stand up in favour of the Winderran dam proposal *was*. Bain had been unusually quiet throughout the proceedings. Now he stepped in to explain the politics of the project, disassociating himself from it. A quick lesson in politics from the master.

'It's a State government thing,' he said. 'Of very limited significance and nothing to do with Canberra except for the purposes of signing off. If it comes before us after the election we'll approve it in a millisecond, of course, if only to support the premier, but the decision to build was made in the heat of the moment. We're happy to sit this one out. Nobody wins with issues like this. It's best to avoid them.'

It was somewhere in there that the comment about having a dog in the fight had surfaced.

'So why do you suggest I stick my neck out?'

'Because you've shown yourself as a rational voice in a difficult place. It doesn't hurt to be recognised for that. These environmentalists are fanatics. Zealots. It's taken a while but people are starting to realise it. They'll never be satisfied. It doesn't matter how much they win they want more. Nothing will ever be enough. Taking them on is a simple way of showing the Party where you stand.'

Helen was more than simply disparaging, not just at the idea of attending the community meeting as a speaker, but of having anything to do with Aldous.

'I never liked him,' she said. 'I don't trust him. He looks like a walking corpse.'

'You can't hold what he looks like against him.'

'Yes I can. He's a politician. What's he doing cosying up to Mayska Coal & Gas? That can't be good from anyone's perspective.

And what do they want from you? I thought you wanted more time to write. You never stop complaining about having to produce your columns, the committee work, the television program. Is this just more procrastination? Or have you decided to throw it away completely?'

Helen, who had not been invited to the dinner and wouldn't have attended if she had, was still recovering from the surgery, suffering now under the strain of radiation. Taking tiny sips from a glass of water in the kitchen when he returned late in the evening. Impatient with him.

On the subject of Mayska, though, she was wrong. The man had a powerful intellect founded on hard learning. He'd spent years in remote north-western Queensland and New Guinea, fossicking, living in caravans and tents with only himself and books for company, taking out mining leases nobody else wanted when he thought there were possibilities. It had given him an unusual perspective on what was important. When China woke from her sleep there he was, in possession of the rights. This, apparently, being how immense wealth is accumulated, not just the original obsession with rocks and the ownership of the leases, but the ability to grasp opportunity when it presented itself, time and again, on each occasion being prepared to risk it all, at least until the construct became so large nobody was prepared to let it fail. Mayska the one amongst a million who could do it.

'What do I want from government?' he said, in answer to Guy's question. 'That's simple: an administration that's open to business. Listen.' Bringing the chair back onto four legs with a crack, leaning forward, 'In our lifetimes we have seen the greatest eradication of poverty in human history. Millions, *billions*, lifted out of abject misery, whole countries, not just China and India – where there is much still to do – but Brazil, African countries like Botswana, the smaller Asians, Vietnam, Thailand, all of them transformed through free trade, nothing else, through being allowed to act in the market.

'There is a great campaign to stop this, the elites in the developed world don't want the unwashed billions to have the kinds of things they have. *The planet can't afford it*, they say, but what they *mean* is that other cultures aren't sophisticated enough to manage their own economies … It's a kind of colonial thinking. A throwback to another time.'

'That's not quite the case,' Guy said. 'It's not that they think them incapable of managing their economies. There are legitimate fears about global warming. I'm sorry to bring it up.'

Mayska waved this apology away. 'Don't be afraid to speak. It's why you're here. But listen, MCG is diverse. We can see change coming just like everyone else. Unlike some others we're not trying to stop it. We've invested in liquefied gas, in electronics research. Whoever comes up with an efficient battery will command the world. Such a battery will be the end of coal. Overnight. You don't think I know that? Technologies change. I want to be the man at the forefront.'

Which was another way of saying he wanted to be the richest man in the world, and to do so he wanted a pliable government in Australia.

Mayska laughed. 'Is that such an unlikely ambition? I am now in a position to make changes to the way the world runs.'

'Peter doesn't like to advertise it,' Bain said, 'but he is Australia's largest philanthropist.'

'An individual like me,' Mayska said. 'I have the capacity to direct funds in ways that are impossible for government, simply because they are top heavy, too slow to turn. I've been given, through my wealth, access to some of the levers of change.'

'So you favour the benevolent dictatorship?' Guy said. Perhaps he *was* drunk, but the man's delusions of grandeur were simply too large. He might own a Giacometti and a Cézanne but he hadn't been looking at them enough. He'd forgotten to notice how frail they were.

'No, you have me wrong. I've told you from where I came.' A careful pause to let that sink in, to be reminded of the flight from Eastern Europe. 'I have a profound and active hatred of repression, corruption, nepotism. But I see the values that sustained the West, that brought it to the fore, in decline. I want to reverse this process.'

Something about the way he said this jolting Guy into relative sobriety. Anyone can say such a thing, and many do; many try to effect change, but few are in possession of the means to do so. Mayska speaking directly to him, saying, *I have these tools in my hands right now.* Here was the point of the dinner next to the tall windows, the ancient brandy in his glass. Mayska was inviting him to be part of the remaking of the world. Mayska was saying *I want you to help me.*

In the middle of the night, woken from sleep as from nightmare, startled awake, he lay in his crumpled sheets, washed by waves of humiliation. That he had allowed himself to be talked into participating in such a farce. The way he had been *treated*. The heat of it burning his skin. The things said about him during the debate indefensible. And at the centre of it, like a crude allegory, this woman, *wistfully* screwing him before the crowd. His own creation turned back on him, not even respecting him for who he was.

Helen doing everything but say I told you so. 'You were conned by the Cézanne,' is what she managed. 'Mayska might be talking about technological change but he's digging up coal as fast as he can while ever the digging's good. The fact he's aware of climate change doesn't mean he's sympathetic to regulation of carbon when it interferes with building his wealth. Probably doing his best to derail rival technologies for batteries as we speak, if he's doing anything at all and not simply bullshitting. I'm not the first person to remark how extreme wealth, like beauty, makes people seem smarter than they are.'

Plotting comebacks in the hours between two and three, that meaningless time when, by common knowledge, it is understood nothing under consideration will survive the dawn and which must, yet, be thought through anyway. No wonder there were alcoholics and drug abusers, depression and despair. And at the heart of it, the kernel of knowledge that he should never have returned to this Godforsaken country, this *oubliette* at the bottom of the world which had brought him nothing but sorrow. A forgotten man in a forgotten place.

His beautiful book, *Correspondencies*, slammed in the *New Yorker*. To have Sheila bring it up on television, to score points. So much ordure coming his way these last years. No real writing for almost a decade. The last novel, which he had thought would be his masterwork (in which *that* woman had starred under the name of Greta), the one he had believed would lift him back into the minds of his readers, would, okay, here we are then, *move the stars to pity*, had been universally ignored. Politely reviewed. *A careful study*. Prolix. *A beautiful confection*. As if he had created a pavlova.

His earlier writing had come out of a sense of trust in his own judgement – a belief he could tell when something was good or bad. Now that capacity, along with any access to originality, appeared to have deserted him. There had been a time when literature had welcomed him, when words had flowed without effort, as if imagination were a well from which it was possible to draw infinite story, all he had to do was describe what he saw in his mind's eye and the words would arrive with facility, running down his arm, coursing across the page from the tip of his pen. He had even tried going back to writing by hand, as if the tyranny of the screen might have been the problem, but not only was it too exhausting to scratch away at the paper, his handwriting barely legible, even to himself, it was as if his body rejected the process, his fingers had become attuned to the machine; time and again he returned to the computer, talking at it, battering its keyboard, fabricating the bones of worlds in the hope that eventually the tipping point would come and out of it a story would appear, something as simple and appealing as a *life*. It had been what he'd done for so long that he didn't know what else to do. The need to be useful. To have his life turned to some purpose. Without it he was nothing.

The problem might be his habitual misanthropy. *There* was a thought to conjure with at three-thirty-seven in the morning, with a demented kookaburra calling the dawn an hour too early, its half-hearted cry dissolving into a heavy-set night of cloud and promised rain, a night in which everything falls back on itself under its own weight and all is failure and shame. Alan rising from his grave to haunt him. Edward there, too, calling from Seattle, to boast of his success in the world of academia. Metaphorically, of course. In reality nobody calls from anywhere and if they did he wouldn't talk to them, he is an embittered old man who had the temerity to think the world was waiting for him, a fool who had been fooled by flattery into thinking he had another turn at utility. *If the fool were to persist in his folly …* but not during the dark hours, not when sleep eludes and all is isolation and illusion.

Helen asleep somewhere in the house, rendered permanently beyond reach by illness and its lessons, as if there were any possibility he might want what she offered anyway. After Alan there had been no more *them*. After Alan it had just been each of them alone in the sprawling house, the complex weave of emotion too broad for resolution or redemption, too raw for forgiveness, from any quarter. Their daughter, the one who hadn't died but undoubtedly, irretrievably, irreversibly, believed she *should* have, navigating the troubled waters until she was old enough to leave, convinced she would never be loved as much as the missing one, which was so unfair, even more unfair than their grief for Alan. But then grief is unfair. So unexpected the intensity. It brooks no interference.

five

Nick

The memorial service for Doctor Miles Prentice was held in a marquee at the showgrounds. Neither the community centre nor any of Winderran's seven churches would have been large enough to accommodate the crowd and, besides, Miles had never willingly entered a house of religion in his life. Even then many were left standing along the sides of the tent, holding the flimsy Order of Service over their heads to ward off the sun.

It wasn't just the marquee, though, that gave rise to the idea of some sort of party. The crowd were turned out in summer clothes, hardly a shred of black in sight, the deceased himself represented by a large flower-bedecked photograph – flowers upon flowers, because in the picture Miles was wearing an Hawaiian shirt with a lei around his neck, smiling broadly, as if he'd just arrived in Honolulu, the photo in fact snapped at a themed party, the giveaway being the piña colada he was holding up to the camera, replete with tiny paper umbrella.

Joy had pulled together a committee to organise the event. Even now she was bustling around in a too-tight black satin dress (in this heat!) making sure the right people were sitting where they needed to be. Placing nervous Nick on the row of chairs at the front for the speakers, facing back into the crowd, horribly exposed. He could see few faces he recognised, this being the thing about Winderran, you thought it was small but there were thousands of people in and around the town you never met, living undisclosed lives. An older demographic, generally, here for the service, but one that cut across all barriers: amongst the retirees and tree-changers were also men with craggy farming faces in sharply ironed short-sleeved shirts and moleskins; frocks on the fleshy women, fanning themselves with programs.

He watched as Guy Lamprey came bobbing his way through the crowd towards him, dressed in an open-necked shirt and washed blue jeans, genuflecting right and left with the air of a politician on holiday. 'I see they've roped you in as well,' he said to Nick, lowering himself onto the white monobloc chair beside him.

He welcomed Lamprey's arrival with mixed emotions, relieved that at least someone he knew had joined him at the front, while at the same time being reminded by his presence of the call-out to Spring Creek a few weeks before. They had not spoken since. The more he'd considered it the more uncomfortable he'd felt about his failure to follow up on what had happened to Cooper, at having accepted Aldous Bain's compromise.

Disregarding such thoughts he held up the folded piece of A4 on which he'd typed some notes for his speech, ruefully admitting to Lamprey that he took no joy in public speaking – by way of an understatement – there being, even then, a sharp terror in his bones.

'Few do, God knows,' Lamprey said, 'but here's hoping I get a better reception than I did talking about the fucking dam. Perhaps even this lot can manage to put aside their differences for a funeral.'

The casual obscenity somehow made more crude by Lamprey's refined voice, its use at an event like this slightly shocking, although who knew what was correct anymore? Funerals, it seemed, had become untethered from ritual, the attendees adrift on a sea of ideas stretching from the traditional mourning of a death to the curious mish-mash *celebrations of a life* so favoured by the secular or multi-faith brigades. Such musings not helped in this case by the choice of music: Jimi Hendrix and Eric Clapton, the Rolling Stones playing 'Time Waits for NoOne *(and it won't wait for you)*'.

'Things would be busy at the practice?' Lamprey said.

'Just a bit.'

The place in chaos. He'd had to cut short his trip to Canberra to try to sort it out.

'Helen and I were hoping you might join us for a meal tomorrow evening.'

'I'm a bit swamped at work,' Nick said.

'Nothing special, we have a few friends coming over, you don't have to stay late, but at least that way you'll get a decent feed.'

'I'd be delighted then.'

'Good, very good,' Lamprey said. 'I wanted you to come, if only as a way of thanking you for what you did the other night ... I understand the young man's on the mend?'

'I assume so,' Nick said, 'I've not heard specifics.'

The crowd filling the rows of plastic chairs. Even at a time like this Nick with an eye for the women. Irredeemable. But then some of them, a man couldn't fail to notice, had seen the occasion as an excuse to dress up, to show some skin.

'But I really don't think I need more thanks. I've rarely been thanked more profusely for anything in my life.'

'Really?'

'Well, I happened to bump into Aldous Bain when I was down in Canberra. Then, when I got back, there was a case of wine on my doorstep with a note from someone at Mayska Coal & Gas.'

'I hope it's something good.'

'Embarrassingly so.'

'Well you deserve it.'

'It's nice of you to say so, even if it's not true. I'll bring a bottle with me tomorrow. Better than anything I'm likely to buy.'

'I look forward to it. Peter has an excellent cellar. So, tell me, how was Aldous?'

Nick not sure how to answer, Bain and his cronies being hardly his favourite people, an opinion their brief meeting had done little to alter. Noting Lamprey's familiarity with Mayska and his cellar. 'He didn't recognise me at first,' he said.

'Aldous is normally pretty good at that sort of thing,' Lamprey said. 'The politician's gift. Actually, I wouldn't be surprised if he was here today, his constituency, pillar of the community and all that.'

On the night he'd arrived Nick had gone around to the restaurant late to say hello to Abie, taking a seat at the bar and ordering a drink, not a little surprised at the place's popularity. He'd always believed in his ex-wife's capability as a chef but here it was now, writ large, her bistro, *Eatery*, still full to the gills with noisy prosperous Canberrans, waiters in long aprons weaving their way between tables, some sort of party going on in the back room.

Someone alerted Abie to his presence. She came out from the kitchen still wearing her apron and sat with him, drinking from a tall glass with a splash of wine at its base, talking about their lives and the children and what he might do with them over the next few days, as if the two of them were civilised people, old friends working out schedules, which in many ways is what they were, the vitriol of their last few meetings – when Greloed, and what Abie saw as his inability to keep his dick in his pants, had been the subject of her not insignificant scorn – papered over for the occasion.

They'd moved on to the topic of her elderly parents when they were interrupted by Aldous Bain who, it seemed, had emerged from the back room to speak to Abie about some detail of the meal, the same tall pomaded creature he'd met in Winderran at the house concert. He glanced at Nick as if trying to place him and failing. Nick, in turn, felt disinclined to help but then, fuelled by a simmering resentment for the position he'd been put in at Spring Creek Camp, held out his hand and introduced himself.

'Ah yes, of course. Different contexts. How delightful to see you again Doctor. What brings you to Canberra?'

'Nick's my husband,' Abie said.

'Hah. A small world, eh?'

When he'd finished with Abie he turned to Nick again. 'Actually,' he said, 'I've been hoping to catch up with you … have you got a moment? Could we go outside? I'd like a cigarette.'

'I'm talking to Abie.'

'Well, another time, then.'

But Abie insisted she had to return to the kitchen, so Nick followed Bain out into the Manuka night, to stand beneath the trees while he lit a cigarette, drawing heavily on it, as if he'd been waiting some time for this moment. He asked Nick if there was any news about Cooper, but without, Nick thought, real interest in the answer.

'I just wanted to say thank you for what you did, that's all,' Bain said. 'We very much appreciated your discretion.'

The man had, for all his loathsomeness, a certain force, as if, not physically powerful himself, he was yet accustomed to command respect, or, failing that, obedience.

'I did want to ask, though.'

'Yes,' Nick said.

'I was wondering if you had mentioned the incident to anyone.'

'I've not. Only because I've been so busy, it's slipped my mind.'

No advantage he could see in letting Bain know how much the incident had disturbed him. 'Why do you ask?'

'Oh, no reason. It's just, we would be grateful if you didn't mention it to anyone. These things have a way of getting out of control.'

'What things?'

'Oh, you know, the family matters of people like Peter Mayska.'

'Were you able to apprehend the perpetrators?' Nick asked. That weird bureaucratic language again, emerging from nowhere, as if Bain provoked it.

'We did,' Bain said. 'And they've been dealt with, not so much the boys themselves as those in charge.'

A certain satisfaction rising at the thought of the thug being brought down.

Their meeting had a curious coda. As they re-entered the restaurant the place fell silent, as if to mark their arrival. The cause of the interruption was, however, not them but the emergence from the back room of Stanley Lonergan, Leader of the Opposition, flanked by his entourage, all well wined and dined, the room appearing to part before them as they made their way through the tables. Nick had never seen him before in person. He was older than he appeared on television, shorter, too, a nuggety bloke, walking with his arms away from his sides like a boxer. Hard not to be awed by him, even for someone like Nick.

'Were you and Miles close?' Nick said, tilting his head towards Lamprey while scanning the faces in the marquee.

'Not really, but we've known each other a long time. Mind you, Miles knew everyone, it went with the territory.' Lamprey's long thin legs spread out before him, taking up space. 'I get asked to do this sort of thing all the time. Often enough I can get out of it, but no chance with this one, I'm afraid.' He pointed to Nick's notes. 'If you want my advice, the best thing to do with that is to read them one more time then toss them away. Almost certainly you know what you're going to say by now anyway. If you get the order wrong who cares? No-one else will notice. Pick a person in the crowd and talk to them. You'll find it easier.'

One of the other town doctors taking the seat on the other side of Nick, leaning across to shake both their hands.

At the same moment Joy stood up to the lectern and tapped the microphone. 'Welcome everyone,' she said, 'on this sad occasion.'

Four or five speakers before him. Telling stories about the deceased that made people laugh. Every joke another nail in Nick's confidence. He could barely listen to what they were saying, sitting there with the sweat running in fine streams down the skin inside his shirt, no use telling himself it was just a question of speaking a few words at a funeral.

There'd been a time, it seemed, when Miles had been known as the *Love God*; this from having been found down the back garden at parties with one or another of the town's wives. *You know who you are*, the speaker said, and everyone laughed; all of them, Miles, the man telling the story, presumably the women themselves, impossibly old for such a tale to stick, although perhaps not, perhaps this was one of the lessons he, Nick, needed to learn: that none of it goes away.

Lamprey strolling to the microphone when it was his turn, taking it out of its stand and holding it like a motivational speaker; no notes; tips of the fingers of his free hand tucked into the pocket of his jeans which, it must be said, hung loose at the back. 'Miles Douglas Prentice, MD,' he said, and paused, looking out over the audience. 'You'd have to excuse a man for being a *Love God*, wouldn't you? Who amongst us, in our heart of hearts, wouldn't want to be one of those?' Letting the laughter settle. 'But jokes aside, today is not just a sad day for Winderran. It's an important day. We should note it well. It marks a great loss to our town, not in the shape of a doctor, even though this was a particularly good one …'

Nick reluctantly admiring Lamprey's poise and timing, thinking, nonetheless, that he'd rarely heard such a load of old cobblers; Miles, whatever else he was, hadn't been a good doctor. Perhaps once upon a time, but these last few months Nick had been picking up the pieces behind him – the badly read tests, the missed calls, the late mornings. It was possible, of course, that this was what funerals were for, papering over the cracks in someone's life, saying good things about them because they're dead and no longer pose a threat.

'No,' Lamprey continued, 'with Miles's passing we've lost an unofficial register of the health of this town, a walking codex of our community's history.'

Giving an account of the three generations of the doctors-Prentice. 'Miles took up the baton sometime in the seventies. These men, grandfather, father, son, overlapped in the practice. What this means is that there's hardly a man or a woman born in these parts in the last hundred years who wasn't brought into the earth by one of them. Hardly anyone who has not, or whose loved ones have not, received their care.

'Miles didn't marry a local girl (which is not to say he didn't try on a few for size) …' More laughter.

Nick folded his speech one more time and stuffed it in his back pocket. Struck by the phrasing, brought *into* the earth. The solidness of it. The certainty of it. He'd not been aware of the history, should have figured it out from the photos hanging in the surgery.

Several years earlier he'd done a course at the hospital in Canberra. Everyone was obliged to do it during their internship; a modern innovation intended to increase their empathy for patients, bravely setting out to teach them how to start to feel all the stuff they'd been so effectively taught not to during their training – either by design or necessity – the anger, guilt, sorrow, which were the currency of any day in a hospital.

The first lesson was titled *What You See Is Never What You Get*. The trainer suggesting they tattoo it onto the inside of their forearms. By the end of the course, several months of lunchtimes later, he'd come to agree with the sentiment, never mind that it was too hard to practise on a daily basis. The message had been directed towards patients anyway, not fellow doctors. Miles had been older and an alcoholic. What were the chances of seeing behind that screen? And yet there he'd been, every day, day after day, perhaps someone not so unlike himself, after all.

When it was Nick's turn he stood behind the lectern, looking out across the mass of faces, taking Lamprey's advice and searching for one to speak to. His eyes finding the nurse, Eugenie, standing at the back of the marquee in a frock and a wide white hat. It shouldn't have been a surprise – some part of him had been searching for her the whole time – but the proposition of speaking directly to her robbed him of whatever it was he'd worked up the courage to say.

'I've had the privilege,' he managed, 'to work with Miles these past few months. Now I have the odious privilege of stepping into his shoes.' Should he risk a joke? *On no account.* 'I can't imagine,' he said, rising to the occasion, 'that even if I worked here for the next twenty years, for the rest of my life, that the whole town would come out to honour me.'

Everyone invited to partake of refreshments prepared by the Ladies Auxiliary, laid out on trestle tables in a tin shed next door to the marquee. The music starting up again, whether by design or chance with 'Sad-Eyed Lady of the Lowlands', with its lilting rhythm and haunting harmonica, it's curious chorus: *Warehouse eyes* and *Arabian drums.* Nick was hoping to escape unnoticed but was waylaid by the appearance of Helen at Lamprey's side, adorned with a kind of turban as cover for her naked scalp, gently placing porcelain fingers into Nick's proffered palm by way of greeting, the curious garb somehow aligning her to Dylan's music, as if it had been for her he'd sat up all night writing the song. *Should I leave them by your gate?* She had, he saw, been crying. It caught him by surprise, a further reminder of Miles, the man. Wondering if she had been one of those wives.

'That was well done, Guy,' she said, looping her arm through Lamprey's, her slightness exaggerated by her husband's bulk, not that he was big, just that she was almost wraith-like, quite possibly not long for the world.

Lamprey putting his own hand over hers, for some reason generating in Nick a deep pang of envy; the longing for a relationship in which both partners support each other, are made larger by being together.

'Excuse me,' she said to Nick, wiping her eyes. 'This is all a bit personal for me. Miles was, as I'm sure you know by now, my doctor. He spoke very highly of you.'

'He did?' Nick embarrassed at the obvious note of surprise in his voice. Casually searching amongst the crowd for Eugenie. He'd gone to the trouble during these last few weeks of finding out who she was, but no more; just a little backgrounding. Married. Reason enough to leave her alone.

He located her in a small group of women, plastic wine glasses and finger food in their hands. All in their finery, as if it was a race day carnival. She met his eyes for an instant (had she been looking out for him?) before turning away. Enough to stop him approaching. Instead he stood awkwardly beside a tent pole, and was thus collared by an older man with a stooped back, whose health he made the mistake of asking after, a retired veterinarian who launched into the history of arthritis in several generations of his family, a man who should have known better.

When he saw Eugenie rounding up two young girls he broke into the man's monologue.

'I have to go,' he said. 'Sorry, pager's ringing.'

Taking a shortcut across the oval, through the parked cars, catching her as she reached her dusty soft-roader, calling out 'Hello,' in a tone he hoped expressed the normality, the innocence, of a casual meeting.

'Doctor Lasker,' she said.

'It's Eugenie?'

'Yes,' she said, tucking her sunglasses up onto the brim of her hat. Blushing.

Really very lovely.

'Nick. Please, call me Nick. I just wanted to say hello. I've been away. I had to go down to Canberra.' Starting to tell her this as a way, perhaps, of explaining why he hadn't pursued her, then realising what he was doing and cutting himself off mid-sentence so as to avoid having to include the bit about seeing children, ex-wife, and all the rest, but thus rendering what he'd said almost senseless, a clumsy non sequitur which he sought in turn to cover by observing she had managed to find a space inside the marquee.

'I thought you spoke rather well,' she said.

'You're very kind. And a liar. I'm not a public speaker. That I came on after Guy Lamprey made it even worse.'

'Well, I'd have to disagree there. But then I'm biased.'

Smiling internally at that, a little surprised that she should be so forthright as to say how she felt about him. The force of her amongst the reflected glare of the parked cars, in the flesh, confirming the feelings he'd had during the days after their meeting. Guessing, now, that she must have felt something similar, if only by the way she stayed to listen to his ramblings despite the presence of her daughters, tugging on her arms. Cursing himself for not having thought of something to say before he chased her across the showgrounds. Standing gormless before this little family.

'So, you're going to take over the practice?' she asked.

'I've not decided. I'll stay for a few months anyway. See how it goes. There's a lot to keep up with.'

'I'm sure there is. Miles was very popular.'

'You knew him?'

'A little. He wasn't very …' she searched for a word, settling on *available*.

For himself he might have chosen *sober*, but then it was probably best not to speak ill of the dead. 'I didn't know his history,' he said. 'He kept to himself. I meant what I said, though, about not expecting to take his place.'

'You're not likely to in a country town like this,' she laughed. 'There's history wherever you look. I should know, my husband was born here.' Communicating her status. Warning him off.

'I should let you go,' he said. 'I just thought I'd say hello.'

'You said that,' the elder daughter said, looking up at him.

'Sandrine!' Eugenie said, squeezing the girl's hand hard.

She could not have been more than twelve, and was dressed as if for a ball, in elbow-length white gloves and a long flowing dress, her hair elaborately braided.

'Do you get out much?' Eugenie said.

Toeing the ground. 'Not really, I'm afraid.'

'Gosh but that must sound rude. I didn't mean it that way. It's just that sometimes, on a Friday night, we go to the *Alterbar* for pizza, listen to music. You could join us.'

Not specifying who 'we' was. Perhaps husband, children and all.

'I'd like that. Get me out of myself a bit.'

'Good,' she said, herding the girls into their seats, the gloved one turning to look back at him, letting him know she had his measure.

~

He'd been at McDonald's with Josh and Danielle when the call came through. The end of a long day, doing *things*: the museum, a walk around the lake, a film, then hamburgers. As if buying their happiness with wall-to-wall entertainment. Danielle still of an age where she wanted to make it work. Josh of an age where he didn't, having brought along some game device from which he was impossible to separate, even to eat the food of his choice. (Abie wouldn't have taken them to a McDonald's in a fit. He'd had to make them promise not to tell her.)

When the hospital rang he all but leapt to answer his mobile.

'I should get this,' he said.

Josh shrugged his shoulders.

It was the Sister.

'Nick,' she said. 'Doctor Lasker, I mean. I'm so glad I've got you. It's Doctor Prentice.'

Tears in her voice. An unusual sound in the presiding nurse, a middle-aged woman of remarkable efficiency, equipped with a lovely dark sense of humour, a trait not to be discounted.

'He's been in an accident, a road accident.'

'Is it serious?'

'I'm afraid he's dead, Doctor Lasker.'

Nick in a plastic booth in the antiseptic homogenised overly lit brightness of the take-away franchise. Danielle watching. Even Josh with one ear cocked, as if such a message might be communicated to everyone proximate without the need for words. Or perhaps it was just they were the children of a doctor, primed for the calls that would take him away.

'What happened?'

'His car went off the edge of the Range. On his way home, we think,' she said. 'Rolled a long way down. Someone saw it happen, otherwise nobody would have known. They had to winch it out.'

An image of a sloping stretch of road at night super-imposing itself on the present surrounds, wet tar reflecting the flashing lights of emergency vehicles, men in hi-viz waterproofs hauling the battered ute up the bank out of the rainforest, all of it imaginary of course, and yet profoundly unsettling; the immediate thought being that Miles had done it deliberately, although why Nick should have thought that, or why Miles would want to have done so, he couldn't have said. He'd been so pleased at the prospect of having a few days away from him. Last seen sitting behind his desk in chino shorts and long white socks, as if he were going on safari. Brogues on his feet.

'I'll come back,' he said. 'I'll be there as soon as I can.'

Both children now looking at him. Wanting an explanation. Their father gone for months at a time. Visiting them for just a few days. Hardly there and now announcing he has to go back north again.

'I'm so sorry,' he said. 'But you must see, it's an emergency.'

'Does this mean you're going to stay up there?' Josh asked, straight to the point, using a tone that suggested Winderran was the ends of the earth. Perhaps it was.

'I'm not sure. I'll be needed for a little while anyway.'

'Aren't there other doctors?' Danielle asked.

'Well, yes, of course there are. There's quite a few in town.'

'So why's it *your* job?' His second child no less alert than the first.

Ticking off the points in his mind. 'Because Miles is … was … my employer, and there was just the two of us in the practice, and we have the hospital emergency.'

'What's going to happen to us?' she said.

'I'll come back down again. Soon. And you could come up and stay with me during the holidays.'

'You'll be working then, too,' Josh said.

'You can visit with Uncle Matt and Auntie Rosie when I am, and do things with me when I'm not.'

'Right,' Josh said. He hadn't stopped looking at his machine, in fact was still pressing buttons even as they spoke. Multi-tasking.

All day Nick had resisted telling him to put it away. 'Couldn't you stop that for a minute?' he said.

No comment.

'Josh.'

'I'll just finish this level.'

'I don't want to go to their place,' Danielle said.

'I thought you liked it there. They've got a swimming pool. And a boat.'

'Denise is a bitch,' Danielle said.

'Don't say that about your cousin.'

'She *is*.'

'It's not nice.'

'It's true,' Josh said, putting the gameboy thingy down to look out the window at the circling cars. A big four-wheel drive having trouble with a reverse park. 'Denise won't let Danielle play with any of her things. They're all spoilt.'

As if this wasn't something he'd thought himself, with the house on the canal estate and the big motorboat, the cupboards full of discarded toys and sporting equipment from forgotten enthusiasms. But then he'd thought the same about his own children, too.

'I don't want you to go away again now,' Danielle said. 'This is supposed to be a holiday together.'

'Okay,' he said, sweet-talking his own daughter, 'I might have to see what I can do. But listen, Honey, Daddy's got a problem he needs to sort out. It's kind of serious and I can't be with you in the way I want to be. Not right now.'

Danielle folding her arms, adopting a resigned expression. 'It's all right Daddy,' she said. 'I can see you're busy. You've got people to look after, haven't you?'

This being, of course, the doctor's dilemma and excuse, both. The perfect reason for not being available, that he was too busy, had sick people who required his presence. And yet, if he was even remotely honest, there was still time for other things.

There were a lot of darks in the Lampreys' house; black kitchen benches, cupboards and tiles, black bookshelves to show up the many-coloured spines of the thousands of books, a broad ironbark table with dark-wood chairs set on a mixed-species hardwood floor. Places laid for eight; guests gathered near the windows with champagne flutes in hand, talking and laughing a little too noisily, nervous at having been invited to share the great man's table.

Lamprey introduced him to the company: the portrait painter Ian Illchild, a bald thick-set individual whose forehead, with its coruscating ripples of flesh, acted as a canvas for his emotions; accompanied by his wife Arlene, mid-sixties Nick would have guessed, but made-up so heavily, like a *geisha* – bright red lipstick on a stark white base – that it was hard to tell. She, less well known than he, but apparently respected for pieces made from found objects, a woman full of bawdy anecdote and raucous laughter. Balancing them one of Miles's ex-patients, Harry Barkham, a great block of a man with thick grey hair and schoolmaster's eyebrows, dressed in loose-fitting beige linen, in possession of both a booming voice and opinions, one of those Winderrians Miles had categorised as suffering from what he liked to call *PIPS, Previously Important Person Syndrome*; accompanied by Deirdre, *his* wife, stick-thin and sharply styled, dressed to match the furniture, giving tight-lipped knowing smiles but saying little. Finally a slim blonde of indeterminate age with, it must be remarked – for they were much on display – formidable breasts, introduced as a potter, something slightly loose about her, as if she were coming apart at the seams; invited, no doubt, to make up the party with him. Or perhaps it was the other way around. Here might be the reason for the late invite, for surely it had been an afterthought. Nick not certain he could deliver the level of conversation required but forgetting his reservations after a glass or two from Mayska's bottle and the late appearance of Helen, emerging from the rear of the house in purple silk, resembling nothing so much as a Buddhist nun, the lack of eyebrows adding to what must have been already a pale and ethereal beauty.

She asked him – they were seated together at one end of the table – to explain why he was in Winderran, *of all places*, as she put it. A question he would normally have let pass but which, when issued from her bleached lips, provoked a version of his history that included Sydney, Canberra, marriage, children, and now divorce; a catalogue that sought to avoid, in the way that a man will when talking to a beautiful woman, no matter her availability, any mention of the other women who surely stand as the stations of the journey, except that Helen's way of listening was so direct he was unable to entirely excise them, and, thus, hearing himself, brought his tale to a halt.

'I seem to be doing nothing but talking about myself,' he said.

'Nonsense,' she replied. 'I'm asking you. I'm always curious as to what it is brings people here. More often than not it seems, in one way or another, to involve love. I think it's something about the place. There's always a story, you see and, at the moment I don't feel as if I have one. I've slipped into a kind of limbo. Just me and my cancer. Too much body,' she said, laughing. 'And I particularly don't want to talk about that today with you, of all people. So, continue. You say you have a brother living down on the coast?'

Blaming Matt for his presence in this part of the world. Telling Helen about his brother's excessive lifestyle, which, he said, he wants instinctively to criticise except that all his injunctions fall away in the face of the family's happiness, the way that he and Rosie always seem to be laughing, always have time to play games with the children, to go out fishing in the motorboat moored in the canal next to the house.

The meal being served by a woman in her mid-thirties with slightly Italian features, introduced as Nina, a distraction in herself, delivering dishes to the table in a no-nonsense manner; far more interesting than the fey blonde (who made the mistake of thinking he might be interested in the various *modalities* she was employing to maintain her health, techniques apparently unknown to, or ignored by, modern science); serving them a whole roast fillet of beef, the meat charred on the outside and cut into thick bloody wedges, the centre all but raw, no contingency for those who might like it otherwise. Helen picking at hers in the way of convalescents, taking tiny mouthfuls, pushing the already small portion around the plate.

Nick dragging his attention away from Nina's short black skirt, bringing the conversation around to Helen. 'What will you do now, without Miles, I mean, as your doctor?'

'You know about my case?'

'I've looked into it, briefly.'

'Well, I have oncology in Brisbane. I'm down there two days a week. They're monitoring me.'

'Which is not the same as having a local GP.'

'No, it's not. But then we weren't going to talk about my health, were we?'

'It's my fault. I'm sorry. I haven't worked out how to be a doctor in a small town yet. I'm either too involved or not enough.'

'It has crossed my mind,' Helen said, pausing for long enough to get him to raise his eyes to meet hers, 'to see if you would ... if you had the time ... take on my case.'

Nick realising how affected he'd become by the wine. So much so that he hadn't noticed their exchange was by way of a job application. Not an afterthought at all. Interviewing for a position he wasn't at all sure he wanted. Too late now.

'I'd be honoured,' he said.

She put her thin hand on his. 'Thank you,' she said. 'I know it's not the most attractive undertaking. But I like you. And I can see why Guy has taken an interest. Unusual for him to pick a doctor, but clearly his good taste hasn't entirely deserted him.' This last said as if to herself rather than him. As if she was fading, which was possibly the case because the next moment she excused herself, standing up from the table, balancing herself with her hands on the hardwood. Trying to brush it off with a laugh. 'All this excitement,' she said.

He went to come around the table to her. 'No, no. You stay here, sit, please. I'm all right. Enjoy yourself. I know that Guy will want to talk to you.' Slipping away, back to from wherever it was she'd come.

After dessert they changed seats. The women gravitating towards one end of the table as in an English novel of manners. The men at the other, with brandy. Nick refusing the latter despite the insistence of his host. 'I've already had too much wine,' he said, 'I have to drive.'

'So, Lamprey, how's the campaign going?' Barkham asked, settling into his chair, that large over-expressive face, folds on folds – you wondered how he ever managed to shave – hovering beneath those extraordinary eyebrows, looking to steer the conversation into an area of interest.

'You mean our ongoing shit-fight,' Lamprey said in a sour tone.

'I hope you're not going to let that meeting get you down,' Barkham said. 'I thought you handled yourself pretty well, all things considered. You didn't have a chance against a mob like that.'

'Did you hear that woman?' Lamprey said, 'Water tanks. I mean, *Jesus wept.*' Leaning forward. 'It's typical Winderran. What this town does best in all the world is split into opposing tribes. I've remarked on it before. Everyone huddled in their little groups just waiting for an issue to emerge so that they can take up positions and throw insults at each other. Everything gets blown out of proportion.' Sitting back, point made, but then, rallying, rising back up again. 'Actually, this might interest you. I've been doing some research. She got her figures wrong. Mixing up gigalitres and megalitres. Easy to do I suppose. You'd need six million houses, not sixty thousand, to store that amount of water. But who can be bothered with facts, eh?'

'Guy here,' Barkham said, pleased with himself, as if he'd scored a point by assisting Lamprey to score one, explained for Nick's benefit, 'performs an essential service in our culture, pricking the wind from those who would set themselves above us.'

'Indeed, indeed,' Lamprey said, 'a windy prick am I.'

A call from the women down the other end to quieten down. 'You men're too noisy,' Arlene said.

'It's just our powerful bass notes, reverberating,' Illchild said deeply, 'you need to lift your game ladies, sing out the higher registers.'

At which Arlene made a fist of ululating and, having started it, was joined by Barkham's wife who, against all expectation, giving possibly her only contribution to the evening, took the vibrating wail to grand new heights, transporting the room.

Lamprey could not have been more delighted, clapping his hands with glee.

'The thing about environmentalists,' he said, when the noise subsided, 'is that it's become like a religion for them.'

'What has?' Illchild asked, possibly a hint of criticism in his voice.

'You name it. Planting trees, for a start,' Lamprey said. 'It doesn't matter where or what type as long as you're putting them in the ground. You can see these fucking orange triangles dotting every hillside in the district like little shrines to their earth goddess. At the same time hardly a day goes by when you're not assaulted by the moronic roar of the machines cutting the buggers down and chipping them up. There are teams of them working around the clock, can't deal with the demand.'

Lamprey, it seemed, wrote an occasional column in one of the weekend papers based around propositions like this, as well as the doings of various politicians, a kind of public diary. Nick hadn't read the column, this week or any other, and wasn't about to start. What he found interesting, though, was how Illchild and Barkham, both significant figures in their own right, acted like a cheer squad, vying for Lamprey's approval. He noted, too, a certain tension between them, as if they might not agree with each other on everything, or be content with their place in whatever mysterious hierarchy held sway, albeit being happy enough on this occasion to demonstrate to Nick who was on the inside and who the *new chum*. None of which was necessary; most of the time he didn't know who or what they were talking about, hadn't been to the meeting, didn't even know the name of the woman who'd got up Lamprey's nose.

'I've been doing a little research on her,' Lamprey was saying. 'She was the union rep at the hospital down the coast for years. Which just about says it all, I'd have thought.'

'Workplace Health and Safety's got out of hand everywhere,' Barkham said. 'They're a law unto themselves, right across the country. It's got so you can't do anything without filling in fifty forms. It's not a wonder we can't compete.'

'You'd have come across a bit of that wouldn't you, Nick?' Lamprey said, attempting to draw him into the conversation.

'Pretty strict in hospitals, what you can and can't do,' he said, non-committedly, hackles rising. He wondered what gave Barkham, or Lamprey especially, with such an ill wife, the qualifications to criticise hospitals. Clearly, at a dinner party general assent was the order of the day, but this was his field. What they hadn't grasped about him – but then how could they have, he'd barely spoken – was that even if he didn't know shit about local or national politics, he was Labor to the core. His father in the railyards at Enfield. 'Not an easy job being a nurse,' he added, 'Underpaid, overworked and good at what they do, in my experience.'

Barkham started to harrumph his way into a contradiction but Illchild got there first, starting to tell a story about Arlene's recent experience in hospital. Lamprey, however, wasn't happy for the conversation to veer into the personal. 'Don't get me started on that chap who owns the land the dam wall's going to be on,' he said. 'Supposed to be a scientist. Talk about crazy.' Looking at Nick, as if to find agreement from him, which Nick would have liked to give except he once again had no point of reference. He'd been up since before dawn. Exhaustion was setting in. He was flattered to have been invited into this circle but doubted it was really a fit. Lamprey didn't need his adulation or approval, he was superfluous to requirement, and yet, at the same time, there was a sense this display was all for his benefit. As if these men needed an audience.

They'd moved on anyway, discussing something Lamprey had said to his co-host on the book show he did on the television.

'Never mind the flak you got for it,' Illchild was saying, 'it warmed my heart to hear someone say something honest on television.'

'A rare thing from politicians of any stripe,' Barkham said.

'I'm not a politician,' Lamprey said.

'Yet,' Barkham said.

'Indeed,' Illchild agreed.

'I do wonder who you've been talking to,' Lamprey said. 'But you, Nick, we're leaving you out.'

'I was actually thinking I ought to be going.'

'So soon? I was going to get you to listen to the sound system, wasn't I?'

'I don't want to break anything up but it's been a long day. I've an early start in the morning.'

Nina emerging from the kitchen at this exact moment, pulling on a coat. Lamprey held up his hand to the men around him.

'You all done, Nina? Shall we call you a cab?'

'Thanks Mr Lamprey. I'd like that.'

'I could give you a lift,' Nick said. 'I was just leaving. Where are you going?'

'Nonsense, Nick,' Lamprey said. 'I'll call Nina a cab. I was going to play you some music.'

'I really must go,' Nick said. 'I'm sorry. Do you mind if we do it another time?'

Dark-haired, dark-eyed Nina beside him in the car, lit by the glow of the dash lights. The road following one of the ridges back towards town, sleeping houses on either side, hidden behind some of the yet-to-be-felled trees. His tiredness mysteriously evaporating.

She lived in one of the new townhouses down behind the shops, not far from the hospital. Ran her own catering business from there. 'Gave up working for others years ago,' she said. 'It never works out. Do you want to come in?'

It felt like a long time since Greloed had gone her own way.

She offered him a nightcap, bourbon. Took out two glasses and placed them on the kitchen bench, added a splash of the brown liquid, viscous against the ice, clinked hers against his, looking at him over the rim as she took a mouthful, leant across to kiss him, her lips at once cold and sweet and fiery against his own.

Nothing to say. Her body neat and firm beneath his hands. Wanting to take it slow but responding to what seemed to be her need to have it happen right there, right then, clothes still half on, perhaps they were winding each other up, each responding to what they imagined the other wanted, to some play of what passion should be like, who knows, but within moments she was up on the bench, her legs wrapped around him, his hands somewhere up inside her clothes, and then he was in, just like that, she holding his face in both her hands while she kissed him, breaking the seal of their mouths to catch a breath.

'Woah, boy,' she said, as if talking to a horse or a dog, panting, her hands on his shoulders, laughing at the corniness of her own language, a deep, easeful laugh which made him laugh too, bringing with it a great wash of relief, a flood of emotion that carried with it all the flotsam of this last year so that he was, for a moment, all but unmanned, slipping out of her.

'I didn't say stop,' she said, grabbing hold.

'I'm not going to,' he said. 'But let's get these clothes off.'

Undoing her shirt, her bra, cupping lovely small breasts in his hands.

'We could try the bed,' she said, leading him there, a woman who looked even better naked than dressed, this surprisingly feminine body joining with his, expressing a wonderful natural joy in the sheer physicality of it all, a woman whose name he barely knew, who he'd seen for the first time but a few hours before.

It was only when they were done, when she was in the shower that he could cast his eye over the ersatz pictures on the wall (a jetty running out into a quiet lake; a Buddha in the mist), the curious collection of stuffed toys on the dresser, the absence of books and the presence of, for fuck's sake, a cat, who'd only then come in to see what the fuss was about. The thing with Greloed was that he hadn't even really liked her when they got together. That's to say he was attracted to her physically but not to who she was. It had happened because of the closeness of their work and the remoteness of their location, because of *propinquity*, she a Swedish nurse on secondment to Australia, he a doctor on the run from several different cages of his own devising, and it hadn't been meant to mean anything, shouldn't have meant anything, she wasn't even his type, slightly plump and strangely adolescent when her clothes were off, with the small high breasts of a renaissance painting and shaved parts, as if her adult body hadn't quite formed though she was almost thirty, practising what she liked to call *emergency sex*, because, she said, its intensity wasn't just a response to the meeting of their bodies but also to the circumstances in which they found themselves. Putting sentences together with a foreigner's exactness. Strange name. Difficult to get his tongue around, hardly the sort to inspire dreams and yet that's what happens, skin rubs against skin enough times and even names as outlandish as hers take on resonance.

He thinks, in retrospect, that she was just trying him on. An unusual notion, but why it should be different for women than men he couldn't say. A study in *The Lancet* suggested the contraceptive pill alters pheromones such that women give out false messages about who they are, to both men *and* themselves. He'd been out there, in the north-west, amongst the red soil and ghost gums, the tall bluffs and wide grasslands, thinking he was *found*, having meaningful interactions with this woman, the landscape, the people, but in fact he'd been as lost as ever, dropping into an infatuation with the wrong person, going out together in the Toyota to get away from the doof music of the settlements, parking for privacy at the end of long sandy tracks where old machines lay half-submerged on riverbanks like harbingers of another age. Crocodiles in the water. Bound to end in tears. His, as it happened. Trapped in another fantasy of his own making. And she, having tried him on, went her own way, taking her energetic little party-self off to some other poor fool on the other side of the world without a thought, without realising how much he had invested in the idea of her. Which was the thing, he no longer seemed to be able to just have sex. Perhaps it was something to do with age but these days this immersion in another seemed to quickly develop ties that bound. Too quickly. Now there he was, in another woman's room, another woman with whom it was probably fair to say he shouldn't be sharing deeply intimate moments, feeling strangely as if in doing what he'd done he'd betrayed the nurse, Eugenie, although clearly that was ridiculous, but evidence, if more was needed, that the process of weaving a fantasy about *her* had already gone too far.

Nina came out of the bathroom, naked, drying herself with a towel, stopped for a moment in the doorway for him to notice her, to see the water still caught in droplets on her skin, to see her breasts, her dark bush, holding the moment before coming to lay herself on her belly, her face next to his.

'I was thinking I should go,' he said, saying it because it was what he thought and because he felt certain she wouldn't be troubled by it, but seeing in her eyes that he was wrong.

'If you want to,' she said, running the tip of her finger along his thigh. 'But me, I thought we were just getting started.'

six

Eugenie

She drove over to see Lindl in the late morning, free for a moment from children, work and husband, following the curves of the Elmhurst Road in summer sunshine, the fields radiant after rain, farm dams full, fat cattle grazing. Taking the turn into the long tree-lined driveway for *Roselea*, the two strips of concrete for the wheels requiring concentration or perhaps just *faith*, pulling her into focus so that when she came back out into the sunshine at the bottom, pausing on the causeway where the dark water pooled against the concrete, it felt, as it often did, as if she had entered another world.

The house, an old Queenslander, was perched on the opposite slope, in an almost perfect position, granted a view down the valley to the sweep of the creek and its dark corridor of forest. Verandas on the north and west and a set of wide steps at the front where a friend might sit with the owners in the evening, drinking wine. Sheds on the left, shaded by a single large Moreton Bay, old bales down to the right, the usual detritus of a working farm scattered about, a water tank on its side, irrigation pipe rolled against a fence. Parking next to Marcus's car. Not a sound except the chooks scratching in the dirt, a currawong calling from down by the creek.

She went up the steps, poked her head in the open door, calling into the dim high-ceilinged hall, always surprised by the sophistication of the interior, the polished wood floors, the antique tallboy, the stillness outside mirrored, but also enhanced, within.

Marcus appeared in shorts and an old t-shirt, grey-bearded, barefoot, smiling broadly, giving her a kiss on one cheek and then, awkwardly, the other. '*Comme les français.*' The accent not so good. Apparently pleased to see her although you'd never really know; of British extraction, politeness before all else.

'You're here for lunch? Lindl's about somewhere.' Singing out her name, listening for a response. 'She might still be down the paddock,' he said, going out onto the veranda. 'Yes, there she is, over near the gully. Are you all right to go down by yourself? Take the path to the left of the bales. Tell her not to be late.'

Lindl, seeing her coming across the paddock, stood from where she was doing something at the base of a small tree, took off her hat and wiped her forehead with her sleeve, waved. 'Is it that time already?' she said. 'I'm so sorry. I'm daydreaming.'

A woman in her fifties with grey hair that she wore long because she could afford to, because she'd managed to retain her presence, carrying a bit of weight on her hips, nothing to complain about, just that it showed in the work clothes, khaki pants and shirt, broad straw hat, dressed as if on staff at the zoo, or maybe the national parks, trousers dirty around the knees, sleeves buttoned at the wrists against the sun.

'I thought we might go for a walk before we eat,' she said. 'What d'you think?'

They met because of the dam. Eugenie had gone to a local forum organised by the State government to spruik the proposal, their token gesture towards community consultation. She'd been directed to sit at a table with five others, one of whom had been Lindl. It was only later she discovered her immediate connection to the proposed site. When the meeting was over they went for coffee. That most surprising and unexpected thing, a new friendship, blossoming; a little mutual admiration club between an older and a younger woman that neither wanted to analyse too closely lest it disappear. There being so much to admire in Lindl, someone utterly different from everyone she knew: an artist who had been wild in her youth, a reader of books, someone who wanted to talk about politics, music and film. Like an emissary from another time.

'So, tell me, how are the girls, how's David?' Lindl asked.

'He's gone again.'

'And?'

'It wasn't so good. Not that it ever is these days.'

The sun very bright out in the paddock in the middle of the day, wishing she'd brought a hat.

'How come?'

'Oh, I don't know, he thinks he needs to be some sort of policeman. Always lecturing the girls: *Homework before screens. Sit up at the table. Don't speak to your mother like that.* Not just the girls. As if things get slack when he's not around. Everyone's relieved when he goes. Which is awful.'

'And you? Are you relieved?'

'He's so stuck in his ways.' Regretting the criticism of her husband as soon as she's made it, rushing to qualify. 'He's no happier than I am. Working in that awful place. He never rings when he's away. It's only me who calls him when I need to. If someone wants something.'

She'd been hoping to talk to Lindl about the curious way she's felt this last week – at once released and groundless, subject to the whim of dangerous forces, strange currents – but they have gone too deep too soon. Out there in the paddock the light was too harsh for that level of engagement and, anyway, though her friend had asked the questions, she hardly seemed to be listening to the answers.

'We'll go down this way,' Lindl said, leading Eugenie over to the fence and through a small gate, into a gully that ran up and away from the main creek. Orange tree guards dotting the slopes, some protecting plants already a metre high. Recently slashed grass lying cross-hatched between them, filling the declivity with its scent.

'This is where we've been concentrating our energies,' Lindl said, crossing over, water welling up between the sheaves of cut grass at each step. As she passed one of the taller trees she grasped a bunch of leaves, pulling on them, letting them run through her fingers in the way another might handle a much-loved dog, giving its fur an affectionate tug. 'We're trying to create a corridor to connect the forest along the creek with the trees on top of the hill.'

'I didn't know you were still planting,' Eugenie said.

'We never stop. Well, I guess we might, one day, but at the moment there's so much more to do.'

'What about the dam?'

'What about it? If it goes ahead we lose it all. If it doesn't then it'll grow. I'm not about to stop because of those arseholes.'

A thick strand of Lindl's hair escaping from beneath her hat. Those startlingly clear eyes, blue-grey, holding her for a moment, as if to make sure Eugenie understood. Although what, she wasn't certain, dazed as much by the breadth of the undertaking as by the heat. Only the first section of the gully planted. Weeds inhabiting the space beyond: lantana and privet, a single camphor laurel halfway up. Mountains of work.

Lindl picked her way over to another gate, pausing to reach inside a tree guard to pull out a cobbler's peg. Eugenie following, grateful when they passed into the cool of the forest proper, trees planted by Lindl and Marcus twenty years before, indistinguishable, now, from the real thing. A mown path leading down towards the creek.

'I guess I'm just surprised,' Eugenie said, 'You know, I've not said anything about it. I figured it was your business … but you haven't been much involved recently. In the campaign.'

There is a committee. The hundreds in the region who oppose the dam reduced to the eight or ten who feel strongly enough to do anything about it. Which is, she guessed, the lesson: there's no, or little, competition for political work, at least until you get to the higher echelons.

'I can't do it anymore,' Lindl said.

Eugenie waited but Lindl offered no further explanation. She'd been right at the centre of things in the beginning but now, whenever the meetings were at *Roselea*, Lindl spent the time pottering in the kitchen, making delicacies for the others, hovering around the fringes, her place at the table on the wide veranda empty.

The larger trees had formed a canopy over the stream, shading the water that was flowing freely after the rain, dark and clean, falling over black rock, running between ferns and clumps of long spiky grass. Just being in this place transformed her mood. Extraordinary that someone might create such a thing, or cause it to come into being. They sat near a small rapid, the sounds washing over them; the movement of water; the grumpy-old-man's-call of a pair of wompoo pigeons in the treetops.

Lindl breaking their silence to point to the other side of the pool where a black plastic box had been attached to the trunk of a palm, incongruous now that Eugenie saw it. 'One of Geoff's monitoring boxes,' she said. 'He's got three of them along here. Recording frog calls at night.'

Geoff was in his late seventies, a biologist, retired now to Winderran, as astute as ever, but with a weakness for over-elaborate dissertations on obscure topics during committee meetings. He didn't trust the Water Board's survey results and wanted to test them himself.

'All very important I know,' Lindl said, 'But frogs have never really been my thing. I mean it all connects of course, but it's the birds that interest me.' She held up her hand. 'You hear that noise? That's spangled drongos. They were late coming this year. They migrate from Papua New Guinea in the spring. All that way. Little birds. I thought maybe something had happened to them. You never know. Land clearing or fires, some fundamental shift in the climate. It's all so fragile. I don't think we know what we're doing most of the time, you know? I just hope so much that we don't fuck it up. I'm not sure I'd want to live in a world without spangled drongos.'

Eugenie unclear as to who the *we* was in this, taking it as people in general. Embarrassed because she didn't even know what these birds looked like. Despite her ever more central role in the *NoDam* campaign the environment remained a somewhat abstract concept. The landscape and its inhabitants not really being her motivating force, which was, surely, more to do with her affection for Lindl than anything else, but connected also, she supposed, to the kind of person her grandparents had made of her, someone who, once engaged, had to see things through, who derived a certain satisfaction from the process itself, no matter the cause; the kind who can't let go; who rewrites the submission a tenth time even though its recipient will only be a nameless bureaucrat; who reads all the literature on the economic and social costs of damming rivers; who makes the phone calls, hands out the leaflets.

'Don't get me wrong,' Lindl said, as if there had been no break from the conversation they'd had out in the sun. 'I'm so glad you're fighting. I can't tell you. But it's just not possible for me. I'm so pleased, too, that you're doing the talking now, that you've taken over the public stuff.'

'I didn't think Marcus was so happy about that,' Eugenie said.

'He wasn't, but he's better now. He's not a public speaker. He's not a politician.'

For all that he was a university lecturer Marcus was a hopeless communicator. Like Geoff, he tended towards long-winded commentary, losing everyone. Excruciating to watch with a microphone. No concept of the sound bite.

'Neither am I.'

'Yes but that's one of your strengths. You've got vitality, you're articulate. People like looking at you. And that's crucial, almost as important as the message, even though it shouldn't be. Marcus wasn't cutting it. Even I could see that. I didn't like him being out there anyway. Not that I like you being exposed either,' she added. 'But, I don't know … you don't seem like such a target.'

Standing.

'We should keep going, hey? It'll be lunchtime soon. We'll go downstream to the second crossing. How're the girls coping, anyway?'

Changing the subject. As if it might just go away after saying something like that. Eugenie trailing along behind her on the narrow track that paralleled the creek and, despite herself, falling into the pattern of child-talk, telling Lindl about Sandrine going into high school for the first time, how Emily was struggling in primary, the difficulty of juggling these tensions as virtually a single mother, as if these practicalities were what she'd wanted to discuss.

The path skirting a small waterfall, maidenhair fern on either side. The sound of voices ahead.

Below the fall was a wide circular pool, broad enough that the sun could find its way to the flashing water. Thick *Lomandra* crowding its edge except on the far side where the stream spilled across a shelf of rock. A man and woman were swimming, their bodies pale in the dark water.

'Bloody hippies,' Lindl said, quietly.

They had little choice except to come around the side of the pool, but it was awkward because the swimmers hadn't seen them, they were engaged in their own little game – not actually having sex, thankfully – just amorous play. It was only when the two women came out onto the flat rocks, where the track crossed the creek and the swimmers' clothes lay in discarded piles, that they were noticed.

'Hi,' the dark-haired girl said, waving. 'The water's lovely, you should come in.'

'Hi,' Lindl replied. 'I bet it is. Just wondering, though, what you think you're doing?' Her tone gentle, but firm.

'Having a swim,' the girl said, stating the obvious. 'We're from the camp.' Gesturing off to the right. 'We thought we'd come up this way, get away from everyone. It's really cool here. Is this your land?'

'Yes.'

The girl swam towards them, rising naked from the water, finding her feet on the wet rock with both remarkable ease and lack of self-consciousness, squeezing her thick hair and pushing it back over one shoulder, proudly full-breasted, dark nipples tight from the cold water, a thick bush between unshaven legs, a natural girl this one, perhaps of Greek extraction, certainly something Mediterranean; a small tattoo at the base of her spine, a series of six straight parallel lines.

The young man, long hair plastered on his scalp, hung back in the water.

'Ange,' the girl said, holding out her hand. 'Hope you don't mind us swimming in your creek. You must be so pissed off with them wanting to build a dam here, hey? I mean, can you believe it? How fucked is that?'

'Pretty fucked,' Lindl said.

'I saw you, at the forum,' Ange said, turning to Eugenie. 'That was you wasn't it? You were really good. How was that guy, hey?

I mean really screwed. He's some kind of writer, isn't he? *Like*, a dinosaur.' Reaching down for a shift-like top and pulling it over her head, rendered more rather than less naked by the thin cloth sticking to her wet skin, the toes of her bare feet splayed on the rock; some sort of feral animal.

'Hey, Will,' she said. 'You can get out. It's all right. I'm sure these ladies've seen what you've got before.' Coming back around to them. 'But listen, hey, can I show you something? You see this thing up here?'

She pointed across the pool to another of Geoff's boxes, fastened with cable ties to a palm tree .

'D'you think we ought to fuck with it?'

'I'd rather you didn't,' Lindl said.

'Is it the government?' Ange asked.

'No, no. It's us, we're monitoring frogs in the creek.'

Ange laughing. A joyful noise, full of fun and self-deprecation.

'Shit, hey?' she said. 'Well, there you go. Will and I were thinking we ought to smash it, you know. Just weren't sure how to do it without being seen. Can't be too careful, hey. We figured the government was watching to see who came here. Recording it all. They're none too fond of us anti-dammers.'

'The scientists will have great fun listening to you and your friend.'

The young man emerged from the pool, but reluctantly, stumbling on the slippery rocks, muscular but hang-dog, trying to cover his parts as he made a lunge for his clothes. His right arm tattooed with a complete sleeve, difficult to tell what the images were except that there appeared to be a sword at their centre. Another significant tattoo on his left thigh, multi-coloured. Projecting resentment in the way only surly young men can.

'So, d'you find any frogs?' Ange asked.

'Some,' Lindl said.

To Eugenie's surprise Lindl offered a round-up of what was going on with the campaign, answering whatever the girl asked, as if she was herself an active participant, as if the information was open to anyone, getting it all mixed up in the process. Although, in fairness, it was always hard to explain to outsiders the way the town operated: there weren't just two opposing groups, each side was made up of different collections of people who didn't necessarily agree on philosophy or strategy. It wasn't an organised campaign, there was no leader, people did their own things. Sometimes it came together, most often it didn't.

Not that Ange seemed particularly interested. Her questions were, Eugenie thought, just a way of inserting herself into things. If she were an animal it would be something burrowing. She had, she realised, taken immediate objection to the girl, possibly because of the way she'd said they were *anti-dammers*, as if anyone could just walk in after all the months of hard campaigning and become one of them, which she supposed, actually, anyone could, in fact everyone was *invited* to. But all the same.

'We planted this bit of forest,' Lindl said. 'We think ...'

'You did?' Ange interrupted.

'Yes.'

'Wow. That's really cool. You mean this wasn't here, before?'

'No. There was a bit of remnant further downstream. This was open paddocks, cattle in the creek. We think there's a colony of Giant Barred frogs living here now ... that's what we're recording. They're critically endangered. We figure there must have been a breeding pair in the remnant and now they've colonised what we've planted. If we find some ... well, that'll be the end of the dam, won't it?'

Eugenie broke in. 'We need to keep going,' she said. 'Marcus will be waiting, won't he?'

Lindl stopping mid-sentence, a little affronted.

'It's all good,' Ange said, 'we need to get back up the camp ourselves, hey, Will?'

The young man had pulled on a pair of heavy denim trousers which he now wore low on the hips, the brand name of his underpants exposed above the waistband. Naked, for all his tatts and his sullenness, he'd been well formed. Dressed, he was risible, clearly in awe of the girl, open-mouthed, nodding his agreement.

Out of earshot they laughed at the queerness of the meeting, the studied naivety of the girl, the doting boy.

'You didn't like me talking to her?' Lindl said.

'You're very trusting,' she replied.

'Which is another way of saying I'm naive?'

Eugenie thought it best not to answer.

'You're probably right,' Lindl said, 'but weren't they beautiful?'

It seemed an odd observation. She'd been so critical of them; the young man's tattoos; his stupid homey trousers; the girl's proud nudity, the unshaven legs and armpits. Some niggling little person in the back of her head speaking in her nan's voice, whispering, *She could be pretty if she looked after herself.* Tainting everything. She'd not seen what Lindl saw.

They came back out into the paddocks, walking up through grassland on an old farm track. Cows in the field on the top side with lovely soft brown skin, chewing the cud, unmoved by their presence, wonderfully content. A catbird calling its weird complaint from somewhere in the forest behind.

'Before, you know,' Eugenie asked, 'what did you mean about being a target?'

'Oh that. It's rubbish, just ignore it.'

'Is there some threat I should know about?'

'You mean other than the decision to resume this land and build a dam on it that destroys thirty years' work?'

'Well, yes. Other than that.'

'It's just me,' Lindl said, coming to a halt, taking off her hat and pushing her hair back, dismissing the question. 'You know how it is, some days I get depressed. I think that's what it is. I mean seriously, clinically. This stuff taps into everything that came up about my mother's family ... the things I found out.'

Lindl's mother had died of cancer. During her last months she had driven down to Brisbane several times a week to nurse her. Then, after she'd gone, Lindl had been obliged to sort through the house, dividing up a lifetime's accumulation of stuff into equal portions. The job falling to her because, of her two brothers, the first was also an artist and wouldn't do it – even if he needed the money more than Lindl – and the second was a lawyer who'd become, in his middle age, strangely rapacious, as if the things he got from the house were more important to him than his relationship with his sister, as if gaining a larger share of their dead parents' possessions made up for some perceived lack.

In her mother's desk Lindl had found correspondence between her grandfather and his family in Germany, the ones who hadn't got out. It wasn't a story she'd known about. That they were Jews had barely been mentioned during her childhood. The letters had affected her profoundly, more perhaps, than Eugenie had realised. One of the things Eugenie loved about Lindl was the way she transformed her life into a series of stories, imbuing each of the characters – brothers, parents, grandparents – with this remarkable vibrancy, pillorying them, yes, but also linking them to figures in art and literature, to history, philosophy, psychoanalysis. To Freud, to Rilke and his *density of childhood*. Sometimes the stories were so compelling that she got lost in them, forgot that Lindl wasn't just the narrator, she was an active participant.

'But I don't want to talk about me,' Lindl said. 'I'd rather talk about you.'

'What about me?' Eugenie said.

'Didn't you want to talk about you and David?'

'Yes.'

'What are you thinking?' Lindl asked.

'All sorts of things,' Eugenie said, so as to avoid saying, straight out, *I'm thinking of leaving, taking my girls, doing a runner.* Now that there was space to speak the problems seemed to be impossible to articulate without sounding self-indulgent or self-serving; as if the long hot haul back up the hill towards the house was some kind of metaphor for the task of summing up where she'd come to.

'Like?'

There was a yellow plastic sign hanging on the wire next to them showing a graphic of a lightning bolt, the kikuyu grass growing thick around the star pickets with their black insulators. It was hot again and she still didn't have a hat. From where they were they could see the camp in the distance, over by the main road.

As a way around it she talked about lack of love, lack of any kind of intimacy between them, David's passive-aggressiveness, his disinterest in his family. The differences between them that fly-in/fly-out only seemed to be making worse. Her belief it wasn't just her, that the girls, too, would be better off out of there.

It sounded as if she were ticking off a list on a PowerPoint slide.

'All marriages are fraught with this sort of thing,' Lindl said, in a tone that suggested she, too, was responding by rote. 'You just have to work through them. They pass.'

It wasn't what Eugenie wanted to hear. The unkind thought surfacing that Lindl didn't understand. That their relationship was one-way: she listened, Lindl spoke.

Her friend, though, was way ahead of her. 'Unless of course,' she said, 'you don't want to do it anymore. Or there're other factors involved you're not telling me about.'

In the early days, before Marcus, when she'd been an artist, a printmaker, Lindl had, by her own account, traded on her beauty, being courted by rich men and poor, intellectuals and morons, sleeping with more than a few of them, not saying which was which. It wasn't, she'd told Eugenie, that she'd necessarily wanted to, it was that she hadn't known how not to, as if the needs of the men who pursued her had precluded her own or, no, that, maybe, her needs *were* the men's needs, which wasn't to say that she'd been happy or even enjoying herself. The only place that she could remember having been happy in those days was in her studio, when she was making art.

'Don't take me as any kind of model,' she said, now. 'Based on what I've told you. I was lucky to even *see* Marcus. He was so upright, so straight, so *solid*, he was almost invisible. In those days, you know, I walked through walls, I walked through people like him for a living and yet one day there he was, the one person I couldn't get around, a person who refused to stay in one place for long enough to give me time to get used to the idea of him.

'I guess what I'm saying,' Lindl said, 'is that sometimes it's hard to see your partner clearly. If there is another man … it's worth considering where *you* are. If you jump ship, you should know why you're doing it. You need to make sure you're not simply shifting partners because you don't want to deal with what's there. You might end up in the same place, only with someone much worse.'

'I'm not leaving David to go to some other man,' Eugenie said, disappointed her friend might think it so.

Disappointed, too, that Lindl wasn't encouraging her to go out and explore the world. She wanted to be told it would be okay to fly from David. Her experience was so much less than Lindl's. She'd only had three lovers before him. Four sexual experiences with men. Going straight from school into nursing and from there into marriage, no room for deviation after what had happened to her. Density of childhood indeed. What she was wondering, now, was if it was too late. Not to have lovers who are intellectuals or morons or something in between, but to have a *life*.

'Good.'

'I don't even know if this man's even aware I exist. He's not the reason.'

Lying through her teeth. The doctor wasn't the reason, but he was a factor. If he wasn't, why else would she have told him where he could find her on a Friday night?

'Excellent,' Lindl said. 'Not that it matters, but do I know him?'

'I don't think so.'

They were almost at the house. Lindl looping her arm through hers. 'Come, we'll have lunch. A cup of tea. We can talk more later.'

'The cure-all,' Eugenie said.

'I'm not telling you what you want to hear, am I?' Lindl said. 'But it's hard for me. The only thing that makes any sense to me these days seems to be nurturing the relationships that matter. Like this one with you. Like the one I have with this piece of land. It's all I have left.'

While they'd been down the creek Marcus had laid out lunch on the veranda; fresh bread, cheese, salad, peeled hard-boiled eggs and cold white wine. As they ate he and Eugenie fell into campaign talk. Their default mode. Who'd said what, who'd written what. Marcus offered up an interesting piece of dirt on one of those who'd chosen to support the dam. Lindl interrupted him part way through.

'Do we have to talk about this all the time?' she said. 'It's all we ever talk about. Going around and around in circles.'

'Yes, darling,' Marcus said. 'But it's important. If we don't fight, if we don't stand up for ourselves who's going to do it for us?'

'Oh for God's sake,' she said. 'Don't treat me like an idiot. Please. I live here. I'm your wife. But all this is so hateful. The way you refer to the other side by their surnames. Lamprey, Barkham, Tweedie. It's like you're all back at boarding school in your loathsome little cliques.'

Something about the force with which she spoke shocked Eugenie. This glimpse into another couple's dynamic. On the way back up the path Lindl had listed the relationships that mattered. She hadn't mentioned Marcus. He didn't respond to her tirade, but she could see him backing up inside and that, also, this might be a kind of default for him, this deference to his wife. It didn't make him appear weak, just vulnerable, and a small ray of warmth for him pushed past all the little irritations of the campaign.

'We did meet the most curious individual down along the creek,' Lindl said.

The naked Ange stepping out of the dark water already become, in her mind, a delicious tale.

seven

Guy

He had met Helen at his London publishing house, a four-storey terrace in Bloomsbury whose once-grand rooms had been cut into small, high-ceilinged offices filled, stacked, encrusted with books and piles of ribbon-tied manuscripts. The sort of place where it was possible from time to time to glimpse a giant of literature slipping in to discuss proofs or to wheedle for an advance. There himself to go through the contract for *Magazine Husbands*. Helen was amongst the group of editors and subs who invited him to join them for a drink at the close of business. They went home together that night, that's how immediate it was; he, the young talent, tall, frail, hollow-chested, smoking furiously, she, at twenty-four, also an ex-pat, precise, pretty, embarrassed that her smile displayed too much of her top teeth and gums, articulate, very much of her time, which is to say pushing the boundaries of what was possible for a woman in England in 1972. She told him later that she hadn't thought she'd ever sleep with an Australian man again. She'd thought, these were her words, this was the way she spoke, this was why he fell in love with her, she thought she was beyond Australian men with their attitude to alcohol, *their incomprehensible embrace of the ordinary in the face of the marvellous.*

He'd been in the city for almost two years by then, scraping by on the royalties from *The Brother* and occasional commissions for book reviews, living on the third floor of a shared house in Hammersmith; not a whit less unhappy or isolated than he'd been when he quit university and took up residence in a converted shed on a farm owned by a group of early hippies out at Mangrove Mountain, where his first novel had come into being. He'd flown to London on the back of it, to construct a reputation in a place where it mattered. Disappointed in, amongst other things, the English girls, so sexy with their proper speech, their buttoned-up clothes, but failing always to deliver on the promise of their inflections, as if it was all veneer, that when those clothes came off they were exactly what you saw and nothing more, vulnerable, naked girls, who didn't know quite what to do. Probably it was his own fault; he wasn't naive about that. He didn't know any better himself. Helen was different: *We're here to enjoy each other,* she said, the word 'here' in this context meaning our very presence on earth. *What happens in this bed, between us,* she said, *this is the important thing.* With her he'd been prepared to allow for such a possibility without the customary aftermath of guilt and self-loathing, to enter into a space of joy with a lover as if, and here was the crux of it, as if it were a *God-given* right. The first time she took him in her mouth, in that pale room with its view over the street, wan winter sunlight plotting soft geometric patterns on the walls, she sliding down his belly to address his cock, doing it so delicately, so caringly, as if she loved it, his *thing,* the actual physical manifestation of it in her hand both so impossibly sexual and deeply disturbing at the same instant – her eyes on his, her lips and hands on *him* – he burst into tears, involuntarily, his body shaking, his cock shrivelling so that she stopped and asked what she'd done wrong, what was the matter, *Wasn't I doing it right?* And he'd had to pull himself together and say, *No, no, it's not you, you're doing it perfectly, it's just no-one's done that before, nobody has ever said I love you in that way, in the deepest part of me.*

Of course he'd written about it. He wrote about everything. His life and everyone he met had no function other than to be transformed into story. In went his childhood on the farm in western New South Wales; his taciturn father and long-suffering mother; in went, too, the hippies with their grandiose illusions about what they were doing on the land; in went the grievous years in the embrace of those oxymoronic sadists, the Christian Brothers, a time during which his misery achieved such heights he'd come to believe himself being tested by Jesus *Himself,* that He had chosen him, *Guy,* to take on His role in this time, that the pain was merely training for greater tests ahead.

No attempt to hide any of it.

The Brother charted the dissolution of a soldier returned from the Second World War, and, through him, his young wife; the two of them in their tiny slab-sided house amid the wheat fields of the Mallee in western Victoria. Along the way it illustrated how neatly the boys brought up by the Brothers fitted the fighting force required to defend Australia against the Japanese, but equally how poorly they'd been modelled for coming back into civilian life; noting the curious way that in the face of repression and unalloyed violence some children turn on themselves, making themselves the problem, while others will take it as a sign that they are marked out as chosen. Guy's characters were damaged people placed in a damaged landscape; both described with painful clarity; the paucity of the world beyond the walls of the little worker's cottage emphasising the claustrophobia within it; the words they said to each other as sparse as the treeless fields. The reviewers hailed him as 'a new voice'.

Those first two books came easily. It was only later that he realised what gifts they'd been and why other writers complained so bitterly about the work. In those years the torment had been elsewhere and the writing had been the special place, the one where all other feelings were subordinate to the process, where for hours at a time he could escape. Away from his desk he'd suffered from a sense of dislocation, a loathing for everyone and their noisome striving after the false gods of the appearances. It might be that he had escaped the Brothers, but the language of the church remained his own, he was rooted in its structures, not simply because he had been brought up to it but also because of the beauty of its cadences, its ecclesiastical sonorities.

Helen changed everything. Bathed in her love, emboldened by his own passion, he'd been free, at least for a time, from the overwhelming need to repel or destroy anyone who came near. For a few days during that London winter he even felt something so extraordinary, so unparalleled, inconsistent and transient, as simple happiness. Walking through St James's Park, passing under the bare branches of the tall limes, he thought himself, for the first time he could recall, both happy and simultaneously aware of it. Until then there had only been the *idea* of happiness, most often seen through a veil of sorrow; happiness, by definition, could only exist as a kind of retrospective pleasure, as a nostalgic re-imagining of what had occurred. This, he had believed, was the correct way to look at it: people who were happy in the moment were shallow, lacking in seriousness and the capacity for deeper feeling. Truth and beauty could only be mediated through pain. Yet there he was, this woman on his arm, the sloping light cutting through the trees, and it was so simple, so banal and yet more real than anything he'd ever imagined.

~

Aldous had been in almost constant contact since the public meeting. Guy had made the mistake of confessing the doubts which had come to plague him. Now Bain was calling every other day, urging him to commit.

'Don't take it to heart,' he said. 'Town Hall meetings are the hardest thing you can do, especially in your home town. And you did well. Down here in Canberra it's different, you'll see, there's a level of separation between decisions and individual consequence.'

'Isn't that what everyone complains about?' he said.

'Undoubtedly. But nothing would get done if it was all personal, would it? It's why we have different levels of government, *and* a Senate. Well, not in Queensland of course, but that's an aberration. Queensland's always an aberration. You can't let emotion rule how you act. We all have doubts, Guy, it's the nature of the beast. But rest assured, we need your sort on the team. We want you on board.'

To reinforce this he arranged a brief 'hello' with the Opposition Leader at a house in Brisbane. Picked him up from the New Farm apartment and delivered him in his com-car to this great spreading Queenslander stepped onto a hill in Hamilton. Security men waiting on the street to meet them, entering Bain's credentials on an iPad. No mention of whose house it was. Some friend of the Party's. An assistant appeared to guide them into a glass-sided lift that raised them to a beautifully restored, painting-rich lobby, and from there to the much landscaped backyard with its swimming pool, its cut sandstone blocks and exquisite hardwood lattices, succulents in tall square pots. Views towards the port and the new high-rise apartments along the river. Lonergan over by the rail in a pale blue polo shirt and shortish shorts, pacing, talking on a mobile, waving them to sit beneath the wide white sail, another one of these small men of extraordinary force, begging the question of correlations between ambition and height; never mind Caesar's concerns about thin men, if it's ambition you're hoping to avoid you'd be more advised to surround yourself with tall blokes. Lonergan, all wiry intensity, even at a distance a burning ego in boat shoes. A former lawyer of course, as they all seemed to be.

They sat on strikingly uncomfortable wooden chairs, long cold drinks gathering dew on the timber. Not a woman in sight, although officially there was a wife, somewhere. What Lamprey imagined, predictably – it was the pool that provoked it, but also the man's tough-guy demeanour, the hair on his arms and legs and in the V-neck of his shirt – were night-time scenes of drunken revelry, a sixties porn party.

Lonergan coming straight to the point, 'Aldous, here, speaks highly of you,' he said.

'Aldous is too kind,' Guy replied.

'Kindness be damned,' Lonergan said. 'What we're after is results and Aldous thinks you can deliver. The Senate's the thing. We need to stop these micro-parties messing with our agenda. We have the policies – reform the public's hungry for. But if I can't get the Senate I'll be just as fucked as the last lot. I need candidates who can own the debate. That's why he's got me talking to you.'

All his life Guy had been writing about status and power in one or another of their manifestations, be it between men and women, adults and children or the behaviour of politicians. Here, now, directly across the table from him, for the first time, was the real thing. He couldn't have been more surprised. He wanted to be cynical and superior, to take notes and avoid being seduced, but his defences were no match for the strength of the man. Mayska had been a piece of work, radiating self-confidence, accustomed to command, but his power, undeniable and fearsome though it was, somehow remained vested in what he had surrounded himself by, in his accumulated wealth. Here, in Lonergan, was, at last, the pure essence of the thing, an individual who wasn't interested in anything as petty as who might like or dislike him, only in his personal agenda and how others might serve its aims. A man gathering it all towards him, raw, coarse, deeply attractive. He'd never encountered such singularity; it was exhilarating and, simultaneously, chilling. The way the man's attention swung onto him with such ferocity, pinning him to the hardwood chair, focusing for a moment before turning to the next thing.

On television and radio his force was diminished. Lonergan had a tendency to pause after a question, as if he was giving the answer due thought, or perhaps, more unkindly, winding through the recently stored talking points for the appropriate sound bite. He had a weakness for agricultural metaphors: *pruning to increase growth, the cut worm forgives the plough*; or, a favourite: *one year of seeding, seven years of grief*, as if the country was a garden and he, already, its keeper. In person there was none of this. He was quicker, more relaxed, humorous, well informed.

'Aldous tells me you think we should be doing more about climate change,' he said.

Lamprey glancing at Bain.

'No point in throwing daggers at him,' Lonergan said with a flicker of a smile. 'It's my job to know what people think. It's his job to tell me.'

Guy tried to brush it off. 'My remarks were taken out of context. Aldous and I were talking with a mutual friend … I suggested he was ignoring the dangers we face.'

'And yet our mutual friend is, as I understand it, working hard on just this problem. Not because he's an altruist. Out of his own interest.' Sitting back in his chair, legs spread. 'The other side like to present us as *denialists*,' he said. 'They call us ignorant. But they're the ones who've got the wrong end of the stick. This whole thing isn't about *climate*. It's about *energy*. About who has it and who hasn't. I'm a realist. At the same time it's more about politics than science. What the other side seem unable to recognise is that, right this minute, we are engaged in a race. It's a race between being destroyed by the unexpected consequences of our technologies and our capacity to invent new ones that'll let us create and distribute energy world-wide without killing us all. One will come out of the other. If we win. But the driving force has to be the market. The market is what has got us this far. Not top-down regulation. You can't regulate us out of where we are. We have to stay the course. Push through.' Speaking in short sentences but without pause. No requirement to think about it, all that already done. The real Lonergan revealed.

'What if the market doesn't deliver?' Guy asked.

'We're fucked then, aren't we?' Lonergan said, laughing dismally. 'But seriously, do you think you can put the genie back in the bottle? That you can stop people reaching out for energy now they've seen what it can do? All those billions in Africa and India? In fucking *China*? Really? Just because you put up a moral argument? No fucking way. Try it and we'll have global war like nothing we've ever seen. Have a look at the environment after that …

'Listen, we might have war anyway, but if we let the market run its course we'll at least have a chance.'

Guy having little or no sense of the truth of what Lonergan was saying, only that, sitting there, sweltering in his best suit, no arguments rose against it. The man's certainty, his drive, the quickness of his brain was all-encompassing, seductive.

'I wouldn't have taken this as your field of interest, Guy,' Lonergan said.

'It's not,' he said. 'I'm a writer. But I've been working in the Arts sector for a couple of decades.'

'That's good. And are you happy about what we're doing there?'

Guy gave a self-deprecating smile, allowed himself what he thought was a smidgin of dissent: 'I'd have to say I'm going to find further cuts to their budget hard to defend.'

Lonergan took a sip from his drink. 'Well then,' he said, 'we won't be giving you Arts, will we?'

Guy nonplussed, stumbling for a comeback.

Lonergan laughed, delighted. 'Listen, Guy,' he said. 'How you sell your ideas is up to you, as long as they tie in with policy. As long as you don't embarrass me or the Party in the process. But don't worry we'll school you, starting immediately. We'll send you off on a training course. Put you through the ringer. Ask you every type of question you're ever going to encounter. Beat the life out of you. You'll have all the help you could need.'

Looking to his left, out at the river. 'Is there anything else?' he said. Standing, offering his hand. The meeting over. Ten minutes. 'Good to have you on board.'

Helen was not amused, even when he made light of his failings in the face of power. Shaking her head in disgust.

'I don't understand how you can get involved with these people,' she said. 'Apart from any other considerations you're not cut out for this, Guy, you're too sensitive. That's why you write. They'll eat you alive. They won't even bother to spit out the bones.'

They were at breakfast, or, rather, she was at breakfast. He'd already been up for several hours. He was talking to Bain on the phone when she emerged from her rooms, her bald head bare, a shawl draped around her shoulders. Carrying her own griefs and concerns. Gliding into the kitchen to consume some herbal concoction.

'Who was that?' she asked.

He shrugged. 'Aldous.'

'The oleaginous one?' she said. 'Is he still at you?'

'Yes.'

'Is there coffee?'

'I'll make a fresh pot.'

'I thought you'd told him no.'

'Maybe I need to do this,' he said. 'Maybe it will be good for me, get me out of this rut.'

He unscrewed the percolator and tapped the used grounds into the bin under the sink. Which was when she said the thing about being eaten alive. As if she could see directly through him, past his self-deprecation to the ambition that had been quickened within. Putting him in his place. A view from a more spiritual plane. One to which her disease gave her special access.

He washed the stainless steel under the tap, flushing out the ashtray smell of old coffee.

'Unexpected consequences my arse,' she said. 'These guys have known what they were doing for decades and have kept doing it, lying to our faces. If you can't see that there's no point in arguing with you. I don't have the energy. It's your choice.'

Spooning fresh grounds into the little cup. Waiting for it. Whatever it was going to be.

'But understand this: I won't be involved. I will not be your political consort. I don't even know if that's the right word; is it men who are consorts? Whatever. I don't want to associate with these men and their self-serving philosophies. It is all men isn't it? You can make your decisions about your life but not mine. Is that clear?'

'The coffee's on,' he said, turning to go. There being only so much self-contained ethereal sermonising a man can take before lunch.

'You're not worried about your past?' she said to his back, bringing him around. 'What they might dig up?'

'I've never hidden who I am.'

'Still.' That calm stare of hers. 'It's one thing to do that as a writer, when you're in control of the material. It's another thing when a journalist stirs around in it trying to find scandal.'

'This isn't America.'

'It's getting more like it every day,' she said.

'It's the least of my worries.'

～

They'd moved in together, into a one-bedroom basement flat, the ground floor of a terrace in Shepherd's Bush. She went to work in the mornings, leaving him there, alone, trying to find his way into the new manuscript.

All through the editing process of *Magazine Husbands* he'd been desperate to start the new work, but now that he had the time and space the ideas refused to animate, the characters remained trite, the sentences fell dead on the page. Frustrated that something which had been so simple was now so hard he took to waiting for her return, pacing the small flat, looking out through rain-spotted windows at the drab back garden. Desperate for release. When she did arrive, he found fault. Her constant cleaning and tidying was symptomatic of a bourgeois sensibility; her chatter about her days, evidence of a scattered mind; her deliberations over clothes, a demonstration of shallowness. He made the mistake of reading to her whatever it was he'd bashed out so torturously during the day. She, in turn, was foolish enough to make comments about it, as if, because she'd studied English Literature, or was some junior assistant editor at a publishing house, she had the right or ability or qualifications to comment sensibly on what he'd produced.

The only thing he wanted from her was total immersion in the physical, he in her body, she in his. He could hardly wait for her to be in the door before he began to undress her. The difficulty was that his former patterns had begun to reassert themselves. When the immediate passion was spent it was replaced by that familiar sense of disgust; at himself, at her, at the act. He'd allowed himself to believe that she had banished whatever forces had previously given rise to this pathology, but in the small dark flat, the more he became accustomed to her, cognisant of her cycles, the intimate physicality of another, the less he could bear to be in the same room, never mind bed, once they were done. He made an excuse to get up, to get a cigarette, say he had to write something, go elsewhere. Her parts, so stimulating to him when he was aroused, now repulsed him; their wetness, their scent, their cloying femininity. He shut himself in the bathroom and washed himself in the sink, covering the sound with the noise of the flushing toilet.

Husbands was well received. Foreign rights were sold, both in America and for translation. There was talk of a film. Requests to speak at festivals arrived, taking the heat out of the struggle with the new book. An invitation to Venice. He found a way to go by himself, but clumsily, managing to tell Helen about it only a few days before he was to depart, making it sound as if it had slipped his mind, as if the journey would be a nuisance, something that cut into his work schedule, making out he hadn't known how much she would want to go with him to that fabled city, excusing himself with a lame story about thinking she wouldn't be able to take time off. Resentful of being put in that position. As if Helen was the problem.

The city was packed. It was spring holidays and barely possible to move in the alleyways. To get on the Vaporetto one had to push, like Japanese in their subways. In an attempt to foster fellow-feeling the writers were housed together in a pension hidden within the labyrinth of the Dorsoduro. The place was less than Guy had hoped for – the room grubby, the shower and toilet down a hallway, the former a pathetic dribble, the latter a smelly latrine whose floor sloped – the whole building sinking into a canal.

Dinner that night was in the courtyard, at one long table, all the significant literary figures gathered at the opposite end. He wondered if their rooms were better than his own. Nobody, it seemed, aware of who he was, or particularly interested in finding out. The abundant wine leading to the kind of raucousness only writers are capable of. Exhausted after the broken night on the train he went up to his room, only to discover it overlooked the restaurant. He lay on the sagging bed, tormented by drunken renditions of *funiculi, funicula* rising from below, wronged at every turn.

Hardly had he slept than he was awake again, grey light seeping in the window. Unwilling to be insulted further he dressed and went out, finding the city transformed; the *Fondamente* all but deserted, Giudecca lying mistily across oily water, a tug-boat passing in the channel. No sign, yet, of the sun. Bent old women in grey sack dresses, characters out of Brueghel, swept the squares with brooms made from bound twigs, gathering litter into carts. Discarded gondolas held conference in narrow canals, tied up to heavy rings rusted into the stone. When the sun did rise it came from behind San Giorgio, announcing its arrival with a great orange glow across a watery sky, the colours picked up by the troubled surface of the lagoon.

In the Piazza San Marco he was, mysteriously, extraordinarily, alone, just him, the pigeons, the stacks of café chairs tied up along the cloisters and a young man in a leather bomber jacket looking up at the griffin perched atop a single tall pillar near the ferry dock. He was an American from the haircut, all but shaved around the neck and sides but long on the top, a blond lock fallen across his forehead.

'You're Guy Lamprey, aren't you?' he said, extending a hand. 'Edward Greave. We're both of us staying in the same dump, I think.' Smiling broadly, as if it was impossible anyone could take anything other than pleasure in their meeting. Something familiar about him that Guy couldn't locate. He was, he explained, an historian, from a mid-western university, in Europe on a Guggenheim, doing research for a book on the mercantile practices of the sixteenth-century city states. He spoke educated Eastern American English, a pleasant accent in itself, redolent of the promise of that country, punctuating his sentences with an occasional toss of the head, a slightly disconcerting tic, akin to the sort of movement you'd make as a way of giving directions. He was to spend the day visiting significant buildings.

'You should come along,' he said.

Guy had never been anywhere. He'd made it to Sydney from western New South Wales and had caught a plane from there to London where he'd found a sad little room to inhabit. A journey large enough in itself. An exploration of the bookshops, libraries and museums of that city had been all he'd managed until he met Helen. With her he'd visited Paris for a weekend, been to Bath and Edinburgh.

'I love your work, by the way,' Edward said. 'I've not read your latest but the first one was terrific. Bracing.'

He was a natural guide, enthusiastic, informed, fluent in Italian, granted entrance through dark-timbered gates to courtyards and villas, the ancient homes of the Medici. In the late afternoon they caught the ferry to Cannaregio to visit a church where they might hear monks perform a piece by Palestrina, not a composer Guy was familiar with. The church had been built by some Doge or other in penance for escaping the plague, or being immensely wealthy, or something else entirely – by that time he wasn't paying attention. He harboured a barely contained horror of churches, no matter the sect, having in fact sworn to himself that once free from the Christian Brothers he would never again darken their doors, naive enough in his youth to believe it might be so easy to shuck off their yoke.

The building's interior was much as he'd expected, fairly grim, although in this case even more so from being constructed of a dark stone that absorbed what small light entered through a bank of high windows. He was, however, unprepared for the beauty of the music; a single voice announcing its beginning, picked up by others, built upon, giving rise to harmonic resonances which filled the whole church, transforming it into another instrument, playing its different parts; the sound separating and coming back together, adding to itself, reverberating, carrying the notes forward and up in a series of ever-expanding steps. Caught by the purity of the moment he thought of Helen for the first time that day, alone in their flat in London, and was pierced by a deep sense of regret that she couldn't be there with him to hear this.

Edward proposed sharing a room. Anything, he said, would be better than where they were staying. When Guy agreed he found an attic overlooking the *Fondamente* itself. Sleep, however, was not to be, at least that first night. When they were at last inside, the door closed behind them, Ed produced a brass snuff box containing a nut of dark hashish.

'The very best Turkish gold,' he said. 'Purchased from a man I know in Florence.'

Guy was a very occasional smoker, nervous of the places his mind went under the influence of this drug, both the intensity of feeling and the inane self-analysis that it provoked, the interminable circular thought about thought, but succumbed, if only to please Edward, who'd sought so hard to please him. He took a long pull and held the musty smoke in his lungs, feeling the drug's warm glow spread through his body, expanding out into the pores of his skin, as if awareness of the moment could be a force in itself, one with the capacity to dissolve etheric barriers which, all unbeknownst to himself, he had been hungering to traverse. Ed taking the joint back and drawing on it himself, his dark glasses gone, those clear eyes – a little close together, as if he were staring intensely into the distance – focused now on Guy; here, at last, the resemblance. Edward had the same pale skin, the same high forehead and the ever-so-slightly lopsided mouth as the boy, Simpson, for whom he'd nurtured a terrible crush that first term at boarding school in Sydney, when he was all of twelve. Could it really be so, that all attraction was based on barely remembered affinities from childhood? Wondering this as Edward leant forward to take his, Guy's, face in his hands and kiss him full on the mouth, kissing Guy, and Guy letting him, Guy responding as if such a thing were the natural corollary of this man's company, of being there in Venice with all its libertine history spooling behind him, as if, when Ed slipped down the length of his body, undoing his belt and the button at the top of his trousers, it was a natural extension of the day.

If it hadn't been for the hash he'd never have allowed it, but what the drug gave him was simply licence to do what he wanted to do anyway. He'd never thought himself capable of such acts, of holding another man's cock in his hands, so different from his own and yet so much the same, so fascinating and erotic, this uncircumcised, squat thing, nestled in its small blond forest; Edward almost hairless on his body except there, very neat, as if he'd been modelled on Greek statues, his beauty encouraging Guy to an anthropological curiosity, noting that far from being repelled he was aroused. Strange revelations indeed. If self-knowledge was the goal then clearly he had been blind to avenues of learning about his own appetites.

Later, lying together on one of the single beds, he admitted that he'd never done this before, even during those years at boarding school when he had craved human contact. 'I was too fucked up for that sort of thing,' he said. 'I couldn't even touch myself without Jesus having something to say about it.'

'Well then, we have a bit to make up for, don't we?' Ed said.

Away from London Guy could see that his frustration with Helen had been as much a reaction to his struggle with the novel as with her. Edward presented the perfect resolution to *that* problem. He allowed Guy to see a man as a woman might, however briefly. Helen would, he thought, understand this, if not forgive it. Edward would be the model for Sheldon, his protagonist in the new work, not Edward the person, but Edward's physical manifestation, standing at the tiny sink, shaving, the ends of the small hotel towel barely meeting across his thigh, emphasising the beginnings of a portliness that would no doubt come upon him in middle age; or, *again*, as he sat naked in the armchair reading, his legs splayed, his cock and balls resting at their apex, such a small part of the whole and yet so significant. It was not that he'd discovered (so late) that he was homosexual, a suggestion as ludicrous as insisting, now, that he was rigorously heterosexual, it was more that he was, that they were – that man in his armchair casually adjusting his tackle – animals, more polymorphically perverse than he'd previously understood, subject first and foremost to their bodies, regardless of how much they might like to see themselves otherwise. Even more interesting was the man's self-satisfaction, his ease with his body and the pleasure it gave him.

They went to each other's sessions. Edward was a skilled performer, bringing history to life, seducing audiences with story. After one of his talks Guy went to congratulate him. Ed, radiant with attention, made to take his hand. For one awful moment Guy thought he might try to kiss him. He pulled away sharply, couldn't help himself, never mind the look of dismay on Ed's face. The shame about what they were doing together might have been subsumed, even absent, in the privacy of their room, but it was intolerable to consider in public.

He made a call to Helen on the hotel's phone, sequestered in its own small box in the lobby. Connection gained through various operators in Italy and London, a process not without its own complications. It had been four days. Helen pleased to hear from him. Embarrassingly so. He had not been certain she would be.

She was alone in the flat. She said she had tried to call the hotel a couple of times. He had to explain why he wasn't there. She wanted him to give an account of everything, who he'd spoken to, how he was being received at the festival.

'I was so worried,' she said. 'The way you left ... I thought you might go there and find some other woman. I've hardly slept.'

'You poor darling.'

'You haven't met another woman, have you?'

'No.'

'You don't mind my asking, do you? I'm sorry. I'm stupid. It's just I love you so much and I couldn't bear it.'

'Sweetheart,' he said, 'I love you too.'

He looked at the old bakelite device on its pegboard, surrounded by scratched numbers and business cards advertising restaurants, tours, nightclubs. He was not often forced to lie, hadn't had much use for the skill since leaving school and home. He could see no advantage, however, in even beginning to explain what had happened. It wasn't of any significance, was little more than research; at worst, a passing indulgence.

eight

Will

Will takes the ute round the camp to have a look-see, no more'n that, doesn't say a word about it to Jaz, not even to Damo and Ren, just rocks up at the gate where a couple of chicks are sitting under a beach umbrella next to a table, flyers and stuff laid out with lumps of rock on them so they won't blow away.

Taking things into his own hands.

A hot day, wind from the west, dry. Leans his arm on the window and says, *What's up?* and the dark one smiles and tells him maybe he ought to come see for himself, points to where he can put the car.

That's how simple it is.

He parks in the paddock and comes back over the gate, easy like, making as if he hangs out in these sorts of places all the time. It helps the chicks are good-looking otherwise it'd be hard to hide his feelings, joshing with them when they ask his name to put on a sheet of paper with the time and date of his arrival, which is the first sense he gets of how the camp's run; casual on the outside, efficient inside. Ange the prettier of the two, dark hair in dreads, olive skin, wearing a man's singlet and no bra, Thai fishermen's pants with the top rolled down so there's a gap between them and the singlet that lets you see the curve of a sweet little belly and the top of some tattoo at the base of her spine. Strong eyebrows and dark eyes, white teeth flashing. He asks where abouts she's from and she says, *Away*, as if that was the end of it but then adding, *This's where I am now. Come and I'll show you what we're about.* She asks the other girl, Ellie, to keep the gate while she's gone, except before they take more than a couple of steps Ellie calls out, *Hostiles!* and Ange runs back to the table and gets on a walkie-talkie and Ellie has a video camera out filming, while for his part, he's about to dive under the fucking table, but sees it's only a four-wheel drive coming along the road, slow like. Nothing written on the door, men in white shirts taking a gander at the camp, coming almost to a stop, letting them get a good look to show they're not worried by cameras or girls in tank tops or him because, he guesses, he looks like one of them with his hair back in its ponytail and his dusty jeans. Some sort of game, he thinks, this with the hostiles. No threat, no bombs, no guns, just faceless men in shirts and black sunglasses.

The camp's been set up on a big flat area near the road, a hundred or so metres above the creek, upstream from where the dam wall's gonna be, which is right where the weir is, backing up the flow. You're not s'posed to swim there on account of it being the town's water supply, but it's a good hole and people always have and now the fucking hippies are in and out of it all day, naked as they come. Ange takes him down there after she's showed him round the camp. Soon as they get there she strips off, just like that, so he can see everything, tits, pubic hair, the lot. He takes off his shirt, no harm in her seeing his pecs and abs, but keeps his jeans on, no way he's going skinny in front of this lot. The tatt on her back is six lines, all together, equal, making like a rectangle right where her hips begin.

Hours later, in the tent, when she's lying on her belly and he's tracing it with his fingertips, she says it's a hexagram from an ancient Chinese book that gives you instructions about how to live.

'That one's the *Creative*,' she says. 'That's me. I write songs.'

It's not like he's ignorant about Asian stuff. One of the rooms at The House-on-the-Hill is set up as a *dojo* for Aikido. Will gets this stuff.

'About, like, protests and the rest?' he says.

'Not so much,' she says. 'I write songs about stuff that moves me. That's what's important, hey? I go where the Muse leads me. I was studying literature at uni and that, but I dropped out. They were, you know, telling me what to think about books, telling me *when* I had to read them. But books are, like, *sacred*, a book comes to you at the time it *needs* to be read and if you're forced to read one when it's not the right time then the message that book has for you gets lost, don't you reckon?'

He nods his head, but he's not big on reading. The only books he reads are manuals and even then he prefers the thing itself, the machine. She rummages around in the back of the tent, she's naked, completely, her gorgeous fucking arse in his face while she's digging in her bag, he can't believe he's there with her like that, he's never had much luck with women, never been like this with one before ever, really. When he was at school he kept pretty much to himself. He had acne real bad. He kept so far away from the girls he couldn't get near them; even if he'd managed to cross the distance he knew they wouldn't be able to see him, wouldn't want a pimply boy from off of one of the local dairy farms, *mud between their toes*, unless they were pissed, or he was, or they both were. Later, in the army, when he'd built himself up, when his face had cleaned up, if you don't count the craters where it'd been, he'd gone to cat houses, but even there it didn't always work out. When you got in the room with the girl it wasn't what you thought it was going to be, no matter that she

144

was selling herself. Perhaps he didn't pay enough; maybe if he'd gone to a better class of place, an officers' joint, things might have been different, but the girls he met were like plastic dolls, seamless. No way in. One time this girl got him off with a handjob, but casually, like she was pumping up a tyre or something. It all happened within the first couple of minutes. When she was done, she wiped up his mess, very efficient, then asked him what he wanted to do next, he still had twenty minutes to go, *did he want to talk?* and he said yes so they sat down together and she asked him about what he was doing and if he liked it and it was about the best fucking thing that had ever happened to him with a girl so he went back the next week to see her again but she wasn't there, she'd moved on.

When Ange took him into the tent and started having sex with him he came in about thirty seconds flat, shooting his load all over the inside of her thigh, not even getting it inside her, like he was some kind of adolescent.

The thing is, she wasn't fazed.

'It's all right,' she says, 'happens to lots of blokes, doesn't it? It'll come back up again in a minute, won't it?' Which it did and this time he was able to do it better, fucking like, well, like a man, looking down at her while he was pushing himself into her and she's making like she's enjoying it, running her hands over the muscles on his stomach and his pecs, saying how handsome he is and making noises like a woman in a porn clip and it's so fucking good he comes pretty quick again. Even then she's all right about it. She brings out this *I Ching* book and three coins and says she's going to do a reading for him. She sits up cross-legged with all that dark hair between her legs, as if it's perfectly natural which, he realises – a stupid little kind of thought, but there you are – that for her it *is*, those breasts, the weight of them, the curve of them with their small nipples with the brown skin around them, the outward swell of her belly with its inset button, is *her* body, she doesn't know anything else, just like him in his body, but even knowing that doesn't make it any less magical. She has this thin band of multi-coloured cord around her ankle, a tiny little silver bell hanging off it, and that's extraordinary, too, because it's on *her*, the light from the torch spilling onto her skin. She smells of patchouli oil and sweat and sex.

She unwraps the coins from a piece of silk, laying the cloth down in front of her, placing the book and the coins on it and performs this little ceremony with her hands over them before shaking the coins out on the cloth six times until she's made one of these hexagrams for him which is pretty, but wouldn't you know it, it's called *Stagnation*, which even he knows means stuck, and he's pissed off at that, as much because maybe it'll mean she won't like him now, as because, in truth, he knows it sums him up, he's still marking time, still caught in that eddy he got washed up in after he left the forces, his life so close to a pile of shit it was all he could do to get out of bed. Just because he's with a bunch of blokes who do training in the morning doesn't make up for it.

The hexagram says it all. Ange reads it out to him, but it doesn't say what he should do about it, least not as he can understand. When she's done with it they lie together and she's small and alive in the curve of his arm.

'Such a *strong* man,' she says. 'Feel those muscles. I like a man with a bit of weight to him.' She puts a hand on his belly just below his sternum, rubbing it around. 'But the *Ching* was right, hey? I feel you blocked in here, like all your energy gets up this far but can't get any further. We need to get you moving in here, eh?'

'I know a way to make that happen,' he says, and rolls over onto her and kisses her and she kisses him back and he's wonderfully grateful that she's not rejected him for his bad hexagram and this time when they do it he's suddenly got all the time in the world and if it's like a porno clip then it's not one he's ever seen because even though they're doing that stuff it's not outside of him, not separate, it's him at her and her at him like legendary wild animals, like fucking gods and he feels the strength in himself like he hasn't for so long and he thinks that what's happening is that she's unblocking him, she's releasing him from the prison he's been in for as long as he can remember.

The truth is, lying with her like that he's prepared to believe anything she says.

In the morning she's still there. In the bed next to him. Naked. Getting in close, resting her head on his shoulder, her breasts against him. After a time they get up so as to go over to the kitchen for breakfast. It's not a big tent, they're getting dressed and he's putting his side-pick in his boot and she says, 'What the fuck is that?' So he gets it out, shows it to her. It's a beautiful thing, spear point, quick draw, made of *AUS8* steel, with a full tang. It has this empty circle in the middle, between the handle and the blade which works as a kind of hand protector but also just looks cool. It slips down inside of his boot like it was never there. He explains to her how you hold it and she takes it and holds it like it's a thing of power, like it's dangerous just to touch, which it is. 'Have you used it?' she asks. 'I mean, have you hurt someone with it?' and he tells her he hasn't but that they train with them, all the blokes carry them, you never know when you might need it, they like to be prepared and she hands it back to him and then kisses him and before you know it they're doing it again and he can't believe it, can't get over how good it is.

When they go over for breakfast he's got this glow on him from what's happened in the tent, it's making the world lighter, it's filling him up to some kind of bursting, but that's not even the total of it because he's also right there in the middle of the camp, surrounded by all these arseholes, and nobody thinks shit about it. He's with Ange so they figure he's okay. He can watch what's going on and take notes, not literally, not with a pen and paper, but he can listen and keep it in his mind like he's on a mission. Damo should see him.

A few days before they'd been hanging out at the house, the four of them, talking about the hippies, the usual shit about them squatting out there, living on the dole, skinny fuckers with dreads, skanky girls with nose rings and shit, all sorts of weirdos coming from who-the-fuck-knows-where acting like they owned the place, this sort of thing, and Jaz said, *One of yous should go over there, check it out, do a bit of recce. That way we could figure how best to mess with them. That'd have to be you, Will, wouldn't it? You've got the hair for it, eh?*

Jaz is the one who calls it The House-on-the-Hill. He pays the rent. Pays for a whole lot of other stuff, too. Not clear where the money comes from. Something to do with a church Damo says. It's an old place out on the east side of town, sat by itself in the paddocks with nothing round it but grass and cows, the best views in the world because the land drops right away there steep as anything. A wrecked car someone drove out into the paddock sitting perched on the edge, it's back door open, like a cardboard cut-out of itself. A shell. Nothing but sea and sky beyond.

Jaz was special forces; he's a big dude, neck and shoulders on him like a steer. Sometimes, late at night, he'll talk about what he's seen, just a little bit, in Africa, Europe, Iraq, Afghanistan. More often he talks about what happened after. When he got into drugs and shit, hit the bottom hard before finding a way back up; how that happened.

You had to have an invite to go there. Mostly it was blokes who'd been with the services. Will didn't even know about it until one night Damo just said, *Come'n I'll get you to meet Jaz.* They'd been at school together. Damo always a skinny kid, this thin streak with a long face and a great snoz, a snoz as wild as he was. When he'd had a few he'd do anything, drove like a maniac. Best driver he'd ever met. They'd be out in the middle of the night doing donuts at Pike's turn-off and Damo'd be at the wheel of his Holden spinning and spinning with the blue smoke from the tyres rising up in the headlights of the other cars and each time he came round you could see his eyes shining out from behind the wheel, his eyes and teeth flashing in this crazy smile, a weird excitement in him like he didn't care, just wanted everything to go faster. Another bastard of a father. But there you go. They went in the army together but Damo'd gone elsewhere. Into the line of fire. Will was in the machine corps. He'd been in some remote camps in Afghanistan when there was fighting going on round them. Shots being fired. People he knew had gotten killed, lost a limb, you name it. His work, but, was in the compounds, fixing the vehicles. He never saw action. He didn't want to make out he'd done more than he had. Which isn't to say it hadn't affected him. When he got back he still had a year or so on his contract and he'd been sent up north building roads for Aboriginals. Doing maintenance on the machines. Couldn't wait to get out, get on with his life. Thought he'd get a job in the mines, earn some real money, looking after the haulpaks and dozers. But when it happened, when he was free, instead of there being *opportunity*, he fell into this pit, living around these people who hadn't the faintest idea of where he'd been or what he'd seen and no way to talk about it. He came back to Winderran because of his mum and ended up staying not because he wanted to but because he couldn't get himself up and at it, like there was this fucking boulder sitting on his shoulders. People he'd grown up with still where he'd left them, working Monday to Friday, getting pissed on the weekend while the world passed them by. Which was pretty much why he'd gone in the first place.

The strange thing is, but, it's home. As if it takes going that far away to know it. He and Damo grew up on dairy farms just out of town. All gone now. Subdivided into hobby farms for these fuckers with Mercedes four-wheel drives to build mansions on. Raise Belted Galloways because they like the way they look.

He and Damo'd spent their time down in the creek, or on the dam, or riding motorbikes round the paddocks. One day they took the bikes out after it'd rained, following an old fire trail into the forest, the dirt shot by the wheels coming up behind them in great fountains, turning them into mud-men, riding for miles and miles with the taste of it in his mouth, which is what it meant to ride dirt bikes, the machine and you and the ground all connected, until eventually they reached a ridge where you got this view through the trees down towards the Brisbane River. They'd stopped the bikes and in the silence after the motors there'd been this feeling, their ears ringing, the mud already drying on their faces, cracking around their mouths as they smiled, extraordinary to be in the forest like that, alone, places nobody else went that they'd taken themselves to, the tall straight trunks of the trees and the view through them and the smell of the eucalyptus in the air. That was the day they decided to join up. They were stopped up there in the forest and Damo'd asked him what he thought and Will had said yeah, he'd do it and Damo said, *Would you? I mean, we could do it together.* And Will had said, *Yeah, that'd be right.*

Damo'd been there when he got back from up north. Different but. Something happened to him. Still wild but more contained. Like a fucking grenade. He's not so far off that himself, but Damo's scary with it. Then one night he tells him about Jaz, like it's some big deal. This ex–special forces freak who's running a house for blokes like them. *You got to watch out but,* he says, *'cos he's got God,* which Will'd have to say didn't sound so good, except Damo says he doesn't rub your nose in it, it's just *there.*

When they go around it's only a few blokes having a drink, smoking some cones, a couple of chicks visiting and it doesn't seem anything special. Jaz a whole lot older than the rest of them, not drinking, and you had to wonder what he was doing hanging around with these younger blokes who're listening to everything he says as if he's some sort of *teacher*, but – and maybe it's the dope or something, the dope *is* strong – he finds himself listening too. He's never met anyone like Jaz. He has a kind of authority that's not been given him by a uniform, or by someone else, but inside.

He tells them there's a war on.

No kidding.

The Middle East, Afghanistan, all that, they're just a small part of it, he says, the war's going on right across the world, it's in Australia too, a war between cultures. He says the Middle East's a fucking trap, the whole fucking Iraq thing was a grand fucking trap they walked right into, and now this thing with Syria's another one. The West going in there's exactly what the fundamentalists want.

'These Islamists,' he says, 'you've seen them, haven't you?' Talking right at Will, past the others. 'You've seen them in the *madrassas*, haven't you?'

Will's not used to being picked out like that. But he says he has, because it's true, he's been in Helmand. He's seen the young men in the doorways of the mud-brick buildings with the big books open on their crossed legs.

'You've seen how they persuade these young men to join them? They work with them, individually, that's what they do. They listen to them, they build relationships with them. These young guys, they've got fuck all, they've never had fucking anything and they can see – they're not stupid – that they're never going to have anything. It's all stacked against them. They can't even get a fucking job and along come these people who talk to them, man to man, about higher purpose, about divine right, about being part of something.'

Will doesn't know why Jaz has chosen him to talk to. As if he, Will, is the only one in the room who understands. It could be the dope. It could be he's imagining that it's him Jaz is talking to, but there's no way of checking on that and anyway Jaz's looking directly at him.

'These guys take the time to listen, that's the thing, to find out what matters to them. They listen and they show how they can help. We've got no hope against that kind of shit, you know? Even if we turn their economies round so they have jobs we're not going to have that relationship with them. In this country we've lost that amongst *our fucking selves*. That's the truth of it. We've killed it off by the way we're living. We think we can just throw fucking technology at our problems and it'll solve them but it won't. We need to get back to what's real. If we don't we'll be fucked. These people want to see us dead. Our technology will not avail us shit against that.'

A couple of days later Damo finds him at his mum's place. He says that Jaz liked him and he can come and live in the house if he wants, even though he hardly said shit the whole time he was there. 'What did he say about me?' he asks.

Damo shrugs his shoulders. 'That you're fucking crazy. That's the way Jaz likes it.'

It's not an offer he's going to refuse. His mum's getting older and shriller by the day, squashed in a little worker's cottage on Burke Street, like there's no hope, like she's been left behind. Hippies playing music at all hours in the rental next door. His father down Maroochydore working for Bunnings, living with a co-worker. *The Bunnies*, his mum and him call them, but not in a nice way. There's not been so much good said about his old man for a long time. Not since the dairies collapsed and he lost his job and went downhill, took it out on his family. It's not something you tend to forget. So he moves out to The House, gets given a bed in the sleep-out, up early in the morning to train with the rest of them, like they were still in the forces, working part-time at the dodgy mechanic's in town so he's often not there during the days and it's better, it has to be better than it was except it's been three months now of not hardly being even noticed, of feeling like he's there but still on the outside, as if there was something else going on in the house that he wasn't part of, that was just over there but out of reach. But then that's what it's been like everywhere for a long time. Like a wall between him and everything else; only difference being that in the house it feels like there's something he wants.

Ange takes him round the camp. Introduces him to people, tells him everything about it. She knows everyone and they know her. Must be a hundred or more people from all over living there, old people going round Australia in their rigs, young people who've come from other campaigns, *battles*, they call them, everyone talking all kinds of shit, global warming and fracking and Aboriginals and land rights, like they've never been up north and seen those folk and how they live, drinking and fighting.

It's all fucking lies, of course, they're professionals is what they are, professional protesters: rent-a-crowds. This is what they *do*. No idea what a fucking battle's like. One bloke from Israel, another from New York. People sitting on bales of hay next to their van beating drums, drinking chai tea, talking shit about the End of Capitalism. The thing is, with Ange it feels different. She believes this stuff and even if he wanted to speak he doesn't seem to have the words to show them how fucked they all are, the ones he's heard Jaz say enough times you'd think they'd just roll off his tongue.

When people ask Will what he does, he says he's a mechanic. He doesn't mention the army, but then they don't ask. When he says he's a local it's like they lose interest, as if someone from around there isn't worth anything, like their opinion doesn't count.

There's a committee that runs the place, organising the water, the dunnies and showers, who works in the kitchen, but at the centre of it there seems to be, really, just one bloke, a Canadian, called Alt.

Will's helping an old bloke with his motor – Ange has gone to do a shift in the kitchen – when he comes over to say hello.

He's about medium height, with a scrappy beard, rangy. He doesn't look any different from the others, wearing loose Indian clothes, dusty feet in sandals, but he's onto Will right away. He leans on the mudguard of the Cruiser, just chatting, but it's in a kind of close way.

'Which part were you in?' he says.

'Of where?' Will says.

'Afghanistan.'

'How d'you know that?'

'It takes one to know one. Just the look of you tells me. I can't tell where you've been but I look at you, how old you are, and I figure it has to be there.'

So he tells him and they talk a bit about what it was like over there. Alt wasn't in Afghanistan, he was in Iraq, like Jaz. Or maybe not. You can never tell with those guys. They keep their cards close. *You* tell *them* stuff, not the other way round.

'So, you still get the nightmares?' Alt asks, just like that, no beating around the bush.

He's got one arm still inside the Cruiser's bonnet. He looks in at the motor and nods.

'And the moods?'

He nods again. *The moods.* Is that what you call them? The fucking rage. And this curious guy, hard like, you can see it in him, he touches him on the shoulder with his closed fist and says, 'It gets better man. In time. Trust me.'

Not so sure what to say to that. Fucking hopes it's true.

'What you doing here, then?' Alt asks and again, like before, there's no notice given, the questions just come and Will's almost caught out this time, as if being there's a crime. He says he's with Ange, but, and that seems to satisfy him.

'We can always use a mechanic,' Alt says.

Around midday Ange takes him down the creek. Not to the weir, further upstream where the creek's still flowing through forest, to a pool where they can be by themselves and this time he takes off his clothes, why wouldn't he, except of course as soon as they're in the water a couple of old biddies appear and stand there the whole time watching while he comes out and dresses himself. Ange there, stark naked, talking to them. Turns out the older one owns the land. It's her who's put up the monitoring box on the tree. Says she's doing it to record frogs. *It's the frogs'll stop the dam*, she says.

After these old girls piss off they're not so much into it next to the creek so they go back up the tent and do it there even though it's hot inside, like being in a fucking sauna. When he wakes up Ange's gone and he's lying in a pool of sweat with his head pounding. It's all he can do to crawl outside, take himself down to the waterhole to cool off.

It doesn't get rid of the headache but at least it's eased. He finds Ange up at the kitchens, helping a band set up for a gig. He sees her before she sees him. She's leaning against a stack of speakers. She's got her hands behind her back pushing her tits out at this bloke she's talking to, looking up at him, head tilted back and laughing. Ange's got this really wide mouth. When she laughs it's like her whole face cracks open, like it's a kind of weather station for what she's feeling. When she sees Will coming the smile just drops right out of it. One side dips into a scowl; you wouldn't think such a small thing could say so much. It gets him in the stomach like he's been hit. He goes up to them but she doesn't even introduce him. It's like he's an embarrassment. He has to hold out his hand to the bloke and say his name to get him to say his, which is, of course, *Steve*. He's the guitarist with the band and he knows Ange from some other place. Will hangs there, waiting for something to happen, for Steve to go tune his guitar or whatever, but he doesn't seem to notice he's not wanted. Ange is off on one of her raves, telling this long story about someone they both know. When she finishes she gives this big laugh and Steve puts his hand on her arm for no reason at all and *leaves* it there. Something just switches in Will, it's like *fuck off dude*, and he reaches out, calm-like, and lifts the man's hand off of her and Ange says, 'What the fuck?' and Steve pushes back, 'Don't touch me, man,' he says. He goes to throw Will's hand off of him and Will simply goes with the movement, this is what Aikido's for, he just lets the man's force take him where he wants to go which, it turns out, is onto the ground, face down, hard, Will coming down onto him to make sure he stays put, his knee in his back, the air going out of the cunt in a great puff of dust, Steve's arm up behind his back, not fucking moving now.

'What the fuck are you doing?' Ange screams, pulling at him, so he lets the guy up. Not so cocky anymore.

'I'm just looking out for you,' he tells her.

Steve takes a couple of steps back, holding onto his arm like he's injured it. 'Hey man, that's not cool,' he says. 'I need to play, man. You can't fucking hurt me like that.'

There's a whole bunch of people looking. Steve brushes himself off, Will hasn't hurt him, barely touched him.

'I don't want you to look out for me,' Ange says. Still fucking yelling. He's screwed up in some serious way. She's really fucking angry.

At least Steve figures out it might be time to go. 'I'll catch up with you later, Ange,' he says, giving a little kind of a wave. Pissing right off.

'You don't get to do that,' she says to him.

'What?'

'You don't get to tell me what to do.'

It doesn't matter that he wasn't trying to tell her what to do. Which is to say, he was, sort of, but not like that. And he doesn't know how to say whatever it is that he was trying to do.

'Just because I've let you fuck me,' she says, 'doesn't mean you own me.'

And that's it. He's in the dog-house. She won't talk to him, never mind that it was her that did it. That night, at the dance, there's a whole bunch of people he's not seen before come in from the surrounding district. A fundraiser. The band's playing loud and everyone's dancing, Ange getting in amongst them. He tries to dance with her but he's not much of a dancer, never has been, and anyway she keeps moving away, spinning around and slipping off between the other people. It's like a game for her, he sees that; he watches her as she goes to the stage and throws herself around in front of Steve, shaking every bit of herself like she wants to have sex with the whole world. He wants her to stop and come back to the tent like she did the previous night, but she won't, she dances on, with everyone and no-one, with anyone except him. Then, when the band takes a break, she goes off with them, leaving him like some dewy-eyed fuck, sitting by himself on a bale of hay.

He can't take it. He finds where he's parked the ute and drives back to The House. Doesn't go in, but. It's late. He walks out into the paddock, out to the edge where the dead car is, where you can see the ocean way off in the moonlight, past the towns along the coast and he sits there with this hurricane whirling around inside him, this giant fucking wind that he has to keep pressed down but which is just too strong, will always be too strong, carving him open to the night. He knows what it is, he isn't stupid, he's jealous, but it feels so unfair because it was so good in the tent before. He fell asleep after they fucked and when he woke up she was someone else.

She was the one made him like that, she would have made anyone like that, she did it on purpose; words coming into his mind, *slut*, *cock-tease* and worse. All this shit bubbling and boiling inside so it's like, up there on the edge of the world, he's never hated anyone quite so much as he hates her and yet the stupid thing is at exactly the same moment he wants her, would do anything for her.

He comes in out of the moonlight onto the back veranda, doesn't see Jaz there on the old couch, the one Ren's dog sleeps on during the day, until he all but trips over his legs.

'Will,' he says, 'Willie Will Bill. Where you been? What you doing up at this time of the morning?'

He's not ready for him to be there. In all the excitement with Ange he's managed to forget about this being some sort of a mission. He's been in this ecstasy that he's not seen before in his sad fucking life and it's made everything around him look good too.

He tells Jaz what he's been doing, about meeting up with a woman and getting on the inside. Jaz listens. Real calm. Asks questions about everything. Gives special attention to this bloke Alt, who Will wishes he'd thought more about at the time; but also how the camp is run; who's there (an Israeli? What does he look like?); about the frog stuff down the creek.

Jaz doesn't ask him to sit so he stays where he is, leaning on a veranda post, talking to this shadowy figure who kind of pulls stuff out of him, as if all the time Will *had* been taking notes and was just waiting for the right questions for the details to spill out. He wonders what the fuck Jaz was doing sitting there anyway, but doesn't ask. You don't ask Jaz things like that.

'Well Billy, you've done good, haven't you? Better than I could've thought. Good on you mate.'

He says thanks. Praise from Jaz doesn't come often and maybe he'd feel better about it if it wasn't that he was so cut about Ange. The moon's gone over the house now, pouring its light out on the hill in front of them as bright as day, so bright you can almost see colour. He's no idea what time it is, close to dawn maybe. If he thought there was any chance he'd sleep he'd go to bed.

'What's up?' Jaz says.

'The chick I told you about,' he says, as if that sums it up.

'I could see something's eating you.'

Jaz's the last person he expects to lend him an ear but right then anything's possible, really, and if he doesn't talk about it chances are he's going to fucking implode. He tells Jaz how she was there one minute and gone the next. About how they'd spent the night together, not the details, just that it had been good. About swimming down the waterhole.

When he's finished Jaz doesn't say anything for a time. He just leaves Will's words hanging there like he's been talking to nothing.

'See those cunts at the camp,' Jaz says, eventually, 'they don't care about anyone but themselves. They don't give a shit if nobody's got a job, it's all the same to them. They'd have everyone living back in humpies if it were up to them. They've got what they want and now they're going to stop any other bastard getting it.'

The thing he likes about Jaz is that he sees things the way they are. It's not just at the camp, but, it's in the town too. These in-comers have taken over everything, filling up the place with their fancy cars and shops, with their fucking crazy ideas of the *land*, as if they'd know a bit of clover from kikuyu, planting fucking trees every which where, like they're fucking *forest* animals so there's no room for him anymore, doesn't matter what he's done for his country in foreign places.

'I'm here to tell you. When I came back I went down. You know about it. You don't need to hear any more of that shit. What I haven't said was why it happened. I won't bore you with it. Thing is, I see the same thing in you. I came back here and I didn't like the place anymore. Australia. You know what I mean? I'd seen all this shit. I'd done stuff which nobody ought to have done. Nobody should've ever have fucking *seen*. I mean it. And I came back here and I couldn't figure what it had been for. Everywhere I looked were just people queuing up to buy shit, filling their lives with junk like that was the meaning of life, filling up their bodies with it, cunts stuffing themselves so hard they have to wear special-sized shorts and shirts.

'You do these things as a soldier which are just, you know, in the line of duty,' he says. 'Nobody's going to pat you on the back for them, but no-one's going to put you in jail for them neither, if you see what I mean. They're things that happened and that's all there is to it, but they have a way of staying with you, and there's no-one can take them away.'

Will's not sure about this bit, he isn't one of those who did stuff they shouldn't have done, seen a whole lot of shit that no-one ought to see. He'd fixed machines. That's all. He's still waiting for Jaz to bring it back around to Ange, to what's eating *him*, but then this thought comes to him – maybe it's because of Jaz talking about people who only think about themselves – that something's bothering *Jaz*, this is why he's up there at four o'clock in the morning on the dog sofa. It occurs to him that Jaz wants someone to listen to *him*.

'You okay, Jaz?' he says.

There's another of these silences. Will allows himself to think, for just a moment, that he's right, that out here on the veranda in the very early morning, they're on the level.

'Nothing for you to worry about, mate,' Jaz says.

Putting him back in his box. He's got it wrong. Jaz could be talking to any fucker. There's this silence into which he wants to put an apology for even thinking what he thought.

Then Jaz says, 'Circumstances beyond one's control, eh? Shit going down. Things I've got to make right. You do your fucking best for people and sometimes it's not good enough. But Billy, I'll say this. You done good these last couple of days. I'm listening to you and I'm thinking there's maybe a way to kill two birds with one stone, fuck with these turkeys at the camp and do a little service for someone else at the same time. That's what I'm thinking.

'I reckon you need to go back. See your girl again,' he says. 'We need someone on the inside. Never mind that crap about her going off with another bloke. You did the right thing to leave. You'll see. Before you know it she'll be begging for you. You can't be seen to want them, no girl wants a man who's weeping for it.'

Hitting him where it hurts. He wasn't weeping for it. Well, maybe a bit.

Later that morning, though, when they're out the back on the grass doing their stretches, all of them out in the early light, getting ready for their run, there's the ping of a text on his phone:

Where r u? Ange

He cleans himself up and gets in the ute. Doesn't matter if Jaz has told him to or not, he's got no choice, he has to go back.

nine

Nick

The *Alterbar* was in a converted church at the bottom end of the street, near the creek, its name emblazoned above the entrance in a red neon font that mimicked Stace's *Eternity*, running liquid in the rain this night, splashing gaudy reflections on the wet concrete path that led towards the building's twin ecclesiastical doors. A surprising number of people inside, collected around old wooden tables, their only common factor being, perhaps, a vaguely bohemian vibe, loose-fitting clothes, a certain studied ease, none of which was any indication – Nick had discovered this about Winderran – of financial status. A three-piece band playing on the small raised area where the altar had once been, singer, piano and saxophone. The place, with its high-raked ceiling and lead-light arched windows, a bit funky, condensation collected on the glass, an exhibition of somewhat garish paintings strung up between them. A bar down one side where he ordered a craft beer from the gay man with significant piercings who asked if he was a member.

He wasn't, hadn't even realised it was a club.

'It's all good,' the barman said, offering him a book to sign.

A quick glance around the room confirming she wasn't there, that, in fact, while he vaguely recognised some faces, he knew no-one. Taking his beer to a small table in the back corner and hunkering down, swiping the screen on his phone to see if anyone wanted him. The singer a long thread of femininity in a deep red cocktail dress, lipstick to match, vamping it up to the mike on standards, projecting sexy innuendo over the top of the noisy crowd. Winding up the set with an extended version of *I'm Your Man*.

He'd barely touched his beer when a woman approached.

'Nick,' she said. 'It's Marie. You remember, we met at Guy's place for dinner, oh, it must be weeks ago now?'

Sliding into the chair opposite, or rather, half onto the chair, so as to communicate she wasn't there to stay, well, unless invited. On that earlier occasion she'd been dressed in something flouncy that gave the unfortunate impression she was both uptight *and* a little fey. Tonight she was in jeans and a simple black top with shoelace straps, cut low enough to confirm but not flaunt that cleavage, her blonde hair loose, and in this guise she was more attractive, more real in fact, smiling at him from kind eyes. Resting a finely shaped hand, long fingers, on the table.

'We're so blessed in this town,' she said.

Tilting his head in question.

'With music,' she said. 'I mean, you don't expect to hear musicians like these in a place like this, do you?'

'No, no you don't,' he said. People in the town, he'd noticed, often found reason to congratulate themselves for living there, which was, he guessed, a good thing, although it didn't always feel that way.

'Do you want to join us?' she asked. 'There's room at our table.' Indicating a group of people further down the room, two or three grey-haired men, a couple of other women, one of whom was looking their way.

She was, he recalled, a potter. Hard to suppress an image of how those fingers, so used to modelling clay, might feel against the skin. Important to at least try not to see every woman as a possible sexual partner. She was not, anyway, so much offering herself – although there was a certain promise in her invitation – as the chance of *company*, conversation, laughter.

'Thanks,' he said, 'but I won't tonight, I'm expecting someone.'

'Well, in that case I'll leave you be,' reaching across the table to touch the back of his hand. 'But if you change your mind, you know where we are.'

She stood up, almost colliding with a young man coming in the door. Nick watched as she wove her way back through the tables. A nice shape to her hips. Miles had said something to him one night in reference to women, how they no longer exerted power over him in the way they once had. Women, he'd said, had become just like other people now … he could relate to them based on who they were, on what they said or thought, as if they were nothing more than attractively shaped men. It wasn't a concept Nick could even begin to embrace.

The young man had made it to the bar. Something familiar about him despite the raincoat draped over his shoulders. Gay, too, at least by the cut of his hair and the stovepipe jeans turned up high on the ankles. The barman leaning across the counter to say something in the young man's ear with what Nick thought was unusual intimacy, although that might have been projection because, in response, the young man produced his wallet, clumsily, using only his left hand, flicking it open to show his ID, revealing, when he turned to face the room, that his right arm was in a cast. Making it all but certain this was Cooper, the boy he'd rescued in the hills to the west of town, except that this young man, for all the similarity, seemed thinner and had just legally purchased a Corona, from which he was now taking a sip, resting his good elbow back against the counter to survey the room with the confidence of someone much older. His reappearance, now, in the bar, inducing in Nick a sense of unease which the dinner with Lamprey and his wife and the chance meeting with Bain had done nothing to dispel.

More people came up for service. The young man made his way to the back of the room. Nick took up his drink, went to stand next to him.

'It's Cooper, isn't it?' he said, holding out his hand. 'Nick Lasker.'

'Doctor Lasker,' Cooper said, 'great to see you.' Sounding genuinely pleased but looking discomfited, nervously glancing around the club, confirming Nick's suspicions that he had, indeed, failed him. Not really anything he could do about it now but say he was sorry. Cooper holding up his plaster to indicate he couldn't shake hands, his beer in the other one, bending his head in close with a curious, perhaps embarrassed, smile on his full lips. 'But you could call me Martin tonight, if you don't mind.'

'I *could*,' Nick said. 'But why would I want to?'

'That's who bought my drink,' Martin/Cooper said.

Which made it possible that Cooper's disquiet was nothing to do with him and all to do with having a false ID, not that it let Nick off the hook. He should have followed through. He'd allowed himself to be got at, plain and simple.

'But it's good, hey?' Cooper said. 'I've been wanting to say thanks, you know, for what you did.' Giving him a broad nervous smile. Something disarming about him, both boyish and knowing at the same time; Nick had noted it before, here it was again.

'How's the arm?' he said.

'Getting better.'

'And everything else?'

'Well, there's still a bit to go ...'

'I'd been wondering how it went for you after that night,' Nick said. 'I didn't think I'd run into you here, though.'

The pianist coming back on stage, a middle-aged man who looked more like a banker than a musician, fiddling with the dials on his equipment then launching into a solo over and around the noise of the crowd.

'I'm up here seeing my dad. Staying at his house. My mother has this thing about maintaining connection. Who knows? It's quite possibly part of their settlement. Like if I don't come to see him she won't get *paid*.'

'He lives here, in Winderran?' Nick said.

'He *visits*. Dad has houses everywhere, you name it: London, New York, a fucking island in the Whitsundays.'

Casually disparaging his father's wealth. Some memory of the family arrangements as told to him in the car seeping back into his consciousness. He'd never been any good at retaining the details of other people's lives, even of those as exotic as Cooper's. The precise nature of the illness or injury of a patient stuck with him but the names of the significant others or the nature of their relationships fell away like once-used phone numbers. It was a trait Abie had hated, seeing it as proof of an endemic narcissism.

When they'd been in the car Cooper had been on morphine. His speech slow and clumsy. In the club he was speaking quickly, almost too fast for clear comprehension, particularly with the music; information delivered in a rush, as if none of it was of any more value than the rest, never mind its personal nature.

'What about you? What are you doing here?' he said, turning his attention on Nick.

'It's a bit odd really,' he said, about to go further, maybe even as far as to mention Eugenie, but catching himself in time. Not sure what could possibly possess him to tell an unknown sixteen-year-old about his fixation. Was he really that far gone?

'It's pretty noisy in here. D'you want to go out for a minute?' he asked.

~

166

It was still raining but the porch provided a small dry area. A bench on either side, a bucket of umbrellas by the door, dripping onto a sand-filled can for cigarette butts. Posters tacked on the wall announcing that on Saturdays there were farmers' markets in the grounds, that this or that band was playing last Thursday night.

The wet grass glistening in the streetlights. A car slowing to a halt, its indicator flashing wetly as it turned into the street beside them. Cooper took a seat on one of the benches and leant back against the wall, his legs extended, looking as if at ease, albeit a bit younger under the harsh light.

Ease was far from what Nick felt. 'D'you see your father often?' he asked.

'This is the first time since this happened,' Cooper said, indicating his arm. 'Tonight was supposed to be the night, you know, for the *big talk*, but when it came down to it Dad – *quelle surprise* – had some crisis going on with his latest takeover. He spent the whole of dinner in his office on the phone to Brazil, left me with my older brother, Michael, who's, like, already old enough to be my father and incredibly straight. He thinks it's his duty to *dispense* wisdom. I escaped out here. So, yeah, we haven't yet had the conversation. That pleasure awaits us.'

'Who's your father taking over this time?'

'They're branching out. Finalising the purchase of CoSecOr. Radical diversification.'

'CoSecOr?'

'Uh … like, the *largest* private security service in the world. MCG pays a fortune for their protection at mine sites, but they also do corrective services. You know, prisons, as well as pretty much any kind of general war-making on demand. It's Michael's plan. He figures it would be cheaper simply to own them. Made a case for it to Dad. I guess you could say the rich are getting richer and they're not all completely fucking stupid. Despite appearances.' Laughing.

'Dad, for example. He's read history. You get massive inequality and sooner or later you get revolution. But hey, if you already own the means of production, why not own the means of protection? That way you can repress the masses for at least a couple of cycles. At least as long as you're alive. I mean, why not make money out of the threat while you're at it? Sell protection to your mates as well. Hell, sell it to the State at the same time. You know how it is … if the State's not going to look after your privilege you have to do it yourself.'

All this coming out at the same speed, three hundred words to the minute or more, a great flow of pissed-offedness at his heritage, a distancing from it, delivered to a near stranger outside a club.

'So is MCG *your* future?' Nick asked.

'Nah. Not my field.'

'Which is?'

'Gaming.'

'Right.' Stretching the syllable out. The best response he could come up with.

'It's okay,' Cooper said. 'Most people don't get it. Dad and Michael don't. They think it's for nerds. They don't understand what you can do with computers. *I* do. We're moving into a new age. People born today are going to live inside them. I mean it, literally. Screens with greater visual acuity than the human eye. Think about what that means. Augmented worlds of extraordinary sophistication. Don't get me started. Whoever owns that is going to own the world.'

Cooper pausing for an instant. Taking a sip of his beer.

Nick wondering if what he'd said was remotely true, about games and security firms, rejecting the possibility, if only because he didn't want it to be so. Noting that for all Cooper's disparagement of his father's wealth he appeared to harbour his own dreams of world domination.

'So, if you don't mind me asking,' he said, 'who's Martin?'

Cooper put the beer aside and leant forward to dig out his wallet, flipping it open perhaps a little too proudly and handing Nick a student card from The University of Queensland. A photo of himself next to the microchip. In the name of someone called Martin Gere. It looked real.

'He's got a Medicare card, too,' Cooper said, passing it across. 'That's as far as I've got. I'd like to try for a passport. That's the holy grail.'

Boasting.

'Is this someone's identity you've bought?'

'Hey! No. He's me. I made him. Well, technically, he was once alive, died when he was three years old. Around the time I was born.' Watching Nick for a reaction. 'It's a speciality of mine.' That smile again. 'It's pretty simple, really. I mean it takes time. I've been doing it for a while. You need to be, you know, a bit *obsessive*. Martin's my favourite. I mean, just the name, hey?' Looking out into the darkness again, caught out searching for praise.

'But why would you want to?'

Cooper picking up the beer and tipping the last of it down his throat.

'Sorry, stupid question,' Nick said.

'It's not for that,' Cooper said. 'Drinking's just a bonus. The internet's a vast place. There's bits of it you don't want to go into as yourself.'

The music leaking out through the doors. Nick finishing his own beer and putting the bottle aside while Cooper talked. The day catching up with him. Even at the best of times the explanation the young man was giving of Tor and VPNs and Block Chain technology would have had his eyes glaze over.

Interrupting him. 'Can I get you another drink?' he said. 'I mean I shouldn't, should I? Corrupting youth.'

'It's just a beer, Doctor Lasker. My ID's watertight.'

'Okay. But you can call me Nick.'

He went back inside. Entering the heat and noise and wash of music. The saxophonist working up through a riff. A small dapper man with a narrow face, wearing a neat little hat, a trilby – the name rising up from some forgotten archive in the brain – tilting back from the waist as he blew into the instrument, climbing the scales, producing a remarkable sound. Several people turning their heads when he'd opened the door, including the woman, Marie. Seeing, with a flush of embarrassment, how this must appear, his refusal to join her table, and then to go outside with a boy half his age. Nothing he could do about it. For all that Cooper was precocious and over-eager he suddenly felt he'd prefer to be with him than in here, trying to fit into a new town, to get to know strangers, to appeal to their better natures.

He ordered another couple of bottles, taking note of his sudden relaxed attitude towards teenage drinking.

'What would happen if you went into these places with your own name?' Nick asked. 'I mean this is what I don't get, all this anonymity. I prefer people to be who they are. People behave better when they've got their name attached to what they're saying. At least some of the time.' Thinking, as he spoke, of Cooper's older brother, abandoned by him for the crime of imparting wisdom. 'I must sound horribly straight,' he added.

'No, you're right. We would be. It's just that privacy's been compromised, hasn't it? Government agencies watch everything, particularly this sort of shit.' Tapping his wallet. 'Don't be fooled it's just *metadata*. If they can get more they do. Never think twice about it. Not *just* them, of course.'

'God, but they must have to wade through some shit.'

'Just think about your browsing history,' Cooper said. 'They have.'

Paranoia and conspiracy being, Nick thought, both enticing and infectious. Like ghost stories, providing shivers of scary pleasure; only now it was *government*.

Cooper clearly deeply in their thrall. Leaning in again, 'But if you want to find out what's really happening, the things people don't want you to know, well you need to come in sideways. It's the one reason I don't mind being at Dad's house. He has a direct line to fibre, superfast, for currency trading. One gig per second. Fantastic encryption. With speed like that you can get around some things you couldn't otherwise avoid, it gives you that edge.'

Nick having come out on the off-chance of meeting a woman and ending up sitting on a porch in the rain talking to a teenager with false ID about gigabits. Which he'd be happier about if the business of Bain had been sorted. Not sure how to bring it up.

'Everything's sort of fine the way it is, *now*,' Cooper was saying. 'But when it starts getting nasty, when they start rounding people up, it would be good to be someone else, wouldn't it?'

'Who's they?'

'The government. The church. My dad.'

'Your dad?'

'Well, Mayska Coal & Gas. That's what buying CoSecOr's all about.' He took a sip of beer. 'You interested to hear what happened to the people who beat me up?' he said.

'I am, yes,' Nick said, more interested than he was prepared to admit. Here it was then, coming back around.

Cooper looking straight at him, no escaping his gaze. 'Zip,' he said.

'I'm sorry?'

'Nothing. Zilch. Zee-ro.'

'I don't understand.'

'Martin's been doing a bit of research,' Cooper said, giving that cute smile again. 'You know how it is, beat me up and what do you know? My curiosity's piqued.'

'It's probably my fault,' Nick said, getting it out there, coming clean. 'I didn't report it. I should have. I was going to, if that makes any difference, I'm sorry. Bain asked me not to. He said your father wanted to avoid publicity and they'd sort it out.' Then told him later it had been sorted, that the thug had been punished. Foolish, he guessed, to ever trust a politician.

'Bain?'

'The local member? He's in the Shadow Cabinet.'

'Oh, you mean Aldous.'

'Yes. You know him?'

'He's a friend of Dad's. I've met him several times. He's a creep. A Christian creep, if you can get creepier than just being a creep.'

Dismissing Bain with a word. The ruthlessness of the young.

'I shouldn't have listened to him.'

'Don't worry about it. Seriously. It's not your fault. If Dad didn't want people to know about it, nothing would have been reported anyway, didn't matter what you did or who you told. That's the way it works. I thought you did good up there at the camp, fronting Jaz like that.' Putting on a deep voice, '"You're in shit so deep you don't even know it." Hot stuff.'

'What was that place anyway?' Nick said, a little pleased despite himself. This was Cooper's gift, he was only sixteen but he could turn things around without trying.

'It's one of those ReachOut schools. If your parents can afford it and are into that sort of thing you do time at them instead of Year 11. You know, rope courses, orienteering, canoeing, cross-country skiing in winter. They operate all over the country. You get assigned to a cohort and move around together for a year. Wouldn't be so bad maybe if they weren't church-based. Hymns at night time. Twice on a Sunday. *The Bible is the word of God made manifest.* I mean, *seriously.* Our lot had the misfortune to end up with that bastard in charge.'

'And?'

'One of their big things is solidarity with the team, you know? They divide you up and then you compete and whichever team wins gets rewarded, the one that loses gets punished, gets given extra work, cleaning the toilets, that sort of shit. Jaz pumped it up, gave no quarter – longer runs, higher jumps, less sleep, pushing us all the time. My mistake was to be not as interested in winning as everyone else. Not being as interested in being a pillock. Being prepared to tell my team mates what I thought about them.'

'So they beat you up?'

'In a word. I was the impurity needing to be purged, the weak link. I'm sorry, I'm not as good at shutting up as I might be. I guess I didn't get how bad the others had it. Not a mistake I'll make a second time.'

A curious understanding of his tormentors, as if he bore them no ill-will. 'I don't get it, though. Why hasn't your father come down on them?'

'Jaz is too useful to them.'

'In what way?'

Cooper's way of talking being to dole out portions of information. You had to keep asking for more. In the car it had seemed obvious what had provoked the other boys: a level of intellectual brilliance combined with flamboyant sexuality, both of which were even more on display at the *Alterbar*, but also combined with something else: a level of confidence that came, perhaps, with being the son of a billionaire. You couldn't ignore this last. The cynicism about wealth was most likely just a teenager trying to get out from under his father's influence – which in this case meant taking philosophic objection to the military-industrial complex, the whole teetering system. What Nick wondered was how long it would last. At what point Cooper would notice his own wellbeing was intrinsically tied to it.

'He's part of their grand program for CoSecOr and the rest.'

A couple of men came out through the high doors, bringing a wash of music with them. Said hello and proceeded to light up, filling the small space with their smoke and their conversation. The rain still coming down so they weren't going any further outside.

'Maybe it's time to go back in,' Nick said.

Only the vaguest possibility of further communication inside, what with the band. They stood at the doorway together. Nick leaning in to yell in Cooper's ear.

'What were you going to say, before about CoSecOr?'

Cooper cupped his hand over Nick's ear and spoke directly into it, but even then Nick couldn't quite get it. The music seemed to have got louder. Cooper waving his hand at him. 'I'll tell you another time,' he said, stepping back and indicating he was going to the bar.

Nick nodded, let him go. The disconnect between what they'd been discussing outside and the lively bar was simply too great. Added to that was the sense that whatever the punchline of Cooper's story had been going to be it wouldn't have justified the events that led up to it; the story was the thing itself. This thought, in turn, pushed aside because, in casting his eyes around the room, he saw that Eugenie was sitting at a table in the corner with a couple of other women. There was, he saw now, another entrance just past the bar, an EXIT sign over the door, which most likely gave direct access to the car park.

Nothing for it. Before he could prevaricate further he went over, putting on his effusive self, the one that could stand in front of a group of women and bluster, make an inane comment about the music and offer to buy them a drink, while simultaneously alert to the subtlest of signs, reading the body language they exchanged as they came to an unspoken consensus about the idea of having him join them – his focus on Eugenie, watchful for any indication of interest.

If there was some she wasn't giving it away.

The other women were known to him. Ann was the nursing Sister from the hospital, Ruth was a physio in town. As always in small communities the medical profession hanging together. 'Don't worry about the drinks,' Ann said. 'There's plenty of time for drinks. Sit. But no talking shop. This is a work-free zone.'

He squeezed around to sit next to Eugenie, coming down hard on what proved to be a former church pew, backed up against the wall.

'Jesus,' he said, leaning in so as to be heard. 'Well here's a blast from the past. I haven't sat on one of these since school.' Putting on his mother's sternest Scot's voice. 'There'll be no slouching here, understand me now, girl!' Which raised a smile, at least, but seemed to lock him, with this approach, into a pattern of humorous remarks that were a long way from what he was feeling.

'My father had us to church every Sunday, rain hail or shine. We had to traipse across Parramatta Road to the Presbyterian Church in Johnston Street. The Stanmore churches were too soft for him. Or *Catholic*,' he said, adding, as if addressing them from the pulpit, shaking a fist for emphasis, '*Idolaters!*'

Shouting it out in that instant of silence at the end of a song.

Several people turning to look.

'Stanmore?' Eugenie said.

'Aye,' he said, embarrassed, although not quite ready to relinquish the Presbyterian minister, as if sticking with the charade might make sense of it to those around, speaking to all three of them under the assumption they might be interested in his origin story, even though the others across the table were unlikely even to be able to hear. 'Mum wouldn't come with us. She'd stay at home to make the Sunday roast. *Her* father was a minister. She said she'd *had enough o' the kirk*. Hadn't banked on marrying my father I suppose.'

'I lived in Stanmore,' Eugenie said.

'In Stanmore? As in Stanmore, Sydney?'

'Well, on the border. My nan told everyone we lived in Petersham because she thought it was more posh, but it was Stanmore just the same. My pop worked in the mill.'

The coincidence allowing them to play the game of exchanging places held in common: the swimming pools in Petersham Park and Leichhardt; the small corner shops; the Academy Twin for films on a Saturday afternoon; the schools. She'd been at St Michael's (a *Catholic!* After what he'd just said), he'd gone to Fort Street. Mapping the two suburbs for each other.

'My parents still live there,' he said, still talking too much, unable to stop. 'They bought a little one-storey in Lincoln Street before I was born. Paid, I don't know, ten thousand dollars. It's worth a fortune now. My brother wants them to sell and buy up here but they're not interested. *We have everything we need right here*, my mother says.'

'My grandparents' house was in Denison Street. I went to live with them there when I was eight,' she said.

Talking on over the top of her until the significance of what she'd said, grandparents, not parents, dawned on him; necessitating questions which she brushed aside.

'I've not been back for a while,' she said. 'My nan's in a home and my pop's dead. I used to go down all the time but it's harder now that David's away so much, me with the girls and all.'

Listening hard to her beneath the noise of the music so as not to miss a thing, at the same time interpreting every word from the point of view of spending time with her. The husband was apparently often away; although what the existence of a husband might mean, he'd have to say, was immaterial at this moment with this woman here, beside him on the hard wooden seat in her striped matelot top and jeans, her wonderful wide open face, clear clear eyes, talking to him.

'I love this song,' she said, turning to listen to the band.

The singer, with her husky voice, embarking on 'Bewitched, Bothered and Bewildered', which just about summed him up.

When he went to the bar for drinks Cooper was there, engaged in his own repartee with the barman.

'Doctor Lasker,' he said. 'You seem to have landed on your feet.' Inclining his head towards the table with the women.

Nick didn't reply, studiously watched his drinks being assembled. Oddly vexed by the suggestion. As if Cooper had assumed too much intimacy.

'Sorry,' the young man said. 'Maybe I don't need any more to drink.'

'Don't worry about it,' Nick said, waving it away. The band as loud as it ever was. 'You were going to tell me why the people who attacked you didn't get into trouble.'

Cooper, coming in close but speaking loud, giving the answer as if it had been waiting there, primed, on his lips. 'Because that's what the program *is*. It's *designed* to pick out the bully boys and girls, not to punish them. They *want* them.'

'What for?'

'Think about it.'

'It's not helping.'

'There's always going to be a need for people who don't mind hurting other people, isn't there?' Cooper said. 'I mean, if you're running a security firm. Especially one that might, potentially, have to police an unruly society – one that doesn't agree with the direction in which you're taking it. But you have to be able to identify who they are, don't you? You have to be able to figure out which are the lunatics and which the useful ones. Camps like that, they're fertile ground. They do it in schools too, of course, they've always done it. But a camp like Spring Creek, full of the children of the converted … it's all hyped up … you've got young people squashed together, physical stress, religion, competition, you get to see their baser natures.'

Hot in the bar. Humid. Men and women from a broad spectrum

of ages in loose multi-coloured clothes enjoying jazz-rock fusion, drinking glasses of micro-brewed beer and pinot grigio.

The barman lining up the drinks, asking for money.

'And that's just the start of it, of course,' Cooper/Martin said.

'A funny thing,' Nick said to Eugenie as he squeezed back in beside her. The two of them isolated by the music, become a small unit, obliged to be close to hear each other, the subject matter irrelevant, the important thing become how to keep it going, employing anything and everything to make her laugh or think him worth the effort of staying where she was. 'I don't know if you remember the first time we met ...'

She, nodding, glancing across at the others, flicking her eyes back to his.

'I came in with a young man with a broken arm? Don't look now, but that's him up at the bar. Cooper.

'I did say,' he said, 'not to look now.'

Bringing herself back to him. Smiling.

'Isn't he too young to be drinking?'

'In theory.'

'Which theory is that?'

'Well Cooper seems to be about twenty years older than he appears. Do you know anything about him?'

'No.'

'Before you arrived I was talking to him outside. He gave this remarkable spiel, conspiracy theories abounding. I mean, he is extraordinary for his age, articulate, confident, possibly *brilliant*. And gay, of course, which shouldn't make any difference but I figure was why he was hassled at the camp in the first place. The thing is he said no charges were laid against the people who beat him up, never mind that his dad's highly influential. The reason was … well, this is what he said … is they're training thugs up there in the bush.'

'Who is?'

'Yes, well, there you have me. It wasn't clear. A multinational security firm? The government? Someone else? The trouble is, while he was talking, it seemed, you know, believable.'

Telling her what he knew about Peter Mayska, which wasn't much more than everyone knew but mentioning the case of wine delivered to his door as a way of illustrating his wealth. Considering the possibility of offering to drink a bottle with her but figuring that was a step too far; a too-open declaration of intent.

'And you accepted it?' she asked.

'I shouldn't have?'

'Do you know how much it's worth?'

'No idea, it's not the sort of wine I'm familiar with.'

'So it was by way of a bribe?'

'I didn't see it that way,' he said, reminded of Bain in Canberra, that pall of discomfort descending again. 'I just thought if you were a billionaire and you wanted to give someone a gift as a way of saying thank you then you'd look pretty cheap if it was Jacob's Creek.' Distressed as much by the ethical dilemma as that the topic was taking them away from the central focus of the moment which was each other, trying to bring it back, saying, 'I was just considering asking you to try some with me.' Which was hardly innocent repartee even though it seemed to work, but then maybe they were already past that stage because, at the end of the set, Ann stood up saying, *sorry to interrupt you two love-birds*, but she had to be getting home.

Eugenie standing up abruptly, as if she'd not been aware of time passing, flushing pink around her neck and shoulders, glancing at Nick and giving him a slightly wan smile before saying that she, too, had to go; everyone finding coats, the three women kissing each other goodbye, making arrangements, starting towards the exit near the bar.

Nick saying he'd go, too. 'I live up next to the hospital,' he said, 'I walked down.'

'In this rain?' Eugenie said. 'I can give you a lift, if you like, I'm going past that way. Save you getting wet.'

Working his way through the tables behind her, Cooper no longer in evidence. Maybe gone home. A driver come to get him.

The musicians were outside, having a cigarette under the cover of a small tacked-on piece of roof. Eugenie stopping to kiss the saxophonist on the cheek, the other nurses going on ahead, waving at them as they ran to their cars. Nick hanging back.

She waved him forward. 'This is my father,' she said, 'Jean-Baptiste.'

Nick shaking the saxophonist's delicate hand and complimenting him on the music which he'd hardly heard all night, realising, a bit slow on the pick-up sometimes, that the man was French. Not knowing enough yet to put the pieces together.

'It can rain for weeks at this time of year,' Eugenie says in the car, apologising for the state of the interior, the children's mess, dog hair; winding the blower up to try to clear the windscreen, Nick glad not to be out in the rain for all sorts of reasons but mostly because he is now being driven by this woman who half turns in her seat as she backs out of the parking space revealing a delightful litheness in her upper body, a taut swelling of breast against her shirt, an expression on her face suggesting both nervousness at being in control of the car and defiance about it at the same time, a kind of I-can-do-this sternness around her lips, communicated by a tight little lift in the corner of her mouth, everything enhanced, as if he's taken a drug, which, of course, in some ways he has. His drug of preference.

'I don't want you to read anything into this,' she says, taking the turn out of the car park onto the road, wet tar gleaming in the streetlights.

'No,' he says. A maximum of three minutes, less, to get him home, in which to persuade her to stay with him, if not for the night then just a little while longer.

'And in that spirit maybe I could invite you in for a drink, or a cup of something? A *herbal* tea?' This last delivered as sardonically as possible

'I don't think so.'

'A man can but try.'

'He can, but shouldn't. I'm married.'

Up the main street, past the medical centre run by the competition, around the curve where the houses had been built below the road, the lights of the new development on the hill glinting through trees. Her hands held at ten to two, very proper, fingers small and neat against the hardness of the wheel, the machine's steel and plastic and glass, its implicit masculinity, accentuating her fragility, the delicacy of her construction.

'Just up here,' he says, 'on the right, then the first house on the left.'

'I know where it is,' she says, easing the car in to the kerb. Leaving the motor running, looking at him, the game they've been playing all evening about to end.

'I could come in for a minute,' she says. 'Just a moment.'

Nick's delight tempered by his sudden awareness of the state of the house, not that it's dirty, or even untidy, just the lack of furniture, the sense of the place as a home. Nina has been to visit twice and even she, with her no-nonsense, we're-here-to-fuck manner, has commented on it, telling him to go and buy a bed, *at least*, which is fair enough, but when does he have the time? And who would help him avoid making the wrong decisions?

Opening the door and stepping aside to let her in and then having to squeeze past to lead her up the stairs because it's a tiny hall and the downstairs is really just garage and laundry, the walls made of purple feature-brick. He can't help seeing it through her eyes. The living room not so bad: a table and some chairs, a framed black and white photograph of a yacht tilting in the wind, a couch which he'd ordered online and didn't disappoint too much when it arrived and, thankfully, didn't require assembling. His laptop on the table surrounded by paperwork and mail. Apologising as he ushers her in and opens the fridge to see what, if anything, there is to drink, only a couple of beers and an expensive bottle of champagne bought to take to a wedding that he was called away from by work.

'Champagne,' he says. 'Or there's that wine I spoke of ...'

'Nothing more to drink, please. And I don't know anything about wine anyway. Perhaps one of those cups of herbal tea? If that wasn't a joke.' Stranded at the end of the island bench in her knee-high leather boots and stretch jeans, her soft leather jacket, spotted with the rain, her thick hair pushed back from her face as if by a strong wind, her whole demeanour as if she is at that moment assailed by forces stronger than herself.

'It's okay,' he says, jocularity dispensed with, come beside her at the bench, 'it's quite safe here.'

'It is?'

'What I mean is I won't do anything you don't want me to.'

'But what if I do want you to? What if I want you to kiss me?' So that she is, all at once, in his arms, her lips against his, no chance of taking even a breath, no room for thought, strategy, consequence, just her against him, his arms inside her jacket, the silk lining warm on the back of his hand, his fingers on the soft cotton of her top, the weight of her shifting beneath his palm, her tongue against his, the taste and scent of her, the complex subtle essence of some perfume sparsely applied hours ago, mixed with her, the musty sensuality of the skin on her neck, behind her ear, back to her lips again, his hands, now, inside the cotton, on skin that communicates the musculature of her back, her ribs, the curve of her spine, all pulled against him while her mouth breaks with his to draw air, to exhale a short sharp burst, almost a laugh, but, then, her hands coming onto his chest, pushing him away.

'Oh fuck,' she says. Looking at him directly. 'I can't be doing this. You know that, don't you?'

He, retreating a millimetre, causing her to grasp his shirt and hold him from further movement, eyes locked.

'I'm married fifteen years. I've never done this.'

One hand inside her shirt, on her skin, the other one on the benchtop. For stability.

What to say? That he was married once, too, but that was over? That he had strayed one too many times? A picture of dark-haired Nina and himself in exactly this situation in her kitchen coming involuntarily to mind. Tell Eugenie that this time it would be different? How would he know? Was the strength of this feeling enough?

Leaning forward to kiss her again, Eugenie's hand finding its way down between his legs, feeling the swelling beneath the cloth.

'Oh fuck,' she says, again. 'I'm going home now. I mean, *now*. Before it's too late.'

ten

Guy

The night train and boat from Venice had him back in London early in the morning, but by the time he reached the flat Helen had already left for work. In the few days he'd been away spring had arrived; the clematis on the back wall was flowering, a bumble bee burying itself amongst the frail petals. He took his typewriter out to the rickety table and set up there, filled with a sense of promise. The sentences, though, came awkwardly, even with the model for a character provided by Edward. It was one thing to recall the way he had stood while shaving, quite another to make that image relevant to the story in a manner that wasn't woefully banal. He stood up from the table, sat down again, went back inside, came out again. No longer knowing how to do this thing. It might be that he'd once known how to trust in the process that led to the creation of a novel, but he could no longer remember how that was so. He was in the same place he'd been before he left, pacing the confines of the flat, stopping to make coffee, eat lunch, read an old weekend arts section in the paper; sitting back down at the table then repeating. Looking up at every sound in the hope of seeing Helen coming in, laden with shopping, putting the bags down and rushing to him.

The afternoon turning to evening. Still she had not appeared. It occurred to him that her lateness was deliberate, that she was punishing him for having gone away without her, giving him a taste of what it was like to stay at home and wait, as if, after all the long winter months of fruitless work, he didn't know what that felt like. He opened the bottle of wine he'd brought back from Italy and poured a glass, went back to the table and drank it, smoking, all pretence at work abandoned.

The long evening faded. The time for a meal passed. He brought his typewriter and papers inside, spreading them across the kitchen table, poured and drank a second glass. When he heard the key in the door he went to meet her, expecting she would come into his arms. Instead she pushed past him, dropping her bag on the floor, throwing her coat across the bench, without so much as glancing at him. Seeing the bottle she poured herself a glass. Only when she'd taken a mouthful did she raise her eyes. She had, he saw, been crying. He asked what the matter was, crossing the small space between them to offer sympathy.

'Don't touch me,' she said.

He stepped back.

She asked him if he wanted to tell her what had happened in Venice.

'What do you mean?' he said.

She made a sound that wasn't quite a word, more an onomatopoeic expression of disgust.

'I don't know where to begin,' she said. 'I think I could have dealt with you having an affair with a *woman*. Some young sycophant who worships your every word. That would have been hideous but understandable. I'm not sure what to do about you sleeping with a man.'

'What are you saying?'

'You're going to deny it?'

'Of course I am. I shared a room with Ed because the other hotel was awful, I told you that. I didn't try to hide anything. I wasn't sleeping with him, except to say we were in the same room.'

'So you weren't having sex with him?'

'No.'

'You can promise me that on, I don't know … *something* you hold sacred?'

'Of course I can. Nothing happened,' he said. 'I missed you. Where would you get the idea I'd been having sex with a man? You know me …'

'Publishing's a small world, Guy. Your lover has a friend. He's been boasting about his conquest. His friend happens to be my friend, which is how I heard about it. Not that that matters, I imagine by now everyone knows, except me, of course, who's locked in a squalid basement flat with someone who can't even tell the truth to the one person in the world who actually loves him.'

She was crying again. Not making any noise, just tears running down her cheeks. The room become smaller than it already was, more obviously beneath street level. She was waiting for him to speak, but the shame of what he'd done, of being caught out for doing it, was too great.

'I don't have to listen to this,' he said. 'I know you're pissed off with me because I went there alone. I'm sorry about that. It wasn't fair. I see it now. That was what I was going to tell you.'

'Why don't I believe you?'

'This is just gossip. Publishing-house gossip, which is even worse. Come here to me, let me hold you.'

Instead she let her head fall forward, putting her fingers to her temples as if to contain whatever was going on in there, to suppress it, pushing the tips hard into her skin. 'You're lying, Guy.'

'I don't have to listen to this,' he said again, suddenly furious, at Edward for talking about it to some third party; at her for bringing it back to berate him with. He stormed along the hall and out the front door, up the steps onto the road where it was now dark, the orange streetlights spreading their weird glow across the bonnets of cars and pavements and onto the little hedges, the litter-strewn front yards and basement wells. The air cold. He went up to the main road, his hands in his pockets, his belly hard with the irrevocability of what he'd just done, telling himself it was for the best, that it was the clean thing to do, he didn't have to buy into this sort of recrimination.

At the pub on the corner he ordered a half, grateful of the coin in his pocket, for his wallet was still on the kitchen bench. His whole life back there. He took a sip of the beer, casting a glance around to see if he was being watched; if his inner turmoil had some external manifestation.

The English never look so good when compared to Latins. There's always a sense of disappointment arriving back on the island, coming off the ferry to fish and chips, sliced white bread, *beer*, a meanness to their interaction with the world, as if everyone is still on rations thirty years after the war, dependent on powdered eggs, dripping and roasted chicory when just across the Channel is a smorgasbord of wine and crisp hot bread, good coffee, of *joie de vivre*; a respect for their writers, well, at least when they're dead.

The men in the pub were old, some even wearing flat workingmen's caps. Nursing their drinks while watching a television slung above the bar. A football game in play, Division One, between Tottenham Hotspur and Arsenal, the rolling roar of the crowd picking up their team's song as the little figures ran on the green. He liked this pub because it wasn't one where the new young drank, it was a real pub, but right then it seemed like the last repository of the desperate and dying. It was, too, he could see this, what he was choosing.

He put the glass down, undrunk, and went back out into the street. He'd left without his keys and was obliged to bang on the door. For a few minutes he thought that she'd already gone, that he'd left it too late, but eventually she opened it, putting on a brave face for whoever was knocking at that time of night.

'Oh,' she said. 'It's you.'

'Yes, I'm afraid it is. I need to talk to you. I need to come in.'

She stood aside, closing the door behind him, waiting until he had made his way past the bedroom – her suitcase out on the bed – and along the passage to the tiny kitchen/dining/living room, with its odd collection of furniture, gathered together at local markets or off the street. The typewriter and his manuscript on the table.

'What is it?' she said. 'I almost didn't come to the door. I didn't want anyone to see me like this.'

'You don't have to leave.'

'Well, I do, actually, but that's another thing. What do you want?'

'I want to try to be honest with you.'

'You want to try, or you want to *be* honest?'

He sat on the old sofa. She stood with her back to the kitchen bench, arms crossed.

'It's true,' he said. 'I did have sex with Ed. I didn't mean to. He got me stoned and made a pass and I went along. I didn't mean it to happen. It didn't mean anything.'

'Good for you,' she said.

'What do you mean?'

'Oh, I don't know. Good for you for telling the truth, at last. Good for you for experimenting. Good for you. Bad for me.'

He had the sense that she was finished with him, was looking for a way to dispatch him out into the world so she could get on with something more important.

'What made you change your mind?' she asked.

'I love you. I went out there on the street and realised I don't want to lose you.'

'Maybe you should have thought about that in Venice.'

'I mean it, I'm sorry. Really I am. I didn't mean it to happen.'

'Do you understand anything, Guy? Your books are full of such close observation, but it's always of other people, isn't it? It's not of you and what you're doing.'

'That's hardly fair ...'

'You're going to talk to me about fairness? You've hurt me, Guy. And then lied about it. To my face. In the middle of all this ... I don't think you get it. This is about honesty, and respect and, I don't know, fealty, being true to someone ...'

'I'm telling the truth.'

'Are you? Bearing in mind that telling the truth isn't the same as being true. But go on, then. Tell me. What happened?'

'It's like I said, he seduced me. He was, I don't know, intelligent, attractive, cosmopolitan. I thought he enjoyed my company, I didn't think it had anything to do with my body. I didn't think it had anything to do with *sex*. Then he got me stoned and kissed me and ... and ... I didn't think it was important. I'm sorry I lied about it. I was ashamed. I didn't want you to know. I was acting badly before I left, I see that, I don't want to blame my work but that was part of it, I was stuck ...'

'So, you're saying this thing you ... what ... *did*, with this man Greave, it only happened once?'

'Yes.' To his surprise tears were running down his own cheeks. He wanted very much to be believed. The idea of having to confess to Helen that it had continued throughout their stay in Venice was more than anathema, it was as though all the shame he'd thought was absent when he'd been with Edward had, instead, just been piled up behind some crude obstruction in his mind, waiting there to pour out and smother him. The other things he'd done with Ed, which had seemed, he wasn't sure what … daring, sophisticated, worldly … she would, he saw, judge as simply *sordid*, the activity of dirty little boys. She must not know about them or about his complicity in them. If she found out there could be no possibility of forgiveness. The weight of this feeling inexorable, all-consuming; shame as a thing in itself. Watching it envelop him, but thinking, also, in one corner of his mind, how he might use it, how it might be possible to describe this crushing sensation and his psyche's desperate attempt to resist the onslaught, creating layer after layer of deceit in its own defence.

'So, let me get this clear, just in my own mind.' Helen still leaning against the bench, gone back to this business with the fingertips at her temples, her hair fallen across her hands. Brushing it back so that she could look at him. 'You had some sort of sex with this man on the first night but then you stayed with him, in the same room, for the rest of the time, for several days?'

'Yes, but that was just convenience. We'd paid for a room together before any of this happened. We weren't going to get our money back if we didn't stay there, were we? I mean I liked him. He's a good man, don't get me wrong, he just happens to be, you know, like *that*. I simply told him it wasn't on.'

'And he accepted that?'

'Yes.'

She shrugged and turned. An expression on her face of profound disappointment. In him. As if she was sad about that, sad he'd failed to live up to what she had believed him to be, what he himself had always wanted to be. He saw, also, that she was unconvinced, and would now pursue this, drag him down through the folds of his lie, bringing further and more awful revelations, one after the other, until she had exposed the full unexpurgated version of his … the word that came to mind was, of course, *sin*, which was outrageous, except that in some way it was correct, albeit it wasn't sin against God or church but against *her*, against what she saw as the sacredness of their bond.

'I'm sorry,' he said. 'Really I am, I'm so sorry. I didn't mean to hurt you.'

'Well you have, Guy.'

Here it was, coming now, the attack.

'Your timing, too, is impeccable,' she said.

'What d'you mean?'

'You think this is all about you? I suppose you do. Everything else is, isn't it? Well, it's not. My mother called last night, at about three in the morning. Dad's had some sort of heart attack.'

'Oh babe,' he said, getting up and going to her, washed by relief at the possibility that her pain wasn't all his fault, that he might be released from the requirement to delve further; he might be able to reverse their roles and offer succour.

She turned herself away from him.

He stood next to her, arms ready to embrace her.

'Is he all right?'

'Yes. I mean, no. He's alive, they're going to do some sort of surgery. His health hasn't been good these last years. He works too hard and drinks too much. I'm flying back to Australia first thing tomorrow to be with my mother.'

'I'll come with you.'

'No. I don't want you to do that. I've already booked my ticket. I don't want you with me. I want to be by myself.'

In the morning, after a sleepless night spent on a camp bed in the living room, standing in the awkward space of the hallway, Helen about to go out to a taxi, he asked, 'Does this mean we're finished? You don't want to see me again?'

She with her bags around her, lit by the dim glow from the high window above the door, the autumn-coloured scarf he'd given her bunched around her neck. She had never been more beautiful than

191

at that moment; the anger and the pain and the trepidation at the coming flight had leached all colour from her face, rendering her utterly vulnerable, but, at the same time, here was the thing, self-contained, a person entirely independent of him.

'I don't know,' she said. 'I need time to think things through. It's not that I don't love you, Guy. I do. But I don't trust you. You've taken that away. Saying sorry doesn't bring it back.'

There is, he has often thought, a powerful hunger for *End Times*. Every generation spawning its own variety of threat, its own species of impending apocalypse. For several thousand years, of course, religion has been at the hard centre of this need, tapping into its possibilities, the Second Coming always imminent. But the slow adoption of the ideas of the Enlightenment and the *rational* – which is to say, the concept that the universe might be comprehensible to the human mind if only we were to observe it closely enough – has undermined many of religion's peculiar concerns, making them largely irrelevant, at least in the West. Which doesn't mean that millenarian passion is spent, only that new and present dangers have to be dreamed up as its cause.

It might, he thinks, be possible to get a column up on the subject. *End Times being no longer on the cards through Revelation and the Return of the Redeemer,* he would begin, *they are now to be visited on us through the agency of environmental destruction. The sins which will bring them upon us are no longer fornication, idolatry and usury, although, clearly, there's still plenty of them to go around, but rather* hubris, *the crime of improving our lot, raising ourselves up to the level of the gods through ever more sophisticated technology. Everybody intrinsically understands this: we will have to be made to pay for our mastery of Nature.*

Christianity replaced by its forerunners – *Pan, Demeter, Gaia* – the old gods rising up in new form to destroy us. The passion for End Times arises, he supposes, out of our innate horror when faced with the meaninglessness of our existence; the ego rebels, it demands a sense of the singular in our lives, a requirement that we must be living not just at *a* point of significance, but at *the* point of significance. And what could be of more consequence than the end of things? Indeed, if we're not living at that time, if we are, after all, *not* the centre of the universe, but simply particles dancing like dust motes in infinite space and time, of no particular import to anyone, then what is left to us?

In the face of the void the hard Right's response is entirely comprehensible: dig up some ancient prophecies from the Good Book to fill the vacuum. Or, alternatively, if you're too smart to believe in fairytales, then call down the Wrath of Nature. Global warming. Or cancer from microwave towers. Even in a town like Winderran, where surely there is a higher than average IQ (but perhaps not, perhaps that, too, is vanity) there are as many crazy beliefs as people in the main street on this Friday morning, going about who knows what business – drinking coffee at tables outside cafés, blocking the road while they attempt reverse parks, dawdling on the pedestrian crossings – trapping him briefly in his car, the window down, looking out at them. Nobody looking back at him with anything other than casual interest, which is as it should be in one's home town, regardless of one's achievements. He's never been accorded special status here. Soon, though, this will change. He will become a Senator, living on the government purse (a welcome eventuality *that*, after the years of slim royalties) with his own staff, an office in Canberra, a travel allowance. A person of influence.

Out of town then, following the line of the ridges, vouchsafed glimpses of the bucolic valleys to the south, rich and verdant, with the obelisks of the mountains standing out of the plain like discarded chess pieces, while out to sea the long sand islands sleep in the late summer sun, the air crystal after all the rain, a kind of perfect day, full of its own redolent fecundity, but rich, also, with the prospect of victory; making his way to the university to do some research. A friend has found something.

Few enough allies in the academic world, but Armistead remains true despite living like nothing so much as a cane toad in his preternaturally darkened building, a modern construction mysteriously lauded for its architectural bravery which is, in fact, no more than a prefabricated concrete and steel shed suffering from a lack of almost all amenity, the walls of Armistead's office only partly softened by the wonderful stacks of books with which they are festooned. To enter his room from the long dim corridor is akin to slipping into an ancient secondhand bookstore at whose centre sits the febrile owner, spreading ever wider in his swivel chair.

'Mr Lamprey,' Armistead says without getting up, his slow middle-American tones softening the syllables, injecting much joviality into his tone. 'How nice of you to grace us with your presence. I trust you were not accosted or assaulted in the corridors by any of your foes.'

'No, Armistead, none at all, in fact I saw no living being in the place, not even that rare creature, a student.'

Hot in the room, the only source of air a loud fan in the corner. One of the building's claims was that its superior design rendered the need for air-conditioning obsolete. As a result the place is freezing in winter and stifling in summer. Armistead swathed in an old football jumper, cut like a tent, many chins emerging from the ragged collar. An alliance between them that goes back to the time when the university was being invested. They have delivered up many favours to each other over the years. Guy takes the chair across the desk from him, the one reserved for visiting students when begging for better grades or more time with assignments. Armistead that unusual thing in Australian academia, an historian. A member of that even more curious sub-species who believe truth lies in the detail. His present project a history of nursing in Queensland. As part of his research he has access to the union's archives, including the minutes of all meetings of hospital branches throughout the organisation's tenure. Strictly limited to use on the university computer system, of course, which is why he's suffered to drive down there.

'You can sit here, Guy,' Armistead says, pushing his broad office chair back so that he can get enough free space between his belly and the desk to stand. 'I'll take myself off to the refectory for a coffee.' Lumbering out the door and away.

Guy going around and inserting himself into the man's lair, into the not entirely pleasant warmth he's left behind, noting the discarded chocolate bar wrappers in the bin beneath the desk, the detritus gathering in and around everything not in immediate use. *Dust in a workspace denotes peace*, Armistead has previously said. Guy only vaguely sympathetic. His preference being for cleanliness and order. But they share a love of research, the gathering of material. The older he becomes the more he relishes it. Nothing too dry for him, not even the minutes of meetings of the Queensland Nurse's Association branches from twelve years ago and their deliberations on Safe Workload Management. Their attempt to institute a policy that *resisted pressures from employers and other staff to undertake work deemed unsafe*. Unfortunately the actual conversations are not recorded, only the outcomes, but even then it is not time wasted, it gives some small insight into the character of Eugenie Lensman, albeit in an earlier iteration.

When Armistead returns Guy gets up reluctantly. Can it be only an hour that has passed? The fat man works his way into his control centre, breathing heavily. A large number seven on the back of his yellow and white jumper. 'You find what you wanted?' he asks.

'A little, nothing of real note,' Guy says.

'Which you can use?'

'It gives me a general sense of the woman's political background. Explains why she's able to hold her own at a meeting. I did find out something else ... her grandfather was a union rep before her ... at the Great Western Milling Company. He's mentioned in a newspaper article about the factory being closed for a week after a worker was injured.'

Armistead digs out a pair of half glasses, something Lamprey thought went out of fashion twenty years ago, and shuffles the bits of paper in front of him. It occurs to Guy that he might have overstepped the mark, that, for all his willingness to help, Armistead is still studying the union's history and might be sympathetic to one of its members. But it turns out that what he's doing is making sure everything is as he left it, that Lamprey hasn't mixed anything up. When he's done he looks up at Guy with rheumy eyes, peering over the top of the rims.

'I've been doing a little backgrounding on the other matter,' he says.

'The listing of the remnant?'

'Yes. But it is *Science*, you understand ... my contacts there are limited ...'

Armistead is being falsely humble. He sits at the centre of a labyrinth of connections within the university and beyond, his life devoted to the battles which rage between faculties and within them, between teaching staff and administration. He is the unquestioned master, minatory and ruthless, rarely, if ever, losing a fight, accumulating advantage in every corridor.

'As we thought,' Armistead says, 'an application was lodged with what used to be called DERM – I'm afraid I can't help you with the new name, it's unpronounceable, although still vaguely connected with resource management – to have the whole riparian strip within the dam site listed.'

'But that's nonsense,' Guy says. 'Ninety-eight per cent of it's been planted over the last twenty years. You can't go classifying that as rare and endangered, or even threatened. And anyway, I thought there was some chance of delisting the original remnant, or at least re-classifying it.'

There's a small bit of remnant rainforest within the dam site. At some previous time it has been listed under the Vegetation Management Act. The assumption has been that it would be deemed insignificant, small enough that it could be ignored or offset with plantings elsewhere. If, however, the new plantings are to be included then real problems might arise.

'Not my field,' Armistead says gently, chidingly.

Lamprey waits.

'But, here's the thing,' Armistead says. 'It seems the application wasn't properly prepared – some technical issue with the process, you understand, not the content. They've made a case, as I understand it, that because it all comes from seed gathered *within* the remnant it represents existing vegetation, of which there's only a tiny amount in the larger catchment. Something like that. It's apparently seen as a good argument.'

'And?'

'Well, the application hasn't yet been progressed.' Taking off the half glasses again to clean them with plump fingers. 'As you know funding's tight everywhere, and the application for extension of the area is not exactly the most popular document on the government's radar right now. There's a process.'

'There's always a process.'

'Indeed. In this case it's been referred to a junior officer for attention. It'll be his job to return it to the applicant to fix up the problems. As it happens I have some connections to this particular department. The supervisor is seeking funding for a project, and would appreciate my backing.' He gives the smallest of smiles. 'It seems possible the return of the application might be delayed, even beyond the time limit for submissions to the environmental impact statement.'

'And there's no paper trail, no emails?'

'None whatsoever.'

'Good man, Armistead. Good man. I really do owe you one this time,' Guy says.

'It's nothing,' Armistead says, brushing the praise aside with the nonchalance of one who knows his own worth.

Guy gets up. Now that he's finished he can't wait to get out of the place. Whenever he sees Armistead the thought comes involuntarily to mind that *there but for the grace of God* ...

Armistead, however, is not yet prepared to let him go. 'You're spending a bit of time with Aldous Bain these days, I understand,' he says.

'What of it?'

'Nothing.'

'Come on, Armistead.'

'It's just a little thing.' The fat man looks up at him. 'I had a bit to do with him years ago. We were in Sydney together, just after I moved. I always thought him an unpleasant chap. Didn't mind the occasional use of muscle to get his own way. Never forgotten that.'

'Tell me more.'

'There's nothing to tell. We were on the opposite side politically, that's all.'

'Aldous doesn't strike me as the sort to get in a fight.'

Armistead laughs at the possibility. 'No, of course not. He had others do it for him, even then.'

There's a four-wheel drive parked out the front when he gets home. Nick Lasker on the couch, jumping up to shake his hand. A couple of piles of stapled-together sheets of paper on the coffee table beside a glass of water. Helen across from him, if anything more reduced than he remembers from the last time he saw her, which had surely been only the evening before. Perhaps it's just that she's in someone else's company, allowing him, for an instant, to see her as she is, so frail that even to be sitting, propped up amongst cushions, seems unlikely. No visible means of support.

'Sit with us a minute,' she says. 'Have you got the time?'

'Of course.'

'You had a pleasant coffee? Did you see anyone?'

She assumes he's been in town, knows nothing about his trip to the university. Probably best to keep it that way.

'Nobody.'

'Did you get my pills?'

'No. No, I didn't. I'll go back in again later. I was distracted. I'm so sorry.'

'Not to worry, darling, I still have some.'

The use of the endearment sounding odd, not just because her voice is so weak.

'Doctor Lasker's here to talk to me about my tests,' she says, directing him towards Nick.

'So, Doctor,' he says, 'I hope everything's looking good?'

'Well, that's the thing, darling,' she says, 'it's not. Not at all.'

The problem had been the intensity of the light. After living in London for so long he'd forgotten how exceptional it was; the different levels of colour.

He'd been travelling for what seemed like days: London, Ankara, Delhi, Kuala Lumpur, Darwin, Sydney, the stops in Asia dream-like affairs, the plane doors opening to hot heavy midnight air, damp and redolent of aeroplane fuel and partly treated sewage, clove cigarettes, the passengers hustled across the tarmac in the darkness to transit lounges boasting a single bamboo-faced bar and closed gift shops, while small brown men with thick moustaches

199

mopped floors under the supervision of soldiers with machine guns strapped across their chests. The cleaners, it was understood, earning so little that they might mop for several lifetimes and never earn enough for the privilege of a single seat on the great silver plane that was ferrying him across the world towards the lover who'd said she wanted to be alone, but whose wishes he was ignoring because that was what a man who loved a woman did. A man like him, *repentant*, who had waited in London for the requisite number of miserable uncommunicative weeks, unable to write anything lucid or even coherent. A man who'd got on a plane and followed her right around the world. To Sydney and a change of terminals, a connecting flight to Brisbane, followed by an indeterminate journey on a rattling train from the ill-named Roma Street Station to somewhere whose name he couldn't even recall but from where he'd finally taken a taxi, costing almost as much as the domestic flight, to this place which didn't seem to be a place at all, just a conglomeration of bungalows huddled together on a wide flat plain behind the dunes, separated one from another by tall paling fences, their roofs festooned with television aerials that mocked the serried white trunks of the paperbarks in the distance, the remnant of coastal forest which, it seemed likely, the whole ugly tile-roofed mess had replaced. The taxi finding its way along neatly kerbed and guttered streets to another of these squat brick homes with its roll-a-door garage, it's aluminium boat on a trailer parked in the double driveway. Important, in the face of suburbs like this, to remember that there is no such thing as normal, that all human beings are, as Anthony Powell would have it, *driven as they are at different speeds by the same Furies* – all people are equally extraordinary – except he couldn't help but think it would be easier to imagine the lives of airport cleaners in Ankara than what occurred in the lounge rooms hidden behind these venetian blinds. Hardly a promising place, this suburb in the provinces of a province at the bottom of the world, in a country he'd thought to have left behind. He, Guy Lamprey, having come back to stand at the ripple-glass door and ring the bell; she, Helen, answering it and finding him there, coming wordlessly into his arms.

Explanations were required. She took him down the short length of street to a thin strip of bush which, when traversed, abruptly, suddenly, astonishingly, revealed the sea. Stepping out of the low scrub into vastness, terrible brightness, the Pacific rolling its waves onto an endless beach, one of those beaches which stretch to the north and to the south without interruption, without headland or bay, one single interminable strip that lost itself in either direction to sea mist, the tide high so that they were obliged to walk in the soft sand up near the low dunes, coming apart and together on the uneven surface, the waves around their ankles, pushing them up the slope with heavy runs of foam. He there in body alone, large bits of him still trapped in those midnight stops, in the long hours in the back of the smoky plane wondering if he was doing the correct thing, when the certainty he'd felt buying the ticket had been lost in that curious plastic limbo, and yet required to be here now, this was the point, called on to come into *presence*, here on the glaring beach, to deliver the message that must be communicated to this woman with the long straight hair blowing in her face who he loved but who'd been sent away from him by what he had done, who, it seemed possible, might still love him, this woman, here, in her rolled up jeans and her white blouse, appearing, extraordinarily, as in a continuum with that person he'd last seen in the hallway weeks ago. Never mind that she was tanned, radiantly healthy now, she was no less separate from him, regardless that her lips, when they'd kissed in the doorway, had been so full of longing.

'I've come to get you,' he said. 'I've come to do whatever it is I need to do to get you back. I want you to come home with me. I need you. I can't tell you how sorry I am for what happened.'

Prepared, now, at last, to come clean if necessary, if that was what it took, to tell her everything that had happened in Venice.

She with other ideas in mind, squeezing his hand.

'What if I said I don't want to go back there?' she said.

'You mean you won't come back with me?'

'No, I mean, what if I wanted to stay here, in Australia? What if being with me involved staying here?'

'Here?'

Stunned by the enormity of the suggestion. This was nowhere. He looked along the beach and down at the sand, coarse-grained, golden-brown, the tips of the waves lapping their footprints, rendering them smooth-edged, ephemeral, the heavy sand absorbing the water as quickly as it arrived. At least, he thought, it was *sand*, not pebbles, not grey and bleak, and, for all the houses hidden behind the dunes, there were few people around, only a couple of surfers out amongst the waves.

'I want to be with you,' he said, the momentum of his journey carrying him forward. 'If that means being here, then that's what it means.'

'I don't want you to say you'll live somewhere with me out of a sense of guilt.'

'It's not guilt,' he said. 'It's recognition. I need you. I don't think I've ever needed anyone before. Not like this.'

'That's good,' she said. 'I like that.'

They walked on. Every few hundred metres the scrub along the top of the dunes was punctuated by a set of wooden steps and a numbered sign, the latter, he supposed, a way of identifying where they were. So that if a swimmer or one of the surfers got into trouble they could call for help. But to whom would they call? Where might help come from?

'I wouldn't ask you to live down *here*,' she said. 'This is awful.

I'm just here because it's where Mum and Dad have moved. There's better places, up in the hills. We could live there. D'you think?'

'I don't know,' he said. 'I'm lost here. You'll have to show me.'

'But do you want to? I mean, really? That's what I'm asking.'

'Yes.'

Turning to him, taking his hands in hers. The wind blowing her hair back from her face, spreading her shirt tight against her breasts, the cloth sharply white next to her skin.

'I can't tell you how happy it makes me to hear you say that,' she said. 'I've missed you, terribly. I don't care about Venice.' Pausing. 'As long as you promise it won't happen again. I'm pregnant, you see,' she said. 'I'm going to have our baby.'

eleven

Will

Jaz comes in the sleep-out and wakes him, *Swell's up*, he says, *You wanna catch some waves?* It's still dark. Four in the morning for fuck's sake. Sometimes it seems like Jaz never sleeps, you can find him out on the veranda any time of night, wrapped in a blanket, just sitting there, staring out into the darkness.

Who's he to say no?

They go down the coast in the ute, just the two of them, Will driving, Jaz beside him in the dark, nobody talking, barely a word spoken. The motorway empty but still lit from end to end. At the headland there's just a smudge of light on the horizon, picking up the underside of a line of cumulus hanging over the edge of the world; cold, too, getting their wetties on in the park, paddling out into the dawn.

The sea's glassy grey, just a skerrick of wind coming in from the west, the tide out, almost on the turn, swell to about a metre rising up in these wicked fucking arcs, feathering along the tops. They catch a couple while the streetlights are still shining on Aerodrome

Road and in amongst the houses on the hill and they're alone out there amongst these near perfect waves, letting their boards slide down the silk of their forward edge, cutting into the moving cliff, always new, infinitely repetitive for whatever it is, a minute, maybe ninety seconds at a time.

Out the back, as the sun's coming up, they sit for a while. Will's no idea why Jaz's chosen him to take for a surf, why anything really. But then that's the way it is most of the time.

'This is what it's about for me,' Jaz says. 'Out here like this.'

Will nods.

Jaz's head is all but shaved, he runs a number three over it every couple of days. Sitting there in the ocean with his great neck rising out of his wetsuit he looks like some kind of sea creature, a bull seal maybe, his face full of lines of shadow. Will's not of a mind to say anything but now the silence has been broken, he gets the sense more's to come. It's not a good feeling. It's similar to how he felt as a boy when his dad was about to tell him all the ways he was failing to be the kind of person he ought to be. In the days when he gave a fuck what his father thought.

'Don't know if I've told you this,' Jaz says, eventually, 'but when you're doing your training for the special forces they give you this exercise. Right at the end. You've been doing this arduous shit for months, running up hills with your packs, crawling through mud, close use of firearms … you name it. All these other blokes have fallen away and you're wondering if you're going to make it, then, last of all, they send you out bush by yourself. They drop you off in the middle of nowhere and you've got to make it on your own. It's the toughest thing. Not the surviving part. That's hard, but you've been trained for it. It's the bit about being by yourself. Nobody knowing what you do or how you do it or giving a shit. Doing what needs to be done because it needs doing. Just you in real time. That's the bit that breaks blokes. It shouldn't be that way, but it is.

'Here's the thing, but. There's harder stuff to come,' he says. 'There's coming back when you've done your time.'

Turning to look at Will, as if he sees right into him, into the darker parts nobody ought to see and it is like it was with his father in one way but in another it couldn't be more different because even though Jaz sees him he's not judging him. It's raw but there's no shame in it.

'But there's the lesson, my friend: sometimes you have to go low. You can't find something you don't know till you get to the place where you know nothing, that's the truth of it, you got to go where you're empty, where there's nothing left. You have to make space in yourself if you want to hear the voice in the wilderness. When Isaiah said, *make straight in the desert a highway for God. Every valley shall be exalted, and every hill made low*, he wasn't talking about hills and valleys, he was talking about what's happening inside you, right now.'

Jaz's God stuff can be awkward. No shit. It comes up every now and then at The House and when it does it's, like, you don't know where to look. This morning, though, out behind the waves, the sun sending beams of light from those low clouds, one on one, it's personal, direct, it's coming straight from Jaz to him and it lifts the hair on the back of his neck. The words get under his skin.

God has never interested Will. He's not like Jaz. He's never thought too much about it. At least until now. Now he doesn't know what to think. Now it's coming at him from all sides. Ange is into spiritual stuff. She's into all of it, astrology, numerology, the *I Ching*, tantra, reiki, runes, chakras, *The Power of Now*. There's not a thing she does in the day that's not governed by *something*. But she won't have a bar of religion. *Organised religion is just that*, she says, angry about it. *Organised. Small men holding onto tiny fucking bits of power. Fiddling about with people's lives. It's about them, not spirituality.*

206

Will doesn't know what to say to either of them. He's not good with people and how they fit together. Never has been. It was one of the things he liked about the army: these things were already decided, you did what this person said, that person did what you said. Even then it could be hard. Machines are more his style. At the heart of a machine is always something he can understand. The first engine he ever stripped down was a red Holden HR 186. He was fifteen. He took it right to the big end, laid it bare so you could see how it worked. The way the pistons at the centre got pushed down when the fuel ignited, causing the crankshaft to turn, and – here was the thing – this movement rotated the camshaft, which lifted one set of valves to let out the spent gasses and another set of valves to let the new fuel in, and because it was all connected, meshed together by cogs, it happened perfectly in time, exactly when it was supposed to. You could even run more things off the same shaft, alternators, fuel and oil pumps, the cooling system. Everything the engine needed being driven by the engine itself. Something wonderfully clean about that, you could almost see the possibility of it doing it without the need for any other input, if you could only get things to work perfectly. You could also see why that couldn't happen, the wear of parts against each other and the weight of the car, all that, but the idea was there. This was where life failed him; too much friction, people rubbing up against each other. You couldn't fix things by making a small adjustment here or there.

The trouble with Ange is that she talks all the time, there's a kind of endless stream of words pouring out of her, like there's no barrier between what's happening in her mind and what comes out of her mouth; important stuff about her mum spilling out with the same force as her worry about where she's put her phone. It flows this way and that so as he can't make any sense of it and after a while he blocks it out even though he knows that's wrong, it's not right to have to ignore her, it's just like it's the price he has to pay to be around her, to have her every now and then give herself over to him, which is when all *his* pain goes away, when it seems like there's some kind of hope.

Jaz points towards the beach, towards the early traffic that's picking up on the road, the houses stepping up the hill, the high-rises to the south, that sea creature's face deeply mournful. 'See this place,' he says, shaking his head in disbelief. 'A land of Godless fucking multitudes. I mean it. People gone soft, wasting away, turned by the media to believing shit about peace and love and the happiness that comes from buying crap, just at the exact moment in history when we need strong men who'll stand up for what they believe and say fucking *enough*, man. You ask these cunts what they believe in, they'll say *nothing*. They'll say exactly that, *nothing*, like they're proud of it. That's where their education's gotten them, pride in themselves over the top of the fucking majesty of something like this.' Spreading his arms out to encompass the waves around them, spouting more scripture, '*Who hath measured the waters in the hollow of his hand, and meted out heaven with a span, comprehended the dust of the earth?*'

Which is just about too much for Will. One quote from the fucking Bible at dawn being enough. Time to fuck off out of there. But then Jaz turns it around.

'Listen, I don't expect you to get this stuff about God. I'm talking about myself. *I* was the crooked way made straight. Maybe you are too. But that doesn't worry me. You can take it or leave it. But I tell you this: there's a change coming. Any fool can see it, *the earth is defiled, its inhabitants have broken the covenant*, and what I'm saying is there's a cost to that and we need to be prepared for when the bill gets served. This training we're doing at The House, it's not for us. We're part of something bigger. We're preparing to be called upon, when the time's right. The question is, Will,' Jaz says, 'are you with us? That's what I'm asking you. Is this something you want to be part of?'

~

At any other time there'd be no question. Even with the religion thrown in Will would jump at it, if only because, at The House, with these blokes, training with them, pushing themselves to the limit, there's a clarity that's been missing for a long time. It's like being back in the army but better because it's men working out together because they *want* to, not because they're told to. There's something larger out there and he's part of it, doesn't matter so much even what it is. He's starting to feel good about himself. It's not that the anger's gone away, it's still there, only focused now, channelled.

At the same time, but, it's tied up with Ange. The two things have happened together and they go in different directions, not just the things they talk about at the camp, the political shit they all fucking believe, but also Ange herself. She's in and out all the time. It's like as soon as she shuts up for just a minute and goes in with him, dives into whatever it is that happens between them, it's all good. Everything that's gone on since the last time, all the wrong words, wrong thoughts, wrong actions, gets wiped clean. They go to this place where it's all new again. But when they come back up to the surface it's like she has to push him away, as if she wants it but can't handle it when she gets it. She turns on him, makes him the cause of all their problems. It's driving him crazy. It's making him so he doesn't know who or where he is, like he's being blown this way and that. Like Jaz says, he's being stripped of everything he knows, down to a place where it's all laid bare. No way to put it back together. None that he can see.

Still, going back up the hill in the ute with Jaz, the boards in the back, he says *yes*. Damo and Ren are in it too, and these are serious guys.

That's good then, Jaz tells him, because he has a little project coming up. Nothing glamorous, mind, but something Will's already been a part of.

209

'See all these fuckers who've come to live here, taking your land, making up laws on what you can and can't do in your own place? This's a way to get back at them. Even up the score.'

twelve

Eugenie

She went to him. There was no use trying to see it any other way. After pouring herself down his stairs and back into her car, liquid with desire, trailing the headlights out through the darkness along the ridges, one hand on the wheel, the other pressed against her lower belly as if to stem the flow from a wound, she had lasted less than forty-eight hours.

The first time she did no more than go to his house. Dropped the girls at their grandmother's, at her mother-in-law's house, if you please, and drove towards him in a light cotton dress, redolent with glorious disassociation, a shivering need, concentrating on *getting there* like some devotee whose practice depended upon holding to only one thing lest all else dissolve around her, refusing, even, to entertain thought about what might happen when she arrived, when she went up those stairs into the house and stood, where she'd been before, at the end of the formica bench, and he poured her cold white wine in a fragile glass and she drank the first bitter sip, cool and delicious on her tongue and he kissed her, not waiting, because they had, in truth, waited long enough, these last two days the most drawn-out foreplay she could imagine, holding him against her, only the thin cloth of her dress between her skin and him, his lips on her neck, his hands on her thighs, sliding up under the soft cotton and onto her buttocks, cupping her there, pulling her against him, lifting her onto the bench so he could kiss her more and then, without words, carry her, bare legs wrapped around his waist, through to the bedroom, not letting go of him, not knowing anymore if this was what she wanted, if this was who she was, if this man was right or wrong, simply lost to the pull of the moment, the imperative of her body. Which was not to say that thought had ceased, had eased or desisted; thought was still working, perhaps even harder than usual, spinning like a mad dervish behind her eyes, it was just that these sensations were stronger than its furious machinations, only the most lucid permutations penetrating to consciousness amid the smell of him, the hard thinness of his body, so much smaller than David in the chest and waist. Noting how they kissed, how sweetly, seductively, he lifted her dress up and over her head, leaving her naked but for a brief pair of knickers and them not for long, wondering how many times he'd done this with women in this room, wondering who she was competing with, how good she needed to be, to look, undoing the buttons on his shirt, his belt, his trousers, driving the dervish back into the furthest corner of her mind, letting her skin talk directly to his skin for just one moment, desperate for that most basic of communications. The constrained force of her desire being inexplicably consummated by a sense of homecoming at the instant when he entered her, as if all the weeks and days and hours since they met in the observation room at the hospital had been pointed directly at this place, where it might be possible, at last, to let go, to open up, free from the bonds of a normal life, exposed without mediation to what lies beneath.

~

The second time they drove together to the coast. It was raining on the Range. She parked her car in the hospital car park as if she was going to work except, instead of turning towards the building, she raised her umbrella and walked, as if she had all the right in the world to do so, out to the street and into the passenger seat of his waiting car. Shaking the drops from the umbrella and folding it into the gap between her seat and the door, arranging her dress, patting it down, a woman in her late-thirties on an assignation with her lover, frighteningly naked beneath the cloth, although not yet ready for him to know that. Going around the business district on back streets to avoid encountering anyone and then out of town, heading north along the switchback road behind the shield of the windscreen wipers, taking one of the smaller winding routes off the escarpment and coming, thus, out from beneath the cloud. Pulling over into a road maintenance site on the side of the hill, lantana tumbling over the steep cut edges of sub-soil, filling the humid air with its scent. Stopping the car because, he said, he couldn't bear to go any further without kissing her; *parking*, like adolescents, in this spot with its view out to sea where the big yellow machines sorted dirt, oblivious to the possibility of discovery because the force of their need for each other would, they understood, protect them. This was the thing, it wasn't just while they were having sex that her life was transformed, it was at all times; the simple fact of being desired and of desiring changed everything, brought to the world a new intensity of light and colour, exposed a larger and more benign pattern within the surface of things.

The sun out down on the coast. Hot. Humidity high.

The restaurant he took her to was in a kind of pavilion perched out in a tea-coloured lake, the table by the rail, a light breeze coming across the water to them, chasing small dislocations in the reflections of the old paperbarks that leant out from the edge to drink; condensation misting their glasses, forming under its own weight small rivulets, the food coming in little parcels, each one a delicacy. Nick across the table from her, alert to her every movement, his knee brushing hers, the formality of the situation requiring that this time they actually speak to each other. Shared geography being, at least, a starting point, a fundamental commonality which might serve to justify the force of their meeting, but also a way into their individual history, the long line of events which had brought them to where they sat.

He told her about his family, about his older brother, about being designated as *the smart one*, being sent to the selective high school and from there, on a scholarship, to university and how, after that, there had never been a moment, really, when there might have been time to question his progress towards being a doctor, only this extraordinary exacting training for situations that no amount of training might prepare you for, so much coming at you so hard for so long that the only thing to do was to face each event as it presented, which was how he'd found himself years later behind a desk in a small windowless room, only his laptop and a pen-holder provided by big pharma for company, listening to the complaints of others, married with children and having affairs, only seeing the patterns in his life when it was far too late. A story which led to her own reflections on childhood, on how, after Yvette had died, when her mother took herself off to India, to Poona, to get in contact with her grief, and from there into hard drugs, and her father went back to France at the behest of the Australian government, she'd gone to live with her grandparents down the road from where, it turned out, Nick was living. Curious, she said, to hear him talk about his childhood there, how, for him, the suburb had been so small, enshrined by the narrowness of its viewpoints, its working-class know-your-place mentality, somewhere to escape from, whereas for her, parachuted into it as an eight-year-old, it had been enormous, all consuming. But then, of course, she had been a small child, carrying *her* grief which was the small grief of a child and therefore hardly worthy of notice. She did not say that. Or only some of it, before he picked up on her comments about the nature of inner-west suburbs of Sydney and went off on some tangent about that, while she looked down into the brown water at the tiny fish playing around the pylons of the building and thought, no longer listening, thought perhaps even for the first time in her life about how she had, of necessity, swallowed that world whole, every bit of it. Donning the school uniform, eating the meals of meat and three veg, watching the sitcoms and soaps on the television that her classmates watched until she was as familiar with the characters as they were, making sure her white knee-socks were straight, her shoes polished. Studying the other girls as much as the curriculum for clues as to what it meant to be normal; working on herself to become *that* with a fierce and unforgiving purpose, in the hope that if she could somehow do it well enough then her glaring differences – to have been unfortunate enough to be raised as a hippie in the backblocks of rural New South Wales; to have been careless enough to have lost a sister, a mother and a father all at the same time – wouldn't be noticeable. But, more than that, if she did achieve normal, if she was especially good, some small part of what had been taken might be given back. A grain of that in her mind, just a little thought in a little brain, but the kind of thing that can set, like with crystals, the pattern for what follows.

In the national park they took the inland track, wanting privacy, walking together on hard-packed sand amid the ti-tree and scribbly gums behind the headland, following the path through groves of paperbarks where tiny red-browed finches darted amongst leaves of spiky grass. Always the sound of the sea as a low note in the distance. Walking, fingers entwined, through scent of salt and bark and leaf. This being one of her most favourite places, where she went when she needed to find herself, to ground herself in life. Inviting him into her place.

'I think it's important to choose where you live,' she said. 'I mean, I don't think it's random. We have this idea we can live anywhere, that we make the choice, but it's not true, there are places that are for you and places that aren't. Sometimes it's hard to tell which is which. The only way to know is to listen.' Wondering if he agreed with that, or thought it was new-age nonsense, wanting to go on and qualify it with stuff about Aboriginal connection to land, the whole philosophical argument that Lindl liked to lay out to justify what was, after all, just a feeling – Lindl, who was the least hippieish of anyone she'd ever met – but holding back from speaking because the magic of the small forest, its tops blown westward by the coastal winds, its branches tightly woven by those same forces, could, she thought, speak for itself. Stopping, once, to lie off to the side of the path amid fox-tail fern and fallen leaves, to look up through fine casuarina needles at the perfect sky. Lying within the creel of his legs, her head on his chest, conscious, how might she not be, of his hardness beneath the cloth, against her breasts, warmed by it but unconcerned, his hands in her hair, gently mussing it, large man's hands pushing their fingers through her thick unruly mane, nothing simple here and yet no other way to be, coming home with him when home is not a narrow concrete-edged suburban street of red-tile-roofed bungalows but somewhere wilder, somewhere before all that, a place like this, a place of air and light and continuous sound, a place where the boundaries between herself and another might, just for one brief instant of time, be thinner, more porous. His heartbeat beneath his skin. Her ear against his chest and that sound is him, her on him, his heart slowing, finding its own solid extraordinary rhythm while somewhere above the wattle birds bark out their curious cries.

~

She had, of necessity, forbidden him to visit, to even text unless she had first texted him. On account of the children and David, the latter due home any day. The very existence of a lover a secret from everyone, even Lindl. On the way back from the coast, in the car, he'd asked her about her husband. That was, she thought, when the real betrayal began, when she spoke to the man she was fucking in cars and forests about the aridity of her marriage.

The third time she went to see him she arrived with only the briefest of warnings. There was an anti-dam meeting scheduled for the late afternoon at the *Alterbar*. She arranged for the girls to walk into town after school, she'd pick them up from her father's house after dinner. But when she met Marcus in the café it seemed at the last minute several people weren't able to make it. They would have to cancel.

The two of them sat together for half an hour, drinking cheap red from expensive glasses, chatting. Marcus didn't want the time to be wasted, he wanted to catch up on aspects of the campaign, but the conversation very quickly degenerated, as it so often did, into commentary on those involved, in this case Geoff Steever.

'The truth of the matter,' Marcus said, 'is that he didn't like our stunt down in Brisbane. You scratch the surface with Geoff and there's a Tory lurking beneath. Doesn't like all this nonsense. It's not his wife who's kept him from coming … I've spent the last hour talking him down … he told me he doesn't think he can be part of the group anymore if we're going to go on like that. His interest's in pure research.'

Eugenie listening, but wishing he would stop. It was, as Lindl had said, just gossip, telling tales on each other. In this case she wasn't even sure of the credibility of the complaint. Marcus and Geoff were very close, they'd known each other for years and tended to vote on things together. It seemed to her that Marcus might be using his friend to cover for his own agenda. It was all too exhausting to contemplate. Not that she thought herself necessarily any better than either of them, it was just she could see a better use for the time: she could be spending this stolen hour visiting Nick, dropping in and ravishing him on his sofa; hot with the idea of it, looking in Marcus's direction but barely hearing the words.

Some years before David had accused her of being frigid. It was not long after Emily was born, when they'd all but stopped having sex. She'd thought it was mutual, an aspect of breastfeeding and lack of sleep. But then, in the middle of a fight about something completely different – something mundane like washing up or warming a bottle or leaving a towel on the floor – David had attacked her. All this resentment about their sex life bubbling up, culminating in this tirade which held at its centre the idea that she was the one in control, the one in possession of the key to the vault of their desire. David digging up this arcane word, this piece of nastiness exhumed from an archaeological site, from some ancient irrelevant culture, still, however, rich in virulence, capable of slipping into the flesh and spreading its infection – *lack of feeling, lack of warmth, lack of sexual capacity* – the latter seeming most unfair because how had her girls come into being if she'd been so unwilling, so cold? *She* could remember the love they'd shared when they first knew each other, and if it had got lost surely its absence could be laid, equally, at his feet. He who'd never been there, never engaged with his daughters, expecting the house to be just so on the basis that he was the one who was bringing in the money, as if she was a fucking maid, never mind that before she stopped work to have *their* children she'd been earning more than him. None of this helping to dispel the understanding that, deep down, she *was* the one at fault; if only because she was a woman. In the café, sitting opposite Marcus, it was finally evident the accusation could not be sustained. Just the thought of Nick's body sent flushes of desire, no, call it what it is, she told herself, flashes of lust, coursing through her body; delicious, hot, revelatory.

Marcus, apparently oblivious, had left off Geoff to talk about Alt, the guy from the hippie camp, who, under different circumstances Eugenie might have been keen to discuss. She didn't have the patience. She stood up.

'I have to go,' she said.

Marcus, broken off mid-sentence, looked up at her in consternation.

'Of course,' he said.

'I'm supposed to be somewhere. I forgot. I'm so sorry.'

Finding the car and sitting behind the wheel to tap letters into her phone with clumsy fingers, trying to defeat the predictive text that wanted to communicate anything but that she would be arriving at his house any minute to fuck him. Sending the message but not waiting for the reply, driving up around to the hospital praying that he'd be there, that the message wouldn't be read by some assisting nurse in one of the observation rooms, panicking at the thought, pulling up a little back from his house, across the road, seeing the lights on up in the kitchen, her heart shuddering with expectation. Nick's flat being seriously weird. As if he didn't live there. Having all the character of a motel room with, true to form, a kitchen built in the seventies, complete with wooden cupboard doors and orange rippled tiles. A mission-brown sink. A figure coming to the window. Nick. Not looking out. For him the window would be a mirror of the room. Holding up a wine glass to the light to see if it was clean. Handing it to a second person behind him, briefly glimpsed, a woman, dark-haired.

Starting the car, doing a U-turn. Back down into wide Peary Street, the angle parks with their bright yellow wheel stops empty now that the shops had closed their doors, only the late shoppers ducking into the supermarket for bread and milk. Telling herself that it could be anything. In shock. Realising, only then, that she knew nothing about him except that he was a doctor. Had been married but was now divorced, as much, he'd confessed, because of his own serial unfaithfulness; noting this at the time he'd told her as being of *interest* – that he had this awareness of himself – but disregarding its relevance to her who had no intention of marrying him. It was just part of who he was and who he was of significance to her. That was all. Left into Leichhardt, back up the hill and left again into Hurley, right into Burke. Navigating a network of the world's explorers for whom the town's streets were named, except, that is to say, the few aberrations honouring local families like those of her husband's: her *own* name now, too, of course, up on signposts so that everything she did in this town was always going to be writ large. The enormous stupidity of going from one man to another.

Jean-Baptiste's street populated by disintegrating little weatherboard houses on stumps, former workers' cottages, stepping up the slope, some in better condition than others, a couple knocked down and replaced by townhouses.

Her father renting a room in one of the cottages, owned by another musician. Moved in there after she'd kicked him out of her house a couple of years before.

Parking the car on the hill. Pulling the handbrake on hard. Going into the house to get the girls. This being all she was capable of, a terrible vacancy in her belly, the sense that she'd made the worst kind of mistake, the repercussions of which were only now becoming apparent but which would, surely, destroy her utterly, could reach out and destroy, even, her daughters.

She needed, simply, to get home, to be away from town, the buildings, the cars, these houses tumbling one on another, crowding thoughts that were already cramped. Music inside. The house, small from the outside, still somehow managing to contain a hallway, three bedrooms, a bathroom and a kitchen/living room in which a practice session was underway, Jean-Baptiste standing by the bench with his alto sax in his hands, still wearing that stupid hat, while Simon, the pianist, worked his way through a solo on the keyboard. The singer, Kat, a dark streak in t-shirt and pants (no bra) at the open glass doors to the deck, a cigarette held out into the open air. How fantastic it must be to have this lot as neighbours. This was something she'd not understood about her father when, as an adult, she'd encountered him again, living in Paris with his mother (her grandmother, for whom her elder daughter Sandrine had been named). She'd been naive, she'd thought the living arrangements a European thing, something an intellectual or an artist from a different culture might do. But if it was so, it was also because he was the archetypical muso, endemically unreliable, still carrying *Bene Gesserit* and that whole generation's sense of entitlement wherever he went – the conviction that the very purpose of their lives was *play*; little changed by a changing world. After she'd gone to find him in France he'd come back to Australia to visit her a couple of times, staying with them, but never for very long. He and David never having quite seen eye to eye.

Winderran, though, with its vibrant music scene, was his type of place and after Sandrine's death – when it turned out her grandmother hadn't owned the flat where she lived in Montmartre, was, in fact, as penniless as him – he'd come back again, this time more permanently. Moving in with them, without formal discussion or appreciation of the different schedules two young daughters might impose – playing music to all hours of the morning, smoking cigarettes and dope, sleeping till midday with a variety of different women, offering regular critiques of her mothering. Infuriating her as much as David so that she had, in the end, asked him to go; *her own father*. Now somewhat reformed, less dope, more meditation and yoga but still the cigarettes and wine. Another burden to be borne.

Sandrine at the kitchen bench, doing homework. Unwashed dishes piled next to the sink. No sign of Emily. The room decorated according to a seventies model that was almost baroque in its own way – paisley patterned throws over the armchairs, pottery water-cooler, dark red walls bearing original art that appeared to have been created under the influence of hallucinogens, but not in a good way. Wind chimes on the veranda. A Persian rug. Realising that it might not be as simple to get the girls out of there as she might have wished.

Sandrine, twelve years old, short boy's haircut on her long face, jumping down from the stool when she saw her, calling out, 'Mummy!'

Simon stopping with the piano mid-chord so suddenly everyone was looking at her. Required to give an explanation as to why she was so early which, she saw, now, she would have to say had nothing to do with having seen Nick at his kitchen window with another woman, was to do with Geoff Steever and a couple of others not being able to make the meeting, except that all this seemed to have happened a long time ago, on another day entirely.

'Fantastic,' Jean-Baptiste said, 'you can have dinner with us.'

'No, really,' she said, 'we have to be getting home.'

Sandrine, by her side, her arms around her waist, objecting. 'But, Mummy, we're—'

'We're going home,' she said, as if she seriously believed this would be the end of it, that Sandrine wouldn't use the presence of the beautiful skinny Kat to embarrass her into doing whatever it was she wanted. The whole parenting conundrum unspooling around her in public once again when she was least equipped to deal with it so that all at once she thought she might burst into tears. 'Where's Emily?'

'Are you okay?' Jean-Baptiste said, demonstrating more awareness than she normally gave him credit for. Perhaps his shift towards the spiritual wasn't all crap. 'You look a bit, I don't know, pale.'

Turning back along the corridor and into Jean-Baptiste's room to find Emily watching a cartoon on his computer, earbuds in her ears. Putting her arm around her younger daughter's shoulders, asking her what she was watching and telling her they'd have to go at the same time as Sandrine came in loaded with her arguments for staying, that Kat had made this or said that. Jean-Baptiste coming in behind her without his instrument to add his weight to it so that she no longer wanted to cry but to scream.

'No,' she said. 'We're going home now. Mummy's had a difficult day.' And, although she hadn't raised her voice, something in the tone must have communicated her state because Jean-Baptiste said to the girls that he thought she meant it, but they'd seen that too and within minutes she had them gathered together, school bags and shoes and hats and empty lunch boxes.

Full dark outside. The girls strapped into their seats. Back up Peary again and out to the west of the town; allowing a certain relief to fall on her. At least until her phone began pinging.

'There's a message for you,' Sandrine said, helpfully. 'Shall I check it?'

'No!' she snapped. 'Leave it alone.'

The business of getting the girls sorted granting a level of calm. The evening routine a balm to the storm inside her, but something that could only really hold until they were in bed and she was by herself again, taking her phone out to the far corner of the veranda, where a signal might be found.

> So sorry, was in the hospital, didn't get your message. Can you still come? N

Which was, of course, so much shit because she'd seen him at the window with another woman, the lie meaning there really had been cause for concern. Meaning, in fact, that she was deeply seriously fucked because somehow or other she'd allowed herself to become infatuated with a man who was totally inappropriate. Worse, she'd acted upon it, been to his house and had sex with him all over the place like some deranged person, tangling him up in the abandonment of her marriage as if that wasn't messy enough. Although, of course, it could be said, thinking this, seeing this, that the marriage had been ready to be abandoned and maybe Nick, *Doctor Nicholas Michael Lasker*, he of the barren household, had been no more than the vehicle with which she might achieve escape velocity from it, a thought which provoked this picture of herself shot into the upper atmosphere, dropping bits of rocket behind her as she went, rising up and up until she could attain an orbit distant enough from the gravitational pull of not just her husband but the entire Lensman clan, indeed from that whole stretch of her life since she'd been a child in the eucalypt forests of southern New South Wales, wandering amongst the grey-barked trees that stretched infinitely across the slopes of the hills, her hand held by Yvette who was telling her stories about what it was she was seeing, filling her tiny mind with a vision of the world which she had never been able to support after Yvette had gone away to wherever it was that sisters went when they got burned up in fires. What sort of orbit could grant her freedom from such influence?

Out on the veranda in the night, her own two daughters asleep, curiously sensitive to her throughout the evening procedures – dinner, television, baths, stories – unusually protective of their mother as if they sensed that she was close to some abyss. The trouble with being shot into the upper atmosphere was that there was nobody there but her, no guides, none of Jean-Baptiste's handy angels to spread their wings around her frail body and carry her through the vast emptiness. Just her, alone, subject to her own recriminations, because who would ever have thought what she was doing with Nick Lasker could have ended well, not just the deceit but also the joy, the sheer fucking pleasure she'd taken in fucking him, in being by his side. There had to be a price for that sort of thing, surely? Her Stanmore grandmother's rulebook seeming, astonishingly, to have made it up into stellar orbit along with her, requiring, sooner or later, to be jettisoned along with everything else, only that she couldn't find the release switch to quite let it go, would have to spin up there with it for companionship a little while longer.

At *Roselea* she parked in the shade of the big fig, going straight down to the old milking bales where they squatted below the road, rusting tin-roofed, still boasting the row of narrow doors along the back wall where cows had once gone in, now permanently shut, the unpainted hardwood washed grey with age, brushed with red lichen. Around the side she found the entrance, a new-made door with a wooden latch, a piece of dowel which you slid to move a fillet of wood, Marcus's handiwork, the kind of thing he did for relaxation when not doing the thousand other jobs the property demanded. Surprised to find the interior all but empty, the walls painted a startling white. The only furniture a couple of chairs, in one of which Lindl was sitting, the big glass doors open in front of her.

Eugenie had never been inside before, had been aware of it as a private space away from the house, hadn't really expected to be invited in, for all their friendship harbouring the lay-person's awe of an artist's workspace. On the basis of a single black and white photo she'd seen of Lindl when she was both young and an active printmaker – standing amongst the equipment of her trade, work benches, pots, brushes, scrapers, prints drying on makeshift washing lines; dressed in a frock and wearing a rolled scarf tied around her head, like a working woman – she'd anticipated a crowded paint-splattered room. But this place was empty, the only sign of any art being a stack of blank canvases leaning against the wall.

Lindl stood, gave her a kiss on the cheek. 'Welcome to my studio,' she said. 'What do you think?'

Eugenie unsure how to respond.

'I had a man come in to line and paint it for me, get rid of the rats,' she said, making a sweeping gesture to embrace the whole empty space, talking about it with a fierce and breezy lightness. 'For literally aeons it was full of stuff, old bits of Mar's farm equipment, boxes that came from the shop, but I got it all moved into one of his sheds.'

'It's lovely,' Eugenie said. 'But ...'

'A bit bare? Yes, it is, isn't it? I had Ian Illchild over here yesterday. I'd promised him some of the canvases left over from the shop. He told me I should spread some colour around. He said it would help. It was one of those things, you know, *build it and they will come*, I thought if I made the space my art would come back ... there being nothing to stop it anymore now my daughter's left home, the shop's closed. The thing is, nothing's come. Well, not nothing. I sit here. Thinking. As if what I really needed was a space for that. Who'd have thought?' She laughed, a fluttering, dismissive, embarrassed laugh which covered, Eugenie thought, more than just the empty space. 'But come, sit with me. What's going on?'

No point in dissembling. 'You probably guessed,' she said. 'I've been seeing another man. Although, in my defence, the last time we spoke it hadn't started.' Saying this to Lindl who, at the time, had disappointed her by advocating the sanctity of marriage when what she'd wanted was permission to see Nick, something, in the event, she hadn't needed help from anyone to do. Now, though, she had to talk to *someone*, the prospect of another long night of tormented thought being more than she could bear. Lindl the only person she could trust not to judge her too harshly, never mind her earlier reticence.

Beneath the present issue of Nick and whatever he was up to – the text messages that had come in during the night, the attempted calls to her mobile that morning (which she'd ignored) and all her conflicting desires (including the need, above all, to *know*, as if knowing more about who he'd been with might help) – beneath those immediate issues lay the need to end her marriage, and the impossibility of that ... by which she meant the practicality of it; how one might even begin to approach such a thing. What her girls would think, how to protect them from harm; but then, also, the question of where she might live, where David would live? Not to mention their finances: they had joint accounts. How David would respond, the terror of that, the fear he might become vicious, take it out on her, or on the girls – there being precedent. It's not that she thought he was happy in the marriage but she knew he was in love with the *idea* of family, in the same way she had once been (what happened to that?), except in his case there was also the factor of his *place* in fucking Winderran and the humiliation he would think she is visiting on *Lensmans* by what she had done, or wanted to do. And opposed to all these anxieties the deep awareness – which she supposed she had to thank Nick for – that the marriage was already over, had been for some time, and the painful discovery which accompanied it that she was, in fact, a person in her own right, who needed ... well, this was another problem – she didn't know what she needed – but she needed *something* and her lack of certainty about what it was contributed to her guilt at requiring anything. All of it informed by a sense of irrevocability and dread at what she'd invoked and, by concurrence, imposed on all those around her by having the temerity to suggest that she was someone important enough to have a say in anything at all.

'You know,' she said, 'it occurs to me that my whole involvement with the anti-dam campaign has been a ruse, a way of untying my marriage by default. Perhaps David's been wise to it since the beginning. That's why he's been so pissed off about it.'

'You don't think,' Lindl said, 'this has all just been stirred up by seeing your doctor?'

'Of course it has,' she said, a bit testily, surprised at the obtuseness of the question, as if Lindl hadn't been listening. 'But that's not the point.'

Lindl remaining frustratingly calm. 'So what is the point?'

'I don't know. That's why I'm talking to you. Maybe I need a room like this to sit in. Maybe if I had a room like this I'd have space to think.' Petulant. Still having not quite dispensed with the idea that her friend might not be as good at listening as she was.

'I'm not being facetious,' Lindl said. 'Don't get me wrong, I'm happy to support you in whatever you do. I mean it. If you need a place to stay, if you need help of any kind, I'm here.'

'But?'

'But I'm worried how David's going to react. He'll see it as you going off with another man. His pride will be hurt.'

'And I should protect him from that?'

'Maybe. Would that be a crime against your new-found honesty?'

'I don't want to lie to him. I might not want to be married to him anymore but it doesn't mean I want to lie.'

Lindl let that hang. Eugenie looked out the open doors, down across the paddock. There was a fence about five metres away to keep the cattle from getting in around the building. Someone, probably Marcus, had mowed the grass inside. The same brown cows from the other day, or ones like them, Brahman-cross, were dotted around the paddock beyond, flicking their giant ears, swishing their long tails, eating grass. Ruminants. You could see why someone might think them sacred.

'What do you think about here?' she asked.

'Stuff.'

'What sort of stuff?'

'We're talking about you,' Lindl said, refusing to be drawn. 'It's not that I want to protect David, or men in general for that matter, so much as protect my friend from the way they behave when they get hurt. But you're right, it was a silly idea. I'm sorry. I was just thinking it might be better to avoid provoking him, to let him down gently. For your own sake, for the sake of the girls. But of course you need to be honest.'

'You think it's all right to leave?' Eugenie said. Still apparently seeking permission.

'If you're asking my opinion I think you're already gone,' Lindl said. 'You were gone when I spoke to you the other day. It's just a matter of how you go about it. And I meant what I said before, about staying here if you need to.'

Tears threatening to well at that. Looking down at the floor to hide it.

'I'm frightened,' Eugenie said. 'That's what this is about.'

'I know,' Lindl said.

They sat. The cows ruminated. The studio had been renovated but the slab floor retained the pattern of its previous use as a dairy. Rough herring-bone indentations sloped towards the doors.

'In the interest of honest disclosure,' Lindl said, not looking at Eugenie, 'what I think about when I sit here is mostly Mum. And my family. It's not entirely healthy.'

'What isn't?'

'My thoughts. They take me down fairly grim pathways. Our capacity for violence. I'd say men's capacity for violence but unfortunately I don't believe it's just them. They're just the agents of it. The convenient scapegoat.'

'You don't mean Marcus?'

'No! No, Marcus is one of the good ones. I'm worried for him, not by him.'

Eugenie waited. Lindl threw up her hands in frustration.

'Some days I wake with this awful sense of foreboding. Everyone must feel like it some time, I suppose. People must have felt this way all through history. In worse times than this. That's what I tell myself, but it doesn't really help. I feel it *now*. At a time when the world most needs to come together in some way, to get over all our petty little hates, we seem instead to be making a great lurch to the Right. Not just in Australia, everywhere.

'Marcus has this idea that it's time for good men to stand up for what they believe in. You've heard him. Spouting his Margaret Meady stuff: *never doubt that a small group of thoughtful, committed citizens can change the world*, the kind of thing you find on the back of toilet doors. The thing about this shit is that it's true, small groups have and do change the world, but the story that doesn't get told is of the millions who fall by the wayside in the process, whose efforts have no effect at all. Who die for nothing. Unremarked, unremembered.'

Eugenie watching.

'What I think is that sooner or later the bullies will shake off their fine suits and start killing people, the way they always have. And they'll start with people like Marcus. I don't think it's the right time for good men to stand up.'

Lapsing into silence.

Eugenie shocked at the force of the outburst. Wondering how to talk her out of this stuff. If it was even her role to do so. Wondering if perhaps Lindl wasn't the one who needed help, by which she meant medication. The nurse in her rising to the occasion. Whether or not one of the amitriptylines might be indicated. Feeling guilty because she, as her friend, hadn't noticed, had been caught up in her own soap opera, her game of doctors and nurses. Wondering what she was doing bringing *her* problems to Lindl to sort out.

'It's why I'm so big on planting trees,' Lindl said, and laughed. 'It grounds me, stops me going down these spirals. Unless of course I think about these arseholes who want to destroy it all.' She laughed again, an even more hollow attempt than the previous one. 'But we were talking about you, weren't we?' Pulling herself up, no irony apparent. 'When you've got to go, you've got to go. There's nothing you can do about it. That's the truth of the matter. A funny thing, though. I was astonished when you said your man was the new doctor. Ian told me something about him yesterday.'

'Yes?' Noting the way her whole mind swung into focus at the very mention of Nick, suggesting she wasn't as indifferent to him as she might have wished.

'I can't remember how we got onto the subject but he was telling me about a dinner he'd had with Guy and Helen Lamprey a few weeks ago. Your doctor was there. It seems he's one of Guy's special friends.'

thirteen

Nick

Joy, the office manager, is a formidable woman. Nick's been a GP long enough to understand that a practice cannot run without an efficient front desk but he's never encountered anyone like her. Of a certain age and substantial girth, she organises the office according to her own established rules, immune, it seems, to his charms (but then the same might be said of him regarding her, this being one of the things Nick has never quite grasped about other people). They have inherited each other and make the best of things, but there is little warmth in their interactions, he knows nothing of her life outside the office, a failing which he recognises is part of the problem, but hardly knows how to rectify. A question about the photo of the young man on the desk at this late stage would only emphasise his previous disinterest. Regardless of her age she is no slouch with technology, updating the system, the calendars, patients' records, referrals, requisition orders for supplies, all without fault or apparent difficulty, while at the same time managing appointments, payments, accounts, the many different health-fund and government requirements, and, even more extraordinarily, getting these things to appear on his computer at will. She can even get a network to speak to a printer.

He does not presume to enter her space; handing patient folders through the door or over the counter, from where they are sorted into various trays, the very obvious *In* and *Out*, but also *Pending*, a series of open-top drawers each one further labelled with her name, as if to distinguish them from someone else's trays, so that there is Joy *In*, Joy *Out*, Joy *Pending*, the latter bringing him up short each of the twenty times a day he encounters it, as if the phrase sums up some central aspect of his life. He had thought, during those few days when he was seeing Eugenie, that joy had, in fact, *arrived*, that this last year had indeed been a kind of pending, a preparation for the actual moment. Now she refuses to communicate with him. No explanation given. It is possible the husband, David, returned unannounced from the mines. He imagines a thick-set individual, broad-shouldered, receding jet black hair cut very short, dark eyebrows and a three-day growth, tattoos on bicep and shoulder, dressed, of course, in hi-viz yellow and dark blue; clothes that she, Eugenie, will wash for him and hang on the Hills Hoist in the garden while, according to the little he does actually know about the man, David watches sport in a lounge room that he, Nick, hasn't ever seen and now, apparently, never will.

Please do not try to contact me

being the only message he has received in reply to the raft of texts he has sent and left for her, each one of which were, in turn, responding to a text announcing she would shortly be arriving at his home to ravish him, a promise she didn't keep or even cancel, and which – though it was impossible she could know this – he wouldn't have been able to entertain no matter how much he might have wanted to because he was at the time, of course, fucking

Nina, although in his defence he would say that this had not been intentional, he had invited Nina to visit for the express purpose of telling her they could no longer continue their occasional liaisons because he'd met somebody. News which Nina had taken with her customary ease, albeit with an attempt to get out of him who the person was, aided and abetted by a series of kisses which degenerated into the act itself. Nina, he supposed, determined to exercise her rights at least one more time as a statement of ownership or, perhaps, a way of saving face, and he being helpless to resist not because he was, in fact, helpless, but rather *hopeless*, lacking any means to say no to a woman in such a circumstance, lest he give offence.

The difficulty – coming into the surgery an hour early, finding he is even ahead of Joy, and that she must have cleaned up before going home the previous night even though it was a late session, the prep room immaculate, the magazines in neat stacks on the waiting-room table, her *Far Side Page-a-Day Cartoon Calendar* turned over to the new day – the trouble is that he doesn't know what to do with himself. Can't eat, can't sleep, can't think straight outside of a consultation and only within one because the process is so deeply ingrained that the protocols initiate themselves automatically. Gnawing at the possibilities, fighting away the awful intuition that she had somehow found out about Nina and wasn't interested in hearing his explanation, should an opportunity to provide one occur; they weren't, after all, in a relationship, there'd never been any discussion about not sleeping with anyone else, and yet, even at the time, he'd known it as a kind of betrayal. If she was just another woman, another in the long series he'd engaged with over the previous twenty years, it wouldn't matter, but Eugenie had never once fallen into that category. Now, he fears, he has become an object of her scorn.

He goes into his office, which is the same one he took on arrival, several months before, puts the laptop on his desk, plugs the various leads into their ports. Nick has always worked for someone else, a medical centre or a private practice, never as his own man. He needs to come to a decision soon about what is happening in Winderran. Miles's rooms, down the end of the corridor, much nicer than his own, remain unoccupied, just as they were when he died, like a rebuke.

His former employer had no heirs and the ownership of the practice is caught in a legal limbo, but it seems possible Nick might be able to take it over as a going concern, with a locum of his own, or, who knows, another partner. He is tempted. Other than his children there is little enough back in Canberra. If he could figure out a way to negotiate with Abie so that he could see Josh and Danielle on a semi-regular basis the prospect of living in Winderran has a certain appeal; although that could just as easily be a result of his feelings for Eugenie. His connection to place always tenuous at best, bound up with the women in his life rather than any sense of *country*.

His brother bringing to this topic a more venal point of view than Eugenie. He thinks taking on the practice would be a good investment. Nick went down to visit on the weekend in a misguided attempt to distract himself. Matt, sitting on a sun-lounge on his tiled patio, his belly proudly before him, explained, between sips of imported beer, that the market was depressed. 'Down thirty per cent if it's an inch,' he said. 'But it'll come back and when it does, Winderran's the sort of place you want to be. It won't stop where it was before the crash, it'll double again. As I live and breathe.' Rattling off percentages like a psychotic calculator. His older brother, the one their father had thought useless, destined to end up sweeping the streets, now beyond simply rich, delighted to instruct his little brother on how to follow him on his path to infinite wealth. The motorboat at its mooring in the canal. As if it was as simple as that.

'I don't have a lot to invest,' Nick said, not prepared to admit what he was paying Abie towards the mortgage on the house in Canberra, or, for that matter, what she'd think about the idea. Speaking of women's scorn.

'You haven't heard of borrowing?' Matt said. 'Interest's at historic lows. Someone like you … you're the darling of the banks. You can't go wrong. Jesus, did you see the people in that town? Last time we were up there you couldn't move for tourists. I'm thinking of buying into the main street myself.'

'You're not worried about the global markets?'

'*Nicky*. Everyone's worried about the global markets. That's what brings the prices down. That's what's going to make us all rich. What did they teach you at those fancy schools of yours?'

'Clearly nothing. So you're not worried?'

'I wouldn't say that.'

'So what are you saying?'

'I'm saying you take the opportunities you're given. Eat, drink and be merry. For tomorrow we die.'

'This,' Nick said, 'is your investment advice?'

The computer sounds a triumphant chord as the screen lights up, his email box automatically filling with missives, many of which call out for attention. Unable to approach them he flicks to a news site but the headlines are all international doom and gloom: India's battle with China over water. Not his business.

He hears Joy come in, and, after giving her a moment to settle, goes out to say hello, only to find there's already a patient in the waiting room, an *alternate* as they're called locally, one of the latter-day hippies, but in this case female, young, barefoot, dressed in what looks like skins, as if she's just wandered in from a teepee or a cave, none too clean, flicking through a woman's magazine, brown unshaven legs stuck out in front of her.

Joy offers to make coffee. He follows her to the little kitchen, standing in the doorway while she boils the kettle. She inclines her head towards the girl in the waiting room. 'No appointment,' she says. 'If you want you can squeeze her in before your 8.45, otherwise you're booked through till lunchtime.'

'I was hoping to catch up on email. But I could. It's not like I want to do that.'

Joy gives him one of her looks, never keen to encourage skiving. 'From the camp, I'd guess,' she says.

'Against the dam?' he asks.

She nods.

'And you, Joy? Do you have a position?' A conversational gambit. He may as well *try*.

The kettle coming to the boil. She ladles several large spoonfuls of grounds into the plunger. If he does take over the practice he'll get one of those things that makes coffee from capsules. They can afford it.

'It's a load of nonsense, if that's what you're asking,' she says.

'I thought you'd be for it.'

The wrong thing to say. She leans on the plunger with her great tuck-shop arms, applying even more force than usual as a result of his *faux pas*, so that he expects any second the thing will explode, spraying hot liquid across the room. He can hardly bear to look.

'Why d'you say that?'

He doesn't know why. Because she's a local, he supposes, but that, too, would be the wrong thing to say. He shrugs. 'Never pays to make assumptions, does it?' he says.

'Right enough. Anyone with half a brain can see the whole idea was made up on the back of a cocktail napkin. This town's future's in tourism, it's in looking after the place, not putting a useless dam in the middle of it.' The plunger has survived her ministrations. She pours a couple of mugs of the hefty brew.

'It's not for me to speak about patients,' she says, glancing up at him, 'but that man Lamprey should know better. He's always thought he was too good for this town, now he's hell bent on destroying it. No excuse his wife's sick.'

'What's he been doing?'

'You don't know?'

'Not exactly.'

'Well I haven't got time for it now,' she says, shaking her head. 'Here's your coffee. Shall I send the girl in?'

'Give me five.'

'Right you are. Mind, she could do with a bath.'

The girl slips into the room crabwise, stopping just inside, against the wall, waiting to be invited forward as if she were a schoolgirl in the headmaster's office, her movements accompanied by the jingle of a small bell on a woven thread around her ankle, the sort of thing you'd put on a cat to keep it from birds. For she would have music. Small, dusky and dusty, dark-eyed, her hair in dreadlocks, carrying with her, for all her shyness, a wild uncouth assertiveness.

He introduces himself, indicates she should come forward, take the chair at the end of the desk. As she sits she shrugs off her jacket, a soft pretty thing of many colours, revealing a cross-tied garment beneath made of something that's not suede but appears to be so, and also that she doesn't shave beneath her arms either, a natural woman this. Giving off a curious salty smell. A silver ring on the longest toe of her left foot.

'What seems to be the trouble?'

'Well, see, I've been having sex with this guy,' she says. 'And now I've got this sharp pain when I, you know, pee. It's come on real quick. I'm trying to figure out if it's because we're, you know, not *simpatico*, or if it's just a natural thing, hey?'

'A natural thing?'

'Yeah, see,' Ange says, 'I've never had this before. With anybody. I live really pure, no drugs, only organic food, I focus my mind on good things, concentrate on my music.'

'So you think he's given you an infection?'

'Well, maybe. But there's other stuff. I'm worried it's a *sign*.'

'Of what?'

'That we shouldn't be together. You know, that we're on a different level, vibrationally.'

Best, perhaps, to tackle the symptoms.

'So, tell me about the pain. How would you describe it?'

'Hot, you know. Like burning.'

He gives her a urine bottle and asks if she'd be able to produce a sample. She says okay and goes out to the toilet, coming back several minutes later looking slightly pale, a urinary tract infection clearly running rampant. No blood in the sample though. Sits down again.

He checks her temperature and blood pressure, that salty smell stronger when he's up close, not unpleasant, just unusual, feral. Running through the standard questions: use of antibiotics; the pill; IUD; sexual partners; history of menstruation. Hoping to exclude alternatives – conscious of his time, the waiting room that will be filling even as Ange takes each enquiry as an opportunity to go off on tangents.

'Will's kind of cute,' she says. 'Buff, eh? Works out with his friends, goes running in the early mornings. He was in the army. Not the kind of guy I normally go with. I figure he's come to me for healing. I'm kind of an empath, you know, I feel the illness inside people, the suppressed hurt at the base of disease. I have to be careful 'cos I take it on. I just don't know if I'm strong enough to deal with his, I'm wondering if that's why I'm getting sick.'

'You mean he was injured? Fighting overseas?'

'No, not hurt like that … inside. It might have happened before he joined up, but being in there hasn't helped, you know, he thinks he has to be tough about everything, which is okay when you're in bed, hey, it's kind of refreshing to find someone like that. But not everywhere else.'

Unusually frank.

'The thing is,' she says, 'I think Will needs me. It's like he's waiting to be rescued.'

'And you're the one to do it?'

'You don't think so?'

'I'm sorry, that's not what I meant,' Nick says. 'I don't know Will. I was just wondering if this was something you do, you know, rescue people, if that's your nature?'

'It goes with being an empath,' she says. 'When I was at school, hey, everyone used to come to me with their problems. Sometimes all a person needs is to be listened to.'

She gives more examples, and Nick attends, but only half-heartedly. Whatever else Ange might be, he thinks, unkindly, it isn't generous with herself. This darkly tanned little girl with her curious smell is someone, he thinks, who puts her own interests first. Feeling sorry for the hapless Will.

'I'm going to prescribe some antibiotics,' he says. 'We'll send your sample off for testing. But you'll need to keep your fluids up, too. I know it hurts to pee but the less you drink the worse it's going to get. Cranberry juice helps.'

Writing her a script.

She keeps talking. 'This crowd he hangs out with,' she says. 'There's this guy, he's like Will's guru or something, has this big house out of town. Rules the roost. Ex-army, a whole bunch of guys, fawning at everything he says. Some sort of Christian thing. Real creepy, crucifixes tattooed on his arm.'

Nick stops writing.

'Will lives with these guys?' he says, as casual as possible.

'Sure. I've been staying there. Listening while they sit round drinking and smoking. *Scheming.*'

'I thought they were into exercise.'

'That's in the morning. In the evenings it's different. In the evenings it's sex'n'drugs and rock'n'roll. In the evenings they sit around and talk about which guns they like. Sorry, *weapons.* They're very serious about that shit. I guess if you lived with a gun next to you for years you might be, but it's weird, hey. After a few drinks one of the guys got stuck into the camp. Said the hippies shouldn't be there, telling locals what they can do. Jaz shut him down, told him to *shut the fuck up.* The thing is,' Ange says, 'Jaz wasn't saying it to be nice to me or anything, he just didn't want me to know what they were about.'

'Which is?'

'I don't know. Something but. You can be sure of that.'

'What do you think?'

'My guess?'

'Yes.'

She leans forward. Delighted to be asked. A girl who could be quite pretty if she wasn't so determined not to be. Bra-less breasts curving beneath the ersatz suede, something a bit pugnacious around her wide mouth, *a mouthy girl*, is what she would have been called back in the day, not even so much for what she looked like as for having opinions, for talking too much. Not sure from where in him such prejudices arise. Wouldn't have taken himself for a person who makes judgements because a girl enjoys rough sex.

'Jaz has got himself in trouble, see. I know this, 'cos Will told me. He's looking for a way to get back on his boss's good side.'

'Who's the boss?' he says, 'God?'

Ange laughs. 'No, his boss at the church. Jaz wants to fuck with the anti-dammers so as to make good. That's why he didn't want me to know.'

'Because you're against the dam?'

Dark-eyebrowed contradictory Ange looking at him with a bit more attention. 'Yeah, 'cos I was at the camp before, see.'

Another of these people who believe in conspiracies. As if life isn't interesting enough the way it is, there has to be another layer or two of intrigue beneath the surface. Which sometimes there is, of course, that's the thing. Who really knows? But you'd be unwise, he thinks, to take advice on it from Ange.

He glances at his watch. It's all gone on far too long. Joy will be fretting. He tells the girl what he's done about her infection, what she needs to do, making sure she understands she needs to take the pills to the end, and to come back to see him if she's not better in forty-eight hours.

'So you don't reckon it's to do with Will?' she says.

'It's caused by bad bacteria in your urethra,' he says. 'That can happen lots of ways, but most often through sex. Best thing to do is get up and have a pee as soon as you finish. Flush anything out that's got in there by accident. That and give yourself a wash. It happens to a lot of women.' Resisting the temptation to say that it's unlikely God is micro-managing the bacterial communities of her vagina to communicate directions about love. Or that even thinking certain thoughts – never mind external forces – might cause bacterial overgrowth. But then these last few days he's not been so immune to these diversions himself. Looking everywhere for guidance.

She gets up, dismissed, pulling on her jacket.

'Thanks,' she says.

'You're welcome. I enjoyed hearing about these guys.'

'You did?'

'Sure.'

'I could tell you more.'

'I bet you could, but I'm out of time.'

'I think I know what they're going to do,' she says.

Intent on getting her out of there. Walking her to the door, prepared to escort her, if need be, all the way to Joy's office. 'Who's going to do what?' he says.

'See, there's a rare frog in the creek. I reckon they're going to kill it.' Stopping in the doorway.

'How?'

'Put chemicals in the creek.'

'If you think that shouldn't you tell someone?'

'I just did.'

At around eleven he takes a break. He makes the coffee himself. Joy comes to check on him in the kitchen, see he's doing it right. Taking up the whole door space with her frame, breathing heavily.

'That girl,' he says.

'I know,' Joy says, 'she really could have done with that bath. And a haircut. But you can't complain really, can you? Heart's in the right place. Camping out there in all that dirt.'

'I don't think she's at the camp anymore. She seems to be in a share house with some ex-army types now. Full of some story about messing with the anti-dam mob.'

Pushing down the plunger.

'Here, let me at that,' Joy says, coming into the small room. 'Hurting them?' she says.

'Not the people. Something about a frog in the creek.'

'How'd she know about that?'

'You've heard of it, too?' he says.

'Of course I have. My brother's place is in line of the dam. Marcus Barker. What did she say?'

fourteen

Guy

After the young man left he stayed exactly where he was. Unable to move. Eventually he roused himself enough to turn on the television, flicking through the channels, failing to be caught by either the late news or an old Al Pacino film, one of the ones from before the actor began to see himself as a serious contender for Shakespeare, although, perhaps that was unfair, maybe he had always been one, what did Guy know, he who'd had the temerity to believe he might prove most royal were he put on, but now found himself sitting in a hotel room, naked from the waist down, a man in his mid-sixties, grey hair on his chest and belly, around his scrotum, useless balls hanging ever lower with age, another whisky in his hand, his eyes glazing at the very existence of film or television, too numb to turn it off.

This anomie, he tried to tell himself, was no more than the result of thwarted sexuality turned upon itself. He had reason to be optimistic; the dinner with members of the Party had, after all, been more successful. He'd forgotten, until he arrived at the restaurant, that Bain had told him the owner was once married to Nick Lasker, Helen's doctor, and that, in one of those peculiar coincidences life seems to delight in throwing up for no special purpose, Bain had even bumped into him there several weeks earlier. No apparent meaning to it, but it must be said that Lasker seemed to surface with unnerving regularity, as if determined to communicate *something*.

A table set for ten, to celebrate his imminent acceptance on the Senate ticket, and to introduce him to several other Senators and power players. Nine men and one woman, the latter being head of communications to the Leader of the Opposition himself and, by all accounts, a terrifying individual, rumoured to possess an unerring capacity to wound, surprisingly young and, on this occasion, very pleasant, introducing herself as an admirer; but then he had, as yet, lacked the opportunity to do anything to attract her ire. The room just large enough for the table and a small area at one end where they mingled, fine wine flowing generously before the food arrived so that even the hardest of heads must have begun to swim. The place lined, floor to ceiling, with black shelves containing bottles of olive oil gathered from around the world.

He spoke for a time to Alexis Corwen, Shadow Minister for the Environment, with whom he'd corresponded but never met, a short neat man also surprisingly, even unnecessarily, young, with the reserved manner of one trained to the sciences who, by the way he held himself, also spent time in the gym, or perhaps jogging around Lake Burley Griffin. Dressed, like all of them, in an exquisite suit, begging the question of tailors; there must be whole workshops of them kept in business by senior members of the government alone.

Guy took the opportunity to put Corwen right about certain anomalies in the final report on the dam, the sorts of things he believed should never have seen the light of day – he'd done little else than research the subject for the previous month, getting on top of it, if only to forestall more disasters. Corwen, though, interrupted him before he could get far, steering him away from the others as much as possible within the confined space.

'Actually,' he said, 'I have good news on that front. I had lunch with my opposite number just today. We seem, remarkably, to all be on the same page on this one. A rare moment of bipartisanship, largely due, I think it's fair to say, to your efforts.'

Guy washed by a hot glow of satisfaction that had little to do with the wine, struggling to retain his composure, shaking Corwen's small hard hand as a way of expressing his pleasure.

'The report will come out next week, or the one after, depending on the cycle,' Corwen said.

This last referring of course to the news, a reminder that all decisions in this place were contingent, that the choice of which projects got up was tied to grubby back-room deals and clever salesmanship rather than merit, and all of these people, even this taut, erudite young man, were engaged in a constant battle to get their little enterprises up, ahead of anyone else. The trappings, the lovely suits and fine wines, were, in fact, quite possibly designed to conceal this, to give the impression that everything was running smoothly, in the hope everyone might forget both the ugliness of the process and that they were all subject to the whim of the electorate. Politics was, Guy thought, something he'd been born to, not so far from what a writer did anyway, sacrificing one or another character in the service of the larger story. The mystery was why he'd waited so long.

When the food arrived it came as small portions delicately placed on large white plates, hard to fathom how so many of these men carried so much weight if this was all they consumed; perhaps they kept buckets of Ben & Jerry's in their offices to binge on against the anxiety. The meat, however, was delicious, perfectly prepared and accompanied by exquisite sauces of varied provenance. Guy made a note to mention it to Nick next time they met.

'When I was born,' he said, indicating the bottles of oil arrayed on the shelves, and addressing as many as could hear him (the room falling pleasingly quiet when they heard his raised voice), 'there wasn't a single espresso machine in the country. Nobody but a refugee would have known what to do with olive oil, never mind an olive, well, except of course, to put it in a martini.' Quickly recovering from the lack of tact in bringing up the subject of immigrants in this company by launching into an old anecdote about martinis and their construction – raising a generous amount of laughter in response. Basking in the pleasure these people took in his stories, in the possibilities the role presented him, in the defeat of his enemies; the enervating pall which had settled on him during these last years sloughing off; forgetting for a moment or two even to observe those present with a writerly eye.

As the company broke up Aldous took him aside.

'Well that went well, don't you think?' he said, sipping the smallest of short blacks. 'Now, I'm afraid I've still some business to attend to this evening, but before I go I wanted to get you acquainted with Michael, over there,' pointing to his chief-of-staff at the far end of the table. 'He has your schedule worked out for the next couple of days. He can run you through it on the way back to the hotel. We're going to put you through the ringer, just a little. Get you up to speed. So that you don't even have to think when you get the difficult questions. I am sorry we have to subject someone like you to this sort of thing, but it's important to stay on message.' Clearing his throat. 'In that regard I did want to have a word. Unpleasant to have to get serious after such a fine meal ...'

'That's what I'm here for,' Guy said, so basted with bonhomie that he could bear to hear almost anything.

'Yes, but these dinners! You mustn't get the idea we do this every day.' Leaning forward. 'What I need to say is that between now and when we announce the ticket you need to watch yourself. And beyond, of course.'

'Of course.'

'I'm referring in particular to who you associate with.'

'Does this mean we'll have to stop meeting Aldous?'

Bain doing him the service of the smallest of smiles.

'Not so much me,' he said. 'You had a couple of nights with our mutual friend a week or so ago, I believe?'

'Peter?' Lamprey said.

'It's come to *Peter*, has it?' Bain enquired.

'I thought,' Guy said, 'Mayska was a friend of the Party's.'

'Oh he is, he is, very much so. A good and influential friend. But I'm sure you understand it doesn't play out so well with the electorate to be seen communing with the zero-point-zero-zero-one per cent. Voters have this ridiculous notion that propinquity to extraordinary wealth will turn your head.'

'So you've been keeping tabs on me?'

'Not so much,' Bain said, laughing. 'But we make that sort of thing our business to know. You can still see him, as much as you like, but not so others notice.'

Guy had spent a weekend in the Whitsundays. Flown there in a private jet, the only passenger, helicoptered on to a neighbouring island then ferried by a man in a thing like a golf buggy to a sun-drenched villa perched on a cliff above the sea. One of several, it transpired, connected to a central building that, in many ways, resembled the one at Winderran, as if they'd been designed by the same architect or at least had the same brief: ultra-modern, lots of glass, polished concrete, re-purposed Australian hardwood. Security systems everywhere, which you wouldn't think so necessary on a small island. This time there were other guests; captains of industry, an artist or two, a minor film star, a sporting personality and several young men and women who didn't seem to fit any category other than to be attractive. At times it felt as if he was acting a part in a house party from a nineteenth-century novel.

It was possible that over the weekend each and every guest had individual time with Peter, but if so he didn't notice it. They had played tennis early one morning, on a court whose outer edge, like an infinity pool, gave way to a view of untrammelled ocean, albeit with a high fence to catch balls. Lamprey had once been an okay player, and found he did not need to be embarrassed, indeed, towards the end of the first set he was up five games to two, all but wiping the court with his opponent. At set point he pushed Mayska outside the back lines with a series of long shots. His host just managing to lob his return over the net. Guy ran forward, scooping up the ball, preparing to drop it on the other side. At the last instant he decided to knock it back to the man. No need to defeat him so forcefully. It was the turning point in the match. Mayska took immediate advantage. He went on to win that set and the next one. No matter what Guy did he couldn't regain the lead, and the more he tried the less successful he became, furious with himself when shot after shot hit the net or went outside the line.

Afterwards, sitting on the little patio of the tennis house, they drank cold sparkling water from bottles and talked, although, Guy couldn't help but notice, Mayska once again tended to dominate the conversation.

'I don't doubt that you think men like me are limited in our interests, that money's everything,' he said, glancing at Guy. 'It's not so. Money has for me only ever been a means to an end. It allows me to hold a house party like this: artists, writers, CEO's of Fortune 500 companies. Courtesans and catamites to entertain. What money does is buy me a better class of associate.'

Guy, still deeply pissed at both losing two sets to zero and at the delight his host clearly took in winning, mused to himself that in reality what it bought Mayska was a better class of audience. Remarking, however, what he'd begun to suspect about the presence of the beautiful young people.

'You don't mind if I philosophise for a moment?'

'Go ahead,' Guy said, smiling through gritted teeth.

'There are two streams of thought about how we've got to be where we are,' Mayska said. 'The first is that the problems humanity faces are both intractable and interminable; when one is solved another takes its place.'

Guy had thought Mayska was being metaphorical when he referred to philosophy, but here they were, before breakfast, discussing *humanity*.

'The second,' he continued, 'is that the problems are solvable; if you could only *legislate* with enough sophistication, then the great issues of poverty and greed, health and welfare, would be resolved. The utopian ideal, if you like. What we saw during the last hundred years was this divergence, a separation on a global scale, into these points of view. On the one hand you had totalitarian regimes who believed that if you could only set up society correctly everything would be all right. I don't need to remind a man like you where *that* got us. On the other you have what I like to think of as the Western ideal, which if you'll permit, I'll sum up as *the problems will always be with us*. We'll conquer one and be faced with another and we'll always be failing, always nearly tipping over the edge of the abyss. The belief that if we have faith in ourselves and our ingenuity, never mind our moral failings, we'll get through.'

Stretching his long thin legs out. Socks around the ankles, barely worn white trainers. Not a gram of extra flesh on him, which, incidentally, made his face somewhat gaunt, or driven, even when he was, as now, pleased with himself. Giving history lessons. Guy waiting for him to come to the point. Expecting that somewhere along the line an explanation would be given for his invitation to the island. What the cost was going to be.

'This belief is central to my business,' Mayska said. 'The larger it becomes, the more problems I encounter, but *at the same time* it also means I can engage better minds to provide solutions.'

Why was it, though, that these self-made men were always so determined to tell people about their business models?

'So why,' Guy said, 'the interest in security services?'

'You have been doing your research.'

'I'm a writer. I follow things through. I don't mind spending a bit of time doing it. I made it my business to read about you, that's all. Except there's not so much that's, how can you say, freely available.'

'But you heard about our acquisition of CoSecOr?'

'I did.'

'And?'

'Well it made me curious. I can see the advantage of it financially, if you have to pay for security you may as well own the company, *and*, in the present climate, I can see the business growing, even exponentially, but I can't see how it fits with what you've just said.'

'But it's entirely consistent,' Mayska said. 'Remember your Hobbes? The *Leviathan*? The State shall have the monopoly on violence and thus eradicate it from the population?'

'Words to that effect.'

'The curious thing is that it's a lesson our government seems to have forgotten. It could be an effect of the long peace, of course, but they've become so enamoured of this idea of "small government" that they've taken to subcontracting out the instruments of law enforcement – domestic and international – to the private sector. Not just here in Australia, all over the West, in the US particularly. What they've failed to recognise is that if you give the monopoly of violence to someone else, even under contract, you no longer have it yourself. Now, that *might* be okay, as long as the interests of the private sector are concurrent with that of the body politic. But what if they're not? Personally I don't want the Leviathan in the hands of people I have no control over. I'd rather be the one holding the gun.'

'Now you're sounding like the NRA,' Guy said, and laughed, as much to defuse what might be seen as an insult as anything else.

Mayska laughed, too. 'Yes,' he said. 'It's true. But I'm not some piece of trailer trash living in Oklahoma, am I? What concerns me directly are security corporations who, given the chance, will put their own interests ahead of my own.'

'Fair enough,' Guy said. 'But what governs your interest?'

'Ah, yes,' Peter said, 'There's the question, isn't it?'

Lamprey waited. Mayska made no attempt to answer. Instead he bent down to adjust first one elegant tennis shoe and then the other, taking his time to get them just right.

It was Guy's experience that if you wait long enough the other person will despair of silence. You wait, and people speak. Peter, though, seemed immune to this anxiety. The silence prevailed, went on too long, even for him.

'So why invite me here?' he said, eventually.

'Ha!' Mayska said, sitting up, slapping his thigh in delight. 'Twice in one morning! I win! You are too soft!'

'What are you talking about?' Guy said, although he knew, just hadn't quite been prepared to believe the man was still playing.

Mayska swung around and punched Guy on the arm, hard enough to hurt. 'Don't take offence,' he said.

Way too late for that.

'Stop,' Mayska said. 'Stop it. I mean it. I order you not to.' Laughing again. 'It was a joke. I like you. That's why I invited you here. No. More than that. I *admire* you. But when we were playing tennis before I saw you. You let me have a point. In the eighth game, you were 40–15, set point, and you gave it to me. Didn't you?'

Guy shrugged.

'But, you see. I was just watching. I was still trying to figure you out. On a good day I think you could beat me, but not if you're prepared to give away games. Is it maybe a writer's thing? Empathy? You feel for the other man, you don't want him to lose? Is that it? I doubt it's because I'm rich!'

Very few people, certainly not those close to him, had ever accused Lamprey of too much empathy.

'And then you did it again … You asked a good question, you waited for the answer, but then you let me go.'

'I did,' Lamprey conceded, but reluctantly. Unused to being lectured on his failings.

'Listen my friend. I tell you this because it's important. You ask me who watches me? People whose judgement I trust, who I hire because I believe in their smarts and that they have the balls to call me on what it is I'm doing. There is no-one else. But right now I need to give you some advice, even though I can see you don't want to hear it, least of all from me. But listen, please. It is important. Don't for a minute think that Bain has invited you into the Party because he likes you. *There* is a man with more killer instinct than the great Khan himself. A vast pile of skulls in his basement. He's been doing this all his life. He will lift you up just exactly as high as he wants to and then he will squash you just as quickly, if it serves his purpose. For him you are nothing more than a tool.'

'I thought you two were friends?'

'Ha!'

'Why then do you have anything to do with him?'

'Because he has power and influence in arenas I do not. And I have the means to influence *him* in some small way.' Not saying what this was. 'Listen, I just say this to you. You have come to this late and from a different perspective. You make a mistake if you think these people want you for your wit or intelligence. I mean,

253

they do, of course, why else? But only in so much as these things are useful to them.'

Warned about Bain by two people in the space of a week. Mayska stood up.

'It's who Aldous associates with that worries me,' he said.

'Lonergan?' Guy said.

Mayska gave him a sardonic look. 'No,' he said. 'The far Right. The religious ones. He thinks he has them under control, he thinks he has me under control, channelling my funds to their projects, but they're a horse that's hard to turn in a tight place.' Stretching. 'Come, we need to get some breakfast. And there is a very beautiful actress staying with us on the island. Right now she will feel as if she is being ignored. Which would defeat the purpose of inviting her.'

Lamprey stayed where he was. 'So, what *do* you want from me?' he said.

Mayska had picked up his racquet. He tapped it against his hairy calf.

'History goes on all over the place all the time,' he said. 'The bits that get remembered have good observers, good chroniclers. That's the only thing that makes them significant. I'm hoping that if you find it interesting you will write about this. How am I doing so far?'

In his armchair in the hotel Guy wondered if Bain knew about the young man who had come to his room. His favourite, Jaydon, had not been available at short notice and the notice had been short because before flying to Canberra he'd thought it inappropriate to indulge himself when Helen was so ill. But the success of the evening had led him to decide to reward himself, vestigial loyalties notwithstanding. Failing to consider how too much wine, too much rich food, and the strangeness of the new boy might affect him.

His inability to perform made him think his original intention had been correct, that the humiliation of his flaccid penis in the face of the beautiful young man was a kind of punishment for yielding to temptation. He felt wrong, dirty, corrupt, useless. Old. He'd declined to take advantage of Mayska's proffered delights in the Whitsundays, if that was what they were, because he'd not been sure there wouldn't be a price to pay and he wasn't yet prepared to sell himself to the billionaire for so little. Was this what he had come to as a writer? The amanuensis of a small man made big by money? A pawn in Aldous Bain's machinations? Was he deluded, becoming paranoid? Is that what was happening now, in the hotel room? Unable to get it up because Bain's foot soldiers (or Mayska's – who knows how large his reach was) might be watching? Nothing like the idea of a camera to dull the spirit. Which did not make it any less demeaning. The boy/man, an exquisite creature, for all his sartorial elegance and slim hairless body, as dumb as a fridge, had ended up kneeling between his legs. Using all his arts. Guy, by no means, an objective participant. He'd had to ask him to stop. The boy had offered to try other techniques. *Did he want to be bound?* The forfeit of his outrageous fee a small price to pay to be rid of him.

Eventually he flicked off the unwatched television, prepared to slope off to bed and tempt the gods of sleep. Reflexively switching on his mobile. Almost immediately it pinged into life. Three missed calls from Lasker. A voice message told him that Helen had had a relapse and been admitted to hospital. Asking him to call, it didn't matter at what time of night.

Already well past midnight. When he rang the number there was no reply. The phone went straight to machine.

fifteen

Eugenie

The girls dropped up at the bus stop, she started in on cleaning the house, furious with everyone: stacked the breakfast dishes in the dishwasher; picked up clothes in the girls' rooms and stuffed them in the washing machine (someone else, as it turned out, would have to hang them out); squirted some evil-smelling chemical around the inside of the toilet bowl, hardly believing its claims of biodegradability; did a pick-up in the living area and returned to scrub the toilet, wipe the sink, despair of the shower. Not done yet: going at the floors with the vacuum cleaner preparatory to mopping, the dog standing hang-dog on the veranda while the machine produced its industrial-level whine so she almost didn't hear the phone.

Joy, from the surgery. Eugenie glanced at the clock on the stove, past eleven – had it taken *that* long – panic rising that something had happened to one of the girls, that all her ugly thoughts about damp towels, abandoned knickers and used tissues and who got to do the shit work around here had brought catastrophe upon her house (when it hadn't even been them she was cross with) ready to drop everything and rush into town, forget any other ideas for the day.

It wasn't why Joy was calling.

'I thought I better ring,' she said, 'and let you know what Doctor Lasker said.'

A different type of panic threatening. Joy, she hoped – assumed – knew nothing about what had been going on. The emphasis on *had*.

'There was a girl in here first thing, looked like she was from the camp. Said her boyfriend was planning to do some damage to the creek. I don't know how serious it is. I tried calling Marcus but he must be out in the paddock. I thought I should tell someone. Just in case there's something to it.'

'What did she say?'

'Can't tell you much more than that. Something about the frogs? You could speak to Doctor Lasker about it.'

'Not sure I should do that. He'd be busy wouldn't he?'

'Oh, I think you'd find he had time to speak to you.'

Having to note that little gets past a practice manager.

'It'd be better to speak to the girl, wouldn't it? Do you have a phone number for her?'

'I couldn't give you that,' Joy said. 'You know that.'

Staring blankly out through the double doors to where the dog was lying by the railing, her big Labrador's head resting on the bottom row of wire as if the thin strand of stainless steel was a pillow. 'Let me think a minute. I'll call you back.'

Putting the phone down. The vacuum cleaner out in the centre of the floor; a basket of clothes waiting to be folded on a chair. The washing machine coming to a halt, announcing the end of its cycle by singing out what someone must have thought was a merry little tune; something to brighten a housewife's day. Barely a word from

David in all this time. Just a single email to say he'd be gone a while longer. No explanation. A surge now, at the thought of talking to Nick, not of panic, but *emotion*, which she almost permitted herself to feel before pushing it back down where it belonged, leaving in its wake an emptiness that felt like nothing so much as dread.

If it were to be done then better done soon.

She called Joy back, asked to be put through.

'Someone's just in there this minute,' she said. 'I'll get him to ring as soon as he's free. Shouldn't be long. You'll be there?'

Where else? Trapped, now, in a limbo of her own making, waiting for the phone to ring. She went to put the vacuum cleaner in the cupboard, but the hose and handle refused to cooperate, tumbling back out, twice. The third time she threw it in, slamming the door, cursing. The everyday resistance of inanimate objects. Everything too much. She'd made the mistake of going on social media at breakfast. Someone had posted a link to an interview with Guy Lamprey on the ABC. He'd been talking about the LNP Arts policy, part of his pitch for the Senate, talking up the trickle-down theory of economics when applied to the creative sector: *The Liberal Party has a plan for the economy. A strong economy means more money for the Arts. When people have disposable income they can afford …* Going on to talk about the dam with equal disregard for the truth: *The hydrology reports are in. They show this is an excellent place to build a dam. It's a great project. Great for the region, great for the economy, great for the environment.* The pro-dammers, some of them real people from Winderran, some of them trolls from who-the-fuck-knew-where, crowing in the comments below.

She went out onto the veranda and squatted down beside Leela. The dog rolling back against her as if understanding her need for touch. Eugenie gathering handfuls of the loose flesh around her neck, pushing her fingers through the fur.

Not having to wait long.

'Yes,' she said. 'How can I help you?'

'*You* called to speak to me.'

'I did. Yes.' A pause. 'I need to tell you straight up this is not about us.' Best to be clear. 'Joy told me you had a girl in there this morning.'

'That's true. But why did Joy tell *you*?'

'Because of my involvement with the dam.'

'What involvement is that?'

'What do you mean, what involvement? My involvement.'

'Which is?'

Dawning on her. 'You don't know?'

Extraordinary that he could be so ignorant of her role; that it might be possible for someone she'd been having sex with not to know the dam had been the central thing in her life for the last year. But then they'd never spoken of it. Their conversations, such as they'd been, had centred around how they came to be where they were, not their daily lives. As if there'd been a ban on the discussion of normal things. He was, of course, a doctor. It's not that they're not smart, just focused on their work to the point of autism.

Reason enough, if she needed one, to avoid him.

'Get Joy to tell you,' she said.

'I will. But, listen, I can take a break for a while at midday. Come around to the surgery. I'll tell you about it then.'

'Tell me now.'

'I'd like to see you face to face.'

'I need to know what this girl told you,' she said, claiming an authority he didn't recognise.

'Maybe,' he said. 'But, equally, I need to see you. I haven't heard from you since you texted to say you were coming round.' Declining to repeat the content of the message, for which she was grateful. 'All I've had is one cryptic text. Now, here you are again, because, apparently, you want something.'

'This is not a game,' she said.

'No, probably not. But I can't talk about it now anyway. I've a patient in just a second. Meet me at twelve. Pick me up outside the surgery in your car if it's important not to be seen with me. Okay?'

'Okay,' she said, because it was too difficult to say anything else, because so many permutations were slithering over and around each other in her tiny brain; the ramifications of seeing him, of not seeing him; the fact of the girl and what that might mean; whether or not his last comment should be construed as sarcasm or sensitivity. That, with just the sound of his voice, she was quivering, light-headed.

No time to deal with the washing in the machine. Only a few moments to shower, change out of her cleaning clothes into a blouse and a pair of long pants, something modest, to run a comb through her ridiculous hair, a bit of eyeliner and a touch of lippy and then into the car. Leela standing by the door wagging her tail and panting, incredulous that, having been used for support, she was to be left behind when the fun stuff happened. Up the dirt and onto the tar, left onto the main road, not letting thought interfere with what she could not deny was a sense of optimism, *I need to see you.* Rushing to him, under the assumption that if she was going to go she may as well go now. As if all this *stuff* that had been sitting beneath the surface these last days, squashed down, was tumbling out every which way, no delicacy to suppression, as they say, let one bit go and out it all comes. Pulling up on the street near the hospital, not so far from where she'd been the evening she saw him at the window. Turning on the radio but getting the midday news, a catalogue of dismay. Turning it off again, pushing her fingers through her hair, looking around to check if anybody was about and catching a glimpse, instead, of Nick, coming down the little concrete path, a slim neat concise man who she's made into something else in her mind.

Strapping himself in, saying, 'Where are we going, then?'

Another of the things she hadn't considered. She turned on the engine, headed back out of town. Not to her house, clearly. Somewhere else. Nick beside her in the car. Broaching the smaller things first.

'Do you really not know about me and the dam?'

'I asked Joy about it, as you suggested. On the way out. She told me a little. The briefest amount. You're really up there in it, aren't you?'

Letting that ride. 'So you're not some sort of spy for that arsehole Lamprey?'

'Gosh,' he said. 'What made you think that?'

'I didn't, not really. But he's a friend of yours, isn't he? He could have been using you without your even knowing.'

'I have been to his house for dinner,' he said. 'That's true. His wife is my patient. She's very ill. Dying if the truth be told. Don't say I said that. But I don't know him at all well. I don't get to socialise much. I don't really pay a lot of attention to what's going on. Perhaps that's obvious. What makes him an arsehole?'

Where to begin?

Forget about Lamprey, she may as well go through with it now that she'd started.

'But you are ...'

How might she put this? Fucking, sleeping with, *having* sex with?

'You are *in a relationship* with someone else?'

'No. I did have a loose arrangement with someone.'

'Until when?'

'The other night. When you said you were coming round. But didn't.'

'I did. I saw you at your kitchen window with a woman.'

Turning off onto the Elmhurst Road as if the car had only one route programmed into it. Taking the track up to the top of the hill above the quarry as a way to avoid that eventuality. Unlikely anyone would be there on a weekday at lunchtime. The best she could do. Stopping next to the little pavilion with its bleak tin roof and scarred picnic table. Very pleased to turn off the car, shaking with the tension. Neither of them interested in the three-sixty-degree view. Nick looking at some aspect of the dashboard while he told her about Nina.

'Did you have sex with her that night?'

He laughed. 'Do you have any right to ask that?'

'I've no idea. But I just did.'

'Well, in that spirit, I guess, yes, I did. If it makes any difference I didn't intend to. I'd asked her around to say I couldn't see her anymore because I was seeing someone else. Break-up sex, I think, is the technical term.'

Saying it brazenly, as if it was, if not *perfectly* okay, at least reasonable, which, she guessed, on some level, it was. She was married. She'd never asked him what his status was any more than he'd asked her about the work she was doing with the dam. Or if she slept with David, which, for the record she didn't, or not often. She couldn't remember the last time. She knew Nina, vaguely. Not someone she'd ever have thought herself in competition with. Too much make-up; tight clothes.

'I'm sorry if I've hurt you. I'm more than sorry. I'm devastated.'

She looked out the window at the view. Retreated, for a moment, to some quieter place where the noise of feeling that had been welling inside her since Joy had said his name could no longer be heard. Moreton Island out along the horizon, an attenuated stretch of low hills, bright sand dunes torn out of its forested banks, yellow, green, blue. The air sharply clear after the rain. Trying desperately to catch a breath, which is what her fucking father was always telling her to do. *Just breathe.* As if anyone had any choice.

'I'm infatuated with you,' he said. 'I can't think about anything else.'

Doing her best to ignore that. 'Tell me about this girl,' she said.

The story he told her about Ange coming in to the surgery giving her a measure of space to deal with her feelings. Or perhaps not, perhaps the story was part of the feelings, that it wasn't just that if he touched her she would have been lost, been anyone's, there, deliquescing in the car on the top of the world, but that the story made that okay, was part of them being together.

'You could talk to her yourself,' he said. 'I could call her. I'm her doctor. I could say there's someone who wants to talk to her.'

'Could you? I mean right now, here?'

'Yes. When I saw how important this was I put her number in my phone.' Hesitating. 'There's something more.'

'What?'

'Well I'm not sure how safe this all is.'

Telling her, then, what he'd somehow never managed to get around to mentioning. About driving up to Spring Creek camp to get Cooper and about the man he'd met there with the tattoos on his arms, the ex-soldier, who'd scared the shit out of him and was somehow tied up with this new threat; the explanation Cooper had given him about the nature of the training camp. The weight of the things Nick was saying – the hint of a larger world operating entirely independently of her and yet having influence in profound and fateful ways – enhancing the sense of being on the cusp of some important revelation, although, again, this could be no more than her hormones, activated by being with this man in the confined space of her car such that it was all but impossible not to touch him. Watching as he dug out his phone and started pressing buttons, swiping through screens, all the tedious technological wizardry that everyone takes for granted. Putting her hand on his on the phone before he could press the green one to dial, bringing his eyes away from the device and onto her, bringing him up against her, this brief tentative touch of his lips, a flutter of trepidation and desire, hers and his, breath mingling, pushing her fingers up into his hair and pulling him towards her, his mouth against hers, not letting him go now that she has him, his hands on her shoulders, inside her blouse, stopping kissing him so she can see what he's doing, watching him undo the buttons so he doesn't tear the cloth which is practical but really she couldn't care less. What was it she said before about the lack of delicacy in suppression? This is what she's been keeping down, or at least part of it, holding a lid on so effectively that she didn't even know she was doing it, maybe David was right about her frigidity, not in a sexual sense but in the way that she seemed to have an ability, sometimes, to cut herself off from things so essential to her true nature, although not anymore, not now in the car, watching him fumble with the buttons, taking over from him, leaning forward to put her arms behind her back to unclip her bra so that there she is, exposed, and there he is, kissing her naked breasts in the narrow space between her and the steering wheel and she's electric in the heat of the car, called by the deepest yearning, cursing herself for the stupidity of her modesty which means now she has to wrestle with jeans, to push them off so that she can climb across gear lever and handbrake, to get on top of him in the passenger seat, get him inside her in a car at midday at the lookout on top of the world, holding onto the handle above the door with one hand, the back of the driver's seat with the other, her knee jammed into the armrest, not caring a rat's if anyone comes, the only thing that matters now is him, in her, here, now, this must be what passion is like, this must be what they've been singing about all these years, that she's never known but knows now, needs to know and be known by. Pushing her hips down to meet him as he rises to her, saying his name aloud as her climax starts, catching her by surprise, that it might happen in a place like this, at a time like this, but more, that what she's feeling can, in fact, increase, that there are still more places to go. Opening her eyes and seeing him there below her, looking down at him looking up wide-eyed at her, and it being all right to be seen like that because he's right there too, no doubt about it, right there with her, going at it stroke for stroke, lunge for lunge, everything concentrated in his and her eyes, his cock and her cunt, everything, the whole fucking world laid out beneath them as she comes in the passenger seat of a Subaru with a man she barely knows but with whom she breathes the very same fucking air.

Across the road from the hospital the Council had constructed a little park with a small rotunda at its centre, the kind of thing more often found in the suburban parks of her childhood, left over from the time when brass bands played on Sunday afternoons. Doubtful that anyone had ever blown a note beneath its roof. This is where she has arranged to meet the girl, Ange, who'd said, on the phone, speaking in a broad accent, slow syllables, that she was still in town, 'Waiting for the pills to take effect, hey.'

Eugenie hadn't connected her to the woman who'd been swimming naked with the gormless man in the creek below *Roselea*, didn't even recognise her at first, coming towards her wearing a wrap-around top and a short denim skirt, her dreads tied back in a ponytail, giving emphasis to thick eyebrows and dark eyes. Dusty feet in sandals. Looking around as if to check nobody was in the bushes. Something a little cute about her, one of those small neat women who walk from the waist down, straight-backed, like a Scottish country dancer. A leather bag over her shoulder and a bottle in a brown paper bag in her hand, the paper pushed back from the top, like a wino, except it was cranberry juice, not port. A decade ago, so as to have something to do with her hands, she'd have lit a cigarette; instead she took a sip from the bottle.

'You were down the creek, hey?' Ange said. 'With that other woman, you know, the one who plants the trees. I don't mind talking to you.' When she'd been speaking to her on the phone, an unknown quantity, Ange had been scared the doctor had told the police.

Eugenie dressed again in her blouse, jeans and up-market sandals, her hair straightened as much as it ever could be, the man she'd just had sex with in her car now back over the road in his surgery with some patient or other while she was here as if nothing had happened. Except of course it had, she was redolent with it, it must be obvious to anyone who cared to look, which was maybe the case because Ange said, straight out, 'So, you and the doctor, hey, you're a thing?'

Perhaps she could smell the sex on her.

'No, of course not.' Denying him already.

'It's okay. I don't mind.'

'You're living out at the camp then?' Eugenie said.

'Was.'

'I thought … when we met you by the river …'

'Nah, couldn't hack it out there. Too rigid, you know? The place's run like an army camp, everybody has their jobs, like on a roster. You can't scratch yourself without getting up someone's nose. Can't say what you think. Has to be *on message*. I'm, like, a free spirit, you know? You can't tell me what to do. I'm staying with Will for a while. Not that it's much better there.'

'You want to sit?' Eugenie said, gesturing to the steps. Not sure of how one did this sort of thing. Settling on the top step, looking out across the grass to the trees on the bottom side of the park, the roofs of the houses that lead down into the town beyond. Ange resting against the newel across the way.

'Is Will the one who's going to do something to the creek?'

'Well … not him so much. I figure it's one of Jaz's things, but Will's part of it.'

'I don't understand why you'd want to tell me this. Isn't Will your boyfriend?'

'Yeah, see, that's the thing. I don't know if you'd call him my boyfriend. I mean we're, like, close. But I'm not sure it's serious. I met him over at the camp and, you know, one thing led to another and now I'm over there at his house, which isn't *his*, it's actually Jaz's and I'm not, like, so keen on *him*.'

'How come?'

'You don't know where you are with him. He's ex-SAS or some shit *and* he's got religion. Happy-clappy shit. Not a good mix, you know?'

'I don't, but okay.'

'I don't reckon he's any good for Will.'

'In what way?'

'Well, he's a randy bugger, for a start.'

'He made a pass at you?'

'He'd have me if he could, never mind Will. Had his hand up my skirt in the kitchen. I mean, right up. While Will's in the next room.' Telling Eugenie this in defence of her morals or of Will, except her outrage rang false, as if she was boasting about it at the same time, letting the world know that men can't resist her. Sitting there with her denim skirt riding up so there's an awful lot of olive-skinned leg on display. Eugenie's response confused by thoughts of Nina, which had to be so much crap after what just happened with Nick, it was just some deep ingrained feminine anxiety bubbling up, making any other woman a threat when she's found a man of value. Although you'd have to say Nick's history didn't help.

'Did you tell Will?'

'Hey, I like Will too much for that. He loves this guy. Worships him. That's why I think he's bad for him. Will'd do anything for him. He doesn't see that sort of shit, he's like *innocent*.'

'And this is why you want to tell me about it?'

'I guess. But it's the frogs, too. They're like *endangered*, aren't they? I mean it's not cool, is it? These guys don't see that, it's not on their radar. I don't want anything to happen to Will, you know? I thought maybe if I told someone I could make it stop.'

Fidgeting. Picking at her fingernails. A *flibbertigibbet*. Her nan's word surfacing out of nowhere. Ange took another drink of juice, finished what was in the bottle. Dug around in her bag for some lip salve. Glanced up at Eugenie. 'What're you going to do?' she said.

'Call some people, I guess. Pick up my kids from school, meet with a few people. What about you?'

'Can I come?'

'Where to?'

'Wherever it is you're going? Just don't want to go back there right now.'

She left Ange in the rotunda and went up to the car, made some calls. Told those she could reach that something had come up and they needed to meet, asked them to tell the others, not meaning to be overly secretive but unwilling to discuss it on the phone. Feeling stupid about it but saying it just the same. Caught in the flow of the strange girl's conspiracies.

She drove into town and dropped Ange at the ice cream shop, telling her she'd be back in a little while, then raced to the school to catch Emily before she took the bus. She didn't trust Ange but she was unable to think of a decent reason to refuse her. Better, in some ways, to know where she was.

Not that she needed to have rushed for Emily's sake. Even after driving through school-time traffic and circling for a park, she was still obliged to stand outside the school gates for ten minutes, watching the children come out. Not her favourite place. Never mind the history of her own education and all its attendant furies, it also meant she had to wait amongst the gaggle of mothers that concentrated itself into little rural/regional cliques, arms crossed firmly over ample bosoms, dressed in slacks and flats, defining who was in and who was out of their groups just as they'd always done, in the same way they had when they were in the schoolyard. Even within the glow of her tryst with Nick she still couldn't curb her critique, remained stubbornly guilty of a failure to imagine any of these women possessed of the capacity to feel what she'd just felt; as if the choice to wear cheap clothes and eat crap food or adhere to Right-wing politics indicated someone's aptitude for love.

Emily all but the last child to emerge, behind even the stragglers, shirt tails out, hat squint, socks around her ankles, unwashed face transforming when she saw her mother. Dropping her bag to come into her arms as if they'd been apart for days not six or seven hours.

'I thought we could go get an ice cream,' Eugenie said. 'If you'd like.'

Emily nodded, as yet unable to speak, still caught in what Eugenie couldn't help but think of as the enlarged joy of the moment. Her daughter possessed of a thespian's world view, given to producing dramatic gestures which in themselves provoked more emotion. The extraordinary fragility of this girl who lived in a world only peripherally connected to things: shoes, hats, bags and coats, meals, all being secondary to whatever was going on in her mind at any given moment, even more than was usually the case for a ten-year-old. Nothing to do with intelligence. She was smart, emotionally as well as intellectually, more so even than her sister, but little drawn to other children's activities. Preferring her own complex imaginary world. Never going to fit in well.

Taking her hand and making for the car as the long line of school buses fired up their big diesels and lumbered out into the shuffling cars. Asking questions about her day but not getting answers and not expecting to.

'Where's Sandrine?' Emily asked.

'She's walking into town with friends. We'll meet her there. We've got to go out to Lindl's.'

'Why?'

'Oh, just dam stuff,' she said.

Making as little of it as possible. Negotiating the clogged main street, finding another park, getting her daughter out of the car again, none of which happened quickly. From a short distance away she saw Ange at one of the café tables, bent over her phone, texting, looking more frail than she had in the rotunda, or for that matter at the creek. Younger, more vulnerable, almost childlike. The thought coming to mind unbidden that this was the real Ange, that, unobserved, the girl wasn't yet anything, was, in fact, only a mirror for other people's projections.

As soon as Ange saw them, though, she bounced up, smiling, full of dark piratical energy.

Eugenie offered to buy her an ice cream. 'My shout,' she said. 'We're having a treat.'

'Sure,' Ange said. 'I like treats.'

Coming inside with them to choose flavours. Emily shy of the wild girl, keeping her mother's body between them at all times, behaviour which might have led Eugenie to some conclusion about Ange's trustworthiness only that Sandrine appeared, coming into the café with two friends. Within moments she had struck up some sort of rapport with Ange. The friends drifting away. As if just the existence of a being such as Ange, with her airy speech and dreadlocks was a fascination.

Outside at the table, eating their ice creams, Eugenie told

Sandrine they were going out to Lindl's, expecting resistance.

'What's happening?' Sandrine asked.

'Nothing, we're just going there for dinner. Ange is going to come along.'

'Cool.'

sixteen

Will

She's not returning messages. It's late afternoon and he's still not heard a word. Must have sent her twenty fucking texts. Still pissed at him. When he dropped her at the doctor's they were having the worst kind of fight, about all the usual shit. When Ange's not happy about something she just cuts him out. It's what she does. No fucking defence against it.

Now, when he could be out looking for her, he has Jaz, of all people, telling him what to do. *Pick the fucking drums up and reload. Try it again.*

They're doing a dry run in the paddock behind the house. Jaz's got them practising unloading the drums out of the ute, emptying them in the creek. You wouldn't think it'd be that fucking hard to manage. He and Damo are taking them from Ren who's swinging the bastards off the back of the ute while they catch them, pretend to open them and toss the lids in the back of the ute (there's nothing to be left behind, no drums, no lids, no fingerprints) lying them down, four at a time. They need to get as much of the stuff in the creek at one time as they can because that way they get a better kill. But also because while they do that, Jaz's going to be up at the house keeping anyone who's there busy, and time's going to be short and it's going to be dark. *This has to be surgical*, he says, *in and out, no fucking around*, but the drums are heavy and they've done it twice already. You can see why they might need to do it two times because there was a fucking mess the first time, all on top of each other, but a third time? It's hot and they're working without a break and the other two are just sitting there watching. And who is it that's telling them what to do? The very same fucker who caused the fucking blow-up in the first place. Who was into his girl in the kitchen that morning. Not that he's going to say shit about it. No point in that. Not now. But if it was any other cunt he'd have already decked him.

He'd driven down to Brissie to get her a couple of days before. She'd been in Sydney to see her mum. Hard to describe how good it felt to meet her at the airport. They'd talked most nights she'd been away, that's how serious it was, these calls which went on and on but were really just Ange jabbering on about her mum or her aunty Ann or her cousins and their babies and what all else. Will standing out the back of The House listening hard because it was her and he needed to hear her voice, even if she was telling him all kinds of shit, but also because he had to know if she'd been with someone else, couldn't live with the idea of it. Not a hint of it, though, just a selfie of her breasts (nothing more) for his pains, *to keep you interested*, she said, as if she really did miss him. When he looked at her beside him in the passenger seat of the Triton, her feet up on the dash, her skirt pushed up, he saw, again, just how fucking gorgeous she was. Sitting there with *him*. Coming to him like a kind of pain, which is how he knew it was real.

What? she said, looking back at him, reaching across to squeeze his balls, *D'you miss me then?* Resting her head on his shoulder as they waltzed on up the Bruce.

He drove her straight to the camp. Hadn't been there since she left. They went in her tent, neither of them giving a shit about it being musty from the rain.

That night, when they went up to eat, she put her arm through his and it felt as if she was actually *there*, she wanted him with her, even after they were done, even with other people about.

The 'kitchens' are just a machinery shed, four bays, three of them open on the front. Hay bales for seats, spread round upturned wooden cable rolls. Alt was in the closed section with the cooks when they lined up to get their food. Will saw him through the servery, saw him watching them. After a while he came over. Sat down. Nobody close by. Maybe that was coincidence.

'So, Will,' he said, 'you been away.'

'Yeah, but Ange is back see.'

'I do. I do. And you've got plans, have you?'

'Not so much, hey.' Nervous. Alt could make him feel like that pretty much anytime, but in this case he was thinking about the twenty drums he had in the back of the ute, wondering if maybe Alt had got wind of them. Jaz had given him the job of buying the stuff. He'd been to pool places and hardware stores all over the shop, from Noosa to South Brisbane, getting them one at a time, paying cash. He'd figured they were safe locked under the tonneau cover. Now he was thinking maybe he ought to have stored them back at The House.

'Just wondering. I wasn't sure we were going to see you again.'

'Yeah, well here I am.'

Alt glanced around the shed. Took out a packet of tobacco, rolled himself a cigarette. Taking his time. 'Here's the thing, Will,' he said.

'I like you. By all accounts you're all right with machines. I think I *understand* you. But I have to say I was glad we weren't seeing such a lot of you.'

'How's that?' Will said.

'We had a few complaints.'

Alt rolled very thin cigarettes. When he took a drag the thing all but disappeared.

'People round here aren't so keen on your attitude.'

'I haven't hurt anyone.'

'Scared the living shit out of some,' Alt said.

That would be this leatherworker dude. Before she went away. It wasn't like he did anything, didn't even touch him, just stepped in and looked at the guy. Not that it was the bloke's fault, he could see that. Ange did it. She didn't even know she was doing it. You asked her what she was up to and she said, *Nothing, I'm just talking to the guy, can't I talk to someone now?* like he was a fucking stalker when anyone could see she was putting out, shaking her head and twirling her hair and pushing out her tits, her shirt falling off, shorts so short you can see the cheeks of her bum, leaning in close, touching the bloke on the arm, you name it. When she does that it's like something in him just goes off. Like she needs protecting from herself. Like she needs protecting *for* him, but she says, afterwards, after he's stepped in, that she hates it, it's bullshit, she never wants to see him again, *I mean, what happens if one of these guys fights back? You gonna pull a knife on him?* and he doesn't have an answer to that, he says he's sorry, but it makes no difference. She's gone. Then later she comes back to him and says *she's* sorry, she doesn't know what it is, but it's like when there's something really good in her life she has to run away from it and she curls up next to him and says, *I like it that you care about me. Sometimes, though, I'm scared.* What about? he asks. *That you'll hurt me*, and he says there's no way he'd do that, no way at all, he's not his fucking old man.

'The thing is,' Alt said. 'I'm going to have to ask you to leave. I don't want to, but I have to. People don't want you round here.'

'What people?' Ange said, fired up. '*I* want him here.'

'Yeah, but that's not the point,' Alt said.

'It's exactly the fucking point,' she said. 'Can't I have a man visit me anymore? Is that what this is? Just because you're a bloke you have the right to decide who I'm fucking, is that it?'

Winding herself up. Loud. Embarrassing *him*. One for the books. Not a girl who likes being told what to do. 'You lot,' she said. 'You're all fucking blow-ins. Will's the only local in the whole camp but he's the one who has to fucking leave?'

'This isn't about where Will's from,' Alt said. Staying real calm.

'It's not?' Ange said. 'Who're you protecting the place for then? Eh?'

Will not able to speak in case he somehow screwed up the raid. But it was like getting kicked in the guts. Alt might've had fucked-up views about stuff but he'd liked him. Something real about the man. Like he really did understand. But when it came down to it an arsehole, same as the rest of them. Jaz was right. They didn't know shit about the way the world worked. Coming in and telling people who lived someplace what they should or shouldn't do on their land. Not even asking to see what people thought because they *knew* they were right. It was like what Damo said, *If we hadn't sold our land to these arseholes they wouldn't have a say in any of this shit.* Never mind the fucking hippies.

Ange wanted to keep on about it, but he blew it off. Said it was okay, he'd go.

'Well I'm going too, then,' she said. 'I'm not staying in this shithole.'

He took her back to The House. Left the tent and all the gear for another day. He'd never seen her so angry. Pissed at him, too. Letting him have it while they drove over there for not taking Alt on.

As soon as he stopped outside, but, she changed. 'You sure this is okay?' she said.

The boys were watching a film on the big TV, sound up loud. Ange kind of slipped in, like she was shy, took a chair at the back, out of the way. Not that they even seemed to notice, didn't want the film interrupted.

When it was over they wanted to know what was up. He told them he'd been kicked out.

'How come?' Ren said.

'Too fucking rough for these cunts. What d'you reckon, love?' he said, turning to Ange, getting a little smile out of her.

'Soon enough they'll get theirs,' Damo said.

'That's enough,' Jaz said.

'Birrup, birrup,' Ren said, making like a frog.

'I said that's fucking enough,' Jaz said.

No doubt about it, Ren could be a dickhead. Too much dope will do that every time.

What makes arseing about with the drums worse is Jaz has a couple of mates, Garry and Clive, up to help. They're sitting on the back veranda. In the shade, watching, offering fucking *advice*. Drinking cans of light though it's only four o'clock and you'd think with all the nonsense Jaz is putting them through alcohol would be off the table. Maybe Jaz doesn't get to tell everyone what to do.

These guys come up from time to time. Not together. Garry's a bikie. A big bloke, getting bigger all the time. He was with Jaz in Bosnia, collects weapons: guns, knives, swords, you name it. Making up for losing his hair by growing a beard and covering every bit of his skin in tatts. Clive's a skinny little fuck with a nearly shaven head and a way of talking out of the side of his mouth. Slowly. Garry likes to think he gives off this don't-fuck-with-me vibe but Clive's the one who has it. One of the things you learn quickly when you get in the army is who to avoid. Clive would be one of them. He works with Jaz in some way up at the camps, or he did until Jaz's troubles came up. They're going to drive the other vehicles.

'What's up with you, Will?' Garry yells out.

Will ignores him.

'You not speaking to me now?' Garry says.

'He's cunt-struck,' Ren offers.

'Shut the fuck up,' Damo says under his breath, for which Will's grateful. This is one of Garry's things, he likes to get a rise out of you. Will's not in the mood. He's close to hitting someone. The thing is, but, the more Garry sees he's getting somewhere the worse he gets.

'Who's the lucky girl, then?' he says. When Will still doesn't bite he says, 'Maybe it's the dog? You been getting into Damo's bitch have you?'

'Lay off it,' Jaz says to Garry.

They're loading the drums back in the ute again. All but done. 'You figure you can get this right now?' Jaz says to them.

'Who's paying for all this shit?' Garry says. 'You still on the government's tit?'

'Sometimes, Garry, you can be a fucking pain,' Jaz says.

'That's okay. I can take my bat and ball and be off home whenever you want. What's getting your goat now?'

'I never was on the government.'

'Technically.'

'Technically,' Jaz replies, 'is good enough for me.'

'So you're saying this one's on you?'

'I'm not saying anything,' Jaz says.

'Well you never fucking do, do you?' Garry says, shaking his head.

Clive's sitting on the arm of the sofa, cleaning his nails with the tip of his blade, his beer in a stubby holder beside him. The blade's a *Hissatsu Folder*. He showed it to Will before. Assisted opening, as they say. What they used to call a flick knife. He glances up at Will with those oval fucking eyes of his and then looks down again.

He'd taken her down the beach to get away from them all. She wouldn't do it in the sleep-out with him. *Someone might hear*, she'd said, never mind how horny they were, which meant he'd spent the night curled up against her in the single bed, barely sleeping, nursing a bone so hard it hurt.

In the car, but, just the two of them, she had her hand on his leg, all rosy-like in herself, happy. Still pissed about what had happened at the camp the night before. Taking it personally. 'Nobody says crap like that to my man,' she said. 'I tell you, that lot have shit for brains. They need to listen to some real people, not just their own fucking ideas. They need to listen to people from round here.'

As if she'd never lived at the protest camp. Going on about it so that he wanted to tell her what was in the back of the ute. Let her know they were onto it. That they had ways to get around these in-comers and their fucking ideas.

They went over the north shore, nobody around on a weekday, found a place out of the way to lie under the trees. Ange wanting it just as bad as him, it really had been a kind of shyness that kept her from it at The House. Sleeping on his arm afterwards, their skin prickly with the salt and the sun. Waking up and going for another swim. On the way back out to the ute he stopped for a shower. She asked for the keys and before he'd given it a thought he tossed them to her and she'd gone and unlocked the tonneau cover to throw her wet towel in the back.

'What's all this?' she said.

'Nothing,' he said, 'just some stuff I got for Jaz.'

She let it go, which wasn't like her, she wasn't one to let much go past, but he didn't think about it at the time, they were hot and hungry, going off to find somewhere to eat.

When they went to bed that night she was sore.

'I can't,' she said, 'It hurts when I pee. Maybe a bit of sand got in.'

He was up at five with the others for the stretches and the run, needing to work off some steam, putting up with their jibes for being exhausted from all the exercise he'd had during the night. Let them think what they want. Ange up and about in the kitchen when they got back, in her little denim skirt and some sort of wrap-around that left her belly bare. The four of them coming in with this kind of wave of testosterone, big men in the small room with her in the middle looking at them over the rim of her coffee mug, ooh-ing and aah-ing at the answers Damo or Ren or even Jaz, or maybe Jaz especially, gave to the questions she asked about their routine. Lapping up the attention.

He went off to shower. Holding it down, telling himself to trust her, because he knew she hated it, he fucking hated it himself. But when he came back out – not sneaking or anything – he just opened the door and there they were, the two of them, alone in the kitchen. Ange in the same place as before, back to the bench, hands resting on its edge, but now Jaz was right beside her, all over her, eating her up. You could see it, clear as if it was written. Ange looking up at him. Fucking purring. Jaz stepped away. Maybe he'd heard the door open. He didn't turn around to look at Will, he just went over to the sink, as natural as you like, and poured the last of his coffee out. It was the way he did that, more than anything, that clinched it for him, made it certain that Jaz had a hard-on for her.

He went into the sleep-out, wrapped in his towel. Shaking with it. Never mind that Jaz had been the one insisted she leave that day – told Will to arrange it because she couldn't be at The House because of the raid – Will knew what he'd seen. He rooted around for some clothes, but when he found them he didn't know what

280

to do with them, just stood there, looking down at the bed where she'd been with him these last two nights, not fucking him because she was sore, or because someone might hear and that someone was Jaz. The two parts of his life that had started to make any fucking sense, to make any of it fucking worthwhile, out there, in the kitchen, *together*.

He wanted to break something, rip stuff off the wall. Pull the fucking cupboard over. Punch something. Scream. Curl into a fucking ball. This is the kind of shit that always happens. Stuff gets dangled in front of him just so it can get pulled away at the last minute. It's happened before, time and again. Someone else always gets the things that were meant for him.

But fucking *Jaz*.

Ange came in. On her way to do something. It seemed he hadn't moved. Was still holding his fucking underpants like he was strangling them. She put her arm around him as she went past, ran the flat of her hand across his belly. All he could do not to grab hold of her. Shake it out of her.

'You all right?' she said.

He nodded.

'You don't look fucking right,' she said, and laughed.

'What d'you want?' he managed to say.

'I reckon I need to see a doctor,' she said. 'D'you know one in town? It really fucking hurts now when I pee.'

On the way into town she asked him again. *You right?* Because he was only just holding it together and it must've been obvious. With her like that in the car he couldn't keep it in anymore. He told her what he'd seen. She wouldn't have a bar of it. *Sometimes,* she said, *you are so fucked up. I wasn't doing anything. Nothing. I'm drinking my coffee and your friend's fucking all over me, asking me this and that. All kinds of shit. Nothing to do with me. You got a problem with him? Talk to him. Don't fucking come to me about it. Be fucked if I know why I waste my time hanging around with you and your fucked-up friends.*

They're all on the veranda. Everyone has a beer except Jaz, but then Jaz never drinks. 'You got your girl sorted?' Jaz says.

'What's it to you?' Will says.

'Miaow,' Garry says.

He and Jaz both look at him. He holds his hands up in mock surrender.

'Is there a problem?' Jaz says to Will.

'Just surprised you need to ask,' Will says. The aggro in him real high now. He's just about ready to take Jaz on, never mind all his supposed murdering skills.

'How's that?' Jaz says, as if he really doesn't understand.

Will doesn't say anything. He fucking can't.

'I just asked if she's found somewhere to stay, is all,' Jaz says. 'Didn't like to have to kick her out. I know you like her.'

Jaz's very fucking calm. Trying to find a way to talk him down but it's just making it worse. The other four watching, listening real close. For some reason Will feels like Clive is the one he has to speak to. That Clive's on his side. Jaz is the one in the wrong, all the fucking way down.

'But then, you know, also,' Jaz says, 'I was wondering who she'd been talking to?'

'What's that supposed to mean?' Will says.

'I'm just wondering if you've told her anything,' Jaz says. 'You know, about what we're doing?'

Turning it around. In a couple of words. Just like that. Making him think maybe he'd read the signs wrong, that when he saw Jaz in the kitchen he wasn't into her, he was interrogating her. That maybe she'd said something to him about what she'd seen in the ute. Some stupid question about the drums. Not without the fucking realms.

'Nothing. I haven't told her anything,' he says.

'That's good, then.'

Maybe this was why Jaz was being so fucking pissed with them during the dry run.

'What did she say to you?' Will asks.

'Nothing.'

'You boys done squabbling?' Clive says, butting in. He has that little smile of his on his face. The one which lets you know he knows he's putting the knife in but because he's smiling you can't say shit. If you say something he's going to stick it further in and twist. Not so different from Garry after all. 'You gonna tell us what we're all doing tonight, then?' he says.

Jaz stands up, shakes himself off. Like a dog out of a creek.

'Right,' he says. 'Now, this is the sitcho.'

Will leans in to listen, but he's not hearing. Jaz is talking about effective action, about surgical fucking strikes. If Will's wrong about what the two of them were doing in the kitchen then he's pissed Ange off for nothing. Maybe pissed her off so badly she won't come back. That's the thing with her, you never know. Which means he's fucked, completely and utterly fucked. Only himself to blame. The reason there's nothing good in his life's because, like she said, he's screwed up. Because he's nothing, never going to be anything at all.

But then again, maybe he *was* right about what he saw. It's not like Jaz is going to tell him he wants to fuck her. It's not like Jaz is going to own up to any laying on of hands. Maybe, too, she did think more about the drums than she let on. There's another fucking thought. Maybe he should come clean and tell Jaz she saw them yesterday. But that would mean calling it all off. Not getting to put it to those arseholes at the camp. To the whole of fucking Winderran. The thoughts spinning in his mind, round and round, none of them better than the other, nothing he can do about any of them, but none of them good for him either, and the anger that's been with him all day comes back to the surface again. The anger feels like his only fucking friend. He'll do this thing with Jaz tonight and he'll try not to take a swing at any of these cunts he's along with, but in the morning he'll piss off, he'll just get in the ute and go. If Ange's there she can come with him, if not, then too bad. That's what he thinks. He thinks he hasn't got any fucks left to give.

seventeen

Eugenie

Lindl was coming in from the paddock when they arrived, drawn up by the sound of the cars, demanding to know what the fuss was about and, in the same breath, typically, announcing she'd make scones, asking the girls if they'd like to help. Ange somehow including herself in this formula, as if the difference in age between her and everyone else relegated her a place at the children's table.

'I could help do that if you like,' she said. 'I mean, if you want to talk to the others ...'

'Well, that'd be nice,' Lindl said, pulling jars out of the pantry, clearing a space on the bench.

They *were* older. In the end only five people gathered around the table on the veranda – herself, Marcus, Lindl, Geoff and Alt. Everyone else either too busy or become disinterested, the tensions within the group starting to affect participation. Eugenie the youngest of their makeshift committee by a couple of decades. Not something she'd previously paid much attention to. Marcus fussing about with wine and glasses, arguing with Lindl as to whether it

285

should be wine or tea. Geoff, in an apparent attempt to smooth over this minor domestic, launching into a convoluted story about drinking at inappropriate hours during his early years at CSIRO. His voice quavering. Probably no coincidence he'd spent his life up to his waist in watercourses. Alt in his usual position over by the railing, watching, holding his peace, smoking one of his hand-rolled cigarettes, one of the few remaining martyrs to the cause. When Ange came out behind Lindl with the biscuits and cheese Alt nodded to her, saying only her name by way of greeting. No love lost there, it seemed.

Eugenie holding off until everyone was settled. Telling them what she'd learned.

'How do they even know about the frogs?' Geoff asked.

'Everyone knows about your frogs, Geoff,' Alt said, giving one of those barks that served him in place of a laugh.

'How come?' Geoff said, not amused.

'Word gets round.'

Neither Lindl nor Eugenie choosing to remind Marcus about the meeting with Ange and Will down by the creek.

'I've only sent the preliminary findings to the Minister, the report's not published until next month. It's supposed to be under wraps.'

'Supposed to be,' Alt said. By choice he dressed in a weird suffusion of Indian garb, American *and* subcontinental, as if attempting to correct historical errors, loose drawstring pants and a collarless working-man's shirt, a soft leather waistcoat with tassels on the shoulders, his hair cut short except for a small braid at the back with coloured thread woven into it, offset by a rather beautiful tattoo of a beast eating its tail that ran around his bicep. Important not to be confused by appearances, he was a man of some authority, a Canadian–Australian who'd worked on more environmental campaigns than she could count. His attention now

286

focused on the story Ange had told her about the drums in the back of Will's ute.

'What do you reckon he's got there?' he asked Geoff. 'Arsenic? Cyanide? I mean if they're pouring that sort of shit in the creek they're going to kill everything.'

Geoff shook his head, dismayed at this show of ignorance of what he regarded as basic science. 'You don't need things like that to kill them,' he said. 'Which doesn't mean they mightn't try, of course, but you'd have trouble buying them in quantity. It's actually pretty easy to wipe out amphibians. Some of the algaecides on the market would effectively kill every frog in a creek.'

'Algaecides?' Eugenie said.

'Pool cleaner,' Marcus said.

'Copper sulphate normally, but also lo-chlor,' Geoff said. 'You can buy it pretty much anywhere. The thing about algaecides is that they're virtually untraceable in flowing water. I don't know the exact quantities you'd have to use, but I wouldn't have thought you'd need much, a couple hundred litres maybe, and you'd get a massive kill. What's more, you'd never know what caused it, where it came from or anything.'

'Even after this rain?' Marcus said.

'Well, I don't know,' Geoff said. 'Certainly the more flow you've got the more you'd have to use. But because the water's up the vertebrates will be *in it*, if you get my meaning.'

'I wouldn't put it past them,' Alt said.

'The thing with these frogs is ...' Geoff said, starting in with an explanation of receptors and non-competitive inhibitors in the family *mixophyes*, the sort of thing which, after a year of campaigning, could make Eugenie's ears start to bleed. Fortunately, though, redirected by a question from Marcus about chains of approval for his research paper.

'The thing is,' Geoff said, bringing himself round. 'If I know what algaecides can do, it's almost certain others do, too. I think it even says it on the label.' Pausing for effect. 'But you understand, if my research ever reaches Corwen's desk it's going to put a halt on the whole project. Corwen can't override the EPBC.'

Eugenie wondering aloud about this, the importance academics such as Geoff and Marcus put on documents like the *Environment Protection and Biodiversity Conservation Act*. As if bits of paper had real weight in the world.

'But they do,' Alt said. 'These bastards, no matter how corrupt they are, want all the documentation correct. They'll do anything to get power and hold onto it, as long as it has some basis in law. There's to be no comebacks later if things go against them.'

'This is only *my* research,' Geoff said, 'The team who did the environmental impact assessment found nothing. If the Commonwealth decide they can't ignore me – and that's a big if – and if they follow up by sending someone here to see this population of frogs and, well, they aren't *there* ... well ... we'd be *fucked*, wouldn't we?' The obscenity clumsy and unusual coming from him, an indication of how strongly he felt.

'Even Guy Lamprey wouldn't kill off an endangered species,' Eugenie said.

'Lamprey mightn't know anything about it,' Marcus said. 'And it wouldn't be the first time it's happened. There was a mine in Virginia that was going to be stopped because of some kind of shrew. The company got around that by simply killing it off.'

'When a project's worth billions, people'll do all kinds of shit,' Lindl said. 'After all, it's only a fucking frog.'

Now everyone had started.

'The trouble is we don't know what they're going to do, or when they're going to do it,' Marcus said.

'Ange seems to think it's tonight,' Eugenie said, craning her neck to see into the kitchen where the hippie girl was rolling out dough with her daughters. Sandrine so ready to be influenced. Possibly there were worse role models. Eugenie just couldn't think of any right then.

'So, what d'you suggest we do?' Geoff said.

'*We're* not going to do anything,' Lindl said. 'We're going to call the police.'

'And say exactly what?' Marcus said. 'That someone says someone else's going to do something to the creek, on the basis of the fact she saw some unidentified drums in the back of a ute?'

'Well it's a start, isn't it?' Lindl said.

'The police won't be interested. You know that,' Geoff said, full of surprises this afternoon. Eugenie glanced at Marcus to see his reaction but could detect none. Maybe there were hidden depths in Geoff she didn't know about. 'This is one of the government's pet projects. D'you really think they're going to post officers here to protect a creek they want to dam? On the say-so of a green group?'

'But we can try, can't we?' Lindl said. 'I mean *look* at us.'

Five people around a table on the wide veranda of a Queenslander, wine and cheese spread out before them. A tiny group of men and women opposed to a dam. There must be a thousand groups like them at any given moment across the country. Older people, generally. Meeting on the second Tuesday of the month in each other's kitchens and old Scout Halls, doing publicity stunts, speaking to the media, writing letters, calling politicians. They weren't soldiers. The only thing they were good at was talking.

'The way I figure it,' Marcus said, standing up and moving things around on the table, drawing an imaginary map of the creek amongst the glasses and plates, 'in this weather, if they want to get twenty-litre drums down to the water they'll need a four-wheel drive. Even then they've got to be on a track. You put a wheel off road at the moment and you're in trouble, doesn't matter what kind of vehicle you're in. There's only three places where they can get access to this stretch of creek by road: the camp, our driveway, and the track that runs along the fence on Mal Izzert's place. Well there's Mal's road too, but to get to it you've got to pass through the farm. I'd doubt anyone's going *there*.'

'You're enjoying this,' Lindl said. 'Aren't you? You men. I see you. You're getting all fired up about it. It's like an episode of *Dad's Army*.'

'We're just facing up to the problem,' Marcus said, affecting to ignore the *Dad's Army* bit but clearly offended. 'This is our creek we're talking about. We have to protect it.'

'Seal the borders!' Lindl cried out. 'Shut down the airports! Call out the National Guard!' Flushed and infuriated, some hidden tension in their marriage suddenly on display.

Alt raised a hand. 'Listen, Lindl's right, we need to contact the police, at least tell them our suspicions. But Geoff's right too, they're not likely to do much. What we can do is keep a watch on the creek, give them a call if something happens. What d'you reckon Lindl? Would that make you feel better?'

'Don't fucking therapise me, Alt. This isn't about me *feeling* anything.'

'I'm not trying to, I'm just alert to your concerns.'

'My concerns are that you old farts are going to get yourselves hurt,' she said.

'Fair enough.' Taking a breath. 'But listen, I've got a few people I trust at the camp. Not all of them are as old as us. We can set lookouts at various points.'

'What will they do if someone comes?' Lindl said. 'Take it up to them? Armed with scythes and pikes?'

'Make a phone call,' Alt said. 'We can all gather at one place pretty quickly. I don't figure anyone's going to want confrontation. And if someone does turn up we'll know they're planning something … we can work on that. Take some licence plate numbers, stir things up a bit.'

'If that's what they do,' Geoff said.

'Well we don't know, do we?' Marcus said.

'It could be nonsense. This girl,' Alt said, glancing towards the kitchen, 'she's not a reliable person.'

'There's an understatement,' Eugenie said, quietly.

'But we have to do something, don't we?' Marcus said, still in field-marshal mode. 'You go back to the camp, Alt. I figure the rest of us can stay here. Keep an eye on things. Call us if you hear anything.'

'What about Ange?' Alt said.

'What about her?' Marcus said.

'I think it'd be better if she stays here.'

The late afternoon sun burnishing the ridges. Everything lush and green, the sound of the creek filling the valley. It might rain for two months during the wet season – until just about every bit of ground was a bog and everything was starting to rot – but here was the upside: when the sun eventually came out you could feel the growth as a tangible force.

She walked with Alt down to his truck. When they were out of earshot he told her his part in Ange's departure from the camp. 'I wasn't so happy having Will round the place,' he said. 'That house he's staying in, I've heard of it. The man, Jaz, *is* ex–special forces, she's right about that, highly decorated, got a Star of Gallantry in Bosnia. Runs training camps in the bush back of here, amongst other things. All very hush-hush. So much so I could find out very little, even from *my* sources.'

'What sort of camps?' she asked, disingenuous.

'On the surface they're ReachOut schools for rich kids. Church-based.'

'But what are they really?'

'Can't help you there.'

'But what d'you *think*? Is it,' she asked, not happy even saying the word, 'something to do with *terrorism*?'

'You don't call it that when it's a program supported by the government, the private sector *and* the churches.' Raising an eyebrow. 'If you ask me it's a training ground for some sort of militia. But for what or whom, I don't know.'

They were out under the big Moreton Bay. Alt's truck a battered old-model Hilux, peeling stickers on the back window, *Save the Tarkine, No to James Price, Lock the Gate*. A catalogue of campaigns. He put his foot up on the bull bar, stretched out his leg.

Only a few months ago a conversation like this would have been inconceivable. Not just the content of what Alt was saying, but her involvement. She had that sense again of there being larger forces at play. It seemed she'd made the mistake of believing she was at the centre of her own life.

'So you're saying there's a real threat here?' she said.

'I don't know. Maybe. Without going into too much detail I'd say these boys present the clearest danger right now. The tactical use of violence. I thought if you're with Ange this evening you could keep your eye on her. Anything you find out might be useful.'

She wondered, not for the first time, what Alt meant by 'his sources'. Where, indeed, Alt came from with all his unusual skills.

He clapped a hand on the bonnet, ready to go. 'It's one of the benefits of this kind of work,' he said. 'Sometimes when you're dealing with a local issue you get to cause serious irritation to powerful people.'

'And that's a good thing?' Eugenie asked.

'Of course it is. It's not worth doing this stuff if you're not making waves.'

~

Lindl was back in the kitchen again, cleaning up. She asked Eugenie if they'd stay for dinner.

'We are horribly spoiled by you. My children and me,' she said.

'It's something I like to do. We miss having children around.'

'Are you okay?' she asked. 'I saw you during the meeting. I didn't say anything, but I saw.'

The remains of the scones, poor misshapen things, on a baking tray on the kitchen bench, her girls now outside at the table where the meeting had been, the hippie chick looking over Sandrine's shoulder at her homework. Emily watching with a kind of awe, seduced by her older sister's conversion to the cult of Ange.

'You know how this sort of thing affects me,' Lindl said, turning to put things in the fridge, talking into its interior, to the shelves laden with half-used jars, as if what she was saying had no importance. 'Marcus loves it, though. The battle. You can see that, can't you? I mean, he says he hates it, but that's for show. Under all that Left-wing pacifism beats a deeply competitive heart. What he doesn't get is that it's the wrong fight; he's taking on people who don't play by the rules.'

'I'm not sure *any* of us know what the rules are.'

'Same as they've always been,' Lindl said. She looked out towards the veranda. 'She's a curious bird, isn't she?'

'Yes,' Eugenie said, amused by this archaic description. 'Although for myself I thought some small animal.'

Lindl laughed. 'A vole?'

'I'm not sure what a vole is. Something from *Wind in the Willows*?'

'You're right, probably not sexy enough. I'd say she's not what she seems. Which is not necessarily a bad thing, but might be.'

'A bit of a mixture, then,' Eugenie said.

'It's possible she doesn't know herself,' Lindl said. 'She's very young, of course. God knows it took me long enough. Some girls never seem to get the power of their sexuality, do they? They kind of sail through as if all the attention's their birthright, getting a shock when the men throw themselves out of their cars onto the street.' Laying out vegetables on the island bench next to a cutting board. 'Ange's one of the ones who both get it and don't, at the same time, if that makes any sense. She goes around milking it for all it's worth while pretending not to know what's she's doing. She's what they used to call *naïf*. I was watching her before, when she was in here with the girls. I think I'd like to paint her. It's not something I feel like doing very much these days, but there's something about her I'd like to capture which might come to light under paint. She does that to you, doesn't she?' Looking up at her. 'I suppose we're all attracted to the damaged ones.'

Breaking up a corm of garlic, starting to peel the cloves and slice them fine, one way and then the other. Always 'throwing something together'. Her hair up in a swirl on the top of her head, a confection so casual and yet so confident, the kind of thing Eugenie would never have been able to do in a million years, not just because of her curls. The remains of the beautiful woman she'd been. A strange thing to think because she was still beautiful. Just older. The perennial strand come loose. Eugenie wanted to reach over and tuck it behind her ear.

'It was you I was interested in,' Eugenie said.

'My damage? Nobody needs to know about my insecurities,' Lindl said.

'Your friends, *I*, I might *want* to know. It might help to talk about them.'

'I don't think so. You're much more interesting.' Squatting in front of the oven to fiddle with its dials. 'How's it going with the doctor?'

'Now you're definitely changing the subject,' Eugenie said, desperate to deflect the question herself. What could she possibly say? Tell her friend where she'd been at lunchtime? She didn't think so.

They played Scrabble. Ange claimed not to know the game but when teamed up with Sandrine they wiped the table clean. Emily supposedly in cahoots with her mother but in reality just snuggled in her arms, barely even willing to go with Lindl to shut up the chooks.

Eugenie excused herself and took Emily off to bed, risking falling asleep by lying next to her in what used to be – still was even though she'd been gone a year – Elianor's room, with its girly things on shelves and walls, brand-name stickers half-torn off the timber chest of drawers, a poster of two surfers looking at a sunset, another of Beyoncé, the singer, in a skin-tight lamé pantsuit, pushing forward her breasts at the same time as she pulled back her arse; presenting from both ends. A popular image that Eugenie disliked even more than it deserved because it seemed to sum up so perfectly the struggles ahead of the delicate girl in her arms, a girl out of step with the world and yet already her own person.

Emily burrowing into her shoulder. Eugenie rocking her a little, whispering sweet nothings. But not a good mother all the same. Already planning, it seemed, to spend more time with Nick, lots of time with Nick.

After her daughter dropped off she stayed a while longer, staring at the ceiling. Letting the day wash over her. Listening to the sounds in the other room. Sandrine's high excited voice. Thinking about the odd way Geoff and Marcus responded to Ange. What Lindl had said about the girl. These old men with, you'd have to think, no further interest in young women, behaving like fools; as if in the presence of some primal feminine force. Something *she* clearly lacked, or if she did possess, was not aware of how to use. Which made her the first in Lindl's categories. The thought slipping into her mind that it was by no means certain a man like Nick would be drawn to her … taken by a wash of both gratitude and trepidation at that; but then it might just have been the power of Beyoncé on the wall.

~

It was after midnight when they heard the motors. Both girls long asleep, the five adults spread around the lounge, cups of herbal tea in hand, the Scrabble board abandoned on the low table between them with its curious matrix of words, CREEK and SLANT and QUIET, the wonderful vowel-employing but hardly game-winning APOGEE. Ready for bed but not yet gone.

Several vehicles, all of them loud, coming down the track.

Marcus up and out the door. Telling Lindl to phone Alt.

Eugenie slipped in to look at the girls. All silent. Toe to toe with each other in the single bed. Sandrine with a grave expression on her face, as if struggling to understand something. Emily, always too hot at night, the covers thrown off, arms akimbo, t-shirt stuck to her skin.

She pulled the door shut as quietly as she could.

Lindl was by the phone, a look of consternation on her face. 'There's no dial tone,' she said.

Geoff standing in the circle of comfortable chairs. Suddenly very old. Fragile. Which she guessed he was.

'It's not just the power?' Eugenie asked. 'Do you have a plug-in phone?'

'The power's still on,' Lindl said.

Obvious now she said it.

Marcus came back inside. Closed the door. Stood with his back to it. 'They're coming here,' he said. 'Turn out the lights.'

'The phone's dead,' Lindl said.

'They'll have cut the line at the top of the hill,' he said. 'No mobile reception down here. They'd know that.' Fear in his voice.

The lights going out.

'Keep back from the windows,' he said. 'Don't let them see you. Keep low.'

The motors throttled down as they reached the causeway. Big diesels burbling. Not stopping. Coming on up the rise towards the house. Headlights sprayed across the windows. At least three vehicles. Spotlights mounted on roll bars above the cabins, very bright. The vehicles beneath them rendered invisible. They swung off the road into the paddock, swaying on the wet ground. Their lights coming directly onto the house. Music blaring. Something with screaming guitars. So loud she could hear it over the motors. A strong bass note, heavy metal music. The white light shining in through the uncurtained windows. Square luminous patterns thrown onto the ceiling. Turning the house upside down.

Eugenie sidled around the walls. She wanted to be back in the girls' room. She wanted to see they hadn't woken up. To hold them. Someone was moving across the room.

Ange was walking towards the door.

'Get down!' she said, yelling a whisper.

Ange turned to her. 'It's okay, I know these guys, I'll talk to them,' she said.

Illuminated by a beam of light. Wearing a weird combination of innocence and gravity, a belief in her own inviolability so formidable it affected everyone around her.

'No,' Marcus said. 'You can't go out there.'

He was still facing into the room. He went to Ange, put his hands on her shoulders and pushed her down onto the floor, out of the light.

'I'll go,' he said.

'No you will not,' Lindl said. 'I won't let you.'

'I'll be damned if I'm going to let them intimidate me.'

He went back to the door. It occurred to Eugenie that it was Ange's example that was driving him, but she repressed the thought.

A gun went off. Five, perhaps six shots. Eugenie dropped to the floor herself. Crawled crabwise towards the girls. Making it to the passage. Leaning back against the wall. The shots, she thought, weren't anything. Guns fired into the air. Designed to scare them. It was working. She couldn't remember being more scared in her life.

A shadow coming towards her. She recoiled, but it was Geoff. He stood over her.

'This is a diversion,' he said.

He seemed in control of himself. Excited if anything. She could hear his breath, short and harsh. 'There'll be others down at the causeway. We need to go there. We'll go out the back.'

Making his way along the hall, turning into the laundry. Not waiting. She stood. Followed him. This was the effect of people who believed in themselves. She ran her fingertips across the closed door of the girls' room, as if to, what, she didn't know, bless them, lock them in safely, communicate her love.

Geoff was holding the back door open. He leant in to whisper in her ear, although with all the other noise such precautions were superfluous. 'We'll go around the sheds,' he said. 'Marcus will keep them up at the house.'

'How?'

'Talk to them.'

As if this was something they'd discussed.

Geoff already moving, making his way around the back of the shed in the ambient glow of the spotlights, circumventing unidentified pieces of machinery. She behind him. The grass long. A sense of dread in every step. She didn't even have a torch. The outbuildings oddly shaped in the referred light.

Past the end of the shed there was only the track. The causeway a hundred metres downhill. The lights from the vehicles on their left side, behind them. Another vehicle was stopped, facing away from them, on the far side of the creek. Headlights off. At least two men moving around behind it. Their actions lit by head torches.

'Get their number plate,' Geoff said. 'Okay? I'll do the rest.'

Simply going on down. Fuelled by God knows what rage. Threat to his frogs, perhaps, accumulated anger at the calculated destruction of everything he'd devoted his life to. She didn't know. Only that she was a pace behind him, similarly charged. At ten metres away he turned on a big maglite torch. She didn't even know he had it with him. Shone it on the men.

'What d'you think you're doing?' he called out, no quaver in his voice now.

There were three men in t-shirts and board shorts. Young men. They had several twenty-litre plastic drums already on the causeway, lying on their sides. Liquid spilling into the creek. White drums with green labels.

The men frozen, caught in the light. Geoff's torch so much brighter than their own.

'You stop that. You're breaking the law.'

Going right on down. Grabbing the closest container and standing it up.

She thought she recognised one of the men. The boy from the creek. Ange's Will.

She was about to say something normal to him, like, *Hey! What d'you think you're doing?* in the way she might address a naughty schoolboy. Except he was reaching into the back of the tray. Picking up a bar. She was just behind Geoff. None of them had seen her in the darkness behind the torch. She ran forward, yelling only one word. *No.* Running in and the bar coming down. As if the momentum of it had just been too strong to stop. As if everything up until then had been moving too fast and too hard for there to be time for it to stop. As if she'd been running towards this exact moment for years.

eighteen

Nick

Nick was already at the hospital when the paramedics called it in. *TBI, probable fracture, severe bleeding. GCS 7, E2 V1 M4, at 0:57. Female, late thirties.* They didn't say a name.

He'd been there for a couple of hours with Helen Lamprey. She'd suffered a relapse, alone at her house, somehow managing to call him before passing out. Major organ failure. The end in sight. He was writing up the report when the charge nurse stuck her head around the door to tell him an ambulance was on its way, pleased she didn't have to try to raise a doctor at that time of night for a trauma patient, a feeling he could only partly share. He would need to be back at the hospital again before seven for his rounds, would have preferred to go back to bed and not be woken again. Going out to meet the big Mercedes as it came under the portico. Stepping up inside to see the patient, lying on her side, strapped into the stretcher to impede movement but turned away from him, the paramedic holding an oxygen mask to her face because, due to the nature of the wound, he couldn't attach it to her head.

300

Asking for details of what she'd been given so far, getting a glimpse of the injury and instructing the nurse to contact Brisbane.

'We'll need the chopper,' he said. 'They won't be able to deal with this on the coast.'

Not taking his eyes off the patient but addressing the paramedics. 'I'm going to confirm the *GCS*. What happened here?'

'Hit with an iron bar.'

'I'll need to get around the other side.'

There being some awful familiarity to the woman's hair. Even with the gore. Slipping backwards. Losing his balance. Almost falling out of the ambulance. Collapsing onto the other gurney, bumping against the paramedic beside him.

'You all right sir?' the man said.

His colleague standing on the ground at the back of the van. Her face at head height to him. Short blonde hair. Blue eyes. Ambulance fatigues. Blue and green should never be seen. Shirt sleeves rolled up. A strong-looking young nurse. Reaching forward to take his pulse. He couldn't form words.

By the time the helicopter arrived he'd pulled himself together enough to arrange passage to Royal Brisbane alongside her. Pulling rank. Familiar enough with the symptoms of shock to know that he wasn't much use to anyone. Embarrassed before the paramedics. *I'm so sorry. I know this person. We had lunch together today.* If you could call it that. Taking nourishment in each other. Not going to explain how he knew her, but not going to be separated from her either. By that time several other people had arrived at the hospital, some of whom he vaguely recognised. Marcus Barker. No sign of the wife whose name he couldn't recall. Eugenie had mentioned them as friends. No sign, either, of the husband, but then there wouldn't be, would there? At the mines.

He shook the man's hand. 'There are children? Two daughters? Is someone taking care of them?' he asked.

'Lindl's taking care of them. They're asleep.' Patting him on the shoulder as if he, Nick, had reason to be in shock. Nobody was supposed to know about them. She'd made him take the back roads around the town so they wouldn't be seen.

The years of his professional life a preparation for moments like this; repeated incidents of high stress having trained him to be able to separate his feelings from his capacity to analyse and assess the patient, not Eugenie, *the patient*, she who had presented with Traumatic Brain Injury; seven on the *Glasgow Coma Scale* (confirmed) although the particulars were slightly altered since the paramedics had done it, *Eyes 2 Verbal 2 Movement 3, at 01:43*, according to his no doubt flawed estimate, a patient who, the latest statistics claimed, had an 89 per cent chance of recovery, although somewhat less of full functionality, the latter not being under question at this instant, that was for later, when she might wake from her coma and the wonderfully named eight-step *Rancho Los Amigos Level of Cognitive Functioning Scale* might be applied; such statistics and measurements being no more than statements of average, nothing to do with an individual case in which an octagonal metal bar has been brought down diagonally across the skull of a woman by a strong young man. Right now it was a matter of the *GCS* and keeping up the vitals, talking to her, for she was occasionally conscious although not *compos mentis*. He'd been asked by a patient, one evening in a Canberra Hospital, how he dealt with traumatic incidents in his work and he'd replied, *We don't see the injury so much. I mean we see it, the blood, the trauma, but only as part of a problem to be solved, we see past it to what is achievable.* Already so removed by then that he couldn't say I.

I see this.

~

In the helicopter. Flying through darkness. Many lights below. A big pair of headphones cushioning his ears. His hand on hers. Her fingers cold but holding him as if she knew whose hand it was.

They'd had lunch at a fine restaurant. Walked in the national park, laid together in the fine-needled shade of casuarinas. One evening at his house, two if you counted the first time she came up with him. The kiss. A thing in itself. Make-up sex in a car. Not much, really, on which to base love.

For nearly ten years, it turned out, they had lived as children in the same suburb. He four years older than she. After school finished both of them going to work in medicine. Never meeting.

At Royal Prince Albert they landed on the roof. Eugenie was taken down in a lift for an MRI and CT scan, then to Intensive Care. Sedated so they could intubate, attach drips and monitoring equipment. Leaving him to sit in a chair beside the bed.

Nobody asked his relationship to her, for which he was glad because he didn't know how he would answer.

Still dark outside. Still part of the same night.

A brain surgeon arrived. Put the scans up on a lightboard and invited Nick to look at them.

'She's sustained a serious blow. You can see here, where the bar made contact and you can see the bone has cracked, here, here and here. There's a bit of swelling going on within the cranium but no more than you'd expect at this stage.'

He glanced at Nick.

'I've seen a lot worse,' he said.

'Which means?' Nick asked, knowing that such questions were both the most common and the hardest to answer.

'Well, the bone isn't shattered. At this stage, as far as I can tell, nothing has penetrated the brain itself. I think she's seen the bar

303

coming and tried to move so it's glanced off.' The surgeon imitating her action, ducking aside. 'There's a contusion on her shoulder which might confirm this. My guess is she'll pull through without too much damage. That's my hope. We won't know until we wake her up, which we won't do for a while. A couple of days at least. Until that swelling goes down. I'm not going to do anything at this stage. If the swelling increases or refuses to go down I can release the pressure. But the bleeding has stopped. I think we'll just clean up the wound and see how we go. The human animal is … but I'm sure you know this … highly resilient.'

The surgeon started taking the scans down and stacking them together, sliding them into their envelope.

'You should get some sleep,' he said.

Nick found a bathroom, washed his hands (again), his face, the back of his neck. Looking in the mirror he saw that he was still wearing the white coat he'd put on at the hospital when they brought Helen in. His stethoscope around his neck. Wondering just how *she* was going. A surge of concern rising that he'd abandoned her like that. Left the hospital unattended. He took off the coat, put the stethoscope in its pocket. He wondered how many lapses of professionalism he'd been guilty of in the last few hours.

He went back to the chair next to Eugenie. Sat, looking out into the rest of the ward. The nurse assigned to Eugenie was balancing on a stool at the end of the bed, the wide report sheet clipped onto its table, making notes. A curtain prevented him from seeing the patient behind him. A glass-walled booth at the centre of the ward. The only part of the room fully lit. Computer monitors glowing. A standing nurse talking to a sitting doctor, their words inaudible. The attending nurses each with their patients. The dead part of night. He stared out at the limited activity, ignored and uncomprehending. He fell asleep, sitting up. One benefit from all those years as an intern.

When he woke it was daylight. The ward full of people, doctors, nurses, nurses' aides, specialists. Six-thirty. He went to the bathroom again and washed, eyeing off the unused shower in the corner. No towels, no clean clothes, no point. Unshaven. He was due at the surgery in two hours but didn't have a car, hadn't drunk anything since before midnight. He looked like shit warmed over.

He found a cafeteria and ordered coffee and breakfast, pulled out his mobile phone, tried to ring the surgery but got no reply. He tried Joy at home. She answered. This, however, meant he had to explain what had happened and where he was. She, of course, knew Eugenie and was appalled. The fact he'd accompanied her – one of their own – to Brisbane did not, for some reason, surprise her. He said he would try and get back as soon as possible. If she could manage to reschedule some patients. Perhaps he could take a train?

When he made it back to the ICU Marcus was there.

'I came down before the traffic,' he said. 'I wasn't going to sleep any more anyway.'

Nick explained what he knew about Eugenie's condition.

'There's a husband, isn't there?' Nick asked. As if he might maintain his innocence with this man.

'Yes,' Marcus said.

Nick lowered his head. 'I'm sorry. I knew that,' he said. 'Does he know she's injured? Where is he?'

'In the Pilbara. He knows but there's a cyclone threatening. He can't get out just now.'

'Right. The thing is,' Nick said, 'I came down with her in the helicopter. I don't have a car and I'm due back in Winderran. I'm wondering if I could borrow yours. I could bring it back this afternoon when I'm finished. I could bring your wife down too, and Eugenie's girls, maybe.'

'If Eugenie's going to be in a coma for a while there's nothing I can do here,' Marcus said. 'I'll drive you back.'

The traffic heavy on Gympie Road, the stop lights streamed for the incoming flow, pulling them up again and again.

Marcus described what had happened at *Roselea*.

'I went out on the veranda. I didn't figure they'd hurt me, which doesn't mean I wasn't scared they might. I was unarmed. It's not, you know, Latin America.'

'Yet.'

'I'm standing there in the glare of their lights, no chance to speak with the noise. I guess they wanted to say something, or hear what I had to say, I don't know, but after a while they turned off the music and the motors, left the lights on. I don't even know what I was going to say. I just thought that if I stayed inside they'd want blood. I mean metaphorically. I mean they'd start smashing things up, shooting at the house maybe and then someone might get hurt. But before I could say much of anything there was a shout from down by the creek. There was another vehicle down there I hadn't seen and it started up, sounding its horn, tearing off up the hill. Some sort of signal I guess. These jerks out the front of the house started their motors up again, made to take off. The trouble was it's been really wet at our place. That front paddock's like an ice-rink. Two of them take off but the third one's gone onto the grass and is spinning around and around. The driver's panicked, and he's flooring it and it's fish-tailing all over the joint, throwing up dirt and mud. The other two have stopped halfway to the causeway. I figure it's because they're waiting for this idiot but then I see something down on the causeway. I called to the others. Just then the ute in the paddock gets traction and lurches off the grass onto the road, sideswiping one of the other vehicles. That's too much for them. They take off, working their way around the obstacle down on the causeway. By that time I'm running down to see what's happening, couldn't give a shit about these fucks in their four-wheel drives. I didn't even take a number plate. I could have, I was standing right next to them when they were stopped. I wasn't thinking clearly. Geoff was down there with Eugenie. Blood all over him. I took one look and jumped in the car, went up the top of the road with the mobile and called emergency. No sign of these bastards. I'll give the ambulance people this: they were there within five minutes. When we got back down to Eugenie they had her laid out on her side next to the drums. Geoff said that they were going to hit him but she got in the way.'

'Will the police get the people who did this?'

'They should do. I mean it should be a breeze. They smashed into each other. That's not something you can hide so easily. The vehicles'll be covered in mud. There's tyre tracks everywhere to match up. They know where to look anyway, because of what the girl told us.'

'You knew that Eugenie and I ... we'd been seeing each other?'

'Lindl knew. She and Eugenie are pretty close.'

'She didn't want anyone else to know. I had to go to great lengths ...' he paused. 'I don't want you to think this is something I do, you know, sleep with other men's wives. Eugenie said she hadn't been happy with David for years, that she wanted to leave ...' fizzling out, loathing the patter emanating from his mouth.

Marcus glanced over at him.

'You're serious about her then, yourself?'

'Is that a test question?'

The day had the sort of brightness only achieved after not having slept. Sunlight bouncing off the cars, four-wheel drives, utes, vans, vast aluminium-bodied gravel trucks, all of them surging forward together with each change of the lights. Everything, at one and the same time, too close and too far away. Passing through little shopping centres stunned into submission by decades of traffic, advertising signs that had lost their meaning from being read too many times by too many people.

'If you want to see it that way,' Marcus said. 'But I was actually asking about you, not her. How it is *you're* doing. I don't figure you spent the night beside her because you're her doctor.'

'Thanks. I'm sorry.'

Was he serious? If there was brain damage, for instance, would he still be there? Did they have enough shared experience to warrant that sort of commitment? He doubted it. But there'd been enough to feel her injury in himself. For it to have got past his doctorial defences and enter into the places within himself reserved for those he loved. They'd been talking about how they got into medicine. In the national park, walking off the lunchtime wine. How they'd managed to get from Stanmore, that strange little suburb moored between the railway tracks and Parramatta Road, to Winderran via hospitals around the country. And why.

'I always liked to care for people,' she'd said. 'I've never spent that much time wondering why. Well, not until recently anyway. Not until my marriage started to fall apart. It seems I've been compensating.'

'For what?'

'Oh, I don't know, the usual.'

'Which is?'

'Family?' Not elaborating the point. 'When you're young you think you can do anything you want. Or I did. Let me say that. *I* thought I could be all sorts of things and I think I thought I'd put on nursing like a coat and wear it for a while. What I didn't realise, I guess, is that after a time you become whatever coat it is you're wearing, never mind what you still think about yourself inside. You've only got one life. You haven't got hundreds of them to choose from.'

They'd reached Carseldine. Marcus pointed to the lights that had brought them to a standstill, again. This time at the head of the rank. 'These are the last ones for about eighty kilometres,' he said. 'It should be plain sailing from here. You can have a sleep if you like.'

Closing his eyes, letting the acceleration of the car push him back into the seat. When she'd been talking like that he'd thought about the way he'd been pushed into medicine and followed it. Giving himself over to it at the expense of everything else. Sex dressed as love as a form of relief from it, getting him into all sorts of shit along the way. Two children now who seemed to always get second best and it was of no account, just for the record, that it had been the same in his generation, when he was a child, that his father hadn't been there for him or his brother, that was irrelevant, you couldn't go measuring things with false comparisons, this was now, not then, and he knew what he was capable of giving and knew that he hadn't been giving it and he'd thought, lying there in the tessellated shade with this new woman, the not-so-distant sea a bass note beneath the sound of the wind in the casuarinas, how it might be possible to do it differently, not just with his children, but with her, as if – and here was the mistake of course, slipping itself in there the way it always did – as if *her presence* might make the difference, that the way he felt for her, the sense of care which welled in his breast when he looked at her, when he was with her, which was associated with sex, aligned with it, but in this case coming from another, more subtle place, might allow him to take a different course.

Then, in the middle of the night, in the early hours of a Tuesday morning she was brought in on a gurney bleeding from the head and it felt like he had been meant to be there for her, that it *wasn't* a mistake, wasn't some false positive, some twisted self-justification to do with sexual gratification or ownership or fear of abandonment, lack of self-worth or *compensation*, it was to do with wanting to provide love for another person, no, not even *wanting*, because it was without volition, it was what it was.

He opened his eyes and looked across at this stranger who'd been up all night, just like him, but who was driving him home now up the Bruce Highway.

'In answer to your question,' he said.

'Yes?' Marcus said.

'I'm serious.'

nineteen

Guy

He slipped out of the airport surrounds and onto the freeway system at speed, turning north on the arterial, grateful for the lack of traffic. Speaking too soon: within minutes he was at a standstill. The northbound lanes caught in the long tail of an accident or roadwork somewhere beyond anyone's understanding. Ten thousand cars easing forward one metre at a time over roads designed to be traversed at a hundred times the speed. Hard not to take it personally.

After ringing Lasker three or four times he'd called the hospital, connecting to a phone at a nurses' station that rang long into the night without recourse to an answering machine, only eventually picked up by a nurse who told him that, yes, his wife had been admitted after suffering a relapse. She was now, though, in a stable condition, resting, but she, the nurse, thought, if she might say it, that it would be good if he could be there.

'Are you saying she's about to die?'

'No Mr Lamprey, I'm not. Not immediately anyway, I don't believe so. But she is extremely ill.'

'Can you put me through to Nick Lasker?'

'No, I'm sorry, Doctor Lasker is not available.'

'Why ever not? He's her doctor. He left a message for me saying, specifically, that I should call him, at any time of day or night. I've been trying to phone him for hours.'

'I'm sorry, Mr Lamprey, but Doctor Lasker's been called away.'

'How can he be called away when he's already on a case? He's my wife's doctor. If she's in crisis then he should be there.'

'Thank you, Mr Lamprey. I'll pass that on to him as soon as I see him.'

The small hours of the morning in a Canberra hotel room.

Getting out his laptop. Navigating the internet for a seat on an early morning flight to Brisbane. Doing something, anything, to cover for the overwhelming sense of Helen's mortality; for his own failure to be there. The disease now in her liver.

The phone on his lap, glancing down to flick through screens in the hope of finding the number for the Party offices in Canberra. Trying not to rear-end the car in front. The drivers all around, likewise, talking to disembodied others via the power of Bluetooth. Only just after nine in Brisbane but ten in Canberra due to Queensland's reluctance to compromise on even the simplest of political imperatives. Time getting away on him.

The switchboard operator condescended to put him through to a secretary who routed him through, in turn, to the media department, one of whose minions was supposed to be picking him up from the hotel in approximately fifteen minutes. Explaining to this unknown individual in the simplest possible language that he was, in fact, in Brisbane, on his way to see his wife in hospital. The traffic at a standstill. Speaking in one-syllable words while concentrating on the movement of a truck a long way ahead, waiting to see it move so that later he, too, might also do so. The heat building. Going back to the radio when the call was over in the hope of hearing a traffic update but thus locking himself into the insufferable chatter of call-back on the local ABC; tormenting him with inanity.

The phone cut in just when there might have been a break for the long-awaited traffic report.

It was Bain. Unexpectedly furious. 'What's this all about, Guy?' he said.

'I'm afraid it's Helen, Aldous,' he said.

'What's Helen got to do with these goons?'

'I'm sorry?'

'Haven't you heard the news?' Bain said.

'What news?'

'About the dam? Where the hell are you anyway?'

'I'm back up in Brisbane, stuck in traffic on the Gateway.'

'What the fuck are you doing there?'

'It's Helen …'

'Listen, I haven't got time for this. You're supposed to be in training today. It's organised. The people, the room, everything. I've got a media storm going on down here. I can't fucking believe it. Some idiots have attacked a conservationist opposing the dam. Up your way. A woman. She's been flown to Brisbane in a coma. Is this something to do with you? Did you tell them to do this?'

The truck he'd been watching, a red Australia Post semi-trailer, way ahead in the queue, had begun to move.

'I don't know what you're talking about,' he said.

'Well you should. Get on to it. Straight away. What the fuck are you doing up in Brisbane?'

'I've been trying to tell you, Helen's back in hospital, she was admitted last night. I'm on my way up there, from the airport. Except right now I'm at a standstill.'

'Right. Hardly the best. Well, make use of the time. Make

some calls. Find out what's going on. Call me as soon as you learn something.'

The radio cutting back in with a song from the seventies, the ancient strains of weeping pedal steel guitar winding out of the speakers in the same way as they had for the last forty years. Pressing the button to get rid of the fucking thing, bugger the traffic report. Unused to being spoken to like that. Bain's indifference to the situation with Helen bringing his own response to the fore. Wondering if he had made the right decision in cancelling the scheduled meetings to rush back. If there was, in fact, any point. The absence of the doctor an unconscionable irritant; how could he make a rational judgement without being in possession of the facts? Was Helen really about to die? Bain's displeasure stinging. It was, apart from anything else, unfair. If Bain's concern was his public image, how much worse would it appear not to be at his wife's bedside? How was he supposed to use the time effectively when he didn't have any staff, wasn't even a candidate yet, never mind elected? Trapped in the car.

The phone again.

This time his daughter. No, *Hi Dad, how are you?* Straight down to business our Sarah. 'What's happening with Mum? I tried to call the house but nobody answered.'

He told her what little he'd got from the hospital.

'Where are you?' she asked, her tone, even through the medium of a mobile phone connected wirelessly to the car radio still managing to convey her disdain at the idea he might be somewhere else than by her mother's side. Getting it from all quarters.

'Stuck in traffic, heading out of Brisbane. I had to go to Canberra yesterday.'

'You *had* to go?'

'Yes, I did.'

'You've always had your priorities,' she said.

Frustration winding up another notch. But then, if he'd expected sympathy he was speaking with the wrong person. Sarah, at thirty-two, was all tight-lipped efficiency and ruthless ambition. For what he was never sure. She had, it seemed, caught the Western Australian disease. Her allegiance solidly with Helen.

Alan would have been thirty-five this year.

The temptation to bite all but overwhelming. Restraining himself. Nothing to be gained by arguing with his daughter.

'You'll come over?'

'I'm packing as we speak. I'll catch a flight late afternoon. I'll go straight from the office.'

All right for her to have business to attend to.

'You'll be okay to get here from the airport?'

'I'll *manage*.'

Not sure why sarcasm was necessary. 'I'll see you then. Let me know when you'll be arriving. I should be at the hospital in an hour or so.'

One of the reasons he hadn't lost control being that, mid-conversation, he'd been taken by the strangest sense that Helen was in the car with him. Right there in the passenger seat. Asking him to calm down. As if the sleepless night was telling on him. As if, in the space of a single phone call, he had bought into some crazy network of belief.

The summer Alan turned twelve they had driven to the farm in western New South Wales, the four of them in the station wagon, two days on the road. The visit was a disaster. It didn't matter what he'd done, sold a quarter of a million copies of his books, hailed internationally as one of the 'top ten under forty' for fuck's sake, built a house on the proceeds, he still wasn't good enough for his father, would never be, the only thing he could have done to get his blessing was to come back and take over the farm, that vast expanse of emptiness and sheep.

He'd never had any time for sheep. The single thing about the place for which he held any nostalgia were the shearing sheds. And, of course, the dogs. The old man never let him have one. *They're working animals*, he said, *not toys*. No discussion or empathy, just an aphorism delivered at best reluctantly, without explanation. One of those famous pronouncements which loomed out of the dark ocean of his father's mind like an iceberg; all the reasoning hidden below the surface. The assumption being that somehow his abstruse mutterings might be able to carry the weight of everything that had gone into their making when of course they couldn't, no simple word could possibly carry that weight; a great poet might, in his lifetime, manage to imbue a single sentence with as much meaning as his father's statements were intended to convey. To Guy as a child they'd been tyrannical rebukes of everything he was. Even as an adult, become a different person, his own man, he couldn't protect himself from them.

After several days they'd been unable to restrain their enmity any longer. An argument broke out at the dinner table from which neither man would resile. The women trying to sort it out between them but if anything only making it worse. As if things had not been said. He ordered the family into the car and drove off, regardless of the hour. His mother on the veranda, arms crossed, asking him not to go like this. Helen in the passenger seat, silent and critical, knowing better than to say, *You're just like your father, you're two of a kind, both as stubborn as each other*, but thinking it so loud he could feel it, the two children in the back also silent, frightened, no doubt, by the ferocity of the exchange. Sarah strapped in, complaining about Alan who was lying across the seat, his feet touching her legs. Driving into the night with furious purpose, scanning the empty road for kangaroos. After an hour or so everyone asleep.

He stopped to pee at one point, standing out on the western plains with the firmament arrayed above him, the air cold, the car's motor ticking down. Nobody woke. He had a drink of water and drove on, given confidence in his decision by the glory of that sky. He loved to drive at night, loved the passage of the road beneath the car. It brought, he believed, a peculiar kind of twentieth-century quietude, something no other human beings in history could ever have felt, special to their time.

Around first light he must have drifted into sleep. He woke, adrenaline filled, to the sound of gravel beneath the tyres. Pulling the wheel. Too late. In the ditch at a hundred and ten. Coming up the other side. The left front of the car rising. Time enough to realise what was happening. That's how long they were in the air. The car come free of the earth. Back down again. Onto its side, spinning, sideways, once, twice. Doors flown open. Objects taken flight. Glass breaking. Noise like he'd never heard: a great rending shriek of metal, once, twice, a third time. Coming to rest upside down in someone's paddock. Wheat.

They were fortunate as these things go. Someone was coming behind, witnessed the accident, stopped.

He never saw his son dead. They found him in the paddock, unmarked, lying on the flattened stalks, his neck broken, thrown from the car during one of its revolutions.

Helen and Guy they airlifted to Sydney. He'd been nearly scalped, had 'serious internal injuries', as well as broken ribs, had lost a lot of blood. Helen had a fractured leg and a broken shoulder, cuts and abrasions. Sarah was, remarkably, almost unhurt.

When he heard what had happened Guy could not see how he might continue to live. Never mind the tubes and wires attached to his body, forcing nutrients and drugs into his veins.

Helen refused to speak to him. Her parents came down and stayed in a motel nearby with Sarah until Helen was well enough to be discharged. They took them back to the Sunshine Coast. Left him there.

His father came to see him. He woke from one of his deep drugged sleeps – they were keeping him sedated because of his propensity for ripping out the cannula – to find the old man sitting there, his good town hat in his lap, his thick arms with the red-blond hairs on them and the sunspots, the stubbed, damaged fingers with the cracks around the joints.

'What are you doing here, Dad?' he said.

'Your mother would have come but she finds the travel hard,' he said. 'So you got me.'

'That's not what I meant.'

'I've come to sit with you,' he said. 'See you don't do something stupid.'

'What, like kill my son?'

His father could have said, 'You already did that.'

If it was a play he was writing that's what he'd have got him to say and then there would have been the great unravelling, the family secrets drawn out, torn from both of them, although what those might be in their case, he wasn't sure, except for a great unwillingness to allow feeling into anything.

It wasn't a play, it was him in a hospital room and Alan dead somewhere, he didn't even know where. Alan dead in a wheat field and his father sitting next to him, as short of words as usual, Guy wondering where in hell *he* got the facility for them, not for the first time when faced with the enigma of the old man, not just his arms and fingers but his whole body swollen in its skin, not fat, but as if someone had pumped him up a bit so that the skin was tightened at the folds and joints, burying those eyes of his which had already sunk back into his head to avoid the quantity of light coming off the land.

'Can happen to anyone,' was what his father said. 'Nothing you can do about it.'

The traffic easing north of the city. Still not flowing the way he wanted it to. Fools to the front of him, scoundrels behind. The old car's air-con struggling with the heat. When he had a Senator's salary he'd arrange to lease a better one. Perhaps even something German. When Helen was gone and he didn't need to listen to her disparagement of prestige cars. *No justification for it*, she would say, *it's just men and their egos.* No appreciation of what could be achieved through fine engineering, no understanding of the flow of ideas which travelled from performance cars down to the sort of thing he was accustomed to drive.

On the half hour he got the state-wide news. A line item announced that a woman allegedly attacked in the Sunshine Coast hinterland was now in a critical condition in hospital in Brisbane. Three men had been arrested in connection with the incident. A fourth was wanted to assist police in their enquiries. The briefest interview with local police. The arrested men, as well as being charged with assault, were being held on two counts of possession of a dangerous substance with intent to interfere with a water supply. Terrorism had been ruled out. Investigations were continuing.

He called a contact at the local paper. The man had the decency to ring him straight back, something that couldn't be said about certain others.

'Charles,' Guy said. 'What's going on?'

'I thought you might know more than me, Guy.'

'Why would you think that?'

'Well whoever these people were they were on your side, Guy. Seems they wanted to wipe out some endangered frog at the dam site. They had a truckload of poison they were about to pour in the creek.'

'For fuck's sake. Who told you this?'

'It's in the police reports. It's already up on our website.'

'But there aren't any endangered frogs in the creek. The Environmental Impact Statement was lodged weeks ago. I've read it.'

'Can I quote you on that?'

'No. You can't. This isn't an interview. I'm out of town and I'm ringing to ask you for information. Not the other way around.'

'So this is off the record?'

The ramifications of his position seeping in around the edge of his consciousness. Nothing decent about the prompt return of his call.

'Yes, very definitely. Listen, I've got a call coming in on another line. I'll have to go.'

Coming up the hill he ran into rain. Nothing unusual for Winderran. When Helen was gone he'd consider moving somewhere else. At least take a flat in Canberra. Or perhaps Melbourne. The cultural life beckoning. It wouldn't be Rome, of course, but nor was it fucking Brisbane.

He parked on the street in front of the hospital. Ran to get under the portico. Pushed into the odd little foyer with its wooden memorial boards to the town's fallen. Rolls of honour. Washing his hands, then on into the wards. The woman in the nurses' station was on the phone, she looked up and, seeing him, pointed down the hall, mouthing the number *Ten*.

Helen in a room by herself. The life gone out of her. On her back with her eyes closed; her mouth, pale-lipped, sagging to one side. A drip feeding a cannula in her right forearm. One of those little things clipped to the end of her finger to record the vitals. A button next to her left hand which she might press for pain relief if she was conscious enough to do so. Unrecognisable as his wife and yet unmistakeable. Barely any flesh on her at all.

He sat in the single plastic chair provided. Hard to get it close because of the height of the bed and the electronic gear she was hooked up to. A device on a wheeled stand measuring her blood pressure; a clear plastic box on another one containing a thing like a caulking gun delivering titrated doses to the drip. LED numbers pulsing. He'd been rushing to get there, as if it was a goal in itself. Now there was nothing to do. All this shit still tumbling around in his head. The dam, Aldous, the dinner the previous night, the young man and what had gone down there. No pun intended. He took Helen's hand in his. Her fingers pale and cold, damp. The skin translucent. Her breath coming in this weird broken rhythm, long spaces between the out and the in so that he thought, for a moment, it might happen right then. That she'd been waiting for him to arrive in order to go.

It was a fantasy. She was still in the grip of life.

When, eventually, they'd sent him back to Queensland he and Helen had barely been able to communicate. They lived as satellites of each other in the house that had lost Alan, caring for Sarah as best they could. A mutual agreement to put her first.

Weeks passed.

One morning Helen came to his office, which by then he'd virtually made his home. Not yet recovered but able to look after his own needs. She stood at the end of his bed, her hands on the wooden baseboard, a thin woman with short hair and a face he wasn't sure he could connect with the woman he'd begged to take him back on the beach thirteen years before.

'I need to talk to you,' she said.

'Go on then,' he said.

'It's about your work.'

'I'm listening.'

'If you write about this I'll never speak to you again,' she said. 'You can write about anything in the world, but this is not for you to use.'

Writing, at the time, he'd have had to say, if she'd wanted to listen, if she hadn't walked out of the room before he could reply, was the furthest thing from his mind.

Time passed. He went out into the corridor and found the toilet. When he came back she was more awake, her eyes open. She looked, he thought, terrified. He took her hand again but she pulled it away with surprising force. The pain acting on her.

He went to find a nurse who came back with him and checked the chart, adjusted the drip. Helen lay with her head towards him, watching. She opened her mouth and he thought she was going to speak but nothing came out, at least no words, just a little dribble of something like vomit which caused her to cough, forcing her to roll onto her side, an agonising process, trying to spit. He got a tissue and wiped away the mess, but clumsily, having to wipe two or three times, unpractised at the task, holding her shoulder as he did so, astonished at how small she'd become. He tried to offer water.

She didn't want it. He thought she was trying to say something. He leant close to her, his ear next to her mouth. Fetid breath. Something rotten within. Dying from the inside out. She said a few words but they were indistinct. He thought they might have been, *Make it stop*.

'She's still in pain,' he said to the nurse.

'She can administer pain relief through the drip whenever she wants.'

'I don't think it's working,' Lamprey said. 'Can you give her something stronger?'

The nurse consulted the chart again. 'She's had as much as her body can take at this time,' she said.

'Is there something else you can give her?'

'I'll talk to Doctor,' the nurse said.

He wasn't cut out for this. It wasn't just that he hated hospitals, their smells, their architecture – why was it they had to be painted one colour halfway up the wall and another for the rest, like boarding schools – hospitals demanded something from him he didn't know how to give.

Make it stop.

'Who is the doctor? Is Doctor Lasker back yet?'

'Doctor Cunningham's presiding at the moment. But I can find out if Doctor Lasker is available. If you'd like.'

'Please.'

His phone rang. Bain. Somehow, for a few minutes, he'd managed to forget about this business. It was all he could do to answer. Trying the sliding door to the garden and surprised to find that it opened, going outside onto a little paved area with a moulded plastic chair and table, some heliconias between it and the next room, a view out across a fence onto paddocks where brown and white dairy cows fed on rich grass.

'Aldous,' he said.

'Guy. What have you found out?'

'Very little. I spoke to a contact at the local paper.'

'For Christ's sake! What on earth made you do that?'

'I went to him for information. As you instructed. Off the record. He's a friend.'

'Don't speak to anyone in the media, whatever you do. What did he tell you?'

'That there's a frog on the endangered species list which lives in the dam area. That someone was trying to kill it.'

'I could have told you that.'

'Why didn't you?'

'Because I only found out in the last couple of days. There's an expert who lives up your way who's done a study. Slater? Sleever?'

'Steever, Geoff Steever.'

'That's the one. Do you know him?'

'I've met him. Ex-CSIRO. Retired. No-one you need to concern yourself with.'

'Just the world's leading authority on sub-tropical amphibians.'

'Was. He's an old man. Listen, the EIS didn't find anything endangered. Steever's probably making it up. One last try for glory. He's thick with the anti-dam mob. They'd do anything.'

'In another scenario,' Bain said, 'we might have said something similar. But the thing is, someone was out there trying to kill the fucking thing. If they didn't exist they wouldn't need to, would they?'

'That's certainly an argument.'

'Fucking oath it is.'

'But for some reason you thought I had no need of knowing this?' Guy said.

Silence on the other end of the line.

'Are you there?'

'Well, that's the thing. Listen, suffice to say it's a disaster. Can you make a statement? Speak to the radio?'

'No.'

'What do you mean, Guy? This is your constituency. This issue is what's *made* you. We're a fucking team, Guy. You need to get on board. One poor player and we're all fucked.'

'As it happens I'm sitting next to my dying wife.'

'Right. Yes. Of course. Give Helen my best wishes.'

'I'm not sure she's taking that sort of thing in.'

'Listen, you don't have to come up with anything yourself. I'll get the office to put something together. For breakfast radio tomorrow. We need you, Guy.'

Hoping that he'd managed to instil some measure of shame in the bastard. Although it would be fair to ask what he was doing there himself, what function he served, sitting next to her thinking about what he might do when she was dead. Where he might live and which car he might buy with money that was going to come from a project which just right then, he'd have to say, looked shaky. An endangered frog might present a problem for the project under some circumstances. An endangered frog which someone had taken it upon themselves to destroy, while doing their best to kill a conservationist in the process, was likely to present an insurmountable obstacle. Might present an obstacle, even, to his own election. He could see that. No doubt the reason Aldous was so angry. Not that it made him any more sympathetic. A skerrick of thought having slipped into his mind while Bain was talking: that he knew more than he was letting on. Drip-feeding Guy the information. A team. Not sure how he had managed to so effectively blind himself to what he was doing, joining up with Bain and Lonergan *et al*. He had always hated teams, particularly teams of men and the threat of violence that lurks, always, at their heart; the bullying to conform to something which could as easily prove to be their worst aspect as their best. The power of the clique tied to its antithesis, the thing they were opposed to or excluded, the *other*. They hadn't even bothered to tell him, even when his name was all over it.

He'd meant to ask about the conservationist.

Helen's eyes were closed but she wasn't asleep. Every now and then a tremor seemed to pass through her, causing her breath to catch, become shorter, harsher, her muscles to tighten, the skin on her face, already tight across the bone, to contract further, her thin lips pulling back from her teeth. He pumped the dongle to release the drug but it had no effect. She turned her head and looked at him again.

He would go and find the doctor himself. Anger so close to the surface. Fury at what had happened, what was happening, at anger itself. Loathing himself for it. Perhaps if he could have something to eat it would be better. The last thing he'd eaten had been the wrap they'd given him on the plane by way of breakfast. There was a vending machine in the lobby. He stood up. Helen's eyes followed him. Unnaturally large.

'I'm going to get something to eat,' he said, saying it loudly, as if she was deaf as well as mute. Like an Englishman addressing a foreigner.

Three or four people on the plastic chairs near the front desk, waiting. Nobody actually bleeding, that he could see. The vending machine carried only the barest minimum. Chocolate bars, potato chips. He bought a Picnic, all his coins could manage. He tore open the wrapper but suddenly didn't want to be seen standing in the foyer eating it. He went back onto the ward, down the corridor to the room, the damn thing open in his hand.

Nick Lasker was standing at the end of the bed in a white coat, looking at Helen's chart. Even in his own present state, sleep-deprived, disorientated, subject to unexpected mood swings, Guy could see the man was exhausted.

He held out his hand. 'Nick,' he said.

Lasker looked at it, as if at something distasteful, then looked at the other one, holding its stupid stump of lumpy chocolate protruding from its brightly coloured wrapper, a crude confectionary turd. He looked back at Helen.

Disconcerted, Guy put the chocolate bar down on the night table. Not sure it would, after resting there, be safe to eat.

'Helen's in a lot of pain,' he said.

'I know,' Nick said. 'She's on the highest dose of morphine we can give her, but it's not having much effect. During the night she suffered a rupture to the abdomen. Under other circumstances we

326

might have been able to operate, but I can't see the advantage. Nor does Helen want us to.'

'Nor I. Is there something else you can give her?'

Nick clipped her chart back onto the end of the bed and went alongside of her, looked at the drip, rested his hand on her wrist.

'Doctor Lasker,' Guy said, no Nicks anymore.

'Yes?'

'She wants this to stop.'

'I know. But there's not much more I can do than I already have.'

'Well you could be in here looking after her instead of chasing after more interesting cases.'

He hadn't meant to say it. He'd thought it, of course he had. But he hadn't meant to say it. And yet there the words were. Out in the open.

In the ensuing silence Lasker remained next to Helen, across the bed from Guy. Gathering himself. After a moment or two he looked up.

'You're under a lot of stress aren't you?' he said.

From the way he said it – the clever employment of psycho-speech, acknowledging the pain of the attacker rather than the thing he'd said – Guy had the sense Lasker was in some way pleased by the rudeness of his outburst, as if it had, in a significant way, changed their status in his favour. Guy started to say something, some rejoinder, but nothing came out. First the words come, then they stop.

'But it's Helen we need to take care of at the moment, isn't it?' Lasker said.

'Yes.'

'What I can do is consult with the Sister about the dosage. We have a responsibility to try to control the pain. To make her as comfortable as possible. Helen asked me to do whatever I can to minimise it. The difficulty is that a stronger dose might have the effect of putting her system into terminal decline.'

'I thought she was already in terminal decline.'

'She is. I'm talking in a more immediate sense. A stronger dose may mean that she won't wake again.'

'Give it to her. I know it's what she wants. She's said so to me, herself, many times. And to you it seems.' Begging favours of the gods of medicine.

'I'll go and talk to the Sister.' Stopping at the door. 'Is there anyone else you want to discuss this with?'

'No. I want what's best for Helen.' Pausing. 'I apologise for what I said a moment ago. I don't know what came over me.'

Lasker didn't respond.

Helen had not stirred throughout the exchange. Now, as soon as the doctor was absent, she went into one of her spasms. Lamprey pressed the pain relief device several times, in the same way and with as much conviction as a man waiting to cross the street bangs the button on the pole. He could do that. What he suddenly found he couldn't do was touch her. Couldn't quite offer that. She'd gone too far, was out of his reach. She had been for a long time, just not as obviously. For many years now they had cohabited out there on the hill, tied together by their mistakes. He was fairly certain she knew he took his pleasure elsewhere, though they'd never discussed it. He never enquired about her. He had thought her sanctimonious, unforgiving, wedded to her grief. He had turned away from her, into his work, and when that wasn't going well, into other things. It might be that she had harboured no opinion about where he took his pleasure, but around his career she'd never been short of judgement, even if it hadn't always been expressed. Her critique of his work in television, of the people he associated with, of his convictions, had been a constant. Like she was his fucking mother. Now, though, extraordinarily enough, she was choosing to leave. Wrestling with some devil on the bed next to him. Taking with her thirty-eight years of his life.

Time passed. This particular spasm appeared to ease. Watching Helen retreat from the fight, physically calming, although still breathing in these short broken breaths, he found himself subject to curious and unpleasant spikes of emotion – washed by waves of frustration, pain, boredom – interspersed with periods where he simply felt nothing at all, this last the most difficult to deal with, his capacity for distance, for indifference, writ large. They were all, no doubt, aspects of grief. He was informed enough about the psychology of the human animal to know that. But the knowledge brought no help.

A young nurse came in, apologising for interrupting. 'Just need to check a few things,' she said, unhooking the chart, taking Helen's pulse.

Lamprey checked his phone. He'd had it on silent. Ten missed calls. A whole raft of emails piling up. Flicking through the headings to see if there was anything he absolutely had to attend to. Addressing the nurse.

'Last night,' he said, 'there was an emergency up this way … I heard a woman was attacked out along Dundalli Creek … was this hospital involved?'

'Oh yes. It was terrible. It was one of our staff. Hit with an iron bar by some young thugs. Cracked her skull. Awful.' The nurse had turned her attention to the machines beside Helen.

'Who was it?' Guy asked, knowing instinctively.

'Eugenie Lensman. She's been here for years. I've not heard how she is yet. We're all thinking of her.' Clipping the charts back onto the end of the bed. 'Doctor Lasker was on duty. He was fantastic. Flew down to Brisbane with her, wouldn't leave her side. A wonderful man. I don't think he's been to bed yet.'

Eugenie Lensman. Brained by some idiot who, according to the local news, was in favour of the dam. Guy slumping back in his hospital chair. Taking it hard. The image from the first time he'd met her coming to mind, at his home, visiting with her father.

Standing by the bookshelves, looking through his library, an innocent who was, at the same time, fundamentally self-contained, her own person, containing multitudes. It was why he'd picked her. Bain, asking if he'd organised this, an idea so clearly ludicrous it didn't bear consideration. Except that he did, in that moment, feel a sense of responsibility. As if, in stealing her for a character, he had in some way created this.

Lasker had left Helen to fly to Brisbane with her.

After taking him on as replacement for Miles, Helen had asked him, casually, 'You don't mind me appropriating your young man?'

'He's not mine,' he replied.

'I thought perhaps …'

'No, I was curious about him, I will admit it. But he won't do. He doesn't understand books.'

'He is a doctor.'

'I know. But a love of science doesn't preclude literature does it?'

'I can't help but see the attraction, though,' she said. 'There's a freshness to him, isn't there? Something uncomplicated and true.'

He wondered if Lasker had already been working with the anti-dam mob even then. No wonder he was so down on him. He, too, thought Guy had something to do with those thugs. Hurting one of his nurses. Or more. Who knows.

The cheek of the man. He had invited him into his home. Given over to him the care of his wife. Now here he was, beholden to him, caught up in the machinations of this town with its smallness, its bitter politics, its strange deracinated history, its residents all inextricably tied up with each other. The whole crappy frontier state of Queensland with its wilful embrace of ignorance and brutality. A province of a province. The decisions Helen had forced him to make which had led him there and everything that followed, all of it spooling out at his feet, slithering and coiling on the hospital floor, impossibly tangled.

⁓

Lasker came back with the Sister. He explained that he was going to record the conversation they would have over the next few moments. The man apparently oblivious to the bile seething around him. He asked if Guy had any objections. *Only to you*, he wanted to say. Desperately trying to concentrate. He said he had none. *Just questions: What is your relationship with Eugenie Lensman? Are you her lover? How long has this been going on?* Lasker fiddled with his smartphone, then, apparently satisfied, explained what he proposed to do. Increasing the dose of morphine would make Helen more comfortable, he said, but it could, also, give rise to catastrophic failure in her system. Did Guy understand this? He did.

'Your wife,' Lasker said, 'has a Do Not Resuscitate order. What this means is that should she suffer from a catastrophic failure the hospital is not to attempt to resuscitate her. Do you understand that?' He did.

Guy added, for the benefit of the machine, that he had asked Doctor Lasker to give his wife whatever pain relief was in his power in order to ease the pain.

Lasker turned off the recorder. 'Now,' he said, 'you're certain you want us to go ahead with this? You're certain that there is no-one else who should be part of this discussion?'

He'd forgotten Sarah.

'We have a daughter,' he said. 'In Perth.'

'Perhaps you would like to consult her?'

'She's coming over here now, she isn't due till midnight, even later.' Looking at his watch. It was only late afternoon. 'If you give Helen more pain relief is something likely to happen quickly?'

'It's not certain, but it could happen in the next couple of hours.'

'I don't believe it would be fair on Helen to keep her in this amount of pain any longer,' he said. 'I don't think Sarah would thank us.'

Saying the words but knowing they were untrue. If Helen was still alive when Sarah arrived she would storm in demanding more tests, more drugs, different doctors, different hospitals. Torturing her mother as a way of appeasing her own guilt at whatever it was that she thought she had done wrong, which was probably no more than survive, a pain that had taken her to the other side of the country to marry some sort of fool.

He checked his phone for messages. Its battery was now flat.

'Please,' he said. 'Go ahead.'

As the drug started flowing Helen's face seemed to relax. Was that a projection? When Lasker and the Sister left he sat down beside the bed again. This time he took her hand in his. A frail bony thing, cold to the touch. In all these past hours she had, he thought, been a powerful force operating in the room, making the decisions. Pushing him away so that she could herself go. An act of will. With the increased dose of morphine she was relinquishing control.

More of this magical thinking, of course; a salve to his conscience. But it seemed a moot point. At least she now looked as if she were asleep, breathing more peacefully.

He sat beside her, just him and her and all the machinery. The anger draining out of him, as if he, too, were affected by the drug. Now, at last, out of this calm, some thread of love rose up in him from beneath the scars. It seemed possible that he had not, in fact, stopped loving her; it was just that for so long she'd been so unavailable he'd got out of the habit of it. They had become, at best, fellow travellers, spectators of each other's lives, shuffling along together because, well, he didn't know why, because, perhaps, for all their lack of intimacy, he knew, fundamentally, that he was a better man with her beside him. It wasn't, now, that he wanted her back or even wanted one last burst of recognition or acknowledgement, it was simply that he could see her, separate from him, doing the business of dying, and that it was her business and nothing to do with him. That when she was done he would be alone and he wasn't sure what that meant, to be rudderless, without guidance, even from afar.

twenty

Eugenie

Much later she had trouble distinguishing between what she experienced within the coma and what happened afterwards. There was no point at which she could say I was asleep *then*, I am awake *now*. There was a long transition period even before the official transition period, the one where the nursing staff played Kim's game with her, where they asked her the meaning of simple childish words, as if she was stupid, words she knew the meaning of perfectly well, just couldn't find the language to say what they were. This was not a story in which the character gets caught up in certain events and then, when they are over, goes back to the life she was living before. The person she became on the other side of the coma was different from the one before. She looked the same, had the same name, the same daughters, the same house, the same job, but she was, she liked to think, larger, by which she meant more inclusive, not just of everybody and everything, but of herself. More at ease, as if there was both less to be done and more appreciation of how those things might be achieved, more recognition of those in her life and less need of them at the same time.

What she remembered was the people who visited. Not so much the conversations with them but their presence, sitting with her. Sandrine – her grandmother, not her daughter – speaking to her in French of course, a wonderful flowing stream of clear pure language, rippling over the stones of an alpine meadow, running between moss and heath while a vast sky cradled the mountains around about – where the sound of the water was the meaning itself as she had always believed it to be, as Yvette had told her it was in *Bene Gesserit* when they played in the wide sandy river bed, in the small clear pools backed up against round granite boulders, the sand on the soles of their feet grating against the hard smooth rock. Yvette telling stories about her, about Eugenie, pronouncing it the French way *Oo-gen-ee,* like it was a tune, stories about the *boy who won* which had morphed, the way stories do, to stories about how Eugenie had won, *local girl wins,* but did not know it, nobody had told her that she was the winner and so she had lived her whole life thinking she had to struggle to survive, to fight against life when all the time she was the one who had been awarded the prize, this was what the people who gathered in her room were telling her, sometimes individually, sometimes in great crowds, streams of people passing in through the opposite wall and out the one behind her as if her bed had been placed on the pavement of a busy street in Sydney or maybe Paris because some of them definitely looked French and they all knew who she was and although she didn't know them she was not afraid or anxious or confused, it was natural that she should be where she was, in a bed like a boat in a flowing river, people washing towards and around her, this was not a trial, they were saying, this wasn't some ordeal whose aim was to teach her a lesson, with all the attendant possibilities of failure, nobody was going to test her on anything at all, this was it, this and this and this, *local girl wins.*

Later, of course, there were more recognisable people. Her daughters, Sandrine and Emily, chatting to her the way girls do

335

who are told to be *bright and cheerful for Mummy because she can hear you and it makes her better to know that you are there*, which it did, but she was sad that they were made to try so hard when outside the sun was shining and the wind was scattering the light in the leaves of the eucalypts that lined the edge of the river, tall white-barked, silver-barked trees whose leaves, too, were silver on the underside, turned by the wind to brush the sky. David, too, hanging in there, for some reason burdened by guilt, as if her incapacity to hear what he was saying was in some way his fault and not the fault of the damn machines that surrounded him where he was working, the sorry bleating of the loaders and the trucks, burying themselves in the landscape. Jean-Baptiste, too, and her nan, she who'd been her mother after Yvette died, Nan there with her, but not her real mother, not her birth mother, who had it turned out already gone past, apparently, gone on and away, a fact which, when she discovered it, made her weep, tears streaming down her cheeks, soaking the bed in which she lay, fixed, grieving for her loss, not one tear of which made the slightest bit of difference, couldn't bring her back but then that wasn't what they were for, anyway, it was just good to cry about it, Yvette holding her hand while she told that part of the story because you need a sister in a situation like that, a sister is the best remedy.

Lindl next to the bed. The doctors must have told her that she should talk as well, that it was possible Eugenie could hear. Lindl telling her about her own daughter, Elianor, gone off to live in Melbourne to study at the university and the fears she had for her which had become co-mingled with the fear she had uncovered cleaning out her mother's house in the form of the letters to and from her grandfather begging his family to leave Europe, which they had ignored, and the horror of what had happened; a story no longer reduced to statistics but become *her* family, and this had, she said, in turn, got mixed up with her grief for her mother and set

336

her off, turned her into a generator, a lightning rod, a lighthouse of fear, beaming it out to the world. She'd been frightened for Marcus, that she would lose him, she even told Eugenie about it, she thought that he had chosen the wrong time to go out into the world to be a spokesperson for what was good and right. She'd been so glad when Eugenie had taken over because it meant her Marcus was going to be safe but all the time it was her, Eugenie, who she should have been looking out for and she blamed herself and Eugenie woke up and said to her, *Get over it*, if she wanted to talk about history there was no doubt worse to come, and if she was going to be claiming blame then she needed to get in line, and that it was silly anyway because it was the best thing that had ever happened to her, the steel bar had cracked open her life and let out all the bits of it that she'd been burying, that she'd forgotten where she'd put, and now they were all together, partying with each other and she was fine with that, but, if she wouldn't mind telling her, Lindl that is, telling Eugenie, where was Nick?

A lot of this, it seems, nobody else heard, and there was no point, really, in trying to figure out which was which. It didn't matter. To argue that Sandrine had not been in the room with her, speaking French, would have been to remove a central part from the puzzle, not just ruining it, but destroying it permanently and thus, in some way, also, the larger thing, whatever that was. The psyche had been scattered to the four corners and her job had been to reassemble it in a way that might allow her, whoever she was, to re-enter the world. And if she insisted that some of the discussions she'd had with David had taken place in a donger in the north-west of Western Australia, perched on the edge of a vast spiralling hole in the ground, carved out of the earth by self-driving haulpaks (she had seen the red dust lying thick on the windowsill, the fake timber panelling on the walls, heard the hum of the air-conditioning) that was okay. It was all right, too, that he had told her, standing in that strange transportable box in his hi-viz shirt, what he'd omitted to mention before, that he'd met another woman in Port Hedland and had been living another life with her for some months. She wasn't cross at all. It was just the way of things, that's what it was; the way all things are part of the way. What she did come to realise, later, when the words started to come back, when the numbers began adding up to more numbers and not to things, was that the moments when she had felt calm, when she had been most at peace with the great scramble of her mind, had been when the doctor had been sitting next to her bed, in those small hours when the room was dark, lit only by the curious glow of the machinery monitoring her progress, when this man had given his attention to her as if his life depended upon it. These were the moments when the healing began.

Acknowledgements

Any book that has taken this long in gestation has had input from many sources. In particular, though, I'd like to express my gratitude to Madonna Duffy, my publisher, for her continued belief in the value of my work, and to both my editors, Julia Stiles and Jacqueline Blanchard; also to my early readers, in particular Mark Newman; as well as to those from whom I sought technical information, Dr Les Hall and Sue Hadfield. Finally I could not have contemplated such a project without the constant love, support and patience of my wife, Chris Francis.

More fiction from UQP

AN ACCIDENTAL TERRORIST
Steven Lang

Winner of the Queensland Premier's Literary Award for Best Emerging Author
Winner of the NSW Premier's Literary Award for a First Novel

When Kelvin returns to his home town on the southern coast of New South Wales he finds himself drawn to a community that lives back in the hills. He meets Jessica, a would-be writer who has escaped the city, and her enigmatic neighbour, Carl. Both are pursuing new lives inspired by the extraordinary landscape around them.

As his relationship with Jessica intensifies, Kelvin is caught up by some of the more radical elements in the community. No one, however, is quite who they seem, and Kelvin makes a decision that will have devastating consequences for all of them. Deep in the southern forests, the story builds to a dramatic climax.

An Accidental Terrorist is thrilling to the final page. It's a compelling account of the everyday struggles of a man trying to come to terms with the decisions he's made and the life he's built.

'Lang structures his story well, the tension and conflict building to a dramatic climax. An impressive debut.'

Sydney Morning Herald

'… hypnotically written and engaging'

Australian Bookseller & Publisher

ISBN 978 0 7022 3520 2

More fiction from UQP

A LOVING, FAITHFUL ANIMAL
Josephine Rowe

It is New Year's Eve, 1990, and Ru's father, Jack, has disappeared in the wake of a savage incident. A Vietnam War veteran, he has long been an erratic presence at home, where Ru's allegiances are divided amongst those she loves. Her sister, Lani, seeks to escape the claustrophobia of small-town life, while their mother, Evelyn, takes refuge in a more vibrant past. And then there's Les, Jack's inscrutable brother, whose loyalties are also torn.

A Loving, Faithful Animal is an incandescent portrait of one family searching for what may yet be redeemable from the ruins of war. Tender, brutal, and heart-stopping in its beauty, this is a hypnotic novel by one of Australia's brightest talents.

'Utterly compelling … This is a striking and highly original novel for readers of Australian literary fiction.'

Books+Publishing

'*A Loving, Faithful Animal* is a novel of startling imagery and power. A beautiful and, at times, shocking exploration of the fault lines that run through families and of the far-reaching – and occasionally devastating – consequences of decisions made by those who govern us.'

Chris Womersley, author of *Bereft* and *Cairo*

'A remarkable work of fiction. Deft, lyrical and deeply moving.'

Wayne Macauley, author of *Demons* and *The Cook*

ISBN 978 0 7022 5396 6